The enemy plane saw Hawk Hunter coming from about a mile out. The giant airship had dozens of windows and glass blisters all over its fuselage. There must have been at least a hundred portholes. Hunter was sure that with so many windows, someone had spotted him coming out of the clouds.

But it really made no difference. Hunter merely kicked in his double-reheat burner and bumped his speed up to 850 knots. The enemy airplane's rear gunners began firing almost immediately, but he was moving way too fast for them to get a bead on him.

He looped around and readied his weapons. On his first pass, he tried to find a vulnerable place under the wing, but his bullets only produced some wisps of vapor and did not ignite any fuel tanks. He looped and went around again, but his bullets only bounced off the two starboard engines. Another loop. Another pass at the engine. No hits. He tried pumping bullets into the underside of the fuselage, but they did little damage.

Hunter made six more futile passes, all burning precious fuel and time. He had not altered the big plane's course at all. They were only 110 miles from the coast. Through the portholes, he could see the enemy airmen laughing and pointing at him.

From somewhere deep inside his brain, Hunter remembered an old tactic the Russians used when they were out of ammo. He pushed his throttle ahead, his engine sucked up a load of gas and he rocketed right for the airship.

Hunter would ram the left-side tail wing until it fell away and took the plane with it . . . or die trying.

THE SKY GHOST

Mack Maloney

Pinnacle Books
Kensington Publishing Corp.

http://www.pinnaclebooks.com

Part One
Water

Chapter 1

August 15, 1997
1300 Hours

The U.S. Navy destroyer *Louis St. Louis* was five hours out of Cape Cod when it got the strange message.

A Navy long-range, antishipping bomber had spotted three bodies floating in the Atlantic about 350 miles off the coast of Maryland and 24 miles from the destroyer's current position.

The crew of the Navy aircraft had no idea who these floaters were. A supertanker carrying aviation fuel had been sunk by a U-boat in the general area several days before, but it was unlikely the three bodies were from this engagement. More than 100,000 gallons of volatile T-stoff fuel had gone up when the supertanker was torpedoed. The chance that any bodies or even body parts remained was nil.

Nevertheless, the bomber saw three bodies and the *Louis St. Louis* was ordered to the area to investigate by Atlantic Wartime Command.

The destroyer was under the command of Captain Eric

Wolf. He was a Naval reserve officer, mid thirties, with a good reputation for chasing long-range missile—firing U-boats away from the eastern seaboard of the United States. Though a handsome man, he was rarely seen without his thick sunglasses. He was of Scandinavian descent; his eyes were sensitive to light. But sometimes the corrective goggles made it look as if he was wearing a mask.

Wolf immediately turned his vessel in the direction of the bodies. The destroyer was powered by double-reaction engines, and at full speed, it could reach the area in a matter of minutes. The superheavy Navy bomber, which was also double-reaction powered, would continue circling until the destroyer arrived.

Wolf went up to the bridge and had the Navy plane's radio signals piped directly to him. He explained the situation to his executive officer, a lieutenant commander named Ed Zal. How had three bodies come to be floating 350 miles from the nearest land? the XO wondered. A huge, weeklong hurricane had just finished battering the New England coast—the Storm of the Century, they had called it. Perhaps these were fishermen who drowned in the storm and were carried far out to sea. Or maybe they were casualties from some unknown combat in the area.

"Strange things happen in war," Wolf told the XO as the swift little warship carved its way through the rolling Atlantic.

"Strange things happen in life," the XO replied.

At 17 miles out, Wolf was finally able to connect directly with the bomber pilot. The aircraft was still circling the area; the bodies were still in sight. The pilot could see no wreckage, no oil slick, no evidence of a recently sunk ship or a downed aircraft. The three bodies were simply floating atop the high waves, each one about 1000 yards from the other.

The destroyer increased speed and closed to within 15 miles. Then came a very strange report from the bomber. The pilot said one of the people in the water was waving up at his aircraft! Wolf asked him to repeat this. Finding three bodies out in the middle of the ocean was strange enough. But for one of them to be alive?

The pilot confirmed his report and had the copilot come on and tell Wolf the same as well. They were flying very low and very slow and one of the floaters was definitely waving up at them.

Wolf called down to his propulsion room and told them to reheat the engines to 110 percent power.

He wanted to solve this mystery quickly.

The aircraft that had spotted the floaters was a U.S. Navy B-201, an 18-engine, long-range, maritime attack plane commonly known as a SuperSea.

It was an enormous airplane. Its wingspan was 960 feet, three times that of its distant cousin, the Hughes Spruce Goose. The airplane was so large, it needed two crews, a total of 60 men, working 12-hour shifts to keep it in the air. Capable of staying aloft for 10 days at a time, it was returning from a weeklong combat patrol in the East Atlantic when it detected the floaters. The crew had shot about 100 feet of insta-film and now the commander of the aircraft, sitting in his luxurious berth just behind the flight deck, was reviewing this footage. Clearly it showed one of the people in the water waving up at them. What's more, a second floater seemed to be showing signs of life too. The COA just couldn't believe it. This was getting stranger by the minute.

Just as the COA requested another reel of insta-film be shot and processed, his surface warfare officer called up to him. An enemy warship had been spotted on the SuperSea's long-range visual display. It was a heavy cruiser, a cloak ship, able to hide its presence from radar and sonar by means of a towed electronic-interference array. But cloaking couldn't fool a TV camera, and the Hughes SuperSea bomber was bristling with them. The SW officer reported the enemy vessel was heading for the bodies in the water too—and at all-out speed.

The COA cursed on hearing this news. Usually a cloaked cruiser would be a prize for him. But his bomber had been on battle station for a week and was depleted of torpedoes, depth charges, and antiship rockets. The plane's 24 machine gunners barely had enough ammunition to load their quad-barrel .50 caliber weapons. The gigantic airplane simply didn't have anything to shoot at the cruiser.

But there was still the matter of the *Louis St. Louis*. The destroyer had not yet seen the enemy ship and was on a virtual collision course with it.

It was up to the SuperSea's aircraft commander to warn them.

The forward TV lookout on the *Louis St. Louis* spotted two people in the water at 1309.55 hours, about ten minutes after first getting the call.

The ship was only about one mile away now, and the waves, which had been calm, were growing choppy.

They were approaching an area of the Atlantic that was known as the Demon Zone. This patch of ocean was infamous. It stretched from north of Bermuda, down to the tip of Florida and then out some 600 miles into the Atlantic. An unusually high number of ships and aircraft had been lost traversing the Zone over the years. The weather *was* different here and prone to abrupt changes. Seamen of all stripes hated operating anywhere near it, Wolf included.

But he had no choice but to continue on.

The "combat-imminent" message from the SuperSea came in at exactly 1313 hours. An enemy cruiser had been spotted, Wolf was told. It was cloaking itself with electronic jamming, towing a separate sled almost as big as the ship itself to do so. The SuperSea's forward TV camera had the enemy vessel dead in its lens. The destroyer would be within range of the cruiser's weapons within five minutes.

Wolf acknowledged the aircraft's report and called his crew to battle stations. They were half a mile from the floaters now—and it was apparent the enemy ship was heading for them too.

He turned around to the massive computer located behind his bridge chair and typed several lines of numbers into its large keyboard. The machine's thick magnetic-film wheels began spinning crazily, the multicolored lights on its control panel blinking like a Christmas tree.

Essentially Wolf was asking the huge computer what he should do—and it took only 35 seconds for the computer to spit out its answer. The destroyer was much faster than the enemy battle cruiser and it was closer to the floaters. But the enemy guns had a longer range and could be very accurate. Therefore, the computer determined, the *Louis St. Louis* would beat the enemy cruiser to the floaters—but the destroyer would fall under the enemy guns' range shortly afterward.

This meant Wolf had to scoop up the floaters—whoever the hell they were!—and then hope to make a fast getaway. Time, then was of the essence . . .

He called Zal to his side and recited a series of orders.

"Deploy starboard rescue boat and retrieval crew," he told the XO. "Order forward weapons crews to ready their stations. Roll out air assets and await my word on launch."

The XO saluted, grabbed a bridge mike and spoke the same words into it.

"Stand by for further orders," was how he ended his message.

The destroyer's starboard rescue boat was dropped into the water a minute later. Onboard was a special squad of Sea Marines, each one highly trained in deep-water rescues.

The destroyer's forward weapons crews began heating the ship's targeting beam. This powerful 200,000-candlewatt light could warm an enemy's hull to a temperature high enough for radiation-seeking shells to hone in on it. The destroyer also had some radar-guided air torpedoes at the ready, as well as half a dozen sonar-guided 188-mm under-water guns.

But the vessel's real ace in the hole was its air assets.

They were Convair FY-1s, vertical take-off fighters. Commonly known as Pogos, each sat on a four-point undercarriage supported by four stubby wings and was powered by a pair of mighty contra-rotating turbo-props on top. These dual propellers acted both as helicopter rotors and huge thrusters; the plane took off vertically like a chopper, and then, when it turned over to the horizontal, it acted like a fighter, one that could move at nearly 600 mph.

The two airplanes were wheeled out from their silolike housings and onto the rear deck of the destroyer. The pilots were already in their cockpits, checking their systems and powering up for launch.

Within a minute, both aircraft were ready to pop. The flight crew chief radioed up to the bridge with this information. The destroyer was now fully combat-ready.

"Stand by," came the terse reply.

It was now 1315.30. The enormous SuperSea bomber was still circling the floaters and simultaneously keeping an eye on the enemy cruiser, now about 25 miles away. Aware that its cloaking device had been foiled, the cruiser was coming on at full speed, its crew rushing to their battle stations.

The destroyer's rescue boat was just 500 yards from the first floater now. Its crew chief was equipped with an extended-lens TV camera and was able to pick up the human form in the water. This picture was fed back to the *Louis St. Louis*. Within seconds, Wolf was viewing the broadcast from the rescue launch.

The man in the water was indeed alive. He was waving with both hands. He was wearing a combat uniform, but it was of no design that Wolf had ever seen. Wolf turned up the power on his TV set and waited for the static to melt away. This gave him a blurry telephoto view of this man.

He *was* a strange one. His hair was long, almost womanish, but he also had a thick growth of beard. His uniform was free of ribbons, stripes, or bars. The TV transmission was black-and-white, so Wolf could not determine the uniform's color. But he guessed it was deep blue—and he knew of no armed forces presently fighting which claimed that color.

The rescue launch reached the man about a minute later—just as Wolf got a report that his vessel would be in range of the enemy cruiser's guns in 30 seconds. The floater was hauled aboard, water-logged and cold. Yet he appeared to be in good shape, considering he'd just been found floating in the middle of the Atlantic Ocean.

Wolf had the camera scan back and forth. He was looking for any minute signs of wreckage, an oil slick, anything that would provide a clue as to how the man got here. But no such clue could be found. It was as if he'd dropped right out of the sky.

Another urgent message from the SuperSea bomber interrupted Wolf's musings. The enemy cruiser was firing its guns! A bright flash was spotted out on the eastern horizon a second later. The destroyer's massive combat computer warned a spread of eight long-range disruption shells was on its way.

Wolf ordered a hard turn to port—and just in time. The squeal of the enemy barrage was picked up by the rescue launch's TV camera. Its shriek filled the bridge's intercom speakers. Two seconds later, the eight shells slammed into the sea 100 yards off the destroyer's starboard bow.

The explosions created a huge swell beneath the surface. This instantly grew into a small tidal wave that hit the destroyer not five seconds later. It struck with such force, the *Louis St. Louis* nearly went right over. Bells and whistles began going off all over the ship. Anything not secured, bodies included, was suddenly flying through the air.

"Evasive action!" Wolf yelled into his intercom. "They might have a radi-seeker. Ice the hulls!"

On the captain's call, a supercoolant called Roxy-5 began flooding through lines built into the ship's hull. The idea was to lower the hull's temperature and prevent it from being warmed by the enemy's own version of a targeting beam.

Then Wolf pushed a series of buttons and was soon talking to the Sea Marine in charge of the rescue launch. It too had barely stayed afloat in the man-made tsunami.

"Can you see the other floaters?" Wolf asked the man quickly.

"We can see one more, sir," came the reply. "He's a half mile to the southeast. He's also alive. He's waving to us!"

A second later another barrage of disrupter shells came screaming out of the sky. They landed just 40 yards off the destroyer's port bow. Once again, the small warship was nearly tipped over by a sudden tidal wave.

Too damn close, Wolf thought. The cruiser was playing with them. The next barrage would definitely be guided by a radi-seeker.

"Roxy team, report!" he barked into the microphone.

"Hull temperature down to thirty-eight degrees, sir," came the reply. "And dropping . . ."

"Double your efforts," Wolf yelled back.

But Wolf knew that hull-cooling or not, they couldn't hold this position much longer. He needed to buy just a little more time, though.

He flipped his intercom switch and was soon talking to the destroyer's air officer.

"Launch air assets," he said.

Seconds later, both Pogos revved up to full power and bounced off the rear of the destroyer. Once airborne, they turned over the horizontal and retracted their undercarriage wheels.

Wolf was quickly connected directly through to the pilots.

"OK boys, two passes, no heroics," he told them. "Just give us time to withdraw."

The pilots replied in the affirmative and clicked off. Then one pilot radioed over to the other.

"OK, sport," he said, "time to make some noise."

The two Pogo pilots increased power and quickly climbed to 10,000 feet above the enemy ship.

Each plane was bearing four machine guns, wing-mounted and synchronously fed. The enemy cruiser below was heavily fortified. From two miles up, it looked like a floating, ironclad castle. Spotting the pair of vertiplanes, it went into a wide circle as part of its evasive action maneuver.

The Pogos turned over and began a murderous dive. As airplanes, they were very noisy and their Super Browning big fifties were known for their bright muzzle flash and high velocity sound. But each Pogo was also carrying a device under its right wing known as SE/X. This stood for Sound Enhancement/Extra. Essentially these were electronic whistles which rang up high-pitched screeches whenever an aircraft equipped with them went into a steep dive.

The combined noise of all this was frightening—that was the point. Despite the cruiser's defensive lockdown, many enemy sailors were standing exposed at their weapon stations.

And now their ears were beginning to fill with the Pogos' ear-splitting screech.

The Pogos opened fire at 7500 feet. Small clouds of antiaircraft shells started coming up at them, but the pilots expertly began spinning and avoided the flak. They passed through 5000 feet and now the pilots could see flashes of sparks atop the mainsail of the enemy cruiser. Their armor-piecing shells were making contact.

The horrifying screech got louder as the Pogos continued their dive, guns blazing. At just 500 feet above the ship, they finally pulled up, each plane strafing the cruiser's bridge before peeling away to the south. Though the bridge was locked up, some of the Pogos' shells hit home and damage to the command center within was extensive. Now the ship had to slow down further—and that was the true purpose of this air attack.

The pair of VTOL-planes returned for their second pass. This time they came in low over the water, concentrating their fire on the unprotected rear of the cruiser. They managed to sever the cable towing the electronic-cloaking sled, causing the assembly to tip over and sink. The enemy cruiser was now very exposed and vulnerable to a variety of weapons.

But the Pogo pilots' orders were for two passes and that's all they would do. They'd bought time for the people out on the destroyer's rescue launch, as Wolf had wanted. Moreover, both planes were running very low on fuel. It was time to break off the engagement and return to the ship.

Still, as the lead pilot pulled out of his strafing run, he aimed his guns squarely on the cruiser's mainsail. A 25-shot barrage severed the secondary radar dish and the ship's VHY radio antenna. It also cut down the main mast, tearing through its flag and sending it in pieces into the ocean.

Looking back down at their handiwork, both pilots could see the enemy ship's colors blown into the sea and slipping beneath the waves.

"That's the only way I want to see the Iron Cross," the lead pilot radioed over to the other. "Ripped and sinking."

"Roger that," replied his wingman.

The crew of the Hughes SuperSea bomber witnessed the strafing attack and radioed down to the American destroyer that their pilots were returning safely.

But the enemy cruiser was still coming on—and now it was launching a recovery boat, too. This one was literally shot off the deck and was heading at very high speed toward the remaining floaters.

Watching all this on his TV screen, the bomber's COA told his machine gun crews to stand by. Then he sent another radio message down to the *Louis St. Louis*. There was something he wanted to ask the captain of the destroyer.

At the same moment, Wolf was talking to the Sea Marines in the American recovery boat. They had the one floater aboard and were coming back. Wolf called down to the propulsion room and ordered more gas be put on the destroyer's double-reaction plant. Then he told his crew to strap in for a quick getaway.

Meanwhile the enemy's high-speed boat had slowed down and was hauling the second floater out of the water. This man appeared to be alive too, but barely. The third floater had drifted far away by this time.

That's when Wolf's air-sea radio began blinking again. It was the SuperSea's COA with his question: Should his gunners strafe the enemy's recovery boat?

Wolf had to think about this for a moment. It was a legitimate question. The enemy recovery boat *was* a vessel of war, and thus a fair target. But it did have at least one of the mysterious floaters on board. And the chances were good the enemy cruiser would disengage once it saw the *Louis St. Louis* accelerate and the SuperSea depart the area. So what was the point of shooting at the rescue boat?

Finally Wolf keyed his mike.

"I don't think that will be necessary," he told the airplane.

The *Louis St. Louis* was 35 miles away from the area just 20 minutes later.

Captain Wolf was in his stateroom, writing up a report on the incident. Behind him, another large computer was whirring softly. He found it a comforting sound. There was a knock at the door. The ship's Executive Officer, the man named Zal, came in.

He handed his own preliminary combat report to Wolf.

"We never got to use our targeting lamp," he said. "We were never in range. Our hull temperature *did* achieve thirty-four degrees though—pretty good, considering."

"They still would have nailed us with a radi-seeker after a third disruption barrage," Wolf said. "But tell the crew they did well nevertheless. At this point, what difference does it make?"

"Will do, skipper," Zal replied.

Wolf fed Zal's report into the huge whirring computer and pushed a button labeled PROCESS.

"I was surprised to see such a large enemy ship in these parts," Zal told Wolf. "I didn't think they could muster enough men or fuel these days to get one out this far."

"A last-gasp patrol," Wolf said with a shrug. "They'll be lucky if they make it back to port. Without their cloaking stuff, they'll be a big fat target for anyone with an air torpedo."

Wolf then looked up at Zal.

"So, where is he?" he asked the XO.

"The man we brought aboard?"

"Yes. Is he still alive?"

"He is—and he's actually in pretty good shape," Zal said. "Probably hasn't had a meal in a while. But other than that, he looks like he just went for a dip in the pool. He should be on the way up from sick bay about now."

Wolf signaled that Zal should close the stateroom door. Then he lowered his voice.

"OK, then—who the hell is he?" he asked the XO.

Zal just shrugged.

"Damned if I know, skipper," he replied. "I don't think he knows himself. He's rather confused at the moment."

Zal took something from his pocket and laid it on Wolf's desk.

"This is all they found on him," he said.

Wolf picked up the rolled piece of cloth and unraveled it. It was a small, tattered American flag. Wrapped inside was a faded picture of a young blond woman.

Wolf let out a whistle.

"Wow, nice babe," he said.

"Look at that flag, skipper," Zal said. "It has fifty stars."

Wolf quickly counted the white stars in the blue field. "Yeah, fifty. What the hell is that about?"

"Last time I checked, the American flag had forty-nine," Zal said.

At that moment there was a knock at the door. Wolf folded the picture back up into the flag and put it in his drawer. Then he signaled Zal to open the door.

Two corpsmen walked in. Between them was the man taken from the sea.

Wolf took one look at him and then did a double take. The man was tall, thin, muscular, probably somewhere in his mid twenties. His hair was very long, his face bearded, but handsome in features. He was obviously Anglo-Saxon. But he looked—*different*. Wolf even removed his thick sunglasses to get a better look at him.

"Well, who the hell are you?" he asked the man bluntly. "An angel who fell out of the sky?"

The man said nothing.

He was wearing sailor scrubs, but this guy was not an ordinary seaman. At least that was obvious. One of the corpsmen handed the man's clothes to Wolf, then he and his partner quickly departed. Zal closed the door behind them.

Wolf examined the set of combat fatigues.

"Well, this is obviously a uniform," Wolf said. "But for what army?"

The man just shrugged.

"I . . . can't say," he mumbled.

" 'Can't say' or 'don't know?' "

"Both, I guess . . ."

The man looked around the stateroom.

"This ship," he asked. "Who does it belong to?"

Wolf put his glasses back on and leaned back in his seat.

"Let us ask the questions first, OK?" he told the man. "Have a seat."

Zal guided the man to a chair opposite Wolf, then he took a seat himself on the couch nearby.

"Do you have any idea how you got to be out in the middle of the Atlantic Ocean?" Wolf asked the man.

The man just shook his head. "No idea."

"Were you part of a ship's crew? An officer maybe?"

The man shook his head again. "I don't know."

"Were you in an airplane? Are you an aviator?"

"Could be one of those top-secret flyboys, skipper," Zal interjected. "You know, the Air Corps Commandos."

Wolf thought about this and nodded slowly.

"How about it, sport?" he asked. "You a secret Air Corps guy? Under orders not to speak?"

"He could have been flying one of the new doodlebugs," Zal added. "Those guys ain't supposed to talk to nobody."

"Any of this ringing a bell, pal?" Wolf pressed.

But the man just shook his head again.

"None of it," he replied.

Wolf stared back at him. Even his voice sounded weird. Yet, just like the man's overall appearance, he wasn't exactly sure *what* was different about it.

The man was studying some of the papers on Wolf's desk. "Can I ask a question now?" he wanted to know.

"OK, sure, ask away," Wolf told him.

"What year is this?"

Wolf and Zal just looked at each other.

"Well, it's 1997, sport," Wolf replied.

A look of surprise registered on the man's face—but it disappeared just as quickly.

"And you are at war, correct?" he asked Wolf.

"You saw that firsthand, didn't you?" Wolf replied.

"But who are you fighting exactly?"

Wolf and Zal looked at each other again. It was a strange question to ask. Maybe it was best to ignore it, they thought.

"Hey, what's with your hair, man?" Wolf asked him

instead. "What army or navy would let you have hair like that?"

The man just stared at the floor. He *was* confused.

Wolf looked over at Zal.

"Well, this is going well," he said sarcastically.

The XO came over and sat on the desk in front of the man. He lowered his voice slightly.

"Look, you ain't a German, are ya, pal?" he asked him.

The man shook his head no.

"Well, now we're getting somewhere!" Zal exclaimed.

Wolf leaned forward in his seat a little. "Are you an American?" he asked.

The man thought a moment and then replied. "Yes."

"Are you a member of the armed forces of the United States of America?"

The man thought another few moments. "No, I am not," he finally replied.

This sent Zal scratching his head.

"So you're a member of the armed services," he said. "And you are an American. But you are not a soldier of the United States?"

The man just nodded. "That's right—I think."

Zal kept on scratching. "Well, now I'm confused," he said.

"Me too," Wolf added.

He turned around in his chair to his computer. He popped the keyboard out, typed in a few quick notes on the interview and then pushed a button that would convert his words into an alpha-numeric language only the computer could understand. Basically he was asking the machine what he should do next.

The computer whirred and blinked and burped and blinked some more. Finally the answer came out on a long piece of ticker tape.

"Terminate interrogation," it read. "Return to port immediately."

Wolf showed the message to Zal, who nodded.

"Listen pal, we've got to stop this right here," Wolf

said. "We'll be bringing you back with us. I have a feeling someone higher up the ladder will be very interested in you."

The man just shrugged. "Do what you've got to do."

Wolf nodded to Zal. "OK, get him fed. And keep him away from the crew. It will take us about four hours to get back into port."

Zal tapped the stranger on the shoulder.

"Let's go, pal," he said.

The man stood up. He really was a strange-looking cat.

"Just one more question," Wolf said. "How about your name? Do you remember that?"

The man thought for a moment, then he finally replied: "Yes, I do. My name is Hawk Hunter."

Wolf looked at Zal, who just shrugged.

"Never heard of you," Wolf said.

Out at sea, on the edge of the Demon Zone, one man was still floating.

Up until a little while ago, two other people had been in the water with him. But one had been picked up by an ultraspeedy warship; the other by a floating iron castle.

The gray, speedy vessel looked like a destroyer—but it was sleeker than any destroyer he'd ever seen. And the iron castle looked too big, too cumbersome to even stay afloat.

But the airplane that had circled above him the whole time was the strangest thing of all. It was the biggest, slowest, oddest-looking airplane he'd ever seen.

But they were all gone now. The destroyer had left the area at incredible speed carrying away one guy, and the black floating castle had departed in slower fashion towards the south carrying another. And then the gigantic airplane had simply flown away, leaving him here, all alone.

He had a huge bump on his head and a long scrape on his left arm. He'd been bobbing in the water for more than an hour now, and he was getting damned cold. He wasn't sure how he got here; his memory was very foggy. In fact, he couldn't even remember his name.

But he was coherent enough to know he was in very dire circumstances. He looked in all directions and saw nothing but water. He could tell by the cloud formations there wasn't any land mass for hundreds of miles. But what could he do?

He couldn't last much longer like this. He had to do something.

So he looked up at the sun and determined which way was west.

And then he started swimming.

Chapter 2

It was now late afternoon.

Hawk Hunter was standing on the foredeck of the *Louis St. Louis,* taking in many deep breaths and slowly letting them out again. Two armed sailors were watching over him from nearby. He was sure to them he looked like someone who needed some fresh air. And a lot of it.

He didn't know who he was. Or where he came from. Or how he got here. His name was Hawk Hunter, that was the only thing he was sure of. After that, it was all a jumble.

And he had no idea *where* he was. Sure, he was on a destroyer and he'd been picked up some 350 miles out in the middle of the Atlantic Ocean. And the people on the ship were Americans and they seemed to be fighting a war against the Germans. And the captain of the destroyer had said it was 1997.

But this ship—it was so strange! And the German ship; it had been even more outlandish. And the airplane which had circled above him while he was in the water: it seemed too enormous to fly. But how would he know these things? How could he know something was strange, if he couldn't remember anything to compare it to?

That was just it. His mind was not a total blank. Some things were coming naturally to him. He knew how to walk and talk and breathe. He knew he was American. He knew who the Germans were, what a destroyer should look like, and that the bigger the airplane, the harder it is to fly.

But what he was doing an hour before he found himself in the water? He didn't know . . .

When the destroyer's captain asked him if he fell right out of the sky, Hunter's brain processed the question as if, yes, that's *exactly* what had happened. He had fallen out of the sky and into the ocean. Not out of an airplane—just out of the clear blue sky. But how could that happen?

Again, he didn't know.

He took another deep breath. His head felt full of stuff. Familiar things. People. Incidents. But for some reason he just couldn't access these memories. He sniffed the sea air and prayed it would uncloud that part of his brain that was hiding all these things *and* the circumstances by which he found himself here, in this strange, but not-so-strange place.

Another deep breath. More questions. Who were those other two guys in the water with him? And exactly what kind of uniform *was* he wearing when he was picked up? And what about . . .

Stop!

Stop. Hunter took another deep breath and let it out slowly. Too many questions were flowing into his head and if his brain got overloaded, then he would blow a neuron fuse for sure. So take another breath, he told himself. Calm down. Be cool. This will all get figured out, somehow.

Maybe.

The ship's captain had said they would make port in four hours; more than three and a half had passed by now.

It was getting dark. The little warship was whipping along the waves like it was a racing boat, so Hunter assumed they must be nearing the vessel's home. But where was it? They were sailing northwest, at least by the moon and the stars. But Hunter couldn't see land anywhere out on the horizon.

Finally, though, he sensed the engines begin to slow. In seconds they were going at two-thirds speed, as if they were approaching land. But again, where the hell was it? They seemed still to be out in the middle of the ocean.

But then his ears began to pick up things his eyes couldn't. Noises. Motors running. Neon burning. People talking, yelling. Music playing. A big band sound—but louder. With echo. And reverb. Was that Tommy Dorsey? Through reverb? Really?

What happened next was simply astonishing to him. One moment they were moving in complete and utter darkness, the next they were sailing off a very bright, very noisy coastline.

What happened?

Hunter looked behind him and realized that the destroyer had just passed through a huge almost-invisible screen. It was at least a half mile high and was being held up by an endless series of slender poles set into pilings about a mile offshore. It was as if someone had put a big curtain along the entire coastline.

"You really are from another place, aren't you?"

Hunter turned around. It was Commander Zal, the XO. He'd been watching him.

"I can tell just by the way you looked at the Big Screen," Zal went on. "You've never seen anything like it before, have you?"

Hunter just shook his head.

"Nope. Never," he said.

"It's called an LSD," Zal told him. "Stands for Light and Sound Dampener. It keeps all light, all radio signals, all TV signals from going out, but still lets everything in. Like a two-way mirror. This way the coastline doesn't have to black out every time it gets dark. Everyone knows about them—they've been around for years. Look at this one. It stretches all the way up to Canada. And it's getting very ratty. But it's still holding up."

"It's amazing," Hunter said. "Sort of . . ."

Now he saw plenty of lights. And heard plenty of noise. He could smell life, lots of it, on the shoreline not too far away. This place—it actually looked familiar to him. Tall buildings. Lots of bridges. A city screaming at the top of its lungs.

Then it hit him—they were right off the coast of New York City!

But wait a moment. This wasn't exactly how he remembered it. The Manhattan skyline was still there—but the buildings were twice as tall and there were twice as many as he recalled. And the Empire State Building was still the tallest one around—and it was at least three times as high as he remembered it.

"They added to it in 1968 and then again in 1979, after the big air raid that year," Zal told him. "You didn't know that either, did you?"

Hunter just shook his head no.

Zal reached into his pocket and came out with a pack of Lucky Strikes. But these Luckies were laid out in a cardboard gold box—like fancy English cigarettes used to be. He lit a butt and then offered one to Hunter, who declined.

"You know what, pal?" Zal said. "Maybe you *are* an angel. Maybe you really did fall out of the sky."

But Hunter did not really hear him. He was too busy looking at a heavily bomb-damaged Statue of Liberty.

"Great Air Raid of 1989," the XO explained. "They ain't going to fix it until the war's all over. Which should be any day now. It's been more of a resistance symbol these past few years—wrecked the way it is. Lots of people have painted it. Photographed it."

They were passing a tremendous amount of naval activity now. Tugs. Ferries. Repair ships. Hunter soon realized New York Harbor was now one enormous naval base. And even though it was past sunset, the lights around it were so bright, it was lit up like a bright, sunny day.

There were at least 200 warships of all sizes tied up at

various points around the harbor. At first, they all seemed very odd to Hunter in shape or design. Some were sleek and long, some were fat and stubby. Some were enormous, some seemed too small. Some were actually two ships linked in the middle as one, like a catamaran. Yet all the ships were covered stem-to-stern with a navy gray paint that seemed very familiar to Hunter. It was so strange. The ships all looked bizarre and different to him, yet perfectly normal at the same time.

"This war you are fighting," Hunter finally turned and asked Zal. "What is it called exactly?"

The XO seemed stumped for a moment. He was a tall wiry guy, not really the poster-boy version of a naval officer.

"What's it called?" he asked. "I don't know, take your pick." He began counting off on his fingers. "The Second Great War. The War. The Big War. The Fifty-Year War . . ."

"Fifty-Year War?" Hunter stopped him. "Why call it that? How long has it been going on?"

Zal stared back at him for a long moment.

"Man, you really have been someplace else."

He took a step closer and pretended to yell into Hunter's ear.

"It's been going on for fifty years, Mack. That's why . . ."

"So it started in 1947?" Hunter asked him.

Once again, the XO was caught off guard.

"Well, no," he replied. "Actually, it started in 1939— Germany invaded Poland . . ."

". . . on September 1st, right?" Hunter interrupted him.

"So, you remember that at least."

"Jessuzz, I guess I do," Hunter said anxiously. "Please go on."

"Well," Zal said. "The Hundred Years' War between England and France lasted longer than a hundred years, right? I guess it's the same kind of thing. Maybe they can call it the Fifty-Eight Years' War once it's over."

But Hunter wanted to get this straight. "So, a war that

started with Germany invading Poland in 1939 is still going on today?"

"That's right, sport," Zal replied.

The XO threw his cigarette away.

"And that's really all I should say to you," he went on. "I've got to get back to the bridge. We'll be pulling in about forty minutes from now."

He signaled the guards that he was returning Hunter to their care and began to walk away.

"Commander?" Hunter called after him. "One more question?"

"OK . . . shoot."

"When this war first started, what did they call it then?"

Zal thought a moment. Then he shrugged.

"Well, back then," he said, "they called it World War II."

Chapter 3

They kept sailing.

Even at two-thirds speed, the destroyer was making at least 100 knots, an incredible speed for such a vessel.

Past New York Harbor. Up the coast of Connecticut, which was now an endless line of huge gun emplacements and military ports. Past Rhode Island, whose shoreline was nothing but oil depots and off-loading terminals. Past Block Island, now one huge airfield. Past Martha's Vineyard—it was bristling with gigantic submarines, many of which had flight decks attached for launching and recovering aircraft.

And all of it looked different, yet familiar to Hunter at the same time.

Eventually the *Louis St. Louis* entered yet another busy Navy facility. This base was located in Buzzard's Bay on the ass end of Cape Cod. Just like the coast of Connecticut and Rhode Island, this part of the Cape was thick with naval activity. The destroyer passed by ships that were so enormous, Hunter couldn't see their decks and thus couldn't figure out what it was they did.

They passed a huge shipbuilding yard. Hunter didn't

have to wonder what they built here. They built aircraft carriers. It said so on a sign painted across an enormous two-towered crane. It read: "AmeriCorp Aircraft Carrier Division. Bigger Is Better."

There was truth in that advertising. These aircraft carriers were gigantic.

What ships they were! There were at least 10 of them in various stages of construction. They were being assembled in sections on extremely high, raised docks. The network of steel surrounding these building platforms was frightening. There seemed to be clouds forming at the top of some of them, they were so high.

The destroyer sailed past the construction bays and up to berthing for the completed carriers. From somewhere back in the deepest part of his skull, Hunter knew what a World War II aircraft carrier *should* look like. Small, narrow, wooden deck.

But the ships being built here were at least fifty times that length. These megacarriers really were "floating cites." They were forty or more decks high, and at least three quarters of a mile long. Each one had three landing and takeoff areas on its vast deck: one at the bow, one at the stern, and a third on an immense island hanging off port side. This overhang alone was larger than a WW II flattop.

One ship was so near complete, it already had its airplanes on board. Hunter saw at least 500 small, swift-looking little fighters of indeterminate origin cluttering the rear deck, while several dozen larger airplanes were crowded on the bow. And still, this behemoth had room on its upper deck for several sets of 16-inch guns, huge weapons more at home on battleships!

The *Louis St. Louis* finally pulled into a tiny berth on the other side of a gigantic oiling station. It took the crew just a few minutes to secure the ship and cool down the double-reaction engines. Then they lowered the gangway and some disappeared into the night. Those who remained onboard were secured to quarters.

Hunter was led off the ship about 30 minutes later, under the care of Zal, the XO. Waiting for them at the bottom of the gangway was a car that looked more like an airplane. It had huge fins in the back, a monstrous grill in the front, tons of chrome all around, and thick whitewall tires. Yet as flashy as it was, its obvious function was that of a military vehicle, right down to the dull green paint and the white star emblazoned on its side doors.

Hunter was put in the backseat with Zal. A pair of plain-clothes Sea Police were up front.

They left the Navy yard and drove for about 20 minutes along a very crowded military highway. The terrain around them could only be described as "urban-beach." Sand dunes and scrub trees were everywhere—as were hundreds of military buildings, supply dumps, and endless rows of multistory Quonset huts.

They finally reached their destination: an air base called Otis Air Corps Field. It was an enormous facility, heavily guarded, with many rows of barbed wire surrounding it. Something flashed through Hunter's mind as they passed through the gate. It was almost as if he'd been here before, but he couldn't remember when—or how.

It took them another 20 minutes and about 14 miles to cross the base. Finally the car arrived at a large red brick building which sat astride the base's longest runway, a 40,000-foot giant. Hunter was hustled out of the car and brought to an office on the sixth floor. The name on the door read: SPECIAL PERSONNEL ASSESSMENT BOARD—NO ADMITTANCE.

Commander Zal and the Sea Police led him into the empty office. There was a table with three chairs on one side facing a single chair on the other. There was a window at the other end of the room. Its shades were down, but light streaming in through the partially open panels painted the far wall with eerie, meticulous stripes.

Behind the table, dominating one corner, was a huge computer. It looked like it had been built back in the Stone Age. It was bigger and bulkier than the one in Captain Wolf's stateroom. It was pockmarked with blinking lights and switches and buttons and no less than half a dozen reel-to-reel magnetic tape spools. It looked like a prop out of a bad sci-fi movie, just like everything else here. A silver nameplate identified it as a "Main/AC-100."

Outside the window, Hunter could hear aircraft taking off. He caught himself trying to determine how many engines each plane had, and whether they were prop, turbo-prop, or jet-driven. But actually what he heard most was a combination of all three sounds, a cacophony that was very confusing to his senses for some reason.

Hunter took a seat. The door at the other end of the dark office opened and three Army officers came in. Two lieutenants and a captain. All three were much too old to be in uniform. The captain was at least 65; the looies not much younger. Despite their relatively low rank, their chests were full of fruit salad—ribbons, pins, and patches. The decorations said they'd been fighting this war for a very long time. They were accompanied by a stenographer who appeared older than they.

Zal handed them a brief report and saluted casually. Then he turned to Hunter.

"Have you ever been to Pittsburgh?" he asked him.

Hunter had to think for a moment. "Do they manufacture a lot of diamonds there these days?" he asked, not really knowing why.

Zal just laughed and shook his head. "No, pal, they don't," he said.

Then Zal reached over and shook Hunter's hand. "Well, good luck, friend," he said.

"Yes, thanks for saving me," Hunter replied.

But it was too late; Zal had already gone out the door.

The three elderly officers read the report silently; the lieutenants relied on their thick reading glasses to get them through; the captain needed the aid of a huge magnifying glass. Hunter watched each man's eyebrows arch and fall with every paragraph. It seemed to take them forever to finish the three-page document, all three were too busy shaking their heads, mumbling, and then losing their place.

The captain was the first to finish. He signaled this by adjusting the enormous hearing aid hanging off his left ear. His name was Pegg. He'd been an Army officer for 55 years.

"You know something? You just plain look different to me," he said to Hunter. "Though I can't exactly put my finger on just why or how that is."

"You look different to me, too," Hunter said.

"What was that?" Pegg asked him, holding his hand by his good ear.

Hunter repeated his statement and added: "You all sound different too."

At this point, the stenographer began pounding away. Only then did Hunter notice her machine was plugged directly into the antique computer.

Then, for the next two hours, he and the three elderly officers went through the whole thing again. The events surrounding his being found at sea. His debriefing by Wolf. His uniform. His haircut. He wasn't allowed to ask any questions and it frequently took the elderly officers several minutes to ask theirs. All the while, the stenographer was inputting their conversation verbatim into the huge computer.

Even as he told the story as best he knew it, Hunter found his troubled mind wandering all over the place. What was going to happen here? Would the three officers find him in need of psychiatric evaluation? Or medical attention? A few days of sleep would probably do him a load of good, whether it be in a loony bin or a hospital.

True, the food might not be to his liking, but he could live with that until his head cleared enough for him to figure out exactly what he was going to do.

* * *

At the far end of the room, opposite the shuttered window, there was a large piece of plate glass that looked like a mirror. And that it was—but it was a two-way mirror.

On the other side, sitting in a tiny office adjacent to the Assessment Board room and hidden from view, were three other men.

They were all dressed exactly the same: black suit, white shirt, dark blue tie. This was their uniform. They were very high-ranking intelligence agents. They were so high up in the spy world in fact, security dictated they be known simply by their code names: X, Y, and Z. They worked for the OSS.

The three agents were much younger that the trio of elderly officers on the Assessment Board. The three senior men were actually a front for the OSS agents, and had been at this facility for years. At just about the same time the *Louis St. Louis* had been ordered back to the Cape, the three agents had been contacted by Atlantic War Command and asked to "monitor" the interrogation of the man who'd been found so mysteriously floating in the middle of the ocean. They'd flown a rocketplane shuttle up from New York City and arrived at Otis two hours before Hunter was finally brought in.

Now, as they watched the interview grind on, the three agents were in various phases of interest. On the one hand, they agreed it was unusual to find someone alive floating in the middle of the ocean, and to have that person unable to recall how they got there or from whence they came. On the other hand, the agents had seen just about everything in the last 10 years of The War. Few things surprised them any more.

What's more, the war itself was nearly over. The American Forces had been battering Germany on all fronts for the past six months. Germany was low on manpower, steel, oil, food, and munitions. Their equipment was obsolete by five years or more. They had reverted to horses to move even the most important items. Meanwhile, America's might was evident just by riding up the coast from New York to Massachusetts. There were no less than 24 Navy bases just in that stretch of coastline. And they equaled only about one-tenth of America's naval forces at the moment. And all that didn't count the Army and the Air Corps.

So the war was almost won, and the three OSS agents were tired of it and certainly didn't want to latch on to something that might endanger their early-out muster plans once the conflict was through.

It was for these reasons that Agents X, Y, and Z sat behind the two-way mirror listening to Hunter's questioning, each with only a half ear open.

But, on another level, it *was* mildly fascinating, especially to X and Z. This person Hunter really knew how to spin a tale—that was obvious. But only one thing mattered to them: was he a German spy or not? Was he someone the Huns wanted to infiltrate into the country at the last minute, before the war was over? They'd been told to expect some last-minute high jinks as the fighting drew to a close. In the 58 years of war there had been no less than seven cease-fires and five armistice signings, all of them against Germany's favor, all of them eventually broken by the German high command. But historically the Germans had let off several big bangs before succumbing. This time probably wouldn't be any different.

But what if this Hunter guy was not a spy—what was he then? And how *did* he come to be floating out in the ocean?

"We could have them call in a psychic evaluation officer," X suggested to Z as the old men continued asking Hunter the same tired questions over and over again.

"You mean hook him up?" Z replied. "Hmm, that might prove interesting. Or at least entertaining. Anything to get us out of here quicker."

X opened a small microphone in front of him. It was patched through the huge computer and into Captain Pegg's hearing aid.

"Call for a psychic eval officer," X said blandly into

the microphone. They watched as Captain Pegg jumped a little, startled by the confidential message that had suddenly popped into his bad ear.

"And get us some more coffee too," the agent added.

The phone rang just once in the billet of Captain Raphael Zoltan.

He wasn't really asleep. He was simply dozing the night away, as he usually did. Zoltan didn't like to sleep, not for long stretches of time anyway. He found it wasteful, and maybe a little too close to the death state for his liking.

The phone call was from the Special Personnel Assessment office; the thinly-disguised OSS interrogation room located about four miles away, up on the northern edge of the air base. Zoltan had heard some OSS agents had been spotted arriving at Otis earlier in the day. Flying in on a noisy rocketplane shuttle was not the way to make your presence unknown. But Zoltan could understand. With the war winding down, everyone was loosening up a little. Even the guys known to some as "America's Gestapo."

Zoltan was asked to come up to the Assessment Board office to examine a subject. Zoltan had heard the rumors too about a mysterious man picked up floating in the sea earlier in the day; the scuttlebutt said he was a highly trained German saboteur feigning amnesia. If that was the case, Zoltan would be able to crack him like an egg.

He got up, got dressed, and packed his equipment bag. A tall thin man in his forties, with slicked-back hair and a pencil-thin mustache, Zoltan's official title was "Psychic Evaluation Officer, First Class." As such it was his job to administer a combination of tests to suspected saboteurs or traitors essentially to get the truth out of them. He mainly did this with a device that was part hypnosis machine, part lie detector. It was called simply the Truth-O-Meter. A suspect would be hooked up to the machine and told to look at the glowing ball that appeared on a small TV screen. This would lull them into a hypnotic state.

Once under, Zoltan would give the subject a lie detector test. From this, he could tell whether what a subject said under hypnosis was a recounting of actual events, a coherent jumble the mind had put together for other psychological reasons, or a set of fabrications..

And if that didn't work, well, Zoltan had other ways of determining what was truth. For instance, he was the only U.S. military officer allowed to carry a crystal ball.

He lugged his bag out of the barracks, being careful not to shatter his collection of crystal globes. His SkyScooter had about an eighth of a tank of fuel in it. Would that be enough to make it the four miles he needed to fly to the north end of the base? Zoltan closed his eyes and put his right forefinger to his brow. Did he have enough butane-2 to push his little flea four miles? The answer came back to him as no.

So he threw his equipment bag over his shoulder and started walking.

The sky was clear, the stars were out and the moon was rising. The base was very quiet tonight; he could almost hear people packing their bags, so soon did everyone think they'd be going home.

He passed a line of CB-319s, gigantic ''Flying Boxcar'' cargo planes that doubled as coastal patrol bombers. They looked like they hadn't flown in months, which was probably close to the truth. Regular coastal patrols had been phased out months ago. There hadn't been a missile-firing U-boat attack on the eastern seaboard in twice as long, so the patrols had been discontinued. Now the big Boxcars looked all dressed up with nowhere to go.

He crossed over one inactive runway and reached the main strip. Here a line of Navy Pogos was gleaming in the moonlight. They looked like they hadn't flown in as long as the Boxcars, even though Zoltan knew at least a couple of Pogos bounced off from Otis everyday, just so the pilots

could get their required flight time in before the anticipated Muster-Out Day.

Zoltan too was counting the hours to the cease-fire; he
wanted the war to end because he believed the economy
of the country and himself would be better off for it. But
cease-fire or not, he was getting out of the service in 15
days on a medical discharge. He had a bad leg, injured
during a 14-day tour of duty in a huge SuperSea combat
platform. He finally got a doctor to go along with him and
with his OK, he would be out of the service for good by
the end of the month.

Once discharged, he hoped to get a head start on everyone and go back to his former profession as a traveling
magician and hypnotist. His daughter was at their home
in the Catskills right now, booking dates for him starting
the first week of September. Last time he had spoken with
her, they had gigs stretching into January already. He really
didn't want anything to happen that would gas those shows.

He walked briskly and was soon within a half mile of the
admin building. Throughout this little journey, he'd been
aware of his moon shadow dancing on the tarmac in front
of him. But now, suddenly, the blue shadow disappeared.
Zoltan stopped. What had happened?

He turned around and saw that a gigantic bank of very
dark clouds had suddenly appeared on the eastern horizon
and had blotted out the moonshine.

Zoltan felt a shiver go through him. Never had he seen
clouds so dark and moving so fast.

Instinctively he hunched his shoulders and pulled his
uniform collar close to his neck.

Then he quickened his pace even more.

By the time Zoltan arrived at the Assessment Board
office, one of the elderly lieutenants was fast asleep.

The other two officers were simply sitting there, puffing
on pipes, not reading, not talking, just waiting.

Zoltan faked a salute and put his bag on the table.

"Where is the subject?" he asked Captain Pegg.

Pegg simply pointed his pipe towards the far end of the table and Zoltan took a look.

He immediately felt his breath catch in his throat. The man sitting at the end of the table was looking back at him in the strangest way. And he looked so . . . different. Zoltan's heart began pounding. The aura in this room was very strange.

Zoltan turned back to the three elderly officers—the second lieutenant was awake by now. Behind them was a mirror, and Zoltan knew who was sitting behind it. He shivered again. There were many strange vibes in this room. Bad ones, good ones. Unidentifiable ones.

Zoltan put his hand to his forehead again, but this time just to ward off a headache. He knew it was going to be a long, strange night.

Zoltan's first duty was to fill out a half dozen very extensive forms.

On these he had to write down, over and over again, his credentials, his military background, his success rate, and so on. The war had been on for 58 years and yet no one had discovered a way to cut down on all the paperwork.

Zoltan's MagicPen ran out of ink halfway through the sixth form and he had to nudge Captain Pegg awake to borrow another writing instrument. All the while, the man at the end of the table sat calmly, staring out the window, through the blinds, at the line of deep blue runway lights beyond.

Finally Zoltan completed the paperwork. He massaged his wrist to get the circulation going again and pushed the documents under Pegg's nose. The senior officer harrumphed himself awake, and the commotion was loud enough to wake the two lieutenants.

Pegg pretended to read Zoltan's paperwork, then lit his pipe again.

"Where exactly do you want to do what you do?" Pegg asked the psychic officer.

Zoltan took another scan of the room. The sleepy officers, the mysterious subject, the three men hidden behind the mirror. All the weird vibes were still here. He had to go to another location.

"A small office will do," he told Pegg.

Pegg turned to one of his looies. "Fred, you want to handle that, please?"

Fred, the lieutenant on the right, rose slowly from his chair, adjusted his back, his hips, and his kneecaps, then walked over to a wallphone and slowly punched in three numbers.

A drowsy corporal appeared at the door about a minute later. Lieutenant Fred told him his needs. The corporal yawned and then gestured for Zoltan to come with him. Zoltan in turn looked down the table at the mysterious subject.

"Would you mind coming with me, sir?"

They marched down the corridor, the corporal shushing them twice, telling them, "Be quiet. People are asleep."

They finally reached a small office at the end of the hall. The corporal opened the door, switched on the light and turned to go. Zoltan caught him by the shoulder.

"Stick around, junior," the psychic officer said, in a rare exhibition of rank-pulling. "I might need you."

Actually, Zoltan almost always worked alone. But something was very puzzling about this particular subject, this man plucked alive from the sea. Just being in the same room with the guy seemed a bit too eerie for him. Zoltan wanted someone else around.

The corporal grumbled as he pulled a chair out in the hallway, sat down on it, and promptly fell asleep. Zoltan sat behind the office desk, gesturing that Hunter should take the chair opposite him.

"You've spoken with a number of people since being found I take it?" Zoltan asked him. "You're probably getting sick and tired of all these questions."

Hunter just shrugged. "I keep putting people to sleep," he replied. "That's probably a bad sign."

Zoltan thought a moment about this reply—but then

plunged on. The man's voice was very odd; so were his features. Not scary. Not frightening. Just odd.

"Do you know what I do?" he asked Hunter.

"Nope."

"I'm going to put you under hypnosis, hook you up to a couple devices at the same time, and ask you some questions. Have you ever been under hypnosis before?"

Hunter's mind suddenly flashed a scene before his eyes. He's on a train, in a large berth surrounded by many lit candles. There's a very young woman standing before him, dressed in a long silk Asian gown. She unbuttons the front of the gown and reveals two beautiful breasts . . .

"Sir?"

Hunter shook himself out of his daze.

"Have you ever been under before?"

Hunter thought another moment then replied: "I really don't know."

Zoltan pretended to take notes. The truth was he wanted to get this whole thing over with as soon as possible.

He opened his equipment bag, lifted out his Truth-O-Meter and his three crystal balls. Hunter looked at the globes and then back at the man as if to say, you've got to be kidding me.

Zoltan had Hunter attach his own contacts from the Truth-O-Meter. One wrapped around his wrist, another around his right ring finger and a third around his head.

Then Zoltan plugged the device in, tested the power, saw it was good, and switched it on.

Then he pulled another device from his bag and connected it to the first. It was a box with a small TV screen in it. Zoltan plugged this in too, did a quick test, then switched it on. The screen came alive. On it, a small yellow light began blinking.

"OK," he said to Hunter. "Now look at the blinking light. Wipe from your mind the fact that you are hooked to the TOM. Just relax. And tell me everything . . ."

* * *

Back in the Assessment Board room, the three elderly officers went back to sleep.

The three men behind the mirror sat silently as well, smoking cigarettes, staring at the ceiling. Though they had no way of knowing it, each man was thinking of the same thing: what he would do after the war.

Agent X hoped to latch on to a lucrative position with the War Crimes Commission; it was already getting formed up in Washington and his contacts were lobbying for him to be hired as an investigator. This would be ideal for him. The position would pay well and be long-term. After so many years of brutal warfare, he was sure that any war crimes trial would go on for 10 years or more.

Agent Z hoped to go to work for one of the big weapons manufacturers once the fighting was over. Their coffers would be flush with money, he was sure—money looking for a place to be spent. His talent would be very helpful in the postwar environment, he believed, especially in finding another war to fight.

As for Agent Y, the silent partner of the three, he wasn't really sure what he was going to do. He wanted to get married, but he'd have to find a girl first. He wanted to build a house near the ocean, maybe further out on Cape Cod. He'd always had visions of a farmhouse right on the edge of a cliff, overlooking the Atlantic.

Maybe he could actually grow something on it and sell it and leave this crazy life behind. . . .

Two hours and 20 minutes later, Zoltan staggered through the door of the interrogation room.

The three elderly officers were in various stages of napping when he burst in. Zoltan fell into a chair, the noise stirring the old men. He was sweating and out of breath.

"My goodness, what's the matter with you?" Captain Pegg asked the hypnotist.

"This man," Zoltan said, hastily lighting a cigarette. "He's just told me the most incredible story."

"Oh really?" one of the elderly lieutenants said.

"Well, tell us then," Pegg said, lighting his pipe.

Zoltan composed himself and drew heavily on his cigarette.

"I'm not sure where to begin" he stammered between puffs, opening up a notebook full of scribbling. "He claims that he is from America, and that he is a soldier of the American armed forces. But not the U.S. Army or Air Corps."

"Well, we knew that," Pegg told him.

"Yes, but he says he's part of something called the United American Armed Forces. And that America has been fighting a series of little wars for about five years, after the world went through a catastrophic war he called World War III. He says the Americans won that war, but were screwed in the peace talks."

"Screwed? How?" Pegg wanted to know for some reason.

Zoltan took another long drag from his cigarette and checked his notes.

"He says that the bad guys sent a bunch of missiles over the North Pole that obliterated the middle of the country. Killed a lot of people, drove a lot more a little crazy. Destroyed the fabric of the government. There was a period of anarchy. A lot of people escaped to Canada."

"Who were these bad guys? The Germans?" Pegg asked.

"I'm not sure," Zoltan said, checking his notes again. "He mentioned so many enemies. Some were called the Mid-Aks. The Family. The Soviets . . ."

"You mean the Russians?" one of the looies asked.

"We're not fighting them," the other old looie said. "Are we?"

"No," Captain Pegg corrected them. "No one is fighting the Russians. There *are* no Russians. Germany owns Russia."

"No, these were different Russians," Zoltan insisted. "Some are good. Some are bad."

He took another massive puff of his cigarette.

"But then he says after a lot of fighting, America made a comeback. Not as the United States, but as a bunch of little countries and territories and such. It was broken up that way. And they began their own armies and navies and things. And then they began fighting each other. Or was it the other way around? I'm not sure. Anyway, then the Second Civil War happened, and then the Russians were finally thrown out. And then the Germans invaded and they were beaten. And then the Vikings invaded . . ."

"The Vikings?" Pegg laughed.

"Yes, he swears it," Zoltan went on. "They had invisible boats and strange weapons and drank some weird drink and . . . Jessuzz, I don't know if the Vikings invaded first or the Germans. Or maybe they came over at the same time. In any case, they were all beaten and thrown out— and then these United Americans battled the Japanese. Or people who were like Japanese."

"The Japanese?" Lieutenant Jeff wheezed, "Why, there's no more peaceful, gentle people in the world . . ."

"I know," Zoltan went on. "But he says they fought them and beat them. Then he fought in a place he called Viet Nam."

"Viet Nam?" Pegg asked. "Where the hell is that?"

Zoltan just shrugged.

"Beats me," he said. "In fact, I don't know half of the places this guy says he's been. But he and his men went down to this Viet Nam place and fought a war there—or maybe two wars, I'm not sure. And well, I just had to stop at that point. I felt like I was going crazy . . ."

Zoltan drew heavily on his cigarette and let out a long, troubled plume of smoke. The room grew silent. Outside, the first rays of dawn were beginning to peek through the window blinds. They'd been at this all night.

"Strange tale," one of the lieutenants said finally.

"Little too late in the war to be bucking for a Section Eight, isn't it?" the other looie said.

"But I don't think he's crazy," Zoltan said, the words leaving his lips just a bit sooner than he wished. "Not completely, anyway."

"Well, how can you say that?" Pegg asked.

Even the stenographer looked up at him.

"Yes, how can you say that?" one of the men behind the two-way mirror asked.

It was X, usually the most cynical of the three. Now even Z sat up and began taking notice again.

Zoltan grew jittery. His psychic radar was flashing warning signals all over the screen. He really didn't want to open up this can of worms. He knew that, just like him, everyone just wanted to go home once the war was over. No one wanted any kind of loose strings, and any excuse to give the military a reason to keep them in after the impending cease-fire and armistice. But, on the other hand, this Hunter guy was so weird, so convincing, he just couldn't be dismissed lightly.

Finally Zoltan said to the three elderly officers: "I know it sounds nuts, but this man, in some manner, is telling the truth."

"That *is* nuts," Captain Pegg scoffed.

"Yes, that *is* nuts," X said in his best old guy voice from behind the mirror.

Z sat a little closer to the one-way glass, as if he might hear better.

"But is it?" he asked X cryptically. "Wasn't there a case a few years ago that . . ."

X reached over and literally put his hand across Z's mouth.

"Cool it, my friend," he told him coldly. "You never know who is listening in."

Z pushed his hand away. "Do you really think someone is bugging us even as we are bugging these people outside?"

X leaned back in his chair and put his hands behind his head. The subject was closed.

"Let's just listen," he suggested.

Zoltan was lighting yet another cigarette.

"That machine of yours has been wrong before?" one of the looies was asking him. "Hasn't it?"

"Nope," Zoltan replied emphatically.

"Nope," X parroted him.

A silence descended on the room again. It was broken only by the erratic puffing of Captain Pegg's pipe.

"Well," the very senior officer said finally. "What should we do now?"

Another silence.

"Get some coffee?" one of the looies asked.

"Talk to him again," Z said into the microphone and thus into Pegg's bad ear.

"Let's talk to him again first," Pegg said.

The looie looked at Zoltan, who crushed out his cigarette and got up to retrieve Hunter.

"I think this has to go higher up the ladder," Zoltan told them.

"Save your breath, Swami," X said from behind the mirror. "That's the last place this is going."

But just as Zoltan was about to go out the door, it suddenly swung open and the sleepy corporal left to guard Hunter rushed in.

The three elderly officers were shaken. Behind the mirror, Agents X, Y and Z quickly sat up again.

"Shit, now what?" Z exclaimed.

"What's wrong?" Pegg asked the young soldier.

"He's gone," the corporal replied.

"Who's gone?" Pegg asked.

"That guy," the soldier replied shakily. "The weird guy. He just got up and ran out of the room. Pushed me aside like I wasn't even there."

Behind the mirror, X reached over and quickly pushed the button on his phone bank.

"Alert security," he barked into the phone. "We have an unauthorized individual on this base . . ."

"Damn, I don't need this," Z grumbled. "Who the hell *is* this guy that he's causing us so much trouble?"

Agent Y, the one who had stayed silent all this time, remained so. But in his head he thought: *Now that's a good question.*

Two seconds after that, the airfield's attack warning siren went off.

Chapter 4

Hunter was running.

He wasn't sure exactly why, but he was running, full-out. Out of the red brick building, across the road, and toward the air base's longest runway. His body was shaking so much, it felt like his head was going to burst. It was as if he had no control over what he was doing. Something very deep, very primal was telling him to run, toward the runways. Toward the airplanes that sat nearby.

He didn't hear the base's attack warning sirens begin to blare. Didn't hear the Intruder Alert Klaxons either. It was as if all sound was shut out of his head, all except his own huffing and puffing. All around him, people were running towards shelters, building basements, even slit trenches that seemed to be dug everywhere. Everyone was running in the opposite direction as he.

It took him less than a minute to reach the runway. Now, without breaking stride, he ran over to a line of Pogo fighters, selected one, and climbed up the access ladder.

There was no one around the plane. No flight personnel or ground crew. It didn't matter to him. He opened the cockpit on the vertical fighter himself and climbed in. The dials and switches inside looked like everything else in this strange world: props from a bad sci-fi movie. Again, this did not deter him. He began pushing buttons and throwing switches and in seconds, the big tail-sitter aircraft began to come alive.

He was now aware of people around the bottom of the aircraft, pointing up at him. One man had a rifle and was aiming at him, but another was pulling it away from the would-be shooter. Hunter hit a few more buttons—oil pressure checks, electrical system readouts—and then pushed the start lever and the huge double propellers at the top of the strange aircraft burst to life.

This served to scatter most of the people buzzing around below him. The cloud of thick black exhaust drove away the rest. The Pogo was shaking so much, Hunter's teeth were chattering. He scanned the rest of the flight instruments, and somehow knew immediately what each one was supposed to do.

Another check of the oil pressure, another check of the electrical readouts. Everything was green. He flipped a switch that read, WEAPONS LOAD. It blinked back on with a message that said: Full.

Hunter then strapped himself in, leaned back in the seat, and reached for the throttle bar.

And then, at that moment, it hit him . . .

He spoke the words out loud:

"What the hell am I doing?"

He didn't know. Just as he was compelled to get up and run out of the hypnosis session and climb into this peculiar airplane, now he was compelled to launch the damn thing and go somewhere to do something.

But what?

He just didn't know.

And could he actually fly this thing? Could he fly at all? Was he a pilot?

Again, he just didn't know.

But something was telling him to go. Now . . .

So he kind of shrugged and took a deep breath and

realized at that moment that he wasn't even wearing a crash helmet or an oxygen mask. But he hit the launch lever anyway.

The big airplane shuddered once, twice. And then, in an amazing burst of power and speed, the Pogo jumped off the runway and went straight up into the cloudless morning sky.

While it was not an unusual occurrence for the base's attack warning signals to go off at Otis Field, it had been quite a while since they had done so.

The vast air base had been attacked a dozen times in this latest phase of the war, the last time being 18 months ago. In that incident, two missile-firing U-boats surfaced about 20 miles out and launched a half dozen concussion rockets at the base's main runway, cratering it badly.

But no defensive measures were taken then or after any other attack on the base for one simple reason: the U-boats were usually long gone before any aircraft crews could get scrambled and any aircraft could launch. The standard procedure then for an attack on the base was for everyone to get to a shelter or a slit trench and stay hunkered down until the attack was over.

That's what most of the personnel at the base were doing now. The shelters were filled and the slit trenches were too. However, the sixth floor of the red administration building still held several people. The elderly officers had retreated to the basement shelter along with the stenographer.

But Agents X, Y, and Z were still on hand, as was a very concerned Captain Zoltan, who was now in their secret room with them. He was looking out the huge unshuttered window to the ocean beyond. His body was shaking. Bad vibes were everywhere.

"What if a German missile hits this building?" he asked the shadowy agents. "We'll all be killed."

Agent X just stared back at him. "You're supposed to

be one who sees the future," he replied snidely. "Do you see this happening?"

Zoltan wiped his brow and nervously tried to push down the creases in his uniform jacket. "No, I guess I don't," he replied finally.

"OK, good," Agent Z said to him. "Then what's to worry?"

But Zoltan *was* worried, though he really wasn't sure why.

"That man, Hunter" he started to say. "He is someone you must not lose track of."

Agent Y was standing at the big window looking up at the Pogo's contrail as it disappeared into the deep blue sky.

"Well, that might be a problem," he said wryly.

The base's attack sirens were now wailing louder than ever. They'd been triggered by a rather outdated system of sonar buoys laid into the seabed about 50 miles off the coast, devices specially designed to detect U-boats. If one was tripped, a warning would go up and down the entire coastline. The sirens were annoying though, so X picked up a phone and called to the base's security office—he wanted the alarms turned off. But of course, no one was in the SO's office to answer the phone.

Agent Z turned back to Zoltan.

"What is it about this man that concerns you so?" he asked the hypnotist.

"He's just a very strange one," Zoltan replied, lighting a cigarette.

"They're all strange," Z said nonchalantly.

"But not like him," Zoltan said. "He's either the best actor in the world or . . ."

"Or what?" Z asked. "Or he's telling the truth? You don't really want to go down on record as believing that, do you?"

Zoltan began to reply, but this time thought better of it.

Instead he just crushed out his cigarette and nervously lit another.

Hunter was at 10,000 feet and laughing hysterically.

Yet he didn't know why.

He was spinning through the air, maxed out on the weird airplane's double-prop engine, laughing and yelping and screaming. He was uncontrollably happy. Either that, or his brain was slowly being starved for oxygen and he was suffering from some kind of narcosis.

Either way, it was euphoric.

The airplane drove like a truck. But he really didn't care. He was doing something here that he hadn't done in a very long time.

He was flying.

He let the g-forces flow through him as the plane climbed higher. The further he got from the ground, the better he felt. This was a battle with gravity, he realized, and for the moment at least, he was winning. And it felt so good, he never wanted to come down.

So he continued to climb—15,000 feet, 20,000, 25,000, 30,000. He was estatic! 35,000 feet, 40,000. He could start to see the dark edge of the stratosphere above him. He believed he could see the stars, the planets. 45,000 feet, 50,000! Damn, he'd done this before. Exactly this! He let out another whoop. He didn't know who he was or where he was, but he knew this is what he'd been born to do, no matter where he'd come from.

He began doing loops. Crazy eights. One-point star-bursts. He felt that at one time he might have been part of a group of airplanes and pilots who performed these things, but only the stunts and his ability to do them remained, and so he did them with great vigor. An upside-down crossover. A controlled stall. Four-point turns. Eight-point turns. These maneuvers, he didn't even know what they were called, yet he was performing them with incredible precision. And all the while laughing uncontrollably.

But then his body began buzzing again—and this time, it was definitely a different vibe.

He was up here to do something, his brain was telling him. That same something that had compelled him to take off in the first place. But what was it?

He put the airplane into a steep dive. Again, the g-forces felt good on his face. He had a panel that read WEAPONS STATUS. But he had no idea what kind of guns the airplane was packing.

However, somewhere in the back of his brain, way in the back part of his skull, it seemed he had a file on this airplane and on its guts. When the Pogo was first built, it was intended to be fitted with two machine guns. But in this place, that all happened years ago. The airplane looked the same, more or less, but what about the weapons? There really was only one way to find out.

He reached over and pulled the weapons lever. There was a bright flash! He was sure the nose of the airplane was about to blow off. There was a huge flame, a huge puff of smoke. And a cloud of sparks.

He quickly disengaged the lever and took a deep breath. Wow!

There must have been . . . wait a minute, was it possible? He pulled the lever again. In amongst the smoke and fire and sparks he detected six telltale streaks. Six machine guns on an airplane? That seemed way too many!

He did a third burst—and sure enough. There were six long fiery streaks. Jessuzz, he thought. What a frigging punch!

He pushed the throttle ahead and the little airplane leapt through the air again. It was oddly shaped, but quick and powerful. He put the Pogo into a spin. And felt the laughter start to gurgle up inside him again. Heavy as it was, the thing handled perfectly!

The plane was strange, but in a great way. It was outlandish, but cool at the same time—though he wasn't sure exactly why he felt both opinions so deeply. Had he flown a similarly outlandish plane before—back wherever he'd come from?

He didn't know.

But suddenly a piece of the puzzle fell into place. Suddenly he realized that he knew something more about himself: He was a fighter pilot. He could feel it. In fact, he might have been more than just an ordinary fighter pilot.

Something was telling him he might have once been the best fighter pilot in the whole world.

But once again, he had to drag himself back to the matter at hand. Why was he up here?

His body vibed again—and he was compelled to look down. And right below him, outlined in black against the deep blue Atlantic, were two submarines. Each was just surfacing. Each had a giant Iron Cross painted on its conning tower.

Their decks were sporting two missile launchers apiece. Crewmen in dark green uniforms were scurrying about these launchers. It was obvious they were getting ready to fire the weapons.

And at that moment, Hunter knew the answer to the question as to why he was here.

From way back deep in his mind, way back in his skull, he heard a familiar voice say: *Time to get to work.*

The pair of German submarines that had just broken the surface were U-boats #153 and #419.

Both were Raeder Class vessels, meaning they were the biggest—and oldest—of the German underwater fleet.

They boasted crews of 311 and 356 respectively. They ran on cogenerating gas turbine reaction power, which made them efficient and gave them superior range. Their weapons may have seemed unusual for a submarine. They carried no torpedoes, no antiship weapons at all. The subs barely had periscopes. These weren't attack submarines.

Rather they were missile-firing boats, known to all as "Zoomers."

What they could do under the right conditions was launch sea-to-surface missiles, the biggest of which was called the Dogglebanger-13.

The DG-13 carried a warhead the size of a small car. It contained nearly five tons of high explosives. It was partially guided by a set of coordinates preset into its nose cone. But with a DG-13, pinpoint accuracy was not a major concern. With its blockbuster-type weapons load, the missile could lay waste to a five-square-mile area. Getting the missile to impact anywhere in the neighborhood of a 2500-foot radius did just fine.

Yes, the DG-13 was a powerful weapon, and the Raeder-class submarines were ideal as a launching platform—but this particular mission was an ironic one for the two subs. It was both their last mission of the war and also their most futile.

Simply put, the German Navy was almost nonexistent. It was close to dead broke. Out of money, out of sailors, out of vessels. The number of German ships that could even make the trip across the Atlantic could be counted on one hand these days, and U-153 and U-419 were two of them.

This attack was also ironic in that the DG-13 warheads being used were the biggest of the war—6.5 ton mammoths developed a year ago by German naval warfare scientists but found to be too costly to go into mass production. So Germany's largest warhead would be used in its last attack on the American mainland. It was a last-gasp mission if there ever was one; a desperate attempt at one last dribble of propaganda before Germany finally fell.

As their commanders back in Lyons had told the U-boat captains: "Make some noise. Then come home."

It was the nature of the DG-13 missile that it was wild on take off, wild during its initial flight, wild when its gyro-pilot took over, and wild all the way down to the target. It was not a tactical weapon—it was much too imprecise for that. Or a strategic weapon either. It was a terror weapon, the last in a long line the Germans had produced over the last half century. Designed simply to kill innocents and inflict pain and suffering. The military equivalent of a bomb in a baby carriage.

The subs had six missiles between them, and thus six targets: Two for downtown Boston. One for downtown Providence. One for downtown Hartford. One for downtown Bridgeport. And the sixth one, a very long lob into Manhattan itself. The two subs were 42 miles off shore. The DG-13 had a range of 110 miles. All they really had to do was point the missiles in the right direction and fire away. If they came down anywhere within a downtown area, casualties would be high, especially at this time of day. The last missile was set to come down in Times Square itself. German intelligence—what was left of it—had informed the Reich High Command that an American victory party had already started in the square. It would be a perfect place then to aim the very last DG-13.

The subs also had one more thing going for them in this final attack: the element of surprise. U-boats firing missiles at the East Coast was nothing new. But there had not been such an attack in almost two years. The commanders of both submarines considered this very good luck.

The deck crews on both subs prepared their first missile and then stood by. Nearly forty tons of high explosives raining down on five Americans cities. That would, the sub captains knew, "make some noise."

Then they could finally all go home.

Or so they thought.

The crewmen of the subs never heard him coming.

This was odd because the Pogo was not a quiet airplane. Its engines were huge and noisy and smoky. It would never be accused of being a stealth either.

But whether the deck crews of U-153 and U-419 were distracted by their mission or thoughts of going home, no one would ever know. The fact is, when the Pogo swooped down upon them, its SE/X whistle screaming, its engine in full growl, the deck hands looked up only at the very last moment. Then they simply froze and saw their end before them.

So the first pass came out of nowhere. The awesome six-gun barrage from the Pogo blew a hole deep in the forward water compartment of U-153. Half the deck crew were killed instantly. A fire in the electrical room directly below the deck roared to life. This explosion blew several more crewmen into the water. One of them was Hans Lans. He was U-153's second-duty cook and first-duty missile aimer.

Lans found himself forty feet away from his sub, burned extensively on his arms and legs and watching in horror as the American aircraft pulled up and out of its murderous dive, disappearing into the thick morning cumulus clouds which had moved in above. Slipping into shock, Hans had a notion to swim back to his sub, burning and smoking as it was. But the screech of the airplane returned and Hans knew getting back to U-153 would soon be impossible.

He watched as the airplane came in level this time, unleashing its powerful barrage on the conning tower of U-419. There was much smoke, much fire, and when it all blew away, Hans could see right through the conning tower of the sub, the bullet holes were so big. Then two quick explosions erupted below decks even before the attacking airplane had pulled up and out of its run.

Lans had to duck underwater to avoid being hit by a huge chunk of flaming metal that whooshed by his head a second later. When he resurfaced, the conning tower of U-419 was gone. All that was left was a smoking hole in the middle of the deck. The sub tipped over, the hole quickly filled with water, and down it went.

That lost his idea of swimming to his companion ship. And now the airplane was coming back again. It was diving on U-153 even as the crewmen remaining on top were desperately trying to get back into the sub. But the sub was diving—and water was pouring in the access holes and the airplane was firing madly again. It was all of a submariner's worst nightmares rolled into one. Lans saw his vessel sinking and heard his comrades dying horribly not 40 feet away.

But then, just as U-153 began to go under, a strange thing happened. Whether it was an electrical short circuit or a stupid piece of heroism on the part of one of his fellow sailors, one of the DG-13s launched off the deck. The huge clumsy weapon staggered off its launcher, stirring up a storm of water and spray. But somehow it made it to the prescribed height of 50 feet, where its secondary motor kicked in and off it went.

Lans felt a sudden and insane surge of pride—or was it revenge?

At least one missile got off, he thought, all feeling in his badly injured arms and legs gone now.

But then he saw the airplane turn over once again and make one long strafing pass over the remains of U-153, killing it for sure. Then with a spin of its wings and a burst of power from its engine, the Pogo took off after the DG-13 missile.

As Lans sank below the waves for the last time, only one thing was on his mind: could the crazy American pilot catch up with the missile before the missile blew apart an entire city?

It was a question the answer to which Submariner First Class Hans Lans would never know.

The truth was, catching the German terror missile was not the problem.

It left a contrail so thick and smoky, it could have been seen at night in bad weather by a blind man.

Stopping the missile once he caught up with it was Hunter's dilemma. He already had two strikes against him. The Pogo's six guns were powerful, but the amount of ammunition that the plane could actually haul into the air was limited. Translation: he was out of ammo.

Even worse, the Pogo's big engine sucked fuel like a toilet sucked water. Whenever he hit the throttle, it was like a flush, and he could watch his fuel needle drop correspondingly. In fact, he was now on the reserve tank, even though he'd been airborne for barely 10 minutes.

So he had nothing to shoot at the missile and he would soon lose the ability to chase it. What could he do?

He knew he first had to catch up with the missile and pull even with it, no matter how much gas it took. So he laid on the throttle and flushed the toilet and watched the reserve fuel needle go down and the fuel warning light pop on. But the airplane burst through the air with renewed power.

It took him but a minute to pull even with it. But already the coastline of Massachusetts was coming into view. This DG-13 was one of the missiles targeted for downtown Boston. Hunter knew he had to act quickly, or the terror weapon would surely hit its mark.

With no ammo, Hunter really had only one choice. He flew a little ahead of the DG-13 and with the last of his fuel, laid on his engine hoping to disrupt the air flow in front of the missile. But the weapon just wobbled a bit and continued blundering on its way.

Hunter tried again, this time putting the ass end of the Pogo just a few feet away from the missile's snout, but again the flying bomb only wobbled a bit and resumed its course.

Hunter had only one trick left. The coastline was looming up very fast. He might not have enough time to do it, but he had to try. Without thinking about it, he yanked the control column up, left, then left again. A moment later he was riding directly underneath the missile. Then, gently, he moved up on its right side. Then with a flick of the steering yoke, he tipped the Pogo violently to the right. His wing smashed against the missile's, jarring it loose from the fuselage. Hunter hit it again, the missile's wing began to flap some more. He hit it again and again. And again. Finally on the sixth try, he hit it hard enough for the wing to fall off. That's when he kicked the Pogo all the way to the right. The missile fell away crazily to the left.

The big bomb spiraled down, impacted on a deserted beach next to a jetty, then bounced up and went into the side of a cliff. Hunter got the Pogo back under control and put it into a very steep climb. The missile went off two seconds later. The explosion was so huge, the flames chased Hunter right up to 4000 feet.

But he didn't care.

He was suddenly laughing again. He'd killed the missile and lived to tell about it.

He turned the Pogo over, and though now dangerously low on fuel, he buzzed the huge crater made by the explosion. Already the seawater was running into it, creating a small lake right on the edge of the famous Cape Cod seashore.

How strange was this, he thought. How fitting as well . . .

Hunter pulled up and turned the plane back towards the inside of the Cape. As he did, he flew above the cliffs and noticed that they were out of place for the landscape. These were the highest places around, and as he passed over one particular place he thought he could see a farmhouse below him and a field that went right up to the edge of the cliff. It looked like a hayfield.

And when Hunter flew over it, he felt even better than when he first became airborne.

Why did he feel this way, he thought, looking down on this little farm with the hayfield at the edge of the cliff.

It would be a long time before he found out.

Chapter 5

The attack sirens finally wound down at Otis.

At the last squeal, people began emerging from their hiding places. The shelters emptied out. The slit trenches too. People gathered in small groups and began discussing what had happened, which was useless, because none of them really knew. The attack warning had gone off, but there was no attack. It wasn't a drill; they would have been notified by now if it had been. Was it a false alarm? It would be a rare occasion if it was.

But something else had happened here. Just as the alarm had gone off, someone had stolen one of the base's Pogo verti-planes. These two events had to be related—the people knew no other way to think about such things. But just *how* they were related, they didn't know.

Only the small group of men on the sixth floor of the admin building knew the answer to that—and even they weren't sure what had happened exactly.

"Well, this guy is long gone now," Agent Z was saying as he scanned the skies all around the base. "Though God knows where."

The phone rang. X picked it up, listened briefly, then hung up again.

"That was an intercepted call from coastal patrol," he told the others. "They report a large explosion over near Nauset Heights."

"He crashed?" Z asked.

"They said it was very big—maybe a German missile," X replied. "There's a hole down there the size of a football field. That sounds a lot bigger than one he could have made."

"Maybe there really was an attack then?" Zoltan wanted to know.

"If that was the case, where did the missiles land, Swami?" Z taunted him, irritated that the psychic officer would even dare to speak.

"It really is a mystery now," X relented. "Too bad that guy is gone . . ."

"Don't be too sure of that," Z said.

They all looked up at him.

"Why?" they asked.

Z was standing at the big window looking out at the coast with his binoculars.

"Because I think he's coming back . . ." he said.

"Coming back?" Agent X and Zoltan said together.

They all rushed to the window, and sure enough, they saw the telltale exhaust trail of the Pogo approaching.

"This is rather impossible, isn't it?" X said, never taking his eyes off the oncoming verti-plane. "He should have run out of fuel long ago."

"Why would he come back?" Zoltan wondered aloud. "That's what I want to know."

Z turned to him.

"You know, for a guy that supposedly possesses so many psychic goods, you're asking a lot of questions . . ."

Again, Zoltan almost said something—but thought better of it, and kept his mouth shut instead.

By now the groups of people who'd been chatting out on the flight line were aware that the Pogo was returning as well. They were pointing and gesturing as the plane approached, all of them just as surprised and startled as the men in the admin building.

Many began running towards the big circle painted on Runway 4, where the Pogos usually landed. A security detail, its vehicles equipped with high-pitched sirens, made their way for the same place.

X picked up the phone and was instantly talking to the base's security officer.

"Arrest the individual flying that plane," he told the man before gruffly hanging up.

The plane went right over the admin building, losing speed and altitude as it did so. As the three agents and the mystic watched, it came to nearly a complete stop. At the same time, it moved its tail down and its nose up and went vertical, just like that.

The Pogo was not a pilot's dream. The reason they were used sparingly was they were a bitch to land. The pilot had to get a hover set and then look over his shoulder and ease the thing down. It was like tapping one's head and rubbing one's belly at the same time, as someone once put it. Up was down; right was left. Some Pogo landings went on for many agonizing minutes; the pilot backing off, going higher, only to complicate his task because the higher one went, the longer and more painful the landing process would be.

But not this pilot—this very surprising individual. He did it completely differently. As soon as he went into his hover, he simply cut the engine way back and the Pogo fell—backward—toward the big circle.

And just as everyone was convinced it would crash, the pilot cranked the engine again, in effect putting on the brakes. Then he touched down without so much as a bump.

It was such a piece of artistry, some people applauded. But then the security troops arrived and the crowd scattered.

The pilot climbed out—and accepted a brief spate of renewed applause. Then he met the security people at the bottom of the access ladder and went calmly to the paddy wagon. The security truck slowly began to drive away.

The phone in the sixth floor office rang a moment later. X answered it. It was the base's top security officer.

"We have him," was the message. "Now what do we do with him?"

It was a good question. X and Z looked at each other. Neither wanted to take on the responsibility of this strange case. What the hell was this guy? A villain? A hero? A spy? A madman? They'd be months trying to figure it out.

No, neither one wanted to get involved in this thing, not so close to what should be the end of the war.

They had better things to do.

So it called for a quick decision, like many quick decisions made when victory was pending. What would they do with this man, now back in their custody?

"I say send him to Sing Sing," X declared. "With the rest of the freaks."

"Sounds good to me," Z replied. He picked up the phone again.

Zoltan was astonished. "You're going to send that man to prison?" he asked. He couldn't believe it.

But they ignored him.

"Make arrangements to transport the prisoner to Ossining Military Prison," Z told the base security officer. He listened for a moment, then cupped the phone and said: "They want to know on what charge?"

X and Z had to think another moment. "Theft of government property?" X suggested.

"Sure . . . or something," Z agreed.

Zoltan lit another cigarette. "I think this is a big mistake," he said. "This man, he is not just an ordinary person. I mean, look at what he did here today. There are some pilots that still can't land a Pogo and they've been flying them for 10 years!"

X finally turned back towards him and fixed him in his steely gaze. "You want to join him in the clink, Swami?"

Zoltan's heart went into his throat. He had no doubt

the OSS agent could get him locked up just as quickly as this strange Hunter character.

So he took the cigarette out of his teeth and drew a line across his mouth. The message was clear: his lips were sealed.

"Theft of government property," Z said into the phone. "Give him, um, let's see. Ten years . . . OK. Bye."

Z then gathered his notebooks and put them into his briefcase.

"Well, that's that," he said, snapping the case closed with a flourish. "Where are we going to eat dinner?"

"Your choice," X replied, getting his coat and hat.

At that moment they both looked up at their other colleague.

Agent Y hadn't said two words during the whole time. He was standing at the big picture window now, looking out on the huge air base, watching as the armored police wagon took the strange man away to prison.

"Problems, my friend?" X asked him.

But Agent Y didn't really hear the question. He turned around and looked at them both, his face blank, as if he was coming out of a trance himself.

"You know what's really strange about all this?" he asked them.

They both shook their heads.

"The strange thing is," Agent Y told them, "I think I might know that man."

Chapter 6

The enormous German battle cruiser slipped into the German-occupied Spanish port of Cádiz at exactly midnight.

The ship had been at sea for nearly two months, a long time these days, and this stop was to be the last of its last patrol. The ship captain's orders to his crew were to cool off the double-reaction engines, destroy all sensitive documents and await further orders.

In days past, when the cruiser returned from patrol, families of the crew members would be on hand to welcome the vessel back. Sometimes there was recorded music, speeches, a small celebration. Reunions. Then preparation for the next cruise would begin.

But there was no celebration this time. No loved ones, no mechanical oompah-band pumping out reverb polkas. This time the return of the battle cruiser had been kept a tightly guarded secret. The port itself had been sealed off. Armed soldiers lined all the docks, the harbors, the roofs of nearby buildings. They blocked off all roads leading in and out of the city itself. A curfew from sundown to sunrise had been declared. Violators would be shot on sight.

These were very strange edicts for the port city of Cádiz, or for any part of Occupied Spain at all. The German Army had rolled into Spanish territory shortly after the occupation of France in 1940 and had been here ever since. Nearly two generations of people of mixed Spanish and German blood had come and gone, and indeed Spain was now more German than Spanish. The people felt this way, and so it was unusual for them to be treated as their forebears had been 50 years before. Curfews, soldiers in the streets, orders to shoot on sight—these things had not been seen in these parts for nearly a half a century.

But then again, how often did a messiah arrive?

The ship was drawn up to its berth by the automated docking system, run by the enormous Mark V computer housed in the largest building in the port. Save for a few of the ship's top officers, and a squad of SSS guards, the crew was confined to quarters. All windows were shuttered. Absolutely no conversation would be permitted, electronic or otherwise.

A convoy of armored vehicles was waiting at the dock. Personnel carriers mostly, three high-speed Tiger-7 supertanks were also in evidence. These frightful machines carried a crew of 10, an enormous 188-mm gun and could travel nearly 80 miles per hour on the open road. These three were just about the last ones left in the German inventory.

There was a stretch Mercedes limousine on hand too, and it was this vehicle which was now driven up to the dock, where the gangplank from the sailing castle had been placed.

A flurry of hand signals and walkie-talkie blasts bounced between the ship and the dock. The port and the city were secured; this was confirmed over and over again. Five massive Messerschmitt helicopter gunships were circling high overhead—yes, the skies were secured too.

Finally, the main hatch leading from the ship's bridge

opened and a dozen heavily armed SSS troopers came out. They were followed by a phalanx of the ship's officers. Then three more armed SSS guards. Behind them, a dark figure, dressed all in black, stepped out.

A hush went over the port. Some fool played a spotlight on the man's face. Thin features, a short beard. Black hair. The man looked directly into the light and the bulb exploded.

Startled, the officers hustled down the gangplank; one quickly opened the limo door. The figure in black climbed in, the door was closed behind him, and the entire motorcade sped away. Out of the port, through the deserted city and to the Spanish Autobahn beyond. They headed north—the entire roadway was clear ahead of them for miles. At top speed they'd be in Berlin by morning.

Two citizens, two middle-aged sisters, did dare to look out their window while all this was going on. All the security in the world could not prevent them, or anyone else in the city, from knowing what was happening. Not even a well-planned German security net could keep hidden a secret this big.

"This man who has come to save us, to save Germany," one sister said to the other as the motorcade flashed by. "They found him out in the ocean."

"Walking atop the waves?" the second sister asked. "Just as they always said it would happen?"

"Yes," the other replied in a hushed reverential voice. "Walking atop the waves. That's exactly how they found him . . ."

Near Bermuda
The next morning

Somebody had finally found the third floater.

It happened about 40 miles off the northern coast of Bermuda. The waves were high and the wind was blowing at 30 knots. A rainstorm had just passed through the area and it was cold for this time of year.

A small rescue launch was sent to pick him up—a very small boat from a much larger one. The rescuers were astonished when they reached the man and found he was still alive. They quickly pulled him onboard.

He was dressed very oddly; right away they felt he was from a different place than they. His skin was very white—he'd been in the water a long time. And he was very thin, as if he were malnourished.

Yet once they laid him at the bottom of their launch, he simply opened his eyes and stared up at his rescuers.

"You're alive." one of the men blurted out. His accent was very thick.

"I know," said the man they pulled from the sea.

"How did you get out here?" a second rescuer asked.

The man thought for a moment.

"That I still don't know," he finally answered.

He looked up at the men. They were in gray uniforms, but they wore long scraggly beards and had oddly curled hair. Their arms, hands, faces, and chests were emblazoned with outlandish tattoos, most of them six-pointed stars.

The man saw their boat was just one of many. Indeed, a long string of boats stretched out before him. Though they were armed, these weren't naval vessels; rather they looked like large passenger ships that had been heavily armed in a very haphazard fashion. They were rusty and old, but their decks were crowded with people. Tough, angry faces on the seamen, gentle, inquiring faces on the women and children. They were all looking down at the man who'd just been pulled from the water.

"What is your name?" one of the rescuers asked him.

The man from the water thought a moment.

"I don't know," he lied. Actually he'd remembered his name sometime during the long night. But he suddenly didn't want to tell these people anything.

"Well, from now on, you'll be known as Rower #1446798."

"Rower?" the man asked, confused.

The rescuers indicated the ship nearest to them. It was a huge cruise liner, which had been rigged with sails, and two huge outboard engines on the stern. But it also had hundreds of holes on its lower hull, down near the water line, and from these holes hundreds of oars were sticking out.

"Yes, a rower," one of the rescuers said. "The Lord has obviously sent you to us. He knows we always need an extra pair of hands to row."

Chapter 7

The cell was 12 feet by eight feet. The ceiling was exactly seven feet and one-quarter inch high. The walls were made of plaster and stone. A single dim bulb hung over it all.

There was a bunk, a chair, a toilet, a sink, and one window. The window faced east, which was good. The morning sun came through on occasion. There were no bars on the window; it was made of thick glass. This was good too, because at night it offered a clear view of the starry sky.

The constellations Ursa Major, Pegasus, and Andromeda had been Hawk Hunter's nightly companions for the past two months. They and dreams of blonds, redheads, brunets. But mostly blonds. Always young, always shapely, they had fed his dreams like ghosts every night since his incarceration.

His hair was very long now, and so was his beard. But his appearance made no difference to him. He was in solitary confinement, segregated from the rest of the prison population. He didn't see anyone other than the same two guards every day. He never went out to the exercise yard; he never went to the chow hall. His meals were brought to him. He washed his own clothes. He cleaned his own cell.

In fact, the only time he left the lockup was to go to the prison library, and this was permitted just once a week. And then he could go only in the middle of the night, when there was no one else inside. He was allowed five minutes to pick out one book, the same two screws watching him at all times.

It took him about two weeks to get over the shock that he was actually in prison and would be for a very long time. No one ever told him what the charges were. But that didn't really matter. He had the three ancient officers and the wacky hypnotist to blame for this and every minute of every day for those first two weeks, he plotted ways to break out and find them and kill them. Hate and thoughts of revenge made his first fortnight in jail bearable.

But eventually, those miserable feelings began to drain away, to be replaced by some a little less dire. He knew he had to make the most of this time in the clink, so he laid out some objectives for himself. The first was to find out exactly where he was.

He had lived another life, somewhere else—this much he knew by now. This world he'd fallen into was a different place, but not a different time. This too he was sure of. But *where* was this? And how did he get here? And what were the differences between where he came from and this here and now? And how could he find out?

His only choice was to reeducate himself. That's why on his first trip to the library he took out a physics book, the only one on the shelves. The text was barely high school level, but he read it cover to cover and at its conclusion, he determined that wherever the hell he was, the same basic tenets of physics seem to apply. This came as a great relief.

Next, he took out a huge book titled *The Greats of Litera-*

ture. Was western culture the same here as there? He read the whole thing. Shakespeare. Dickens. Joyce. Everything was as he remembered it. Then he read a book on the great philosophers. Confucius. Plato. Homer. All of them, just the same.

Next came the psychologists: Freud, Jung, Skinner. And it was in Jung that he found his first clue as to the difference between here and there. Nothing in Jung's writings mentioned the subject of Coincidences. This was very strange. In Hunter's place, Jung had spent much time pondering the meaning of coincidences. He'd coined the term "synchronicity," or "meaningful coincidences" and brought to the fore, at least for discussion, the notion that there might be a spiritual connection to even the smallest coincidental event.

But here, in this place, there was none of that, in Jung or anywhere else. For Hunter, the omission was as glaring as if he'd read $E=MC^3$ or that Scrooge was a sweetheart. What is a world without coincidence? What are the ramifications of that? In all his reading and rereadings, he could not come up with a suitable answer.

He went on to read basic math, basic English, and basic religion books. Everything matched up. One and one still made two; subjects came before verbs, and some people thought the world was created in seven days. Nothing was different.

Then he started reading the history books.

And that's where it got strange.

For the most part, the early history of this place was the same as his, but there were some unusual exceptions. The first thing he discovered was the Athenians had beaten the Spartans in the Peloponnesian War, not the other way around. And then the Battle of Chaeronea was fought in 332 BC, not 338. And that Julius Caesar had conquered England the first time the Romans invaded, not the fifth. And the First Crusade had failed to capture Jerusalem.

The American Revolution played out as he remembered it. but there was no War of 1812. The U.S. Civil War lasted only two years, with the North soundly defeating the South. A second war erupted with Mexico in 1886. There was a Spanish-American War, but most of the fighting had been done in South America. And then, in 1901, the U.S. fought a bizarre war against Italy.

World War I went off just as he recalled it, as did the Great Depression. Then on September 1, 1939, Germany invaded Poland. World War II was on.

But then the real twists began. First of all, Germany attacked France two months after defeating Poland, not six. There was no Phony War then. The British Army was surrounded at Dunkirk—and there it was destroyed. Next, the Spanish allowed the Germans to change the railroad gauge throughout their country and soon the Germans rolled through and captured Gibraltar. This essentially sealed off the Mediterranean, making it a German lake. Germany invaded England next and was successful. They won in North Africa and took over the Middle East oil reserves too. Then Germany attacked and defeated Russia in eight short weeks. Throughout all this, Japan stayed neutral, having no expansionist plans of its own. Instead they fed both Germany and America technology and became very wealthy in the bargain.

It became clear that in this world, the Germans didn't make any of the classic blunders that had sealed their fate in the version of World War II that Hunter knew. They were a formidable enemy, not a stumbling, bumbling giant and had made great strides on the battlefield long before America could do anything about it. By the end of 1943, Germany held all of Europe. By the end of 1944, they held all of the Middle East, all of Africa, and huge chunks of Asia and the Subcontinent.

Then, in April of 1945, Hitler died, not by a bullet in the mouth, but of a simple heart attack. Admiral Canais took over the Third Reich and after that, Germany became "respectable." Any Jews not incinerated were freed. Wartime restrictions were eased. The SS was eliminated, as was the Gestapo. Neutral countries began trading with the vast German Empire.

And the war calmed down.

For 10 years.

Then came something called the Uprising of Kent. This was essentially a revolt in German-controlled England, which after three years of guerrilla fighting and substantial help from the U.S. and other countries, succeeded in ejecting the Germans from the British Isles in 1957.

But the Germans came back in 1961, were thrown out again in 1963, were back in 1967, and were tossed out in 1971.

In between all this, and through various U.S. presidential administrations, the American support for its British allies never wavered. But it did become a drain—both financially and technology-wise. American troops fought with the British for so long, the two forces were eventually integrated, becoming simply the Allied Forces. But despite much valor and sacrifice, the war never really stopped, it just laid dormant for periods of time, flaring up whenever the Germans felt their nerve growing back again. Not total warfare. No clear-cut victories. No unconditional surrenders. Just a long series of appeasements. This is why the conflict had dragged on for 58 years.

And this is why everything looked so odd, yet familiar to Hunter. The U.S. Navy looked the same in its infinite dabs of gray paint because it *was* the same. But it was its ships' designs, and the whole concept of bigger-is-better, that made for a strange world. (Especially for a person like Hunter, who knew somehow that sizing-down was usually the way to go when technology starts to spurt.) Twists and turns, both political and technological, had dictated certain weapons systems be built over others. So this was a world of Pogo verti-fighters and gigantic sea bombers and monstrous aircraft carriers that were supposedly impossible to sink. America built big and long-range, because in this world, that was the best way to protect its own watery borders.

The latest phase of the war started in 1987, with another successful invasion of England by Germany. Control of the North Sea oilfields was the spark this time. Germany craved oil, and the North Sea held more than their Middle Eastern and Russian deposits combined. But this particular invasion of the UK had been very brutal. Many people around the world were outraged. Allies on both sides mustered up and the fighting began anew.

Two new weapons made the Germans especially formidable this time. First, their aircraft engineers figured out a way to build a bomber that would reach America, drop a substantial bomb load, and return, all in one trip; it was the Focke-Wulf 910, the world's first 10,000-mile bomber. This was something the Americans had been working on with vague enthusiasm for years—the great length of the war put the emphasis on some military advancements, at the expense of others. The American long-range bomber was one of them. By 1987, the Germans had finally beat them to it.

The Huns, as many had taken to calling the Germans this time, also developed a new line of missile firing U-boats, like the pair Hunter had destroyed off the coast of Massachusetts. While their long-range bombers made only scattered appearances in the early part of this phase, pulling off some spectacular bombings of Boston, Miami, and New York, the "Great Air Raids" were actually infrequent ones. On the other hand, the German subs were very effective. They were able to surface close to the American seaboard and launch DG-2 missiles up to 300 miles inland. This set off extensive anti–U-boat spending in the U.S. War Department.

These two weapons forced America to devote a lot of resources to continental and naval defense. Thus when the war was back on in 1987, the support for the United Kingdom was less than in previous outbreaks.

That's why it took 10 long years to finally squeeze Germany. Blockades, constant fighting, diplomatic activity, and Germany's own voracious appetite for fuel and raw materials slowly took its toll. Eventually, the Reich went bankrupt. It couldn't pay its bills. Support dried up. Friendly nations went away. And that's why the Americans and their allies had been on the verge of defeating Germany once again when Hunter was thrown into prison.

But that was two months ago. What had happened since? Hunter didn't know. He had no access to newspapers, or radio, or TV. If and when the war was really over, he assumed that word eventually would have filtered down to him here in prison.

Or would it?

Chapter 8

The Bahamas
One week later

The OSS agent known as X pulled his Panama hat further down on his head and let out a yawn.

The tide was coming in. Already he could feel the warm sea lapping at the legs of his beach chair. He would have to get up and move eventually, he supposed. But then again, the tides moved very slowly down here. He might not have to do anything for another 30 minutes, or maybe even an hour. That was fine with him.

He felt a soft finger on his lips and opened his mouth as it commanded. A grape of some sort, peeled and deseeded, was put on his tongue, the soft finger retreating very slowly.

X took a bite. The grape exploded in his mouth.

"Mmmm, very nice," he said.

"It's from my own special patch," the gorgeous brunet on his right whispered in his ear. "I grew it myself."

Another finger touched his lips, this one from the left. He opened his mouth and felt a straw go in.

"Suck," the voice of the gorgeous blond whispered in his left ear.

He did so, and his mouth was soon filled with the sweetest champagne he'd ever tasted.

"Excellent vintage," he said.

"A case of it will be chilling in our room tonight," she cooed.

X pulled his sun hat down a bit further and readjusted himself on the lounge chair.

The water was lapping his toes now but he didn't care. He had peeled grapes, he had champagne, he had the sun. He had a prime piece of beachfront property on Exu, the most exotic of the Bahamian Islands. He had two unbelievably sexy females that would do anything he asked waiting at his beck and call.

This is how he chose to celebrate Armistice Day.

If it was 10 A.M. here in the Bahamas, then it was 5 P.M. in Paris, and that's where, in less than 30 minutes, the so-called Fifth Agreement was due to be signed.

From what X had heard, it was a simple document. Germany agreed to pull back to its pre-1987 borders, release all POWs, pay war reparations in installments lasting 100 years, and reduce its armed forces by two-thirds. It had been six weeks since a cease-fire went into effect; now, finally, the Allied Forces would be getting something in writing.

A war crimes tribunal would convene in about a year, and while X knew that a secret agreement had been struck in which the very highest-ranking German officers would remain untouched, there were several thousand middle-level officers and many enlisted men who would be tried. He'd already secured a position on its investigation staff. The trials would cost billions; the tab would be paid by the world community. This meant a lot of money would be available for people like him.

Another grape was placed on his lips, then the champagne straw was inserted again. He chewed and sucked and then heard a giggle and opened his eyes for the first time in two hours to see the two girls leaning over him and gently kissing each other on the lips.

"Wow," X thought softly. "What a way to end a war."

When he opened his eyes again a few minutes later, the girls were still kissing, still caressing. The blond had removed her top and was now assisting the brunet in removing hers. X laughed a little bit. The girls were fondling each other's breasts.

This is almost too good, he thought.

And no sooner had the notion popped into his mind than he realized it was the worst thing he could have thought.

For when he opened his eyes again, he saw the jinx had already taken affect.

Coming down the beach, walking right toward him, dressed in the worst cabana-wear possible, was his colleague, Agent Z.

He was carrying his briefcase in one hand and a yellow envelope in the other. X knew the yellow envelope contained a CFG—a confidential flash-gram. A kind of top-secret bulletin.

Shit . . .

Z walked right up to him, and with the wave of his hand, shooed the kissing beauties away.

"What's up?" X asked him.

"Just a curious little thing," Z said, plopping down beside him and taking a swig of champagne.

"Yes?"

"The German delegation to Paris?" Z said. "They were supposed to land at Rue Airport more than an hour ago."

"Yeah? So?"

"So," Z went on. "They haven't arrived. Not yet, anyway."

X sat up a little and lifted his hat from his brow.

"They get a late start?" he asked.

Z shrugged. "No one knows. We haven't had a good set of eyes in Berlin for a month. That was part of the cease-fire agreement."

"What's the last thing you have?"

Z opened the yellow envelope and took out six photographs. There were aerial shots of Berlin, taken, X could tell, from a high-flying spy plane. Z handed one photo to X. It showed the Berlin airport. A large plane was sitting on the main runway. There were huge Iron Cross symbols on its wings. This was the airplane of the German High Command, the people who were supposed to be flying to Paris to sign the peace agreement.

"This was taken early this morning," Z told him. "That's their airplane. It looks ready to go. But that picture is several hours old already."

But X wasn't really listening to him. Nor was he looking at the picture of the Berlin Airport. Instead, he was staring at another photo, one which showed downtown Berlin.

"What the hell is this?"

He directed Z's vision to the photo. Z didn't see it at first. X pushed the photo even closer to his nose. Only then did Z see what X saw.

He was very familiar with aerial photos of Berlin these days. Essentially, the city was a series of concrete bunkers and reinforced military buildings, architecture made to be bombproof—a successful strategy as it turned out. For except for a few scattered raids several years before, the German capital had been spared aerial bombardment throughout this phase of the war simply because there was a lack of vulnerable targets.

But now looking at the photo, Z realized that something strange was going on within the city.

Sprouting up among the bunkers, he could see the beginnings of new skyscrapers being put into place. Steel skeletons growing on dozens of previously vacant lots. Spires like those found on theaters or museums could also be seen in the early stages of construction.

Even more revealing, the streets around the new buildings and the blocks and blocks of bunkers were thick with traffic, both civilian and military.

"What the hell is this?" Z asked.

"Odd time to start some urban renewal," X said.

He studied the four other photographs and found similar disturbing clues on them. The face of downtown Berlin was changing right before their eyes.

"I thought these guys were broke?" Z went on. "There are so many trucks on those streets, they must have found a million gallons of gas somewhere."

But now X had seen something else. The tops of many of the bunkers and military buildings in the center of the capital looked as if they'd received a new coat of paint—but just on the roofs. Not all, just some. He pointed it out to Z. Again, it didn't make sense.

Not until X happened to put two of the photographs together. And that's when he saw the painted roofs actually formed a pattern. He put a third photo beneath the first two, and like a jigsaw puzzle, the pattern became clearer.

Four long arms, twisted at the middle.

The fourth picture was added, then the fifth and finally the sixth. And that's when the pattern became crystal clear.

By painting the roofs of selected bunkers, the Germans had in effect created a huge swastika, several miles in length, and situated perfectly on an east-to-west axis. Obviously it had been laid out just so high-flying spy craft could photograph it.

"Jessuzz, look at that." X couldn't believe it.

"What? Why?"

"It's a swastika," X told him coldly. "And why? Well, shoot me if I'm wrong, but I think they're sending us a message here."

Z just looked at him. "And that message is?"

"I think," X said, "they're telling us: Fuck You."

It was strange, because at that precise moment, they both felt the ground shake. Not a lot, but enough to notice. The ice cubes in X's drink began to tinkle. The last wave to hit the beach landed a little funny and off-kilter. Even the two beauties, necking on a blanket nearby, noticed it. They came out of their clench long enough to look over at the OSS agents.

"Are there earthquakes in the Bahamas?" the blond asked.

Both agents shook their heads. They didn't know.

Then, a moment later, they heard another sound, another rumbling. They looked up and could see an aircraft was coming out of the north, quickly descending out of the clouds. It was an octocopter, a massive eight-rotor helicopter capable of carrying up to 200 passengers.

This one was heading right for them. They watched as it took about half a minute to get to within 150 yards of the beach. Then it went into a hover and came down about 100 yards away from them, dislodging X's sun umbrella from its mooring, knocking over his drink tray, scattering his selection of grapes, and blowing sand all over the two amorous bathing beauties.

X shielded his eyes against the billowing sand, watching his little piece of paradise simply blow away.

The octo finally set down and its rotors began to slow. A door opened, and a familiar figure jumped out and began running toward them.

It was their colleague, Agent Y.

"Well, the party's really over now," X said.

They both knew something must be up for Y to come all the way over from the mainland in such a big aircraft.

"Hear the latest?" he asked the two agents.

"Yes, sunny all day," X replied sarcastically. "You came all the way down here for that?"

"The Germans just iced Paris," he said.

"Iced?" both X and Z asked.

"Flattened," Y was more specific. "A missile barrage of some kind. They've killed everyone in a 20-mile radius. There's nothing left. Not even the Eiffel Tower."

X and Z just stared back at him. "You've got to be kidding," X said, slipping into denial.

"You think I'd come all this way just to pull your crank?" Y asked him.

"Jessuzz, he's serious," Z said, the news just beginning to sink in.

"When did this happen?" X wanted to know.

"About an hour ago," he replied, looking out to sea. "They said it was so bad, we might even get some shock waves, maybe even a tidal event."

X and Z looked at each other. The jolt they'd just felt. The Earth had moved. Literally.

"They've killed a million people, maybe two, or even three," Y told them, his voice sounding almost as if he was in shock. "Including the President, the Cabinet, maybe as many as 200 of our top military guys. This is big trouble."

"Bastards," Z swore. "Got everyone in one place at one time. Then, zap!"

"We've all got to get back up to D.C." Y told them. "There's going to be a national emergency declared any minute."

X pieced the photos back together on his lap. The huge swastika looked even more ominous now.

"Boy, when these guys say 'Fuck You,'" he said, "they really mean it."

The next month was a living hell for Agents X, Y, and Z.

The war was back on. Battlefronts which had been dormant for months had suddenly come to life.

The Germans attacked viciously everywhere—a massive simultaneous Blitzkrieg was begun, including yet another brutal invasion of England.

Caught napping, with its leadership gone, the American forces could only retreat, trying to save as many men and as much material as possible. And among the turmoil and uncertainty, there was the question: How? How had the Germans been able to do it, so quickly, so secretly?

Called back to active duty, X, Y, and Z worked 24-hour days sifting through the mountains of intelligence that suddenly wound up at their door. Books would be written, all three knew, about the stunning resurgence of the German military. Not only had the Germans won back all of the territory they'd lost in the past two years of the war, they went on the offensive to win new objectives: all of Africa, all of India, all of Siberia. And of course, all of the British Isles.

Within two months of the Deception at Paris, the Allied Forces held two lone positions that separated Iron Cross Europe from the American mainland: Iceland, and the Azores.

On Christmas Day, 1997, Germany launched a massive combined air-sea assault on the Azores and won them in three days. After the stunning victory, a German military spokesman told the world press: "We are just trying to win the war."

As the OSS's top intelligence agents, X, Y, and Z were ordered to make some sense of the astonishing German resurgence. How was the enemy able to come back so strong, so quickly from the brink of defeat?

Finding out would be a daunting task. The German war machine, always excellent at security, had become more secret than ever. Even stranger, German society was rebounding at the speed of light as well. New building projects were exploding all over the Reich. Huge candlelight parades were held in German cities night after night, usually involving tens of thousands of citizens marching around and around in the shape of enormous swastikas. Roof-painting continued throughout Germany too. Along with forest-cutting and field-trimming, the Germans were carving huge twisted crosses across their landscape as if they were trying to communicate with peoples in outer space or on other planets.

What's more, throughout the renewed fighting a vast array of new German wonder weapons had been revealed. One was an artillery shell which was fired some 50,000 feet in the air where it exploded and rained thousands of smaller lethal shells on large concentrations of Allied troops below. Hundreds of Me-462 jet fighters, Arado heavy jet bombers, V-6 and V-7 rockets, some carrying poison-gas warheads, had also been used by the Germans.

The worst wonder weapon of all, though, was a block-buster high-explosive warhead called the DG-55. Just three of them were enough to devastate Paris and kill 3.2 million people on what was supposed to be the Armistice Day. The warhead was so big, there was no doubt one would be able to sink one of the Navy's new megacarriers or any of the current line of megaships. The U.S. Navy then was effectively stuck in its home ports.

There was no arguing then that the speed at which the German war machine had been revitalized was astonishing, almost unnatural. From the brink of surrender to a position of dominance in such a short time was unheard of.

What was the spark that relit Germany? How had the resurgence been so complete, so massive, so quick?

In among the many American reversals on various battle-fields worldwide, this was the deepest, darkest mystery of all.

The three agents interviewed hundreds of American military and diplomatic people, often bringing them down to a small, dark, intentionally intimidating room in the subbasement of OSS headquarters and giving them the third degree. This in the lack of German POWs, of which there were none. There was even a shortage of suspected Germans—spies and saboteurs, real or imagined—that the trio of agents had never had a problem securing before.

But even from all these interviews and interrogations, there was little clue as to what or who was behind the German resurgence.

It became so bad, the agents were forced to turn to the Main/AC military-affairs computer, the machine which was hooked into every ship, airplane, supertank, and platoon-size Army unit throughout the U.S. military. The computer kept instructing the agents to whittle down time and events and try to isolate the one specific day, the one specific hour that could be pinpointed as the day the tide turned back in favor of Germany.

It took many more hours to fulfill this task, many long nights of arguments, frustration, and bad coffee.

But then, finally, the agents narrowed in on an answer.

The date, they found out, that things began to change turned out to be August 15, 1997.

The day three men were plucked from the middle of the Atlantic Ocean.

Chapter 9

The first day of January, 1998, found Captain Eric Wolf in mixed spirits.

He'd just been promoted. His previous exploits in the Atlantic war against the U-boats had not gone unnoticed in Washington. Wolf was about to take responsibility for strategic operations in the entire Atlantic Wartime Command. It was an enormous job of great challenge—especially in light of the recent German resurgence.

The person who was in the job before him had met a rather inglorious end—he'd dressed in his best uniform and then jumped out his Pentagon office window. It was 15 floors down. The pressure of running the Atlantic war had become too much for him. When Wolf was appointed to his post, they gave him the deceased man's office. The first thing Wolf noticed was that all the windows had been nailed shut.

He'd been on the job two weeks now. He'd slept an average of two hours a night in that time. His section was being swamped with reports of renewed German activity up and down the east coast. There were tales of huge new German vessels, battleships, cruisers, flying boats, and submarines. American shipping had ground to a halt; 33 ships had been sunk since Wolf took his new job. Not only oceangoing vessels, but coastal cargo haulers, barges, even pleasure craft. The Germans were getting close again.

Wolf's job was hampered by the fact that he had very few resources, such as antisubmarine planes and ships, or men to operate them. Like everyone else, he was the victim of the premature muster-out before the Deception of Paris.

So when he'd received the message to report to the OSS main office this particular morning, he'd assumed it was for some kind of briefing. Perhaps yet another new design of German warship had been spotted in the Atlantic, or a new kind of U-boat weapon was in the offing.

But when Wolf arrived at OSS HQ, he was taken to a basement office where three men awaited him.

These characters were rather grim and war-weary. The room itself was very dark and smelled of bad coffee.

He was told to sit down.

"Captain, we've called you here to discuss an incident which happened in August of last year," one man began.

Wolf had to think a moment. So much had happened between August and the present.

"You were ordered to investigate some people found floating in the middle of the ocean," the man continued. "Do you recall?"

"Yes, of course, I remember," Wolf replied—as if he could have forgotten that day.

"There were three people in the water, true?"

"Yes, that was the report," Wolf replied, now becoming very curious as to why the OSS men wanted to know about this strange incident.

"The man you picked up," he was asked. "What do you recall about him?"

"He was very odd," Wolf replied right away. "Definitely a military man. But I was never sure exactly what military he belonged to. I just assumed he was part of a secret unit or something . . ."

The three men just looked at each other wearily.

"And the other two people in the water," one asked him. "Did you ever get to see either one of them?"

Wolf just shook his head. "No," he replied. Then he got brave. "Why do you ask?"

But the OSS men wouldn't answer that question. Not in a million years.

There was a long silence.

Wolf shifted in his seat. "Is that it? Do you have anything else for me?"

The man closest to him turned and looked him straight in the eye. "Did you have any chance to recover either one of the other two men that day?"

Wolf thought a moment.

"No," he answered truthfully. "We were under attack. They were too far away. The Germans were very close. They'd fired on us twice, and I'm sure they were preparing to fire again. My Main/AC told me I should withdraw after retrieving the one man."

"And it is your testimony that it was impossible for you to pick up the second man, the one the Germans eventually got?"

Wolf felt a chill go through him. "Testimony?" he asked. "Why? Is this a trial?"

"Maybe it is," one man growled at him. "So just answer the question."

Wolf began stammering, stopped, and took a deep breath. He knew the OSS was capable of just about anything, especially these days. However, he felt it was best to simply tell the truth.

"Yes I guess it is . . ." he finally replied. "I went the way the computer told me to go. Those were always my standing orders. So I didn't attempt to retrieve either of the two remaining men."

That's when one of the OSS men lost it completely. He suddenly began pounding his fist on the table.

"Goddamn it man, couldn't you have at least tried?" he screamed at Wolf, before his colleagues were able to restrain him. "Do you have any idea how things would be different right now if you had just made that extra effort!"

Wolf was stunned.

"But . . . I was just following orders," he heard himself saying. "The Main/AC told me to . . ."

But one of the agents held up his hand and cut Wolf off. Then he got up and slowly opened the door.

"That will be all, Captain," he said. "For now . . ."

Chapter 10

Two weeks later

The sound of a key turning in the lock of his cell woke Hunter from a very deep sleep.

The door opened, and the faint light from the bare bulb in the hallway flooded in.

His two guards peered in at him. What did they want, he wondered. It wasn't time to go to the library. His breakfast wouldn't come for another two hours. Maybe he was being executed today . . .

That's when he realized there was a third person with them. He was an officer in the Air Corps. Brown suit jacket, tan shirt, brown tie and cap. He was old. Very old. Wrinkled face, white hair, red nose. His officer's bars actually reflected some of the spare light from the hallway.

Hunter recognized him right away. It was Captain Pegg, the ancient officer from that day at Otis. One of the guys he'd wanted to kill.

Pegg indicated to the guards that he was OK, and they let him into the cell alone. Hunter was slouched in the corner now, both bemused and confused.

What the hell could this be about?

Pegg laid his topcoat on the bare cot, then took a seat in the creaky wooden chair across from Hunter.

"You're not a chaplain now, are you?" Hunter asked him. "Come to give me instructions on how to meet the Maker?"

Pegg cackled—and for a moment Hunter thought that he might have actually known this guy before. Back where he'd come from. It was a strange, stray thought.

"I'm hardly a priest," Pegg told him.

He studied Hunter for a moment. He looked different from the last time he'd seen him. It was the very long hair and the beard that was so off-putting. He could have been an artist's model for a religious card, Pegg thought.

"I'll get right to the point," Pegg told him. "In the past few months, the war has taken a terrible turn for us. The Germans have made headway on every front. They've grown stronger. Bolder. Smarter. This time last year, people were chilling the champagne for the victory party. Now, there's worry about whether we can hang on through the winter."

Hunter's ears perked up. The last he'd heard, the U.S. was about to put the sword through the German heart and finally be done with this final phase of World War II. What had happened? And why was this bird here telling him this?

The guy read his mind.

"Why? Well, the official answer is, 'We don't know,'" Pegg said. "Unofficially, there is new leadership at the very top of the German High Command. All we know is that the enemy has been revitalized to near miraculous proportions, everywhere."

Hunter sat up a little more. What the hell *was* this all about?

"Why am I here?" the officer asked the question for him. "It's simple, really. After your actions that day at Otis, you got a file down at HQ that fills its own drawer. Anyone who's ever read it concludes that you are either a kook, an illusionist, or a guy from outer space.

"But the plain fact is, we need people who can fly airplanes, and that's just about the only thing anyone I've talked to agrees you can do."

"So?"

"So, I'm here to offer you a way to get out of this place," Pegg said.

Hunter sat all the way up now.

"How so?"

The officer just shrugged. "It's simple. The Air Corps needs pilots, and we need them now. You don't even have to be good. We're that desperate."

He let his voice trail off.

"Flying I can do," Hunter replied. "But where exactly would I be doing all this flying? Cargo humping?"

The officer laughed and shook his head. "You think we're going to spring you just to have you flying shit from Shiloh?"

"That would be my guess," Hunter replied.

"Well, your guess would be wrong," Pegg told him. "The guys who were shipping shit are now flying bombers over London. That's where you'll be going too. If you survive the flight over there."

"You make it sound so inviting," Hunter told him. "Maybe the food here isn't that bad after all."

The man smiled and appreciated the joke, but then got serious. "Let me tell you something," he began. "This is a one-time offer. Your choice. You'll start at the lowest rank possible, and you're guaranteed to see combat, a lot of it, very quickly. No one will know who you are, or where you came from. But the way I see it, if you choose to stay here, someday someone down at HQ will decide that it's time to start shooting all the spies and traitors and kooks we've got locked up here. Especially if the Germans keep their steamroller going.

"Now, there's about a dozen people in other prisons

that are being given the opportunity to serve out their sentences in combat. That's how bad things have become.''

Hunter just shook his head. Renegades and criminals released from prison to help out the struggling war effort.

''I think I've seen this movie,'' he finally told the officer.

Pegg signaled for the guards to come get him.

''So? Is it a deal?'' he asked Hunter.

Hunter thought for only a few more seconds, then nodded slowly.

''To tell you the truth, to get a decent bath and some new clothes?'' he replied. ''I'd do just about anything.''

Captain Pegg left the prison 10 minutes later.

A black, nondescript military car was waiting for him outside. He nodded to the driver, then climbed into the back and settled in beside the car's only other passenger.

''How did it go?'' the man known as Agent Y asked him.

''He bought in,'' Pegg replied with a cough. ''He'll be on his way within the hour.''

Y breathed what might have been interpreted as a sign of relief—but was actually one of exhaustion.

He hadn't slept in so long he couldn't remember the last time he'd closed his eyes. Hidden away in their tiny subbasement office in Washington, D.C., he and his two colleagues, X and Z, had continued to pour over intelligence reports from the front, trying to find more clues as to why the German resurgence had taken place.

In many ways, it seemed to be a fool's errand, especially to X and Z. Akin to painting the life rafts as the *Titanic* went down, was how they put it. To X and Z, the reason for the German resurgence really didn't matter in the end. The war was back on, and America was losing it, and that was it. It was fate.

But Agent Y was a different kind of person. He believed the tiniest incident could have an affect on the whole. He and his colleagues had narrowed down the first day of the

German resurgence to August 15—the day that Hunter and two others were found floating in the Atlantic.

True, many mistakes had been made by the U.S. military since then, downsized and caught off guard as they were. But could all that be reversed? Could a small twist here change the course of History? If a butterfly flaps its wings over Brazil, does it eventually cause a hurricane over Cuba?

Y didn't know. But if the man the Germans had retrieved from the sea was so special that he put the Reich back on its feet and on the offensive in just a few short months, then perhaps the biggest error the U.S. had made so far was keeping the other man pulled from the sea that day locked up in jail.

And that's what Y was here this day to change.

"Do you think he suspects that he is being sprung for reasons other than the fact that he is a pilot and a good one?" the OSS man asked Pegg.

The elderly officer thought about the question, and then just shrugged no.

"Well, that is the reason he's getting out, right?" he asked Agent Y. "I mean, what other reason would there be?"

"Yes, of course," Y mumbled, his thoughts more on butterflies and hurricanes and the fact that he already felt a strange connection with this man Hunter. "What else could it be?"

Pegg cleared his throat and leaned back, and promptly fell asleep.

Envious, Y just slumped further in the seat and told the driver to get going.

He had to get back to Washington before X and Z knew he was gone.

Chapter 11

One hour later, Hunter was as far away from his cramped cell in Sing Sing as he could have ever imagined.

He'd been allowed to shower and get dressed. Then he hustled to the meal hall, where he ate an enormous bowl of oatmeal alone. Then he was given a flight suit for a U.S. Air Corps officer that looked more like something from a movie prop department.

Then he was blindfolded.

He was led outside, where a car with a perforated muffler was waiting by the front gate of the prison. It was now about 7 A.M. He was stuffed into the back seat of this car with three other people. The driver, a man with a mild English accent, told them there would be no talking during the trip. Then he gunned the engine and they were off.

The car drove for more than eight hours. Some of it was over very bumpy roads, some on a very crowded highway. The car was moving very fast, and the driver laying on the horn every 10 seconds or so. Hunter knew they were moving northeast. Not a word was said during the trip.

By mid afternoon, they were by the sea. Hunter could

taste the salt in the air. The distant sound of waves crashing echoed in his ears. They turned due north and the road got very winding, yet fast. Hunter slept, but even in his dreams he was trying to figure out where he was going.

After an hour on the winding oceanfront road, the car finally stopped. The door opened and a hand came in and pulled him out. The other passengers, who had endured the same long ride in complete silence, were taken out as well.

They were at an airfield, Hunter could tell. The stink of aviation fuel was something he could never forget. The air was thick with it here.

They were led away from the car and toward an aircraft. Hunter could hear the whine of its engines in pre–warm-up mode. He could sense that this aircraft was large—very large—judging by the smell of gas fumes in the air. But he also knew it wasn't a fixed-wing aircraft.

He was put into a large cabin, along with at least six other people, three of them carrying guns, obvious by the rattling. Hunter was placed on a benchstyle seat, facing forward and belted in over his lap and shoulders.

Then, the aircraft's engines came to life.

The rumble started somewhere around his feet, went up through his ankles, his torso, his chest, neck, eyes, and ears. It was so loud, and so deep, his body began shaking with sympathetic movement. The air itself was fluctuating, the growl was so intense.

"Oh Lord," Hunter heard one of his fellow travelers say. The voice was hauntingly familiar. It was an Irish brogue. "They've put us on an old Beater. Did they really take us out here just to kill us like this?"

The aircraft lifted off a moment later. It did so not with any kind of grace, but with a huge bang and a tremor that set the bench's bolts to rattling. The engine noise only got louder as the aircraft groaned itself into the air. For the first time he could recall, Hunter found himself actually fearing a takeoff—that's how steep and shaky and sharp the ascent was.

But this feeling quickly passed, and he felt awash in another sensation entirely. He was flying—again. For the first time in a long time he was actually moving through the air. Now his heart was beating faster, but for a different reason. Suddenly all the months in the prison, all the uncertainty of who or what he was—suddenly it was all gone away.

He was in the air. That's all that mattered at the moment.

But what exactly was he flying in?

That question was answered a few moments later.

It came without warning. One moment, Hunter's eyes were blindfolded—the next, the blindfold was gone. A crewman had removed it and handed him an olive-drab ski mask. "Put it on," a voice said. "It gets mighty cold up here."

Hunter did as was told, grateful the blindfold was gone at last. But his eyes could see nothing but white light for the next few moments. He was next to a window, facing the sun, and the rays were strong and they stung his still-fragile retinas.

But eventually his vision cleared and he was able to distinguish shapes and colors. The wind was suddenly in his face. The most horrendous noise filled his ears.

What the hell was he flying in exactly? It was very large, painted dull gray inside and out. It had very long thin wings sticking out from underneath the cabin where Hunter was sitting, but he could see no power plants or engines on those wings. The roar of the engines was coming directly above his head. So he looked up, and saw the blurred flare of a rotor blade, spinning right above him. It was one of many.

Goddamn. They were on a helicopter—yet it was the size of a jumbo jet!

"Damn us and bless us," Hunter heard that brogue say again. He finally turned and looked at the guy sitting next to him.

He was a small fireplug of a man. Pale face, except for

the red nose. He looked like a leprechaun on steroids. Hunter's jaw simply fell open.

He knew this man—but he didn't know how . . .

The man stared back at him too—it was obvious he was having the same sensation.

Finally the man stuck his hand out.

"How ye be?" he asked Hunter. "Mike Fitzgerald here."

Hunter felt his skin go cold. His mouth went dry. The hair on the back of his neck was suddenly standing at attention. He unconsciously moved away from the man, all the while unable to break the lock of his gaze on him.

Jessuzz, he knew this guy. Somewhere back in his memory, he knew him. He may even have been good friends with him. In fact, they had gone to hell and back together, several times.

But he was also sure about something else.

He was sure that this man was dead . . .

The helicopter flew on into the night.

The weather got bad, and the engines on the huge chopper growled even louder. The cabin was unheated and unlit, just like his jail cell, and Hunter was too stunned, too confused, maybe even too frightened to converse with the man next to him.

So he didn't.

He simply kept his eyes left, looking out the window and watching as monstrous black swirling clouds enveloped the huge helicopter.

The flight lasted four hours. Hunter had slept, fitfully, his mind fighting what his body demanded. But his dreams were full of dead birds, corpses coming to life, and everyone speaking in Irish accents and asking him why he thought everything was so weird.

When he awoke, his ears detected a slowdown in the huge chopper's power plants. The man who'd spoken to him was still beside him, cold and not moving. The temperature inside the passenger cabin was below freezing. He was convinced the man was dead.

But now the helicopter was descending rapidly and the screech of the huge engines began waking up the other passengers. Eventually the man on his right stirred too.

Hunter wished he hadn't. He would have preferred the man stay dead. Because if he wasn't, then Hunter would be certain that this strange place in which he'd landed was indeed hell, or some kind of hell, where the dead come back and your life is a succession of idiots, old men, prison cells, and flying on airplanes you are certain are going to crash.

Yes, at that moment he thought he finally had his answer. He had died and gone to Hell.

What had he done to deserve this, he wondered as the chopper simply fell out of the sky, quickly and not under any kind of control. What had he done in his previous life to wind up in eternal damnation?

He didn't know.

Somewhere in among these gloomy thoughts, he heard a voice come over the cracked intercom speaker. The voice was unintelligible, but the others took the message to mean they should fasten their seat belts—quickly. The aircraft engines were screaming like banshees now, and the thick clouds outside gave no clue as to how high they still were or how fast they were actually falling.

Hunter grabbed for his seat belt and redoubled the clasp, and in the next second there was a huge boom! The chopper shuddered from top to bottom—and each man's head hit the ceiling, seat belts or not.

A second later, they were down.

The incredible down wash from the big chopper's blades had created a huge snow squall. That's why it looked as if they'd been flying at 10,000 feet when in reality, they'd been about 10 feet from the hard surface.

"Did we crash?" someone asked.

Hunter thought, maybe we did. He forced the door open

and jumped out. The others followed him. He rolled and scrambled as far and as fast as he could.

When he looked back at the helicopter, he saw the top rotor assembly was smoking heavily. A pair of smaller helicopters were buzzing about it, spewing purple-K foam from nose-mounted nozzles onto the hot engines. Finally the Beater's blades stopped spinning and the whirlwind died down, and Hunter realized they'd landed at a huge air base out in the middle of a very frozen, cold forest.

Gander. Newfoundland.

Somehow he knew that's where he was.

Two trucks appeared out of the last of the snow squall. They stopped, turned around, and backed up to where Hunter and his fellow passengers stood, shivering in the freezing temperatures. Two men jumped out. Hunter's fellow passengers were given uniform packs that were clearly marked: Tropical Combat Issue. Each man was handed a flight helmet and a pair of gloves. Then they climbed into the first truck. As the drove away, the last man on board, the one who'd said his name was Mike Fitzgerald, gave Hunter a ghostly salute.

Now it was Hunter's turn. He was given a pack that read: Polar Combat Issue. Then he was put into the back of the second truck, alone.

The truck drove to the opposite side of the base and stopped outside a barracks. An officer appeared from within. He was wearing so many layers of clothing his face was all but obscured. He checked Hunter's pack and then took a long time just staring at Hunter's long hair and beard.

"No one had a chance to shave you up?" he asked him. "Or give you a buzz?"

Hunter just shrugged.

"No sir," he replied.

"Well, there's no time now either," the man said.

Outside the truck a slow rumbling began. Hunter's ears began to hurt, the dissonance was so extreme. This was not some monster helicopter he was hearing. These were airplane engines winding up. But it sounded as if an entire squadron of aircraft had suddenly turned on their engines all at once.

The noise became so loud, so quickly, it became impossible to talk, impossible to think.

"That's your ride now!" the officer managed to yell above the growing din. "Go!"

Hunter climbed down from the back of the truck to find the sun was brightening ever so slightly on the horizon.

But then it became dark again. Something in the snow and the wind was moving in between him and the horizon. It took a few moments for him to realize that it was another airplane. This one larger and more frightening than the chopper which had brought him here.

It was a fixed-wing aircraft, at least twice the size of the Beater. Its wings held eight propeller engines on each side. Its design looked vaguely familiar to him, especially its snout, which carried an extended radar dome that looked like a long black nose. C-124 Globemaster was the designation that suddenly popped into Hunter's head—but this airplane was bigger than the vague memory he had of that airplane. Much bigger.

And the problem with this plane was it looked to be in worse condition that the aptly named Beater helicopter. Much worse.

First of all, the 16 piston engines were all smoking mightily, not a good sign at all. They were sparking flames and bits of flash and sparks too. The underside of the wings were soaked with aviation fuel. One spark in the wrong place might touch off a fuel line and then a fuel tank and then things at the base would get very warm very quickly.

What's more, the plane itself looked horribly beat up. Its numbers and insignia were faded, some of the windows were cracked, one was even boarded up with a piece of plywood.

Hunter felt a very long chill go through him. The last thing he wanted to do was get on this flying piece of shit. But he was in the army now. And he would have no choice.

He hustled out onto the frozen tarmac, ran up the ramp and packed himself into the rear cargo hold along with boxes of Q-rations, bottled water, cases marked AERIAL BOMBS, and barrels of aviation fuel. A half dozen soldiers were thrown on board with him. They were wearing GI issue winter clothing and carrying enormous field packs. None of them looked over 16 years old. From their insignia, Hunter determined they were a unit of Air Guards, infantry soldiers attached to the Air Corps.

They sat inside the hold of the big plane for more than a half hour. Not talking not moving, just waiting. This wasn't a delay. It was simply the time it took for the air-plane's engines to warm up properly. Normally Hunter would have been concerned at the sight of the gas and the bombs—but at this point, he found it a morbid comfort. At least he knew that if the plane went down it would go down big and quick. The aviation fuel and the bombs would take care of that.

Hunter was near a cracked window and watched as the ground crew went to each of the engines on his side, staring up at the contra-rotating propellers for a few minutes with huge fire extinguishers in their hands. And just for com-fort, a deicing crew in a cherry picker–type truck was wash-ing down the enormous wing with what looked to be the most ineffective deicing agent imaginable.

Hunter was a betting man—or at least he thought he was. Looking out on these preflight operations, he figured the chances of this airplane ever getting into the air were slim. The chances of it actually arriving at its destination—whereever that might be—seemed infinitesimal.

But eventually all 16 engines were turning to someone's satisfaction. The noise and the shaking were enough to make Hunter's teeth rattle—and ironically, with all the pyrotechnics about, there was no heat in the cargo cabin.

In the end, there was no warning. The huge plane just rumbled once and started moving forward, very slowly.

Hunter sat back and held on, but kept his eyes out the cracked window. The airplane picked up speed; the interior rumbled even more; jostling the rations and the gasoline, the bombs and the passengers. Hunter wished he'd seen the runway they were about to use—he'd have been able to tell how long it would take for a plane this size to actually get airborne. He guessed it would have to be at least five miles long.

They started rolling faster.

He looked around the cabin. Concern was written all over the faces of the young Air Guards. He wondered what they saw on his.

It seemed to take forever, but finally, somehow, some way, the airplane began ascending. Yet no sooner had the wheels left the ground than two of the eight engines on Hunter's side began spouting flames. Not smoke. Not exhaust. Flames!

Yet the big airplane just continued climbing. It went up steep and noisy, jostling the passengers and the gasoline even more severely. Hunter couldn't take his eyes off the burning engines. In seconds, the innermost engine was literally engulfed in flames.

But still the airplane climbed higher and higher. Into the thick white clouds.

Climbing, like it was going up to Heaven itself.

Part Two

Fire and Ice

Chapter 12

Somehow, Hunter fell asleep during the long, perilous plane ride.

Head leaning against a barrel of gasoline, feet propped up on a case of aerial bombs, it was exhaustion, not bravado that sucked him down into a deep and disturbing slumber.

He dreamed heavily while he was out—but there were no beautiful girls in these dreams. Instead, there was water. Tons of it, cold and surging. So much water it was rising above the mountaintops. An ocean in the middle of a forest. And he was riding a motorcycle through the air above it. And there were streaks of lightning all around him. And he was wearing someone else's clothes, someone else's boots, and eating someone else's food. And there was an airplane and he had to get to it, but it was always just ahead of him and he couldn't make the motorcycle go quick enough through the air, because he had foolishly attached bombs to it. Bombs a little girl had given him . . .

Who was she?

He was jolted awake before he could find out. A change in the engine noise and a sudden loss of air pressure both served to knock him back into consciousness.

Jessuzz, where was he?

Hunter hastily wiped the sleep from his eyes and some frost from the nearest window and peered down. Only then did he realize the plane was nearing its destination. Below he saw an island in the middle of a cold, cold sea. Lots of mountains, lots of snow, lots of ice. And once again, somehow he knew exactly where he was.

Iceland.

From 20,000 feet, the place looked very small and very, very dark. The plane began circling. Hunter sat back and held on. Scattered throughout the cabin, the Air Guards too were in various states of distress. The airplane sounded like it was literally coming apart at the seams now, all 16 engines screaming at once in the ice-cold air.

Then the plane began to fall. It rattled, it rolled. It stalled. It fell some more. At one point, Hunter thought he could actually hear screams coming from the cockpit.

Through some very high winds, through a blinding snow-storm, toward a pair of very faint lines of landing lights, the plane plummeted.

After 10 long minutes of horror, it finally hit the ground with the finesse of a boulder, bounced once, then came down again. Then it rolled and rolled and rolled. For four miles at least it rumbled along, as if it didn't want to stop here. Everything inside the cargo bay shifted again, this time toward the front of the plane. Gasoline spilled, Q-rations were crushed. Air Guards were thrown about like rag dolls. Finally the right-side landing gear collapsed, blowing out 10 of the 18 tires. Only then did the gigantic plane finally skid to a halt.

The interior began filling with smoke. A fire truck mate-rialized out of the darkness and its crew commenced foam-ing down the engines and the smoking landing gear. They did this in such a routine fashion, it looked like an hourly event. Someone opened the side cargo door and Hunter made a beeline down the access ramp, scrambling out with the battered and bruised Air Guards. It was a replay of his terrifying flight on the Beater. Everyone wanted to get as far away from this flying beast as possible, pilots and flight crew included.

Maybe this flying stuff ain't that good, he thought suddenly.

Only at a safe distance did Hunter stop and take stock of his new surroundings. He might as well have been standing at the North Pole itself. There was snow, snow, ice, and more snow. Even the runway was made of packed snow. And snow was falling in near blizzard conditions. The only indication of civilization that he could see was way, *way* across the frozen tarmac. It was a small clutch of buildings, each one with a chimney and steamy smoke pouring out of it. There seemed to be lights on in every window on every floor of every building—and even from this distance, Hunter thought he could smell food.

The Air Guards saw the same thing and formed up and started walking. Hunter tagged along, but soon lost the 12 soldiers in the blinding snow; they vanished like ghosts in the gale, even though they were only 20 feet or so ahead of him.

Alone, cold and weary, it took him nearly half an hour to reach the buildings. The wind was blowing very hard and it was not going his way. He was forced to walk backward most of the way.

When he finally reached the front door of the first building, he stopped and took a deep sniff. The scent of beef stew was on the wind. He also detected the smell of beer, whiskey, and maybe even a whiff of marijuana.

At least he'd chosen his destination well. Above the door was a sign that read: 2001ST FIGHTER SQUADRON—OFFICERS CLUB. In papers contained in his Polar Combat Pack, it said he was to report to the 2001st. Now Hunter's stomach began to rumble. He felt like he hadn't eaten in days. Was this place open? How many people were actually inside? He could hear music, but no voices. He couldn't see through the window; like everything else, it was frosted over. So he knocked once on the door and then went in.

The place was empty. There was music playing on a juke

box, and there was booze and hot food steaming behind the bar. But the club was deserted.

The only person in evidence was the bartender. He looked up as soon as Hunter came in, but just as quickly looked away. Hunter dropped his bag in the corner and made for the bar. The bartender timidly washed an area in front of him.

"All we got is beer and whiskey," he told Hunter. "Which will it be?"

"Both," Hunter replied. "And how much for a bowl of stew?"

The bartender just stared back at him.

"This is also the officers' chow hall, rook," he said. "It doesn't cost anything."

This was good; Hunter didn't have a penny on him.

The beer proved watery and the whiskey was bitter but Hunter quickly drained them both, trying his best to shake off the chill from the awful flight in. He got two more drinks and a huge bowl of stew. And even though he had his pick of any seat in the house, he took his food and drink to a table in the farthest corner.

Just like you can tell an army by what it eats, you can tell an army by what its mess hall looks like. And on closer look, this place was a dump. And the stew sucked.

This was not good.

The club was so dark it was almost solemn. There were no trophies in evidence, no plaques, no insignia depicting the reverie of the men who were assigned here. This place was supposed to be the watering hole for an entire squadron of fighter pilots. But where the hell was everybody?

Bad as it was, Hunter finished his stew and ordered another beer. No sooner had he returned to his seat, than the door flew open and an Air Corps officer came in. He marched across the room to the mantel above the fireplace. Here was placed a huge, ugly ceramic mug that was shaped into the face of a devil. The officer turned the mug around so its demonic features were pointing outwards.

Then he cleared his voice and bellowed to the empty hall:

"Squadron briefing in 30 minutes. All pilots report."

With that, he turned on his heel and went back out the door.

Hunter looked up at the bartender who blinked and then looked away again. Hunter stood up and scanned the room once again.

Indeed, it was still empty.

"Well, I guess he means me," he said.

Twenty minutes later Hunter was sitting in the 2001st's squadron briefing room—alone.

A military family tree of sorts was painted on one wall of the room. The mural showed the area in southeast Iceland where the frigid base was located. It was actually an island off the coast, surrounded both by water and snowy tundra—there was no evidence of any of the famous Icelandic hot springs here, at least not according to the painting. It was just snow and ice and mountains and water.

The island was nearly a perfect oval, and there was a ring of 12 air bases built around its periphery. All had American flags and various unit numbers painted above them. The bases were laid out like pearls on a necklace, each with several long runways, each one about 10 miles from the other. A quick count revealed that 32 bomber squadrons, totaling more than 800 airplanes, were supposedly on station here. Each base had its own strange Nordic name.

The base where the 2001st Fighter Squadron was located was called oDrjmlendk. Or as Hunter would learn later, in slang, "Dreamland."

Below the painted map, in quotes, someone had tagged the entire arrangement of air bases "The Circle."

Next to the mural, the wall was plastered with photographs. They were pictures of pilots, some of them candid, some striking heroic poses, but mostly regulation photos.

Below each one was a man's name and a date, followed by the letters "KIA." Hunter didn't have to be a cryptologist to decipher what these initials meant. This was a wall of the dead, and there were so many photographs, the morbid gallery stretched completely around to the other side of the room.

After another 10 minutes, the same officer who had made the announcement in the Officers' Club walked in and climbed up onto the slightly raised stage at the front. A small plaque on the podium identified him as Major A. Payne, Briefing Officer. He was a pudgy but solid man in his mid forties, red of face, and thin of hair. His uniform seemed baggy on him. Off to his left was the omnipresent Main/AC computer, whirring and burping as usual. Behind him was a movie screen. Hunter was sitting fourth row, aisle seat. There were more than 400 chairs in here, he guessed. But at the moment, his was the only one that was occupied.

The officer ignored Hunter at first—like the OC bartender, it was like he didn't even want to look at him, that if he did he too might share his fate. Instead he kept his eyes glued to his wristwatch. At exactly 0300 hours, he looked up and finally took a long gaze at Hunter. Then he just shook his head.

He switched on a device that resembled a movie projector and the movie screen behind him came alive with blotches of brilliant but blurry colors. The officer focused the device's lens to reveal a map being projected on the screen. It showed the northwestern corner of England.

"The target for today will be the electrical power plants in Manchester," the major began. "You will be flying fighter escort for the 999th Bombing Group."

As the officer was saying this, the map suddenly came to life. Small but distinct cartoonlike icons of bombers began popping up on the screen. The animated planes rose up from the southern Icelandic coastline and formed up into neat boxes about 50 miles out to sea.

"Weather over the target area is expected to be cloudy,

with breaks. Winds on the ingress will be twenty-two knots southeast, sustained.''

Now animated clouds appeared and began moving across the map of England.

"Approach to the target will be from the northwest," the major continued. "The drop site is approximately one square mile."

Now a blue ring appeared on the map and the highlighted section became a zoom-in. It showed in some detail the city of Manchester.

"The 999th will drop their bombs on the center of the city, as a large power generation plant is located there. It will be a drop-on-leader release."

Again, the cartoon played out to show thousands of bombs dropping from hundreds of planes and the targeted city exploding into flames and smoke. It was all amazingly lifelike, yet almost humorous at the same time.

"Enemy fighter opposition is unknown, but could be heavy," Payne said, completing his briefing. "Full ammo loads and reserve tanks will be mandatory."

The major finally looked up.

"Any questions?" he asked the near empty hall.

Hunter stood up. "Yes, I have a question."

The major seemed annoyed. "Yes?"

"Sir, I'm the only one here."

The officer took his glasses off and rubbed his balding head.

"I know that," he said.

Hunter just stared back at the man.

"But it seems like such an important event as a mission briefing for an entire fighter squadron would demand mandatory attendance," he told Payne. "Wouldn't it?"

The officer took a breath and let it out slowly.

Then he told Hunter calmly, but through gritted teeth: "There *is* no one else."

And that's when it hit home. Maybe it was the three beers and two whiskeys that were clouding his judgment, or maybe it was the bad stew sitting like a rock in his stomach. But finally it dawned on Hunter what was happening here. The empty officers' club. The wall of deceased pilots. Pegg had been right when he said the Air Corps was desperate for pilots. Very desperate.

The fact was, there really was no one else in the 2001st Fighter Squadron.

Hunter was it.

Chapter 13

The sun came up—so to speak—about 90 minutes later.
Hunter had been directed to a prep room, given a pile
of insta-films and a device called a Boomer on which he
could watch them. The films were copies of previous missions flown over Manchester, England. Each one played
out on the Boomer's small TV screen using the lifelike
cartoons similar to the briefing film he'd just seen.

At 0400 hours he suited up, and at 0415, began the long
trudge out to the frozen flight line where a lone fighter
waited silently in the snow. What kind of planes did the
2001st Fighter Squadron fly exactly? Hunter wasn't sure.
Some kind of big airplane had shown up on the insta-
films. But even though he would soon be flying one himself, Hunter didn't know the aircraft's name or lineage.

Now, the closer he got to the fighter, the more it looked
like a weird combination of two planes he was somehow
able to recall. The plane before him had the distinctive
cockpit, nose, and tail section of the famous P-51 Mustang.
But it also had the swept-back wings and air intake of the
equally famous F-86 Sabre jet. The plane was more than

twice the size of both these aircraft and from the looks of it, powered by a jet engine of enormous proportions.

The weird bastardization did impress Hunter for a moment. It was interesting that in this strange place in which he found himself, that many airplanes had followed a kind of aeronautical Darwin's theory. Survival of the fittest. It was as if some airplanes he'd known back in his other place had mated and mutated into completely different animals.

He reached the airplane and was met by a very junior member of the ground crew, a kid who wasn't even old enough to shave. He seemed very surprised to see Hunter walking out to the flight line. The plane, the kid told him, was called a F-151 Mustang-5

They did a quick walk around. The kid told him the Mustang-5 had four machine guns on board, two in each wing, and a cannon in the nose. The machine guns were at full load, the cannon had exactly 25 shells and usually didn't work very well.

At that point, the wind and snow began to blow so hard, Hunter couldn't even talk to the kid anymore. He climbed the access ladder alone and strapped himself in. He fiddled with some dials, did some standard checks and then fired up the plane's huge engine. The thing literally bucked to life. Soon every bone in his body was vibrating. He increased the RPMs and gradually the big engine smoothed out and the vibrations died down. Hunter had no idea what shape the engine was in—it sounded OK, but not great. One thing was for certain: the cockpit heater was a piece of shit. It was blowing absolutely frigid air.

Hunter did a full diagnostic check, following a manual he found laying on the seat. From what he could surmise, everything was working as it was supposed to.

He gave the kid the OK sign and the kid unchocked the tires. Then Hunter dismissed him with a salute.

Then he waited.

The airplane was bucking and bronking and the wind was blowing and Hunter sat wondering in the freezing cold cockpit just how he'd managed to get himself into this position. Fall out of the sky, go to prison, transfer up here to a frozen hell, meet a dead man on the way. How crazy had things become? How crazy would they get? Finally the radio crackled to life, relieving him of the burden of replaying all the recent events in his head. The voice on the other end sounded like it was coming from Mars.

"Flight Zebra One, are you ready for take-off?" the radio asked.

Hunter looked for the microphone, found it under his seat, and responded. "Roger Tower—one question: any idea where I'm supposed to go exactly?"

"You are to link up with the 999th 55 nautical miles southwest of here. Homing beacon set to 76.9 hertz. Got it?"

Hunter was now searching the cockpit for anything that looked like a homing beacon. He found it eventually over near the auxiliary fuel pump activator.

"Click it on and it tells me where to go?" he asked the tower.

"That's right," came the reply. "You are now cleared for takeoff."

It was strange what happened next, because Hunter just rogered off, popped the brakes, and then started taxiing. It was really was a stupid thing to do—or it seemed stupid. He had no idea what he was supposed to do, how this plane flew, what its limitations were, or even its range or ceiling. There had been no time to read the thick manual. But something inside him was just telling him: Do it. Take off. Find the bombers. Fly the mission.

Was it instinct? His unconscious? The onset of insanity? He didn't know.

So he gunned the engine and began taxiing. He made the runway in less than a minute. Another gun of the engine and the aircraft settled down nicely again. He took a long look around. Obviously there was no other traffic he had to be concerned with. So he hit full throttle and the Mustang jet began rumbling down the runway.

And rumbling. And rumbling.

His speed was going up, but so slowly, it seemed to take forever for him to approach takeoff velocity.

He pushed extra throttle and still hit only 95 mph.

The end of the runway was coming up very quickly now. The wind, the cold, maybe water in the fuel. They were all working against him.

Deep concern suddenly flooded his chest. Maybe this flying stuff ain't so great after all—those words had come back to haunt him again. But then, again from somewhere deep in his mind, from a place that seemed to be located way in the back of his skull, a voice told him that to get into the air all he had to do was tap the brakes, raise the nose and go.

It was an old aviators' trick that had drifted to the forefront of his brain. So Hunter tapped the brakes and the nose flared up and it was just the kick the airplane needed to jump off the ground.

The engine coughed once, then twice, but somehow it pushed enough air through the turbine to burn enough fuel to keep itself going up. Hunter let out a quick sigh of relief. He was flying—again.

He brought the jet up gently, no time to show off here. The cold air was wicked, but apparently this engine could swallow anything. Soon he crawled up the gear and pushed more gas. The beast responded better than he would have ever thought. He pulled back on the control stick and climbed.

Up over the frozen field. Up over the nearby mountains. To the layers of crystal air above. It was now close to 5 A.M. The day was already into its perpetual twilight; it wouldn't get much brighter anywhere in Iceland today. But he knew it would grow lighter the further south he went.

He climbed some more and the absurdity of the situation began to wear away, to be replaced somewhat by that sheer delight of being airborne. Again the feeling from the back of his head told him that doing things like this—taking off in a strange airplane to fight in some unknown battle—

were not that alien to him. In fact, he seemed to have vague memories of doing things much worse, more dangerous, even more foolhardy than this.

But how could that be? What kind of a person had he been that things like this didn't bother him, didn't phase him? He didn't know—and oddest of all, at that moment, he didn't feel the need to dwell on it very much.

The mission, whatever it might be, was the most important thing to concentrate on now.

As he climbed, the sky began to clear of darkness and mist.

Below him now was the very cold North Atlantic. He could see the wave caps even though he was passing up through 7500 feet. The wind was brutal up here— *22 knots my ass!* Hunter thought, hunkering down in the cockpit and praying for the heater to finally kick in.

When he reached Angels-10, he turned southeast and switched on the homing beacon.

This should be interesting, he thought.

A TV screen came to life on the left side of the control panel. It was so small he hadn't even noticed it before. It displayed a very crude, yet somehow discernible picture of the sky ahead. In the middle was an amber circle. When Hunter turned up the power, this circle began pulsating. He steered a little left, and the ring stopped blinking and became whole. That was simple, he thought. Too simple maybe?

He flew for about 20 minutes, keeping the amber circle together and going where it told him.

The sun gradually grew brighter, and the clouds less dark and threatening. Soon he found himself passing through thick white cumulus clouds—huge, billowing ones—miles across and miles high.

As he passed through 15,000 feet, his body started shaking again. A moment later he began coming out of the huge cloud bank. His homing beacon was brighter than ever.

When he finally broke through he found a great surprise waiting for him. Off to his left, he saw a group of bombers. They were of some undetermined type. Long wings, long snouts, high tail wings, lots of jet engines. Yet again, on closer look, they bore a resemblance to another pair of airplanes whose memory was locked somewhere back in Hunter's head. The nose was that of a B-24 Liberator, an airplane from his version of World War II, he supposed. The fuselage was thick, almost square, and the wings rode on top, just like the Liberator. But the wings themselves were swept back and extremely long, and the tail section was several stories high, just like another hazily familiar airplane. Long, immense, powerful. It was called . . . a B-52, yes, that was it! Hunter shook his head as if to clear it. These bombers were both astonishing and bizarre. They were a cross between a B-24 and a B-52, and maybe twice the size of both.

There were 36 of them, flying in three box formations. They were painted in a typical blue and white polar camouflage disbursement pattern; the tail wings bore the numbers 15/999. He'd found the 999th Bombardment Squadron.

His beacon glowed again. Now he looked above him, and saw another dozen of the big B-24/52 bombers. These were painted all black, some with ferocious nose and tail art. Then he spotted another group way off to his right. And another group below them. And another beside them. He'd come up in the middle of a formation of more than 100 bombers!

His surprise grew. When he'd left Dreamland field on his own, he'd had the vague notion that he would link up with a few scattered bombers somewhere and they would drop a couple of strings of bombs quickly and then make for home, absurd as all that was. Now looking all over the sky made for a very impressive sight, frightening even. What he was seeing in every direction was substantial power. Not enormous. But substantial.

Maybe this wouldn't be so bad after all . . .

But the shine came off a little when he checked in with the Group Flight Leader and announced he was joining the package. The man actually laughed when he heard Hunter was flying out of Dreamland and representing the 2001st Fighter Group.

"Don't tell me they finally scraped up someone to join the party?" the man asked.

Hunter explained, in shorthand radio talk, that he was a new replacement, on base less than 10 hours.

The Flight Leader replied: "OK, rook. Then just don't get in anyone's way."

By this time Hunter was pulling up alongside the massive lead bomber. The thing was so big, it was like something from a nightmare. Its fuselage and wings seemed to go on forever. The disruption it was causing to the airflow all around it was enormous.

He finally drew even with it and was able to look inside the multitiered cockpit. To his astonishment, he saw half a dozen bearded, unkempt faces looking back out at him.

This was a bomber crew?

The people peering out at him seemed more at home in a cave or a barroom. They had long hair and beards. They wore a patchwork of moldy uniforms. Many had their service caps on backwards or not at all. And incredibly, Hunter could see a bottle of liquor being passed among them.

Was he dreaming?

Was this really happening?

He called over to the flight leader.

"Am I correct in assuming that I am the only fighter cover today?" he asked.

"That's the situation, rook," came the slurred reply.

The words hit Hunter like a ton of bricks. Why he expected more fighter planes to show up, he didn't know. Payne certainly didn't mention any in his briefing. And as far as Hunter could tell, there were no other fighter squadrons operating out of oDrjmlendk.

But really? Just him? Just one fighter pilot left in this whole fucking crazy world to protect more than a hundred gigantic bombers? At least one of which was being flown by drunks?

"That's the situation," the Flight Leader's voice crackled in his ears, as if he'd read his mind. "Welcome to the War . . ."

Hunter managed to get one more question off to him, though. "What exactly am I expected to do?"

"Just stay awake," came the gruff reply. "And if you see any enemy fighters, shoot 'em down."

The flight down took about two hours.

Though it was 900 miles to target, the big bombers were traveling at .9 Mach without even breathing hard. This was an incredible speed for planes so big and bulky. Hunter's airplane itself was giant for a single-seat fighter, but his gas tanks—in the wings, in the body, and in three massive drop tanks below—gave him more than enough fuel to cruise at 550 knots. He was gaining grudging respect for the Mustang jet. It ran smoother than it looked, and its fuel consumption was surprisingly efficient—as it would have to be.

Even after two hours at near Mach speed, his tank was just passing down through three-quarters full, and he still had his reserves attached.

So maybe in some ways, bigger *was* better, he thought. Still, something about the whole size thing in this strange world was very alien to him.

They first spotted land at about 0715 hours. This was the top of Scotland. Hunter's homing screen actually popped up with animated landmarks, similar to the moving, cartoonish briefing map. The first city of any import he could see, both on the TV screen and out his cockpit window, was Glasgow, the capital of Occupied Scotland.

Once this was clearly in view, the homing beacon turned the entire group due south. They flew at 45,000 feet right down the North Channel and were soon above the Irish Sea. It looked wild and cold, but oddly, it seemed a little green too.

Once they'd passed over the Isle of Man, the homing screen began blinking again. The entire group now turned east.

A moment later, they made landfall.

They approached the target, Manchester, from the northwest. Along the way, billows of smoke could be seen rising from the city of Blackpool, apparently hit earlier that day. Bradford and Leeds were on fire as well. The smoke was so dense from these two cities, they joined together in an acrid black blanket hanging in the sky above.

The group flew right over another earlier target—a massive power generating station at Bolton-Bury. It too was burning. The smoke was so thick here in fact, that the city's defenders had turned on dozens of searchlights. Their weakened beams stabbed up through the smoke at Hunter's group. And Hunter did see some flak bursting way off to his right. But there was nothing of consequence being thrown up at them here. He got the distinct impression that any antiaircraft crews left below were either out of ammo, out of power, or dead.

The group gradually passed out of the smoke and continued inland. Hunter had positioned his Mustang out on the right flank of the lead aircraft. He was flying the lowest position in the entire package now.

The real clouds got thicker, just as predicted by the insta-film mission tape, and soon Hunter was flying blind once again. He snapped on the homing device and this gave him a shadow's view of the bombing group, just enough for him to keep a proper distance away from them.

When they broke out of the clouds again two minutes later, Hunter could see the outer reaches of Manchester itself.

It too had been hit recently by bombers from the Circle.

The center of the city was supposed to be the 999th's drop point. But there was no more center of the city. No homes, no discernible streets, certainly no power plants that he could find. All that Hunter could see was a deep burning hole in the ground.

The Flight Leader gave the order for his bombers to pull into drop formation.

They were just above Manchester now, and entering the same kind of artificial night they'd encountered over Bolton-Bury, so thick were the smoke clouds from the previous bombing.

Hunter pulled close to the lead bomber again. He saw the bombardier inside the big plane give a thumbs-up sign. The lead plane's bomb bay doors snapped open.

Then, suddenly—a very urgent voice came on the line. It was the flight leader again.

"God damn it! Hold on here . . ." he screamed out over the general radio call.

Hunter tilted the Mustang-5 to the left and saw an unbelievable sight coming up from the edge of the burning city. It looked at first like a gigantic flower burst, made of smoke and long towering streaks of flame. Then it transformed into a fireworks display going off with hundreds of enormous sparks rising up from it.

And suddenly Hunter's headphones were filled with voices. They were thick with slurred words and high anxiety.

"Jessuzz, what the hell . . . ?"

"How many are there?"

"What the fuck is happening here?"

Hunter knew the answer a few seconds later. These were enemy interceptors, hundreds of them, heading straight up towards the bomber stream.

But what were they exactly? Hunter's long-term memory kicked in again. They looked like nothing more than tubes with short stubby wings attached. But hanging off their noses were huge cannons, and the flare of their exhaust plumes spoke of their extremely high velocity. They were

Natters. German rocketplanes. Frightening in their simplicity. More than 300 were climbing up to meet them.

And they were moving so fast, if Hunter didn't act, they would be among the bombers in seconds.

He let his instincts take over. Putting the nose of the Mustang straight down, he dove into the swarm. The next thing he knew he was turning, twisting, firing his guns, jinking this way and that. He was so close to some of the ascending Natters he could actually see the faces of the German pilots inside. He could even see their expressions. They all looked exactly the same—shocked that a single fighter was trying to protect the large bomber force, and amused by it as well.

There were so many of them, Hunter's mind was racing at the speed of light, trying to figure out an advantage. In the end there really was only one: the Natter was a rocket plane and this meant it carried a load of highly volatile rocket fuel on board. One bullet in the wrong place and the thing became a flying fiery coffin.

Against such overwhelming odds Hunter knew he literally had to make ever bullet count. So he began shooting at the enemy aircraft in very short bursts, trying to line up two, or even three Natters at a time and sending a burst through all of them.

It was a good strategy because soon the sky all around him was exploding with the German wonder weapons. He cut through the swarm with a ruthlessness that surprised even him. He was downing two or three planes with a burst here, icing up to four and five with a burst there. Each time one exploded that meant another life snuffed out, another pilot lost to the enemy. There would be no parachutes seen in this battle.

It went on for what seemed like hours, but in reality was less than a minute. Incredibly, Hunter had downed at least 20 of the rocket planes, and driven off maybe twice that number.

But then he finally pulled up and looked back up at the bomber group. That's when the real horror hit. Though he'd done all that was humanly possible—and then some—many Natters had still gotten through. And they were ripping into the bomber stream like jungle cats into a prey.

Hunter quickly looped around and began chasing the rocketplanes as they were rising into the bombers. The German aircraft were good for only one pass—their engines stayed lit for five minutes, tops. Where that gave them incredible speed, it also meant the German pilots had to make every shot count as well. And this they were doing. Even as Hunter was picking off the last of the climbing swarm, the thick of it continued to stream through the planes of the 999th. The bombers' gunners were firing furiously at the rocketplanes, but they were moving so fast, their shells just couldn't catch up to the tiny lethal aircraft.

Soon as many bombers were falling out of the sky as were Natters. Pieces of flaming wreckage were raining down all around Hunter's airplane. He began steering madly to avoid it all. He even saw men falling, some dead, but some still alive. Hats off, beards flowing, heads and bodies bloody, they were dropping like insects into the burning city below.

What madness was this? Hunter looped again and began chasing Natters that had already made their strafing pass and were now trying to get away. He picked off half a dozen this way, adding to his already enormous count, but it was too little too late to help the 999th.

The Natters all eventually blew through, and those still in one piece simply descended back to earth, firing the retro-jets with the last of their fuel and setting down anywhere it was soft and grassy. In all, the ferocious attack lasted no more than 90 seconds.

Hunter's stomach felt like it was made of lead. He leveled off and did a quick, terrifying count. There were just 70 bombers left. Forty-four bombers gone. Just like that. In less than two minutes. Twenty men per bomber. More than 800 killed. No parachutes, no crash landings. No survivors. Just a fiery death four miles up.

And that's when Hunter saw some real heroism at work, fueled by alcoholic spirits as it may have been. Those bombers that remained made a wide turn, got back on course, and went over the city again, this time from the southeast. At exactly the right moment, they began dropping their ordnance loads. Now hundreds of big black iron bombs were raining down on Manchester, hitting the center of the city, which was now a growing ball of flame. The more bombs that went into the conflagration, the higher and more widespread the fire became. And now the surviving bombers, suddenly lighter as the titanic weights were gone from their bomb bays, rose up 2000, 3000, 4000 feet or more, like they were being pulled up on a string to the sun.

Then they formed up tight again, passed beyond the burning target, and as one, swung around west and made for the Irish Sea.

Hunter put the Mustang right on their tail. He was sucking on his oxygen mask now like there was no tomorrow. His uniform was bathed in sweat. He looked around the cockpit for a barf bag, his stomach gurgling, his brain screaming to make some sense of this very nonsensical situation.

He knew it would be a long ride home.

Chapter 14

Hunter set down back at Dreamland Base two hours later.

He'd thrown up twice on the return journey, an event that he had no recollection of ever happening to him before.

It didn't help that he was exhausted. Six months of sitting in jail had obviously softened him up. After the nausea, exhaustion began taking hold again. He had to resort to holding his breath for two or three minutes at a time, just so he'd gasp for about five minutes afterwards and force oxygen into his lungs and thus keep himself awake and not puking.

It was still perpetual dusk when he bounced in. He taxied through some thick snow to the 2001st's deserted flight line. The same dog-faced kid who'd served as his maintenance crew appeared out of the snow and choked off the Mustang-5's wheels.

Hunter killed the engine and waited for the access ladder to be placed. He waited and waited and waited. Then he wiped the fog from his cockpit glass and saw the maintenance kid driving away.

Hunter just shook his weary head, popped the canopy, and climbed out on his own. He threw the puke bag into the wind and it disappeared in the gale. Then came a 10-minute trudge to the ops building. The bitter cold served him like a bucket of ice water in the face.

He went to the briefing hut and found only Major Payne waiting inside.

Payne barely acknowledged his presence as Hunter collapsed into the same chair in which he'd sat earlier this long day. The officer watched his wristwatch for 10 long minutes, again as if he expected more people to show up.

But of course, no one did. At exactly 1000 hours, he stood up and addressed his audience of one. Reading from a single sheet of paper, he said:

"I have been cleared to tell you that today's operations against enemy-held territory have been deemed highly successful. More than seven targets were hit."

Then he finally looked at Hunter.

"OK," he said. "What did you see?"

Hunter told him just about everything. The Natters. The destruction of so many bombers. The 999th's brave second bombing run. The only thing he left out was the sight of the booze and the unkempt airmen.

The officer took it all down. At the end of it, he just looked up. "That it?" he asked Hunter.

"Yes," Hunter replied, truthfully.

"Had enough yet?"

Hunter was surprised by the question.

"No," he heard himself say.

"OK," Payne said. "Same time tomorrow. Dismissed."

With that, Payne left the room.

It took Hunter another 10 minutes of trudging through the blinding wind and snow to make it to the officers' club.

By the time he reached the front door, he was numb again. Nothing made sense here—well, not exactly anyway.

He recalled reading somewhere, at some time, about

the pressures that pilots during his version of World War II had felt after flying bombing mission after bombing mission and seeing their comrades shot out of the sky and then the destruction they were causing below.

Many had to either block it all out completely or go nuts dwelling on it. Hunter was somewhat convinced that he was already nuts—living inside of some grand illusion. So he decided that he would have little trouble blocking it out. Plus, he was just so tired—and hungry and sober—to deal with it.

That would soon change, he promised himself.

With that one thought in mind, he went through the OC door.

The place held a few more people this time, maintenance and logistics officers from what Hunter could see. Barely a head turned when he came in. He made his way to the bar, ordered a triple whiskey and the hot meal of the day. It was beef stew again; the bowl was the size of a small trough. He took the food and booze to the same corner table and began to feed.

About halfway through his meal, the lights at one end of the hall dimmed. Someone came out and put a microphone on the small stage in front of him. A spotlight appeared, focused on the back wall, and then took on a red tint. The microphone squealed, then a tall, affable guy walked calmly out on the stage.

"Welcome to today's matinee performance," he said into the mike in a deep tenor. "I'm Colonel Crabb . . ."

The man's announcement stopped Hunter in mid bite. *Colonel Crabb?* Why was that name familiar? He took a closer look at the man. He was in a uniform, but it didn't look too regulation, even in this crazy place. It was a cross between an Air Corps colonel's dress blues and a very tacky tuxedo.

His hair too looked a little off the books. It was swept back and highly moussed. He was holding a conductor's baton in one hand, a glass of something in the other.

"We have a great card of entertainment for you today,"

the Colonel said, as many of those in the chow hall moved their chairs closer to the stage. "The first number is called 'Dance of the Fawns.'"

There was polite applause from the crowd. It seemed like they were familiar with the piece.

Hunter swigged his drink. 'Dance of the Fawns?' What the hell could this be?

A small jazz band was assembled in the corner. On a cue from the Colonel's baton, they struck up a 12-bar blues theme.

Then the curtain opened to revealed a stage decorated with the tackiest sets possible. A cutout tree. A crayon-colored bush. Blue aluminum paper as a forest stream. Then four dancers tiptoed on to the stage. They were young, nubile teen-age girls. They were dressed in layers of silk and satin, and as the music struck up, they began dancing. There was little sense to the movements, little effort to keep in time. But the main objective of the dance was aimed at their disrobing. Bit by bit, the girls peeled off the layers of silk scarves and satin skirts, and soon they were simply naked.

The band hit a flourish and the girls took a bow and pirouetted off the stage, to be replaced by four more. This quartet pranced out and began disrobing in exactly the same way.

It went on like this for an hour. The audience was absolutely entranced. The girls were all beautiful, if dangerously young. The music was intoxicating. In the corner, occasionally accompanying the band on the congas, was Colonel Crabb. Lording over it all, one of the naked girls propped up on his lap, a smile of satisfaction creasing his face.

He looked so familiar . . .

He moved only after the lights dimmed, and the girls from the eighth dance left the stage. Marching up to the microphone, now with two young girls, one on each arm, he tapped the microphone and said: "And now a word from our sponsor."

At that point, a couch was brought up to the stage. Two

more girls appeared, sat on the couch, slowly disrobed
each other and engaged in 20 long minutes of sensual,
highly erotic kissing and touching.

At the end of the segment, the Colonel reappeared and
held up a sign over the heads of the lip-locked girls.

It read: Fly United . . . Airlines.

The audience applauded, the girls left the stage, and
Crabb announced the second interpretive ballet of the
show: "The Eight Temptations of Lolita."

The audience applauded again. Hunter ordered
another triple whiskey. The day's events began slowly wash-
ing away.

What a strange, strange place he'd found himself in . . .

Chapter 15

Hunter stayed in the officers' club for many, many hours, getting drunk, watching Crabb's "culture revue."

When he could no longer see straight, he stumbled to the 2001st officers' barracks, selected the first bunk he came to, and fell asleep.

Thankfully, he did not dream . . .

He woke up the next day cold and sore. His stomach felt like it was turned inside out. He looked around the barracks—it was a long Quonset hut containing at least 200 beds—and found that it was indeed very empty.

He located a coffee machine, made a pot, and drank half of it. Looking through the empty barracks, he saw each bed was made, corners tight. Each had a pilot's cap placed squarely on the pillow and a pair of boots down at the foot. Hunter laid his hand on the bunk next to his. It was ice cold. Then he turned around to the bunk he'd slept in and saw a pilot's cap on the floor and a pair of boots under the bed—just where he'd drunkenly thrown them the night before.

A shiver went through him. He'd slept in the bed of a dead man.

Thus began his second day in Hell.

He found the shower, and stood underneath the spigot for 20 long minutes, waiting for warm water that never came. Then he dried off and returned to his bed. He found a storeroom, and from it he took a new package of clothes, from the thermal underwear on out. Everything was colored light green.

He found a yellow duty roster that had been pinned to a board near the front door of the barracks. It was the daily assignment for the 2001st. It was long enough to hold at least 200 names. His was the only one on it.

There was a bomber mission taking off from one of the other Circle bases in less than an hour. He had to get briefed and get airborne to ride shotgun for them in less than 30 minutes.

The last thing he noted was that his rank had been penciled in as that of a lowly flight officer. Hunter understood this to be somewhere way below second lieutenant and barely above sergeant.

Though he wasn't sure exactly what his rank had been in his previous life, he was sure it was higher than this.

Payne was waiting for him once again in the big briefing room.

It was empty, like before. Again the officer barely acknowledged Hunter's presence. It was as if he himself would die just by setting eyes too long on Hunter. Maybe that was his experience, Hunter thought. Payne seemed like a good officer, stuck in the most gruesome position possible. Hunter looked at the gallery of dead pilots and wondered how many Payne had known personally.

Probably all of them, he thought.

They ran through a quick mission film—the target today was the city of Laxey Bay on the Isle of Man. One hundred and thirty-three bombers would attack a power plant on the island, one which supplied a lot of electricity via undersea cables for Occupied England and Ireland.

Payne was as brief as he had been the day before. When the mission film was over, he looked about the room and then his eyes rested on Hunter, sitting in the same seat as the day before.

"Any questions?" he asked.

Hunter just shook his head no.

What was the point?

"OK, then," Payne said. "Good luck . . . and good-bye."

With that, the briefing officer slowly walked off the stage, leaving Hunter with the distinct impression that Payne didn't expect to see him alive again.

Hunter walked back out into the snow and wind and cold again and was surprised to see that it was actually a little brighter this morning.

It gave him an opportunity to see more of the base. There were 18 hangars in all, laid out in a box with streets running like latticework between them.

Some of the hangars looked as if they'd been worked everyday until recently—tire tracks and oil-stained snow outside the now-locked doors being the clue. But there was a small group of aircraft barns at the rear of the place that didn't look as if they'd been used in years. In front of one of them, the snowdrifts were as high as the hangar door itself.

Hunter's mind flashed a message for him: Something strange was sitting in one of those barns. Something that might turn out to be very helpful to him someday.

The snow picked up again and all but short visibility became lost. Head down, Hunter fought the gale for another few minutes until he finally found the flight line.

Only one plane had been dragged out onto the preflight area, of course. The same Mustang-5 he'd flown the day before.

The same dopey maintenance kid was there too, eyes barely open, snot frozen to his nostrils. He looked at Hunter oddly as they met at the plane's access ladder.

"Going up again, huh?" he asked with a long, noisy sniff.

Hunter ignored him. It was too cold to chat. He began his preflight walk-around.

"I heard it was rough up there yesterday," the kid persisted.

Hunter was manually working the flaps, knocking pieces of ice from between the control surface hinges.

"Is it ever any other way?" he replied to the kid, trying to nip the inane conversation in the bud.

He completed the walk-around and then climbed up the access ladder. This time the kid came up the ladder and helped him strap in.

"I've seen a lot come and go," he said, sniffing and belting him at the same time.

"Mostly go . . ." he added ominously.

Hunter finally turned to him. "Hey kid, what is it with you? You want me to put you in my will? You want my boots or something?"

The kid was startled. He wiped some of the frozen snot from his nose.

"No sir," he said. "I just wanted to say . . . well, good luck up there."

With that, he banged Hunter twice on the helmet and disappeared.

Hunter fired the Mustang's engine and the thing came to life with surprising verve. He did a weapons check. His four machine guns were full, and the cannon was packing the same 25 shells. He did a fuel check: his main fuel tanks were full, and he was carrying three drop tanks with 500 gallons each. He switched on the homing TV, it came right to life too. He hit the radio check switch. It came back green.

Then he hit the heater switch—and the same old cold air came blowing in.

"That didn't last long," he murmured.

He taxied and took off without incident, once again

tapping the enormous fighter into the air with a touch of the brakes.

It was a very cloudy day. Hunter climbed as fast as he could, hoping that increased engine use would heat the plane up, but it was no soap. The heater was blowing air even colder than before. Finally he just gave up and switched the damn thing off.

He passed up through Angels-22 and finally broke through the soup.

He keyed the homing TV and was soon locked on a solid beam. The circle got tight, the screen came alive, and he was soon looking at long lines of contrails cutting across the deep blue morning sky. The sun was reflecting off the lines of frozen ice crystal, giving them an oddly warming hue. Hunter shivered when he saw this. It reminded him of just how cold he really was.

He laid on the throttle and the double-reaction engine kicked in response. He rose to 32,000 feet, the g-forces rippling his face and invigorating his body. He had the bombers in visual range within a minute.

This was not the 999th from the day before. These airplanes were from the unfortunately numbered 13th Heavy Bombardment Squadron.

They were flying enormous aircraft, larger than the B-24/52s from Hunter's previous mission. He took a moment to study these airplanes and again, saw an example of the odd aeronautical Darwinism at work.

As with most combat aircraft he'd seen here in this strange world, these looked to be a combination of two airplanes, memories of which were allowed to leak out of the back of his skull. These planes were very long and thin. They had enormous wingspans with six contra-rotating props on each side, back-mounted, pusher-style, along with a set of four jet engines way out on the tips. In this way the plane resembled what Hunter remembered as the B-36 Peacemaker.

But the snout of the aircraft was tiered and had an arsenal of weapons sticking out of it. So did the fuselage, which looked very thick and rugged and was lousy with machine gun stations. The flight deck, the canopy, the dozens of gun blisters, the high tail, and even the partially retracted landing gear were all reminiscent of a plane Hunter recalled as the B-17 Flying Something-or-Other.

So these were B-17/36s. Even his swiss-cheese brain knew that was another very bizarre combination.

He called up to the flight leader, and unlike the day before, he received a very crisp response on the first try.

"This is Section Leader Tango One," a very official-sounding voice responded. "I read you, Cover."

He and Hunter exchanged a flurry of information on headings, weather changes, heights, emergency frequencies, and so on. For the first time since this whole bad dream had commenced, Hunter found himself authentically impressed. He hit the throttle bar again and zoomed up to meet the column of B-17/36s.

For some reason, he felt the adherence to military protocol, and the confident no-nonsense tone to be very reassuring. Why was this? Had he been a hardass back in his previous military career? A by-the-book kind of guy?

He didn't know.

He reached the head of the column and moved up parallel to the flight leader.

These airplanes was very spit and polished, none of them bore the garish nose paintings of the day before. Nor were they painted in the dull blue polar camouflage of the group, the ill-fated 999th. These planes looked like they just rolled off the factory assembly line. They were bright, shiny, reflective metal.

The pilot of the first ship gave Hunter a friendly salute, which he returned. All of the faces looking out at him now were clean and neatly dressed. No beards and booze here.

Normally, Hunter's instincts told him, for the 132 bombers in this flight at least a couple dozen fighters would be riding shotgun. They would normally take up positions about 5000 feet above the group, riding lead, flanks, and rear.

But there were no two dozen airplanes to guard this column. It was just Hunter. For this reason, he chose to take a position about a half mile ahead of the column at only a slightly higher altitude. Like the scout in front of the cavalry column, leading the way.

Though he was just as cold and just as confused as the day before, he did feel different today. The esprit de corps of this bomber group was goosing him into a better frame of mind.

That's another reason he took the lead point. If anyone was going to take a shot at them, they'd have to take a shot at him first.

That's the way he wanted it to be.

They reached the approaches to the North Channel exactly two hours later.

The weather had been cooperative and the skies friendly. No surprise with this group, everything was exactly on schedule.

To Hunter's left, Scotland, still foggy in the early morning sun. To his right, northern Ireland, covered in clouds and raining as usual. Still, it did look emeraldlike this morning, and not at all uninviting. Hunter wondered for a moment if he was Irish, or of Irish parents maybe.

In the same thought he hoped the Irish were on the right side of this war against Germany. He knew that Eire was occupied, but just how much resistance were the Sods putting up against their perpetual enemy's enemy? He didn't know.

Twenty minutes later, their target came in sight. The Isle of Man was a substantial chunk of land in the northern part of the Irish Sea.

The target, a double-reaction power station, provided juice to nearly all of Occupied Britain and Ireland. To knock it out or even damage it would put the Germans in the dark, at least for a while anyway.

In any case, it beat bombing an already bombed-out city like Manchester.

Hunter keyed in on the bombing group's interplane frequency and heard a symphony of crisp orders and responses. The group was tightening up, proper prebomb etiquette. The gun crews were testing their weapons, again, another routine item on the checklist. Various things involved in bomb-dropping itself—bay doors, fusing systems, gyros, and of course bombsights—were being checked in a very methodical, professional way.

There was a whole new feeling running through Hunter right now. These guys of the 13th had pride, man. They were ready to do the job, come what may. And he was sure they had to be astute enough to know that it would probably get rough over the target, especially with exactly one fighter plane riding cover.

Hunter knew he had to do everything in his power to help protect them.

Everything . . .

It happened about two minutes later.

Hunter was checking his own fuel load, at the same time watching a fuzzy yet discernible picture of the Isle of Man on his homing TV. As he understood it, the earliest warning they could get of fighter opposition would be from the "Homer." The camera would pick up a large number of rising indications, run a crude memory check on them, radio this data back to the Circle and if the Main/AC computer back there caught on, it would positively ID them as unfriendlies. All this took a while, needed 100-percent electronic and atmospheric cooperation and the Main/AC couldn't be too busy when the call from the group came in. The problem was every Main/AC everywhere was always too busy because everyone seemed to rely on them, or were tied to them slavishly.

This is what had happened the mission before—and why the Natter attack had been such a surprise.

And this is what happened today.

But in the end it didn't matter—Hunter detected the swarm of enemy aircraft even before some of them left the ground.

It all started when his body began shaking.

It was so intense at first, he thought something was wrong with the Mustang-5. His eyes flash-scanned the control panel and saw no red or blinking lights. He pushed the systems diagnostic button and everything appeared green. Only then did he realize he was shaking and not the airplane.

The feeling was not a new one, just a forgotten one.

The tingling at the end of the fingertips. The buzzing at the base of the skull. Eyes suddenly looking in all directions at once. It was an intensity rivaling that of his first time airborne in the Pogo—but definitely with a very different vibe.

Trouble is coming, a voice was saying crisp and clear in his head, even more so than the voices of the 13th Bombardment pilots. *Do something about it . . .*

The next thing he knew, Hunter was diving.

He'd slammed the nose of the Mustang-5 down to the floor and now he could see the northern coast of the Isle of Man coming up at him very, very fast.

And up ahead, about 45 degrees in his field of vision, he saw them.

At first he would have sworn they were a flock of birds, and in a way, they were. They were just heads and wings really, white, almost reflective. They were not trailing any smoke, any exhaust or flames at all. They looked, for want of a better word, graceful. And they weren't the particularly ungraceful Natters.

What were they then?

Hunter increased power even as he was passing through Mach 1 in a dive. These things were swooping up towards the bombers and he was moving so fast and had dove on them so unexpectedly, they hadn't seen him yet.

He keyed his homing TV and got a split-second bead

on one of them close-up. The German Iron Cross was painted on its wings. And there were serial numbers on its very short tail. And he could see a bubble-type canopy at the very front of the snout. And underneath each one, he saw a load of antiaircraft rockets.

And suddenly the name just popped into his head. These things were Horton flying wings.

Hunter's breath caught in his throat—not so much upon the realization that a swarm of weird deadly interceptors was rising up to attack the bomber group, as that something his psyche had warned him so early that they were coming.

How could that have happened? It was the same feeling which had caused him to look down at the two U-boats that day, and he supposed, that got him through the knife fight with the Natters the day before. But never had he had the feeling this intense—not in this place anyway.

But the feeling was more than just an early warning system—this vibe had given him an outstanding advantage that every pilot wanted more than anything else if he was about to get into a dogfight.

He'd seen the enemy—and they hadn't seen him.

The Horton flying wings were designated Ho-IXX. They were built of tubular aluminum, and their wings were sturdy plywood. This gave them a swiftness never before seen in a German interceptor, another example of the great leap forward in the Reich lately.

They were powered by two massive BMW-Juno 5000 engines, double reheat monsters that made up nearly 60 percent of the strange aircraft's weight. These made the planes extremely powerful and maneuverable.

But to cut down the weight even further, the aircraft's small cabin wasn't pressurized. Instead the pilot wore a pressurized suit and a helmet that really was out of a sci-fi movie. Again the extra lightness gave the little wing a measure of grace.

But there was a problem. The German flying wings were

interceptors—platforms from which missiles could be fired into a bomber stream with great accuracy. But there was a difference between interceptors and fighters. Fighters could do what interceptors could do—shoot at bombers. But the fighters could also dogfight, due to their weapons. Usually interceptors could not.

And this day, in this world, the Horton wings were purely interceptors.

And the Mustang-5 was a fighter.

Hunter kept on diving, way down, right to the deck. He streaked across the beach on the northern tip of the island, turned the big plane over and then started climbing again.

Now he had three advantages. He was behind the enemy, they didn't see him and his plane was a better fighter than theirs.

It was odd because the Hortens were flying in a long chevron formation, almost mimicking the shape of their wings themselves. Hunter could see their strategy as clear as day. They would rise up into the bomber stream—knowing the bombers would have to be going very slow while going into their bombing runs—and start flooding it with their antiaircraft rockets.

It was also obvious the Germans had brought the wings in to specifically defend the power plant on the Isle of Man.

Hunter could just barely see the bomber stream coming into view now. He was so low, and the sun was so bright, that spotting them was a little difficult. He increased throttle and began to climb. The 12 wings were laid out for him in perfect fashion.

He climbed more, sneaking up on them—3000 feet, 4000, 4500 . . .

Still they were completely unaware of him. The bombers he figured must be at 22-Angels by now, their bombing altitude. Clouds had moved in. They were hiding the bomb group! Excellent!

Hunter opened up at exactly 5000 feet. His four guns screamed streaks across the sky. For whatever reason the plane was overloaded with tracer bullets—and he found it a great, if familiar aid. His first barrage tore into the first pair of wings.

And that's where Hunter found his fourth advantage: like the Natters, the Horten wings were loaded with a very volatile rocket fuel known as S/W-Stoff. Hunter knew it was highly flammable because all it took was a few hits and the first wing just disintegrated, even quicker than a Natter.

He tore into the second one, then a third one. They too blew up immediately. He turned and knocked off a fourth wing. It too went up like a matchstick. But this is the last one he would take by surprise. By now the rest of the Horton group saw him and began evasive action.

With the precision of an aerobatics team, they broke into a starburst. Each one turning over in an opposite direction from the others.

This did not slow down Hunter though. He simply picked the two wings closest to him and dove on them. He hit one just as it was at the bottom of its loop. There was no explosion this time—Hunter drilled a barrage right into the cockpit and killed the pilot outright.

He continued on through his own loop and wound up on the number two man's tail. One quick barrage from his four guns tore off the plane's tiny tail. It was enough to make him lose control. The pilot knew he was cooked and pulled his ejector seat. It worked—but it horribly cut his neck on the way out.

Hunter could see the blood spraying in all directions as the chute opened and the hapless pilot began to descend.

Now he had six left. They were scattered all over the sky—and all thoughts of going after the bombers were gone.

But suddenly and very unexpectedly Hunter began vibrating again. What was this? He turned and saw another swarm of aircraft coming up right at him. These weren't graceful or elegant or anything even close to it. These airplanes were down and dirty motherfuckers—they looked it and they sounded it.

But again, what were they exactly?

They were very strange looking. Big, swept back wings, two- or three-man canopy. Wide bodies. Jet engines. This was a German hybrid: an Me-110 fighter-bomber and a Me-262 jet. Again, to Hunter, it looked like those two airplane designs had been melted down into one. Appropriately enough they were known as Me-666s.

They were coming on very fast and two were gluing themselves on Hunter's tail.

Damn—he'd fallen for something here. These fighters were protecting the interceptors, an odd but effective tactic.

And he'd made a huge mistake. He should have suspected the Isle of Man would be defended in depth. But it was too late to worry about that now.

In the next second, rockets were whooshing by him. And bullet streams. Not only did he have one of the beasts on his tail, but a wing had come around and got on his six o'clock as well.

Now what? As suddenly as the thought hit his brain, he began spinning. Around and around, the Mustang-5 was screeching back in protest but kept turning. For a moment, Hunter felt like he was back in the Pogo. Turning, twisting, and avoiding anything fired at him.

To the brutal turn he added a back-breaking climb. The bolts were coming apart as he pulled at least 8gs, way too much even for the rugged Mustang-5 to take. He kept spinning and climbing and like lions after the swift feet they tried to catch, the Me-666s gave up on him.

Hunter pulled back around, drenched in sweat, and somehow managed to throw a stream of slugs into the wing that had been pursuing him. It exploded.

But then he saw the Me-666s were rocketing past him and up to where the bombers should be.

Hunter felt a shiver go through him. Combined, the Horton wings and Me-666s would slaughter the 13th.

He couldn't let it happen.

He pushed the throttle ahead, did an inverted loop—
and began climbing . . .

If anyone had been there to see it, the next two minutes
were a display of aeronautical ability like none ever seen
in this place—this strange, but not-so-strange alternate
universe.

Hunter quickly caught up with the remaining Me-666s,
and splashed one with a 10-shot tracer barrage.

Then he turned up and under two more of the swift,
mean-looking aircraft—they had rear guns, radar-controlled no doubt, and they started firing at Hunter, but
neither scored hits. The Mustang-5 simply seemed to move
out of the way at the split-second before any enemy shells
could hit it.

It was a strange thing, almost eerie to see. The American
jet jinking, jagging, ducking, spinning, going every which
way except in the path of the enemy bullets.

All the while the Mustang's guns were firing and shred-
ding the tails off of a pair of still-ascending Me-666s. The
two planes each lost a half a tail section. Both had no
choice but to fall away.

Next the Mustang did a 180-degree loop that seemed
impossibly tight, and impossibly g-straining. The big jet
somehow turned inside the small swifter flying wings, nail-
ing one with a long steady burst, then just catching the
other with a quick short one. Either way, the result was
the same. The wings were packed with fuel—rubbing two
rocks together would have blown one of them up. Tracers
were catastrophic.

The Mustang then rolled once again and kept climbing—up toward the clouds, again where the 13th Heavy
Bombardment Squadron should be.

There were three Me-666s left, and two wings. The American airplane once again pulled hard gs, got on the tail of
a Me-666, squeezed off what looked to be as few as 10
bullets from each gun—perfectly placed to rip the star-

board wing off. The pilots bailed out even before the huge perforation in their fuselage caught fire.

The Mustang-5 pulled 8 gs backward now—winding up in a head-on with a flying wing. Two short bursts—the German pilot was dead. The wing beside him tried to break away. A dive and another close-in shot by the Mustang-5. After that, it was elemental. Sparks hit S/W-Stoff. Wing explodes.

Now there was just a pair of Me-666s left but even two could cause havoc in among the steely-eyed bombers of the 13th Heavy.

Hunter pulled incredible gs screeching out of his dive, somehow looped right up again, and a burst of his tracers which seemed to have the right amount of English on them. They went right through the pilot's compartment, killing both.

That left only one.

Again, if there had been any witnesses to this most astonishing air combat—any who lived, that is—what they saw next would defy adequate description.

It was again an exercise in rather superhuman flying and optical illusions. For at one second it seemed as if the lone Me-666 was pulling away from the Mustang-5—just as a matter of the angle and being in the right place at the right time, it was far away from the rampaging American jet.

It might also have seemed not impossible that this lone German fighter could still plant an antiaircraft rocket barrage into the 13th Heavy Bombardment squadron and do catastrophic damage. Or the German plane could have easily just turned away and retired at its leisure. After losing every one of its colleagues, no air commandant would fault the last plane from leaving the field of battle, if just to tell the tale.

But whichever way the German pilots had decided to play it, they would never get to act, because in the blink of an eye, the Mustang-5 seemed to disappear from one space in the sky and reappear in another, this one looking right down the throat of the German attack plane.

Any witness might have argued whether there was a long burst from the Mustang, or a short burst, or even no burst of fire at all. Because it seemed as if the German airplane, in trying to get out of the way of the suddenly diving fighter, simply seemed to come apart in a flash of fire and smoke.

Not quite an explosion, not quite a disintegration either. The plane's atoms just chose that moment to disassemble catastrophically, taking the atoms of both crew members with it.

And after that, the sky was suddenly empty again. Very empty.

Inside the cockpit of the Mustang-5, Hunter was not cold any longer.

He was sweating bullets. The canopy was fogged up from his exhalations, many of the dials and switches frozen in place from the continuous onslaught of g-forces.

He was sucking on his oxygen mask like he'd just run the marathon. But there was a grim satisfaction to his heavy breathing too. He'd done similar amazing flying things in another life—this he was sure of now. But that was really secondary to him at the moment.

What was foremost was he'd broken his neck, almost literally, and risked his life more than a dozen times inside of four and a half minutes to protect the 13th Heavy Bombardment Group from harm and allow them to perform their mission.

Too bad they weren't around to appreciate the effort.

That was the hard, cold fact Hunter slowly came to as he searched the sky for the 132 gigantic bombers.

It was a useless endeavor for the first few moments. It seemed as if the squadron of bombers had vanished into thin air while he was battling in the cosmic dogfight.

Only by flying higher, up to 35-angels did Hunter finally spot them. Not going in over the target, as their mission called for. Nor had they all been shot done by yet another phantom squadron of German fighters.

No, the 13th Heavy Bombardment Squadron was now heading northwest, back out over the North Channel, making for the open spaces of the ocean and a return trip home.

That's when it hit Hunter like a hammer on the head. For while he was breaking ass and elbow and risking life and limb to protect them, the 13th Heavy Bombardment Squadron, at first sight of the enemy interceptors, had turned tail and run away.

Three hours later, Hunter was slumped in a chair in the 2001st's briefing room.

Payne was standing at the podium, the usual tortured look on his face. Behind him, the Main/AC was whirring softly.

"These are very serious accusations," he was saying to Hunter.

"They are not accusations," Hunter was firing back. "They are the facts. The truth. No room for interpretation. No need for it either."

"You are claiming that an entire bomb group left the field of battle for no reason at all," Payne said, trying to spin Hunter's story a little.

But Hunter wasn't buying it. He was cold, he was hungry, he was tired and he was very pissed. But he was not a fool.

"No—they had a reason," he retorted. "They were cowards, they ran away."

He slipped further down into his seat. He was beyond exhaustion now.

Payne was shaking his head—but not quite in disbelief. More in futility. Plus, he was hiding something. Hunter could feel it.

"And I'll bet it isn't the first time they've done it either," Hunter continued wearily. "They looked to be in pretty tight formation as they were flying away from me."

Payne tried again. "But you still have to admit that no one was on hand to verify your story," he told Hunter.

That's when Hunter lost it. Payne was either the war's biggest pussy, or he was hiding something very big. Hunter flew out of his chair and made three threatening steps toward the officer.

"Do you actually think I'm making this up?" he challenged him.

Payne's face turned red. "Do I really have to read you the book of etiquette, Flight Officer?"

Hunter's anger entered another realm at that point. He was so mad, he actually calmed down.

"I'm reporting an act of major cowardice and you're going to pull rank on me?" he asked Payne.

Payne just stared back at him.

"Shame on you," Hunter said, grabbing his gear. "And if you want send the Air Cops to arrest me—for insubordination or whatever—then I'll be in the OC, getting wrapped."

With that, Hunter walked out of the briefing room, leaving Payne alone, staring out from the podium onto the empty auditorium.

Chapter 16

The next day broke cold and windy—but with no snow.

After making good on his promise to get drunk, Hunter ate some of the OC's sucky stew and watched Colonel Crabb's culture offering of the day, "Daughters of the Witch Queen."

To Hunter it looked a lot like "Dance of Lolita Island," but he was drunk, and really in no shape to play theater critic. So he sat there and watched and drank and added his applause to that of the bartender and a couple maintenance guys and Air Guards any time one of the girls lost all her clothing or when they completed a song together.

Once again, he couldn't remember walking back to the barracks, opening the door, flopping on his bunk. But he did recall reading the note that was posted on the roster board—someone had slipped in and planted it there.

It said the regular morning briefing would be "rescheduled" to after the assigned bombing mission—a military dodge if there ever was one.

There was a mission assignment package waiting for him too and with drunken fingers he opened it, read that he was flying again at 0400 hours the next morning. Only then did he fall into unconsciousness.

That night he dreamed he was in a tropical jungle. There was a pyramid in a clearing and hundreds of natives were bowing around it. He was at the top of this pyramid, a headdress and mask over his head. The people were bowing to him, chanting to him. A beautiful girl and a monk were nearby. Even in his dream Hunter had to ask the inevitable question: was he some kind of Inca god in his former life?

He woke up, took a shower, drank some coffee, got dressed, and only then did he remember the briefing pack he'd read the night before.

He was flying cover for yet another bomber squadron this morning. They were the 3234th squadron, from Base Six of the Circle. The bombing raid was to be over a target not in Occupied England but Occupied Ireland. They were taking off in 30 minutes.

Hunter trudged out to the flight line. The Mustang-5 was waiting for him, apparently just as he left it.

But there was a surprise waiting for him. When he reached the airplane he discovered not just Dopey the maintenance guy hanging about, but two others, Sneezy and Sniffy. Between them they didn't total 50 years old.

The access ladder was waiting for him this time too. And the jet was turned on, its engine already warming up. When Hunter did a quick walk around, the three kids followed him like a mother duck. Everything looked OK. The wings had even been deiced.

Hunter climbed up into the cockpit and Dopey helped him strap in, while his compatriots waited nearby, looks of anticipation on their pimply faces.

"Everything went to green on the diagnostic series this morning," Dopey told him. "We also recalibrated the gun sights and greased the feeder links."

Hunter just looked up at him. "Thanks, kid," he said finally.

The kid strapped him in, hit him twice on the helmet

with much enthusiasm, and then disappeared down the access ladder. But a second later he was back again.

"We fixed the heater, too," he said before he saluted and disappeared again.

Hunter reached done and clicked on the heater switch. Sure enough, the cockpit was flooded with ultrawarm air.

Hunter returned the trio of salutes and then began taxiing. His new fan club actually waved good-bye.

Getting off the ground went well.

With the ice finally off his wings, the takeoff run took only two-thirds the distance.

Hunter climbed, and began sucking on the oxygen mask. He knew enough to know that the big O was the best cure for a hangover. As he rose above the airfield, for the first time he was able to get a glimpse of some of the other bases around the Circle.

There were two bomber bases about a mile from Dreamland. Then a cargo unit was located directly over the hill. Then another couple of bomber bases. The rest was sealed in mist and blowing snow.

He rose to 20,000 feet and turned on the homing TV. Sure enough, way up ahead of him was yet another bomber group.

But there were to be many different things about this outfit.

Many, *many* things.

They were the 3234th, located on Base Six, way on the other side of the Circle. They weren't crudely impressive like the 999th or brass-plated cowards like the 13th.

He made contact with the flight leader and was surprised to see only 12 bombers in a loose formation. They were flying the B-17/36s like the 13th, but they were hardly shiny. Instead, they were painted in white and blue camo.

Hunter pulled square with the leader as usual—but was surprised to see the windscreen of this airplane, and all the others, was tinted. It was so dark, it was impossible for him to see in.

He keyed his radio and sent over his call sign. The reply was full of static. Hunter tried again with the same result. He was certain the fault lay in his own radio set. It was something he'd have to bring up with his fan club once he got back.

He could hear just well enough to read his radio checks and then to inform the flight leader he was moving up to the point.

A wag of the wings was his only reply.

He took the point as promised and played the mission tape again. The cartoon showed Ireland and the weather and where the hit was going to be.

It was another power plant, but this one was deep in a valley which, according to the mission film, was suspected of bearing heavy AA fire.

Hunter sucked on his oxygen mask a little deeper. This was not going to be a routine mission here, he could tell already. It was going to be rough going in, rough flying over this valley of flak, and rough going out. No wonder Payne chose not to brief him in person.

So he took the next 90 minutes of the flight to read over the mission paper and watch the tape and try to attune his inner senses to give him warning of the first sign of trouble.

But the ride down was uneventful—eerily so. They arrived sooner than expected, a great wind on their tails. At 20 miles out, the flight leader ordered the 12 aircraft to bunch up.

They did, expertly forming into two chevrons of six each. The flight leader gave another order, and now the chevrons began to stretch and stretch and soon the whole squadron was flying in a single file line.

Hunter was watching all this over his shoulder. Before him was the fog and the rain and the east side of Ireland and the target they were supposed to hit. But this was a strange formation to complete this task.

Then the bombers started diving . . .

Hunter couldn't believe it at first—but down they went,

the 12 bombers, one right after another, dropping into the Irish mist.

Hunter knew his place was with them, so he looped over, cut speed, and dove down to join them in the murk.

The reports that the valley was thick with ack-ack guns had not been exaggerated. No sooner had Hunter broken through the clouds at 3000 feet when he started picking up muzzle flashes. Again, it looked like a Fourth of July celebration. There were so many streaks of fire and smoke and muzzle flashes and explosions, the glare off his cockpit glass was nearly blinding.

The two lead bombers had already started their bombing runs. It was nightmarish to see the two huge airplanes whipping along not 500 feet above the ground, bomb bays open, somehow swinging and swaying their way through the solid wall of flak.

Again Hunter felt his airplane kind of take over and go where it wanted to go. He came in right on the bomber number two's tail, and opened up at the ground. There was no aiming necessary here—anywhere his long stream of tracers went hit something belonging to the enemy.

The flak guns were like trees interspersed among the dens and dells. Some were locked in place, but many others were mobile. Flak trucks and towed wagons were much in evidence. Hunter zigged and zagged—flak was exploding all around him, but he was literally steering through it.

He found the road that led to the power station and began firing at anything that moved on it. The road was the targeting point of reference for the bombers, so he was cleaving a path through it in which they could fly. The problem was there were so many guns below him it would be impossible for the enemy gunners to miss the bombers coming in so low and so slow.

Hunter had to evacuate the area to let the big planes come in and do their work. The hail of fire that met these two big planes was incredible.

Streaks of light were tearing right through the two huge bombers, but they were not deterred in their bombinrun. They came right in over the power plant and let loose a string of bombs that practically went right through the chimney.

Both planes managed to run the gauntlet and come out the other end battered but still flying.

Hunter looped again. He had about a five-second window before the next pair came in. He took out a towed flak wagon and a row of trucks in one long barrage. Then he had to get out again.

The next two planes came in, even lower, even slower. They stayed steady and true—right to the end.

It was strange how they both got hit in almost the same place at the same time. Both caught on fire, but side by side they continued the bombing run, dropped their ordnance, and then tried to climb out of the valley. But neither made it. The strain and the flames were just too much. They both hit the hillside at almost the same time, their demise signaled by two identical fireballs.

Hunter screamed over and came down on the 188 mm gun that had pinged them and destroyed it—but it was too little too late. The pair of airplanes were now no more than two craters in the side of an Irish hill.

The next three pairs of bombers came down harder, faster, and dropped their bombs right on the money. By the time they pulled up, the power plant was engulfed in flames.

Climbing out of the valley of death, their multitude of engines screaming, the diminished bomber squadron formed up at 7500 feet. Then, in something Hunter could not believe, they grouped in a tight formation, and rode right over the place where the two planes had gone in.

Braving the still-lethal flak, they flew a last tribute to their fallen colleagues.

Then they all turned northwest and, with Hunter watching the rear, headed for home.

Chapter 17

Over the Atlantic

The enormous Hughes B-201 Navy Superbomber had been on combat patrol for 16 days now.

In that time, it had seen action off the French coast, over Gibraltar, off the Ivory Coast, near the Channel Islands, and briefly in the Scapa Flow. It had sunk three German supply ships and heavily damaged a destroyer. But this had not been a pleasant flight for the big plane. It had been aloft for so long, the paint was actually peeling off its wings. The electrical system had not worked correctly since the third day out, and the domino effect from this was everything from spoiled food to stuffed toilets.

The crew was exhausted and demoralized. This flight was nearly twice as long as their usual combat patrol, and yet the prizes of war had been very few, and they had nearly been shot down several times already. But just like every other American aircraft still flying, the big plane was being pressed to the limit. That's how bad the war had been going.

The crew knew better than most how the tide had turned

so dramatically in favor of Germany in the last few months. In fact, there were some who actually blamed the commander of this particular aircraft for the German resurgence.

As the story went, the OSS, at odds for months as to determine the cause of the dramatic German comeback, had reached a startling conclusion: the resurgence could be traced back to the day that the B-201 SuperSea spotted three floaters in the mid-Atlantic, then watched as one was picked up by an American destroyer, and another by a German battle cruiser.

Though no one knew exactly what the connection between the two events might be, the thinking was that if the COA had sunk the German rescue boat, the German revival might not have happened, strange as that sounded.

This was all very top secret, of course, but someone at Atlantic Wartime Command had let the aircraft commander know, and rumors soon started swirling among the crew. This led the commander to take to his stateroom for long periods of time, drinking brandy from the airship's medicine supply. To see their once proud if haughty COA reduced to this further demoralized the 42-man crew. One story swept the airplane at midflight that the second-in-command had actually found a suicide note written by the COA discarded in the trash.

It got so bad, many crewmen had started whispering about the airplane itself being cursed. A morbid betting pool had even been established. What would happen first: would the COA blow his brains out or would the airplane crash? Many were simply convinced the airplane would never make it home again.

Its latest orders did nothing to squelch the notion that the B-201 was a cursed ship.

The exhausted crew had just navigated the big plane around the enemy-held Azores when they received a mes-
om Atlantic Wartime Command. HQ was diverting
turn route. Instead of putting down at their usual
e in Ship Bottom Bay, New Jersey, the plane was

being directed to a base in South Carolina. This would add four more hours to the crew's already-backbreaking ordeal. What's more, the weather they were expected to go through would guarantee to toss them around some. The forecast between mid-Atlantic and the Carolina coast was for heavy rain and very high winds.

No surprise either that it had them flying through a section of the infamous Demon Zone.

The lumbering B-201 was two hours west of the Azores when an urgent call woke the aircraft commander out of his latest drunken stupor.

The crew had just turned the big plane slightly to the southwest, in hopes of missing the worst of the mid-ocean storm, when its air defense officer reported seeing unidentified objects on his long-range TV screen.

There were five in all, he first reported. They were flying at 25,000 feet, some two miles below the B-201 and heading in the same general direction.

Normally the ADO would have done a visual-data check on the unidentified aircraft. This was a Main/AC computer-generated search of the airplane's TV-video records made in an attempt to match up the blurry objects with something similar stored in the big plane's video logs. But right away the ADO knew there was nothing like these objects in the plane's video library—or anyone else's for that matter.

Quite simply, the airplanes they had spotted were gigantic. Bigger than the B-201 SuperSea. Bigger than anything in the U.S. aircraft arsenal. In fact, they were so big, the ADO's first estimate that the airplanes were actually 15 miles away from the SuperSea proved to be wrong by exactly half. When first spotted, the mystery planes were more than *thirty* miles away from the SuperSea. They were so big they simply looked closer.

This was a strange turn of events aboard the B-201. To see something flying that was bigger than themselves was just one step away from being impossible.

Yet here were five aircraft that dwarfed them.

And they *were* airplanes—that much the ADO did know. On the long-range insta-film he'd shot, one could clearly see wings and fuselages and fronts and back and tail sections—all the components of an airplane. But the wings were enormous in length, and they held more than 20 engines—on one side!

The noses of these aircraft were huge, bulbous. They rode atop the front part of the fuselage like a penthouse atop a skyscraper. The fuselages themselves looked to contain eight to 10 decks or more. There were oceanliners with less room for accommodations.

As soon as the aircraft commander got over the astonishment of the gigantic airplanes, he screeched a radio message down to the air defense officer.

"Who do these planes belong to?" he demanded of the ADO.

The ADO had anticipated the question, but the truth was, he didn't know. With the highly secretive—some would say paranoid—nature of the U.S. military these days, there was a chance these flying behemoths were just another in a long line of secret weapons to come out of the war effort in the last half century.

The problem with that scenario was simple though: if these were American airplanes, being tested way out here in the Demon Zone, there would be no way that Atlantic Wartime Command would have vectored the SuperSea to fly anywhere near them.

This led the ADO, along with the B-201's intelligence officers, to reach the same conclusion: The monstrous airplanes must belong to the enemy.

But the greatest surprise was about to come.

As the ADO watched, another five airplanes appeared. These were just as large, just as frighteningly grand as the first five. The two groups merged, and like clockwork, separated into pairs—one new arrival with one from the original group.

But now what was this? Long hoses were being let out

of the rear of the lead airplanes and somehow were connecting to the noses of the trailing ships? Hoses? Stretching between two airplanes four miles above the ocean? What madness could this be?

The entire SuperSea crew was now aware of what was happening below them. Peering out the many bubble windows adorning the bottom of the B-201, the crew members gasped in horror at the sight of the huge airplanes. They seemed too big to be flying. Too big to be real. And the connecting operation of the hoses. What was that all about?

"Could they be transferring fuel?" one crew man wondered.

It seemed ludicrous, even though the airplanes deploying the hoses *did* look like flying tanker-ships, as opposed to the trailing aircraft, which looked more like troop-carrying planes.

But that answer would never really be discerned—at least not by the crew of the B-201. As it turned out, the premonitions by the crew that the airplane would never land safely again were about to come true.

No one on board the B-201 saw the enemy fighters coming.

No one was looking for them. And why should they? The SuperSea was out in the middle of nowhere. Far from any airfield, and certainly out of range of fighter aircraft.

But suddenly there were 12 of them. They were the latest German wonder weapon: the Messerschmitt BF-909, jet-assisted, dual-prop fighters built for quickness and heavy firepower—but not particularly long range. They came out of a cloud on the B-201's left, flying line abreast. They all opened up with machine guns and rockets at precisely the same moment, at 1200 feet out. The combined fusillade tore into the SuperSea. The flight deck was hit, as were the double-heat engines and the remaining magazine stocks. The German fighters laid on the fire until 300 feet out, then they finally broke in all directions.

Only one strafing pass would be needed. The B-201 simply blew up two seconds later. The huge airplane split in two, the front half spinning away in a ball of flame while the rear continued flying on for a few seconds before beginning the long last plunge down.

Bodies could be seen falling from the wreckage, some with parachutes, some without. It didn't make any difference—they were all on fire. The major part of the wreckage hit the water nearly two minutes later—it took that long for the mighty airship to come down.

But not nearly long enough for anyone left alive onboard to radio a Mayday call. Two enemy fighters swooped down and checked the smoldering, sinking wreckage, then rejoined their comrades back up at 22,000 feet. They formed up into four chevrons of three each and together disappeared into a huge cloud bank to the south—the same place the tandem aircraft had gone just minutes before. They would quickly link up with the huge airplanes and be retrieved by them, the fighter pilots hooking onto arresting hooks carried beneath the big planes' wings and attaching themselves there. Then together they would complete the airborne refueling exercise, once again in secret.

No one at Atlantic Wartime Command would ever know what happened to the Navy B-201 SuperSea. And with the war effort going so badly these days, no one had the time or disposition to find out, especially since the plane disappeared inside the Demon Zone.

In the end, the B-201 and its crew of 42 would simply be listed as "lost en route."

Chapter 18

Dreamland Base

Hawk Hunter woke up the next morning hungover, restless, and cold.

He'd had a troubled sleep. The bombing mission over Ireland was still very fresh in his mind and it had caused him to have strange, nonsensical dreams. Of the three missions he'd flown in as many days, this was the one that haunted him the most.

Now laying awake in his frigid bunk, he wasn't sure why this was so. Something deep inside him ached whenever he thought back on the mission. Seeing the two bombers get hit and go in at the same time. Then their colleagues daring a tribute over their fiery graves. More Americans had certainly died during the 999th's attack on Manchester. And more hate and disgust had built up in his soul for the cowards of the 13th during the aborted attack on the Isle of Man.

But this last mission—it seemed very stuck to him even after another marathon drinking session at the OC. Why?

He finally rolled out of his bunk, his feet hitting the

cold, cold floor. The empty barracks was not heated very well; neither was the water. Hunter took a brisk, frozen shower, then stumbled into his clothes.

Outside, the wind and snow were blowing so fiercely that he was certain there'd be no flying today. He checked the duty roster at the main entranceway to the barracks and saw nothing had been written on it.

This was good, he thought.

There were a few things he wanted to do.

He braved the fierce wind and snow and trudged over to the OC. Here he found Major Payne.

The officer was sitting alone, staring into a cup of coffee. He was the only one on hand for morning mess.

"Did I miss the crowd?" Hunter asked, walking up to his table.

Payne barely looked up.

"What's your beef today? You're not flying. No one is."

"No beef. I just want to make a request."

"And that is?"

"I want to present myself formally to the CO of the Wing," Hunter told him. "His office is here, I understand?"

Payne froze for a second.

"Why would you want to do that?" he asked.

Hunter just shrugged.

"Don't all new men get to shake hands with the Old Man?" he replied. "I mean, I've been here three days and have flown three missions, and haven't heard anyone even mention the top guy. You do have a Wing CO right? Someone in charge of all these bases?"

Payne sipped his coffee now, even though it was obviously ice cold. Outside, the wind and snow were howling at full throttle.

"You know, I've verified your enemy kill claims," Payne told him, changing the subject slightly. "You realize you've shot down more enemy fighters in three days than this entire squadron did in three months, back when we were winning this thing?"

Hunter just shrugged again. "Lot of targets," he said. "I just point the guns and shoot."

Payne glared up at him. "Don't give me that," he said. "You've shot down almost 50 aircraft, for Christ's sake."

"Are you complaining?"

Payne's hand came down just a little too hard on the table. It made his coffee cup rattle.

"I just think it's weird," he told Hunter. "I mean, this squadron was about to close up shop. We were about to go home. Me, the logistics guys, the mechanics. The weather people. We had no more pilots. We had nothing left to do. The bombers were just going to be on their own and we were going to be done with it.

"Then you show up—from God knows where—and you start emptying the sky of Huns. If those dipshits in the War Department weren't so busy looking for a place to hide, they'd have pinned a chestful of medals on you already."

"What's your point?" Hunter asked him. "I'm just doing the job."

Payne's face turned crimson red now.

"The point is, I've done some checking up on you," he said through gritted teeth. "And you didn't come up here through regular channels. No one knows who the hell you are back at Air Corps Command. That could mean you were sent up here by the OSS. And maybe that means you're a spy."

Hunter almost laughed. "A spy? For who?"

Payne looked like he was going to burst.

"Don't you get it?" he asked angrily. "We were gone, me and the rest of the people in this crappy little snowball club. Gone, man. When we ran out of pilots, we were going home. Those were the orders. We didn't even have to call ahead of time. If you hadn't shown up, we'd be home now. *Home.* But then those assholes at the OSS throw you into this mix—for whatever damn reason—and we get stuck here, running this whole thing for one guy."

"And I can't accommodate you by getting myself killed, is that it?" Hunter asked him, trying to stay calm.

Payne started to agree—but caught himself.

"I just wanted everyone to get out of here, in one piece," he said instead, a little quieter. "You've seen the photos on that wall in the ops room. Can you imagine what this place was like just six months ago? We had *won* the damn thing. We were packing our bags and getting ready to kiss some girls in Times Square. Then we were going home to our families. And then the roof fell in. And I was getting calluses on my hands from hanging all those pictures. Standing out on the runway and waiting for a flight to come home—and no one did. Any idea what that's like?"

Now it was Hunter's turn to shut up and just think. This was turning into a whole different thing here. The affect he'd had on the 2001st in just three days *was* rather dramatic. Sending him up here because the Air Corps needed pilots was one thing. But how could Pegg and the people he worked for possibly know he'd shoot down so many enemy aircraft and thus become such a valuable commodity that he would put a monkey wrench into any 2001st muster-out plans?

"I mean," Payne went on, "you're like a squadron all to yourself. We can't close up shop here while you're still around. My question is, where the hell were you six months ago?"

Hunter felt all the air go out of him now.

"I don't know," he replied simply.

But Payne really didn't hear him. Or he didn't get what Hunter was really trying to say.

"Yeah, neither do I," the officer just murmured.

Then he looked up at Hunter—tears were forming in the corners of his eyes.

"I saw this place die," he said. "Not just this base, but the whole Circle. They would have been writing books, making movies about us, this place, if the war had ended six months ago like it was supposed to. But now it's turned into a bad dream. I know what you saw with the 999th that day. Those guys have been flying drunk for months. And I wasn't surprised by what the 13th did either. They're the biggest gang of cowards I've ever come across. They've actually institutionalized cowardice."

With great embarrassment, Payne wiped his eyes.

"I just wanted to get my boys home, what was left of them," he whispered. "That's all."

Hunter stared back at him. His first impression of Payne had been the correct one. He was a good officer and probably, deep down, a good guy.

"That's all anyone wants to do," he told him.

They were quiet for a few uncomfortable moments. Outside, the wind blew and the snow fell. Payne went back to staring into his coffee. Hunter shifted from one foot to the other and wondered if it was time to retreat.

But then Payne surprised him.

He looked up from his coffee and said: "You know something? Maybe meeting the Old Man is exactly what you need."

It took them 15 minutes to walk just a quarter of a mile down the flight line. The wind was so fierce, at times it would blow Hunter back two steps for every one he managed to take.

A couple of times Payne yelled something over to him, but Hunter couldn't hear him. He just kept his head down and kept walking.

They finally reached the so-called Command Hut. Appropriately enough, it was shaped like an igloo, one built out of tin sheeting and rubber insulation.

"This was HQ for the entire Circle," Payne yelled over to him, Hunter hearing him this time. "Everything for the twelve bases came right out of here. If they were ever going to make a movie about this place, the first shot would be right here, right at this front door. Because this is where it all used to happen."

Used to . . . Those words stayed with Hunter.

They went inside and took two minutes to pick the ice particles from their faces, hands, and coats.

Then they went into a huge Situation Room. This place, where all the planning, logistics, and paperwork for the entire Air Wing based at the Circle would normally be done, was empty. The desks, chairs, phones, maps, charts, everything that should have been bustling with activity, instead was covered with dust.

They walked silently into the next room, which was supposed to be the CO's briefing room—the place where all the big plans were supposed to be made. But this room was still and dusty too. A second lieutenant was sitting in a chair by the door to the Wing Commander's office. He was unkempt, his uniform a mess. It looked like he hadn't moved off his seat in years.

He looked up at Payne and Hunter and barely nodded to them. There were no salutes.

"He's not too good today," the lieutenant told Payne.

Payne opened the CO's office door and Hunter followed him inside. It was very dark in the office. Just a single light on a desk that was as dusty as all those outside.

Over near the window, a man sat in a chair. He was absolutely still. The silence in the room was almost painful. Even the wind outside seemed to be dulled by it.

They took a few steps in, then Payne closed the door behind them.

"You see how he is right now?" Payne whispered to Hunter. "That's the way he's been for the past four months."

Hunter took a good look at the man. He was probably in his mid fifties. He was small, wiry. He looked like a fighter pilot.

But his face was like ice. He was not moving, he seemed dead. But his eyes were open, and his chair was rocking ever so slightly.

His name was Jones. General Seth Jones.

"Catatonic?" Hunter asked, the word barely passing his lips. Payne just shrugged.

"You tell me," he said. "The docs couldn't figure it out."

Hunter felt his chest tighten up. There was a strange feeling in here. It was as if the CO, this man slowly rocking in his chair, wasn't even here.

Payne knew what he was feeling. "Yeah, gives me the creeps too." he said.

With that, Payne retreated and left Hunter in the room alone. Hunter walked over to the man in the chair and saluted.

"Flight Officer Hunter, reporting for duty, sir," he said.

The man did not move. Not a muscle. Hunter took a closer look. His face was creased with two channels running down from his eyes. Were these tear tracks?

Hunter tried introducing himself again. Still nothing. He stood there for a long moment, wondering just what movie this was from. He got right up in the CO's face. The man was breathing, he was alive at least. But he was in some kind of catatonic state.

In his lap was a pile of reports. It was as if he'd been reading them when he went into his spell.

Though Hunter was sure it was against a couple hundred regulations, he picked up the first report and started reading it.

It was a postmission briefing report from four months earlier. It told of a particularly hazardous job the Air Wing had to perform.

This was when the war had started turning back in the Germans' favor. It seemed like a routine mission—maybe too routine. It was over occupied France. Four hundred and sixteen bombers, 82 covering fighters. They were hit by 250 Natters, the first day the German rocket planes had appeared in combat.

No one came back.

The next day, the Wing was sent out to hit the 20 or so airfields where the Natters were based. It was a panic mission—and the Wing paid the price. One bomber out of 317 made it back. No fighters returned.

Hunter picked up the third report. This spoke of a massive 800-plane raid that the entire Air Corps, desperate for a victory, sent against the Natter bases along the French coast.

More than half the planes came home that day—because more than half the pilots turned around before they even crossed the coastline. Those that did were simply slaughtered by the rocket planes. Nearly 400 airplanes—both bombers and fighters—went down.

That's when Air Corps Command stopped all bombing missions over the Continent. They simply couldn't take the bomber losses. Even worse, the American side had been so certain the war was winding down—again—that they'd actually started pulling bombers back to the U.S. and mustering out their crews! Now they had almost no pilots.

The final blow came in the next report. Apparently bucking HQ's orders, Jones, the Wing CO, had gathered some intelligence on his own and had put together a huge strike of bombers, training bombers, even cargo planes carrying bombs.

They went off to hit a Natter assembly plant in occupied Belgium. They ran into bad weather coming in on the target and that had thrown off the aiming mechanisms in the lead airplanes. Still, the Wing unloaded 12,000 tons of bombs on what they thought was the Natter factory— but it wasn't. They hit a hospital for POWs instead. Then, on the outbound leg, they were attacked by hordes of Natters, Me-666s, and Horton flying wings. The Wing was decimated.

How bad was that day? One crew, it was reported, was so in the thick of it and so freaked out, they detonated their unused bombs and blew themselves up as well as five other planes around them.

Once again, no airplanes returned.

That's when General Seth Jones sat down in his chair. He hadn't moved since.

Hunter took a deep breath and let it out slowly. Well, that explained a lot of the strangeness around here. Obviously the CO was a highly respected man back in the States and the last thing the Air Corps wanted to do now was sack him—morale would plummet even further. So they just let him stay up here, sitting in his chair and allowing what was left of the Wing to fly hit-or-miss missions over the UK.

Waiting for the end.

Hunter saw one final piece of paper in the CO's lap. In many ways it was the most astonishing document of them all.

It was a letter of authorization from Jones naming an officer at Wing HQ to be his Adjunct-General. Hunter read the fine print and apparently this was a position where the so-named officer would in effect take over all duties for the CO. He would run the operations. He would run the missions. He would pick the targets. Everything.

Yet the place where the officer's name was to be filled in was blank.

Hunter studied the letter. It was slightly stained, slightly dog-eared. It was obvious at least one person had read it besides the CO. And if one person was aware of its contents, then the entire Wing would be.

So to Hunter's mind, it wasn't that no one had seen the blank line to fill in—there simply hadn't been any takers.

And why should there be? No one wanted to be the Captain of the *Titanic*. So they were just waiting around for the patient to die.

Now it was Hunter who sat down and became motionless in a chair. Staring out the frosted window, looking at the same view the catatonic CO had watched for nearly four months, he thought about his very strange life.

He was from somewhere else. He wasn't sure where, but he had to assume that if he got here from there, then maybe somehow, someday, he'd be able to get back.

But how and when would that ever happen? He didn't know, but deep inside he was certain it wasn't going to happen while this screwy war was still going on.

He would need a great mind to get him back to where he came from, and the way he saw it, all the great minds were either working on the war or in hiding.

So, in the logical sway of things, it would follow that the quickest way for him to reach his goal, was for him to do whatever he could to shorten this war. Somehow. Some way.

It was a long shot—he knew that. But what was the alternative? Sit back and wait for the end? He wasn't exactly sure yet what kind of a person he was back in his old life, but he knew at least he wasn't someone who would just give up and wait for the book to be closed. Not without a fight. Not without trying something, no matter how outrageous.

He looked down at the letter of authorization. The CO's signature was just a scribble, and the ink had stained, but it was still written by a man who knew he was fading fast— and wanted to do something about it.

And maybe this was what Hunter was supposed to do, he thought. From the back of his skull, a voice was urging him on, telling him, yes *this* was exactly what he should do.

And then, a plan began formulating in his mind.

He sat there for at least half an hour. The wind blowing outside, the frozen officer not five feet away.

Then he simply stood up, folded the letter, and put it in his pocket.

Then he left the office.

Chapter 19

It was 1800 hours, six o'clock in the evening.

Dreamland base had been shut down tight all day as a fierce blizzard blanketed the Circle bases and halted all operations.

Alone as always in the large, ghostly barracks, Hunter had spent the day finally reading the manual on the Mustang-5. He was glad he had it, if just to pass the time, but he really didn't learn anything new. Flying was doing, and if you're doing then you were past learning.

The day also gave him time to build the plan which had germinated in his visit to the CO's office earlier. Even he had to admit it was a monster of an idea. Multifaceted. Dangerous. Outlandish even. It made him wonder once again: Just who the hell was he in his previous life that he would even dream up the sort of scheme he was now contemplating? There was no answer to that, he guessed— so he didn't dwell on it.

Instead, he just went with the flow.

A third set of thoughts had played on his mind all day too. It had to do with the last mission he'd flown, the one over Ireland with the 3234th. Why would it not let go of him? He didn't know.

But in a strange way, that's what the first part of his plan was all about.

The wind abated a little and Hunter took that as a sign that he should get moving. The weather here was unpredictable to say the least. He had to take advantage of any break in the squall.

He put the manual away and raided one of the barracks' clothes lockers. He liberated two sweaters, an extra flight suit, two woolen hats, and a pair of thermal gloves. None of them appeared to have been owned by any of the deceased residents of the barracks. This was just fine with him. He climbed into the clothes, being careful to layer himself as he did so.

He'd secured a quart bottle of Hard Jack from the OC's reticent bartender earlier in the day, 180 proof no less. He also bought a thick piece of dried pepper beef, a favorite of the maintenance crews. It was enough food and booze to man a small party. Now he took a long slug of the booze; it went down like gasoline. He took a bite of the beef, and it tasted worse than the booze—at first anyway. Thus fortified and bundled, he went out the back door of the barracks.

The bitter wind greeted him like a punch in the mouth. Another quick swig of Jack dulled that pain. Another chaw of beef would keep his mouth moving, important for what lay ahead.

He took a deep breath and took a look around. The wind had died down to a mere gale. It was cloudy as always, and some snow was still falling—but it would not be difficult for him to find his destination.

Over the snowy hills to the north, the glow of lights was intense, amplified by the low cloud cover. There was a definite orange tint to this glow. Halogen, Hunter guessed correctly. The lights were about half a mile away.

Then he turned to his left. Off to the northwest, there

was another glow. This one was greenish, about two miles away. Beyond that, some more orange, and beyond that some more blues and greens. All around him, in an almost 360-degree sweep, the lights from the 12 bases which made up the Circle Wing glowed against the night sky like the aurora borealis.

He took another slug of Jack, a third mouthful of pepper beef, and then started off, up and over the first hill, trudging over the hard-packed snow and ice.

He would head towards the orange lights first.

The hike was not as bad as it could have been.

Sure the wind was blowing, and ice crystals filled the night air. But Hunter soon discovered he had the ability to put himself into another state of mind for the trek, just as he was able to put himself in another place while riding the long flights home from the UK bombing missions.

If he didn't dwell too much on the wind and the subzero temperature, then it ceased being windy and cold. The stars helped too. The sky was hardly clear, but there were some occasional breaks in the overcast, and sometimes they were big enough for a patch of stars to peek through. The night sky was much different up here, near the North Pole, than it had been in the view from his prison cell. The stars seemed brighter, and there were many more of them. The clouds moved quickly and gave him only tantalizing glimpses of the most impressive constellations, but these were enough to keep him entertained during the long, icy march.

He reached his first destination 55 minutes later. He topped an ice hill and suddenly, there it was before him. Four huge runways, a couple of dozen buildings, a half dozen maintenance hangars. About 100 B-24/52 bombers, lined up wing-to-wing on the frozen tarmac.

It was Circle Field #3. Home of the 999th Bomber Squadron.

* * *

Hunter made it to the edge of the base, stripped off his overalls and hid the bottle of Jack. There was no fence, no barrier preventing him from just walking on to the base. Just like his own airfield, security here was nonexistent.

He made directly for the base's officer's club. He found it quickly and was heartened to see the lights burning within. He pushed back his hair, took one more gulp of the icy air, and went through the front door.

The place was livelier than the club back at the 2001st. Much livelier. There were two fights going on when Hunter walked in. The floor was wet with booze, spit, and even blood. Fists connecting, bottles breaking, the mayhem seemed routine. But many people were just sitting around too. Clutches of unkempt pilots at out-of-the-way tables, eating, drinking, playing cards. The air was thick with both cigarette smoke and pot. This was obviously the normal state of affairs for this place.

Hunter drew few glances coming in, and quickly made for the bar. He ordered a whiskey, drained it, and then ordered another. Then he asked the bartender a question.

"Who's the big cheese here tonight?"

The barkeep didn't reply. He just nodded to a man sitting alone in one corner of the hall. His back was to everyone else.

"What's he drink?" Hunter asked the bartender.

"Anything," was the reply.

"Give me two," Hunter said.

The bartender did so. Hunter walked over and put the two massive glasses of whiskey on the table, next to the six full glasses already there. Apparently everyone was buying drinks for this guy.

The man looked up. He just stared at the new glass of whiskey in front of him. Hunter sat down.

And then it got a little weird.

He intended to ask the man about the current state of

his depleted squadron—but before the words could get out, the man looked up at him.

Hunter nearly dropped his glass. The guy was in his mid thirties, just a touch of gray in his hair, a lot of Irish in his face. He was a little chunky, but very tough-looking.

And Hunter swore that he'd met him before.

"Who the fuck are you?" the man wanted to know.

"Do I know you?" Hunter asked him.

The man just stared back at him, and slowly took a long sip of whiskey.

"You one of my new pilots?" he finally asked Hunter, still sizing him up. "I wasn't told I'd be getting any . . ."

"I'm from the 2001st," he told the man. "You know? Right over the hill?"

This barely registered on the man.

"You here to borrow a cup of sugar?" he asked derisively—but Hunter could tell his heart was not completely in his bitterness.

"I'm the fighter guy who flew with you three days ago," Hunter said, tasting his own whiskey.

The man laughed and took another swig. "Oh, that was you?" he asked. "Showed a lot of initiative, my friend."

It might have been as close as he would come to getting a compliment out of the man.

"Just trying to do the gig," Hunter replied. "You lost a lot of guys that day."

The man swigged his drink and snorted.

"Where you been, pal? You read the papers? We've been losing guys like that for the past four months."

"Any interest in trying to change that?" Hunter asked him point-blank.

"Besides staying on the ground you mean?" the man asked back.

"I mean finally doing something that will have some kind of effect on all this, instead of wasting eight hundred lives dropping bombs into a big hole in the ground," Hunter told him.

The CO drained his glass of whiskey and let out another drunken cough.

"Anything is better than what we're doing now," he said.

"Your men feel the same way?"

"What's left of them, yes."

The man started on another drink. Two drunks went flying through the air right in back of him. He didn't flinch a muscle.

"How many aircraft do you think are still operational here?" Hunter asked him.

The man shrugged and burped.

"We got about a hundred and six that can still get airborne," he replied. "The whole Wing, counting trainers and cargo humps? Maybe eleven hundred or so. It was six thousand this time last year."

"You think there's enough pilots left to fly all those planes?"

"Barely," was the man's reply. "Why all these questions?"

Hunter just shrugged. "Might have something cooking. Maybe a different way of doing business."

The guy laughed again.

"You? How can you change anything?" he asked Hunter. "You're the newest guy on the Circle."

"Leave the details to me," Hunter told him.

The guy drained his drink in one great swallow and started on another.

"Well, whatever you have in mind, count us in," he said with a slur. "It will be entertaining, if nothing else."

Hunter finished his own drink, and then stood up. "Someone will be in touch," he said.

But the man didn't hear him. He was already nose-deep in his next glass.

Hunter headed for the door. Step one in a long process was complete. But one thought still lingered.

He passed by the bar.

"That guy," he asked the bartender. "The CO. What's his name anyway?"

The bartender snorted a laugh too. "If you don't know who he is, you must be very new around here."

"I am," Hunter replied. "So?"

"That man's name," the bartender said, "Is Captain P.J. O'Malley."

Ten minutes later, Hunter was trudging through the snow again.

He'd retrieved his bottle of Jack and his extra clothes and had started out over the hills once more. He was fairly drunk by now, dangerous in such freezing weather, but OK with him. The wind was not blowing, and the air was not cold. He'd convinced himself of that, and thus it was so.

About a mile away, he saw yellow lights. They were his next goal. And he was inside another state of mind again too. But this one had nothing to do with the stars or constellations.

His feet were stepping through foot-high snow. *Crunch! Crunch!* The noise he made with his boots seemed awfully loud.

That guy back at the 999th—his Irish face, his drinking habits, his old-at-35 demeanor. Damn, Hunter knew him. Knew him and had drank with him and had fought with him. He could feel it in his skin, in his bones and way, *way* in the back of his skull.

But who the hell was he?

Crunch! Crunch! The snow was getting deeper and the ice harder but Hunter trudged on.

The voice in his ear back on the huge chopper. The man named Fitzgerald and that familiar Irish brogue. He was sure he'd known him too. But who the hell had Hunter hung around with in his previous place? A bunch of Micks? Is that why he was drinking so much? And what was next? A fistfight? A brawl with a Protestant?

The phenomenon of thinking he recognized people was the exact same feeling as déjà vu—whatever the hell that was. Maybe, though, it just happened to be that the two people with which he'd had this deep impression were Celtic. If it happened a third time, that might hold the key.

But that guy O'Malley, back at the 999th. He looked *so* familiar.

Crunch! Crunch!

The yellow lights were slowly getting closer, even as the wind became stronger. It was hitting him on the lee side now and he used it to move him along.

Crunch! Crunch!

What was it going to be like when he reached the yellow lights?

Forty minutes later, Hunter came up over the hill, taking his last swing of Jack and chewing his last piece of beef.

The first thing he saw on the other side were the frozen runways. Once again there were no fences, no guards patrolling the perimeter of the airfield. No less than eight dozen B-17/B-36 bombers were waiting in the snow beyond a group of buildings.

Appropriately enough, they were bathed in the yellowish lights.

Hunter let out a long cold breath. His second destination was now before him. Circle Base Four. The home of the 13th Heavy Bombardment Squadron.

The 13th's operations hall was filled to capacity.

Every seat was taken, and some people were standing along the walls. No less than 16 officers were sitting atop a slightly raised stage at one end. Each one was crisply dressed. Each one had his own microphone. Cameras were running from three angles. Someone tested the mikes, and there was a squeal of feedback. The lights dimmed. The premission briefing had begun.

A huge moving map was projected on the screen behind the officers. It showed the British Isles.

Someone hit a special effects button and dozens of little cartoonish flames began popping up on the map. Obviously these were the targets intended for the 13th the next day.

Now little weather clouds were coming into view. They were thick over the North Sea, but clear over the British Isles. This brought a smattering of applause from the assembled bomber pilots.

Another switch was thrown, and now dozens of bombers were popping on the screen. Each one was unique, and they each bore different numbers, different paint schemes, different nose art. They looked oddly realistic. Even their little propellers were turning. More applause; some hoots. The individual pilots began busily writing down exactly where their particular airplanes were in the animated formation.

The briefing continued. The cartoon bombers neared their targets. Numbers up and down the sides of the screen showed bombing routes for individual packages, approach and egress paths, and projected weather for the ride home. At the very end, the words *Enemy Air Activity* flashed onto the screen. This brought a hush from the pilots. Then came the notation: *Details Currently Classified.*

This definitely took the wind out of the room. The place became very quiet, and finally the animation ended. The screen disappeared into the ceiling and the curtains were closed—but the lights stayed down.

"OK," someone called out finally. "What are we *really* going to do?"

Thus began a very strange discussion among the pilots. What the person meant was, where was the 13th *really* going to drop their bombs? In the ocean? Or on land somewhere?

"If we find the right place, with some buildings on terrain," one pilot said, "we can turn on the cameras and at least get some photos of it. It would be a better way to prove we flew the mission than just dumping our loads into the sea again.''

"But where is such a place?" another pilot asked. "What piece of land can we unload over that's not within range of some enemy aircraft? We can't bomb the Faeroe Islands again. We've got too many films of bombing seagulls already."

It was a real dilemma for the 13th. When the Wing CO went catatonic, most of the squadrons around the Circle just began operating on their own. Doing their own thing. Some flew regular missions. Some went overboard and showed initiative beyond what could be expected. Some sent up only a few airplanes. Some sent up the whole kit and caboodle. Some didn't fly at all.

The 13th was different. They all wanted to fly their 50 missions so they could go home as heroes—so flying was never the question. However, they were all of the ilk that they didn't want to risk their lives while fulfilling their mission quotas. So they became very adept at dumping loads and not meeting the enemy at all. They'd bombed the small Faeroe Islands many times already, just to get smoky film as proof of completing their mission. Most of the time though, they just dumped their loads at sea.

The mission to the Isle of Man two days ago had thrown a monkey wrench into this method of operation, though. For the first time in a very long time, some fighter support showed up. Small as it was, it had come as a shock. It also gave them a witness, which was the last thing they wanted.

So they had to improvise that day. They actually flew the mission, hoping that the enemy would do them a favor and shoot down the hero. When they saw him dive into two dozen German interceptors, they figured that was enough. They all turned tail and headed for home, dropping their bombs at sea. As far as they knew, the guy went down somewhere over the Isle of Man.

"How about dumping at the very northern corner of Scotland again?" another pilot asked.

"That makes damn good film, or we can edit some stuff together again and . . ."

And so the discussion went on. Two hundred pilots and officers, using big words and lots of military terminology, trying to figure out the best way to be derelict in their duty for yet another day.

Finally they decided that next time they went up, they would simply dump their bombs at sea.

That done, the top officer, the man who had led the mission over the Isle of Man two days before, came to the podium and asked: "Any questions?"

Only one hand went up. It was way in the back, in the last row. It belonged to someone who'd come late to the meeting.

"Yes?" the 13th CO asked.

"How come you guys are so chicken?" the voice in the back shouted out.

A gasp went through the hall. All heads turned. The man stood up. It was Hunter.

"Excuse me?" the very surprised voice from the podium asked.

"I said, why are all you guys so chicken? So yellow? What's the secret?"

Some of the pilots stood up—but none advanced toward Hunter. As he knew they wouldn't.

"You're uninvited here, sir," the CO called out from the stage.

"Too bad," Hunter replied, feeling more than a little of the Jack.

With that, he walked down the aisle, climbed up to the stage, walked over to the CO, grabbed him by his starched shirt collar, and hissed at him: "Guess who I am?"

The CO was instantly shaking in his spit-polished flight boots.

"I . . . I don't know," he stammered.

"Well, here's a hint," Hunter said.

He drew his fist back and let the guy have it, right on the jaw.

The man was more stunned than hurt. Another gasp went through the room. But again, no one moved.

"Hey, what is this?" the CO yelled.

Hunter didn't reply. He just hit him again.

This time the guy went down like a sack of bricks. He quickly scrambled to his feet—and Hunter hit him again.

And again. And again.

Hunter kept hitting the man, the man kept getting back up and Hunter just kept hitting him again.

It got to the point where the guy's lips were bloody, both his eyes were blackened, his cheeks were puffed out like a doll. And Hunter's hand was getting sore just from hitting him.

So finally he just stopped. He reached down, grabbed the guy, and said loud enough so the fancy microphones could pick it up, "I was your fighter cover the other day," he said, "and if you chicken bastards ever try running out like that again, I'll shoot you all down myself. Got it?"

There was silence in the hall.

Hunter slammed the man's head into the podium.

"I said, Got it?"

A murmur rose up from the crowded room. It sounded deep and ashamed. "Got it," the voices said.

Hunter slammed the man's head on the podium again and then let him drop to the floor.

Then he climbed down off the stage and left the hall unopposed.

Phase two was complete.

Colonel Crabb was the only person on the Circle who had his own car.

It was a DeSoto, of course. One of their latest all-weather vehicles, called the VistaWagon. It was a combination limousine, all-terrain vehicle, and taxicab. It had huge seats inside, a well-stocked bar, a small kitchen, and an outstanding music system. Outside it was able to move through the ice and snow thanks to six huge heavy-treaded tires and a host of Accu-drive options.

Crabb had just left Circle Base Eight, had cut across the hills, and picked up two of his girls at Base Five. They'd been booked there for a "private" performance of a dance called: "Nursery Rhyme #17—Jill & Jill."

It was one of Crabb's favorites.

Now he was climbing another hill, keeping his car on the very narrow ice road while six of his dancers lounged in the back, all in various stages of undress.

Crabb had been driving these dark snowy paths for nearly a year now—he'd been "entertaining" at the Circle bases for that long, and while the pay was good, he was kind of stuck here. While the crowds for his type of entertainment would undoubtedly have been bigger back in the U.S., he felt it was his duty to stay here now that things had changed so drastically. He felt his services were needed more than ever.

But in all his times of driving the back iceways, never once had he picked up a hitchhiker.

But there was a first time for everything.

He came upon Hunter walking alone just as it began snowing again.

Crabb beeped twice; he recognized the young fighter pilot from the 2001st's OC performances. On the first beep, Hunter whirled around, and with perfect timing, stuck out his thumb as if he were indeed hitchhiking.

Of course, Crabb stopped.

"What happened to you?" he asked Hunter. "Land your airplane at the wrong place?"

"No one back there would know what to do with it if I did," Hunter replied, indicating the yellow haze of the 13th's airfield about half a mile back.

"Only place we don't play," Crabb told him. "Tried it once. The girls got scared, and I never got paid."

"Not surprised to hear that," Hunter replied.

"Need a lift back to The Dream?" Crabb asked. "I'm going that way eventually."

Hunter looked inside the vehicle and saw half a dozen dancers from the Colonel's show huddled among the rear seats.

"You sure you got room?" Hunter asked.

Crabb winked.

"Sure," he replied slyly. "But I'm afraid I'm gonna have to ask you to sit in the back. That OK?"

Hunter took another look in at the girls, huddling together, young painted faces smiling back at him. He took a sniff. They smelled great.

"Yeah," Hunter said climbing in, "I think I'll manage."

"I got one stop to make," Crabb told him. "Over at Base Six. That OK?"

Hunter started to comment what a coincidence that would be—that's just where he wanted to go. But he stopped himself and just nodded.

"Yes, that's fine with me," he said instead.

There were no lights blazing in the ops hall at Base Six. Not electrical ones anyway.

Crabb pulled his car up to the front of the place and dimmed his headlights.

"Quiet here tonight," he told Hunter. "Not that that's so unusual."

"Can you give me about 20 minutes?" Hunter asked him.

Crabb turned off the car, flipped the auxiliary heater on, and lit a cigar. Two of his girls crawled up to the front seat with him and took up positions on his lap. It would be warmer that way.

"Sure," he said, turning up some cool jazz on the car's boss sound system. "I've got a little bit of a wait here too. Take your time."

Hunter disengaged himself from the girls in the back and climbed out of the DeSoto. Crabb was right, the base was very quiet. This was the home of the 3234th Bomber Squadron, the people he'd covered on the haunting mission over Ireland. Their bullet-scarred bombers were lined up nearby. The wind was whistling through the holes that hadn't been patched yet.

The line of bombers out on the tarmac was cold, dark, silent. Covered with snow. Maybe they wouldn't have to fly tomorrow either.

There was a glow coming from the ops hall that was flickering, orange. Eerie. Hunter walked around the back, unlatched the rear door, and slipped in. Down the darkened corridor was the ops hall. The door was open.

Hunter quietly walked over and peeked in.

He'd come in the middle of a memorial service. The hall was about one-quarter full. There were lit candles everywhere. The room was very dark. Everyone inside had their heads bowed. All seemed deep in silent prayer. Leading it, hidden in the shadows, was the squadron's commanding officer.

This was obviously a tribute to the crews of the two planes that went into the Irish hillside the day before. Hunter took off his cap. He believed it would be a long time before he saw valor and heroism like that again.

This made the flurry of punches to the mouth of the 13th's CO even more appropriate.

Hunter thought a moment about what he wanted to say to these pilots and crews.

That they were the best he'd seen since coming to the Circle? That they were the bravest? The most fearless? He could tell they were also one of the smallest units left in the Wing—next to the 2001st, of course. There was a sad connection to size and bravery here, in this frozen, God-forsaken place. Among the bomber groups, the 3234th had probably lost more people than anyone else.

But actually, these people had a big place in the plan Hunter was formulating in his mind. Perhaps the linchpin.

So he waited until the prayer service was through and then stepped back to let the private moments within the hall really be private.

It was over in another minute or so. Some murmured voices, some scattered sniffles, then a final amen.

Then the crews picked up one candle each and filed out of the front of the hall. Only when he was sure they were all gone and only the commanding officer was left on the stage did Hunter go in.

The lights were still low and Hunter was so quiet on his feet that the squadron CO didn't hear him until the last moment.

"Excuse me," Hunter half whispered. "Do you have a minute?"

The CO spun around—this was very strange—and Hunter found himself staring into two of the deepest, most beautiful blue eyes he could ever recall seeing, in this world or the last one. And that's when it fell into place. Now he realized why the mission over Ireland had haunted him so.

Yes, this was a strange place he'd fallen into.

The sterling aviators were cowards; the effective ones were drunks.

And the brave ones were women.

Much to his surprise, five minutes later, Hunter was in the officers' club of Base Six sharing a drink with the very lovely, very female squadron commander.

Her name was Captain Sarah James. She was beautiful. Brown hair cut short, but attractive. Big eyes. Big lips. Big smile. She was solidly built, yet still very feminine. She was sweet. A real flower. Hunter liked her.

They talked. About the mission over Ireland. About the Circle Bases. About the cowards at the 13th and the drunks at the 999th. They talked about the war. And about General Jones.

But mostly Hunter wanted to know how she and her women pilots wound up here.

"We were transit pilots," she explained over their second glass of watery beer. "They had us humping new bombers out of here about half a year ago—back when people thought things were winding down and the war would soon be over. We wanted flying time, a lot of the men pilots wanted early muster—so that's how it started.

"Then, when things went so badly, so quickly, the Air Corps began scrambling for pilots. We flew in those shit-kickers you saw us flying and they told us to stay. We remained intact as a whole unit, and to our surprise, they activated us. Gave us a week to drop flour sacks in the snow and sent us into action."

Her eyes went down to the table.

"Everyone in your squadron is a woman?" Hunter asked.

"Yes," she replied, adding with a smile, "as far as I know."

But then her smile faded; she knew what his next question was going to be.

"How many?" was all Hunter had to ask.

"Well, I prefer to say there's forty pilots and twenty crews left," she replied. "But there were four hundred and eleven of us when we first arrived."

And now in those beautiful blue eyes, Hunter could see the pain of every loss.

"You know what the problem is," she said, bucking up with a swig of beer. "The problem is no one wants to really win this war. They just want it to end. There's a difference."

Hunter swigged his beer too. "I'm with you on that," he said.

She went on: "The whole concept of victory has been lost to us. People don't realize that to really end the suffering and misery, you've got to swing a wide path. Not just drop a few bombs here and there and hope it will go away."

As she spoke, Hunter's mind was going in two directions at once. He admired her for her stand, her character, her guts. And what she was saying made sense on many levels. But she was also very attractive, and extremely sexy in a way he was sure she didn't even realize.

Yes, now the vibrations he felt in his body weren't all

coming from his cerebrum. These were emanating further south.

But he was drunk and the adrenaline was still rushing through his body, and he knew himself well enough to recognize that now was the time to retreat.

He finished his beer. Then he got up to go.

"Duty calls," he said. "If the weather breaks, I'm sure I'll have an early flight tomorrow."

She was sad, he could tell.

"We're on stand-down for two days," she told him. "Got to fix the planes."

Hunter was suddenly very glad to hear that. Suddenly he didn't want anything happening to her, or her squadron.

"Things might be shaking up around here," he told her, talking completely off the top of his head. "I figure the best way to get out of this thing is through the front door. You interested in hearing more about that sometime?"

She looked up at him and her eyes actually glistened. Damn, she was nice.

"I'm interested in hearing anything you have to say, Flight Officer Hunter," she replied.

Her words hit him like a piece of three-inch flak to the chest.

"I'll make sure of it then," he replied.

Then he shook her hand and went out the door as gracefully as he could.

Crabb was still waiting outside. Hunter walked over to the cab and climbed in. At about the same time, two of Crabb's dancers were coming out of the back of the 3234th's officers' club, leaving from a separate room in the back. It was obvious they had just "worked."

It took Hunter a few seconds to put two and two together.

Crabb's dancers were all females—the 3234th was made up entirely of females. Interesting . . .

Crabb knew what he was thinking.

"Hey, everyone likes ice cream," he said, as the two girls

climbed in and added to the crowd in the back. "But not everyone likes the same flavor."

Hunter could only nod in agreement. He closed his eyes and saw those big blue ones again.

"Yes, I guess you're right," he said finally.

It was strange how it happened.

How the second-to-last piece of a big puzzle Hunter was trying to put together in his head just fell into place—and all because Colonel Crabb took a wrong turn.

But if there are no coincidences here, then why did Crabb, who'd driven these roads many times before, take a right instead of a left?

There was no way of knowing, but that's what happened. He went right, not left, and soon they rumbling down a snow-covered roadway that got seriously narrow very quickly. It was so slim Crabb had no room to turn around. He cursed, he spat, he cursed some more.

Nearly asleep, cuddling with Crabb's beauties in the back, Hunter hardly noticed anything at first. Only Crabb's profane rumblings alerted him that something was amiss.

They topped a hill, and Crabb finally stopped the car.

"Not a fucking snow flake falling and I get lost?" he was swearing. "I've driven these roads in blizzards before and I've never gotten lost."

Everyone looked out the windows. They weren't really lost. Not technically, anyway. All the bases of the Circle were glowing, and it was just a case of picking which one was Dreamland—where the 2001st was stationed, and where Crabb and his nubile employees usually laid their heads.

Dreamland had a reddish tinge to it. That could have been it right over there. But the 999th's base next door had an orange tinge and that looked to be all the way over the other side of the mountain. And the appropriately yellow-tinted home of the 13th Squadron looked to be even further east of that. It didn't make sense.

"The place is laid out in a fucking Circle!" Crabb was grumbling. "How can you get lost?"

But Hunter really wasn't listening. He was looking down the road instead. There was another base down there—perhaps Base Eight or Nine, one of the places no one ever talked about.

Hunter could see the runway from here, but obviously this was not an operational place. It was simply an airstrip and a few buildings. But flanking the runway were dozens of large, low-level structures. They were built of gray cement. Iron bars crossed the steel doors. Each one was built about 100 yards from the next, and there were rows of them. For some reason, Hunter recognized the pattern. These were magazines. Buildings where bombs were kept.

He was mystified by this. There was a well-known shortage of aerial bombs at the Circle. If these magazines were full, then why was there a shortage? Had someone forgotten what might be stored out here? It was entirely possible in this very crazy place.

He told Crabb he'd buy him dinner if he proceeded further down the road. Dinner at the Dreamland OC was no enticement, but Crabb drove down onto the base anyway.

"I've never been down here before," Crabb said, a little amazed at himself. "I'm not even sure what base this is."

There was no security, no sentries or guardhouses or roadblocks. They drove right on to the runway and headed for the first row of bomb-storage houses.

Hunter got out and examined the door of one with the aid of Crabb's flashlight. It was padlocked, but that proved no problem for Hunter. He had the lock picked and sprung in a flash.

As soon as he opened the door, part of the mystery was solved. This magazine did indeed contain bombs—lots of them. So did all the other magazines here. And yes, they'd been forgotten in the crush of paperwork and madness and apathy which had descended on the Circle Bases.

But these weren't iron bombs or antipersonnel bombs or cratering bombs left here to be buried by the snow.

They were firebombs. Incendiaries. Weapons whose sole purpose was to start fires.

And there were thousands of them.

Major Payne was sleeping when he heard the knocking on his billet door.

He thought he was dreaming at first. In his dream, he was here in Iceland, but he was in a huge cavern underneath it and there were two submarines there. They had brought a huge, very unusual looking jet with them, and for some reason it was hidden underneath the ice.

And then he discovered he was the pilot of this plane, and that it was smaller now and had wings that moved and might have had a name like B-1 or B-2.

And he was given orders to fly this plane out of the ice cave and go bomb a place in Russia. The fate of the world depended on the success of his mission.

And so he got into the airplane and started the engines and the ice began to fall, and he turned to his copilot, whose face he could not see and asked: "Why are we going to bomb the Russians? There are no more Russians . . ."

And the copilot just reached over and started rapping the top of his flight helmet really hard, and that's when Payne woke up and realized someone was knocking on his door.

He stumbled out of bed, took notice of the invigorated gale outside, had a stray thought that no one would be flying again tomorrow, and then finally opened the door.

It was Hunter.

He looked drunk. He looked cold. But his eyes were on fire.

"Christ, it's two in the morning!" Payne whined as he fumbled for his glasses.

"I want you to read something," Hunter was telling him.

"There are no flights today," Payne kept right on going, grabbing his bathrobe. "Go back to bed."

But Hunter boldly stepped into the officer's billet.

"Read this," he was telling Payne. He was now holding a piece of soggy paper in his hand. Payne could barely see it.

"What the fuck is it?" he demanded of Hunter.

It was the letter of authorization from the Wing Group CO, the man who still sat frozen to his seat a few buildings away.

Payne gave it a cursory once-over. He'd seen it before of course.

"Yes, so?" he asked Hunter.

"So you told me the other day that all you wanted was to bring everyone home, right? Everyone in the squadron who was left alive?"

Payne just nodded. "Yes, so?"

"So this paper will make it happen," Hunter said. "There's only one way out of here—and it's not in retreat. There are people here that are so brave they don't know what day it is. They are risking their lives—and losing them—for nothing. Don't you see? It could go on like this for years—and in the end the result will still be the same. For whatever reason, the Germans made a comeback. It was dramatic, that's true. But we haven't done a damn thing to stand in their way. We are rolling over like puppy dogs because historically that's the way things have always gone.

"But its not the right way—it just *seems* like it is."

Payne took off his glasses and just shook his head, as if he couldn't believe Hunter was standing there saying all this stuff.

"Make some sense please, Flight Officer," he told him.

"Tomorrow," Hunter said. "Tomorrow I'll make some sense. But now, we have to do something about this letter. It's the first step to solving a lot of problems. I know it is."

Payne took the letter again and read it over—especially

the last paragraph, where it stated that anyone signing it would in effect become the CO for the entire Circle Wing.

"What are you suggesting exactly?" Payne asked him harshly. "That you sign this thing and take command?"

Hunter just shook his head. "No, not me," he replied. "It's not my style, and besides, I'll be too busy."

Payne's face grimaced.

"Then who the hell do you want to sign it?" he asked.

Hunter pulled a pen from his flight suit pocket and handed it to Payne.

"You," he said.

Chapter 20

The weekly cargo plane from Gander touched down at Dreamland base at the height of yet another snowstorm.

It came in, like most planes did at the fighter base, slipping and sliding, two of its 10 engines on fire, the rest of them encased in ice.

The base's emergency crews rode out to the newly arrived aircraft at a somewhat leisurely pace and hosed down the offending engines.

And as always the crew fled—getting away from their flying beast as fast as they could.

One passenger stumbled out of the back. His hair was smoldering, that's how close he'd come to being consumed.

He was carrying two large suitcases and kept dropping them as he ran. Finally one of them burst open and the insides fell out onto the snow. A bottle of red hair dye. A tacky tuxedo. Three crystal balls.

It was Zoltan. Formerly Captain Zoltan of the Air Corps Psychic Evaluation Division, now Zoltan the Magnificent, USO performer.

He picked up his stuff, grabbing all he could in the

blinding snow and then looked around the frozen base in a quiet panic.

"What the hell am I doing here?" he asked.

His daughter had first inquired about this gig months before, just after Zoltan got mustered out of the service because of his bad knees—or was it bad legs?

The problem was neither he nor his daughter could see into the future—at least not far enough to realize that an American victory was not in the bag, as everyone had assumed way back then.

He was playing a rubber chicken date in Westchester when he first heard about the Great German Deception in Paris. His initial disgust was an economic one. His daughter had been working on a postwar European tour for him and a five-night stand in Paris was to have been the topper.

But that idea was killed as soon as the place got flattened, and frankly, after that, the whole entertainment dollar thing went right down the tubes. People went back to buying booze and things they could do at home. The audience appeal of a traveling psychic show was pretty lean when it appeared the country was about to be invaded. You would have thought that people would flock to a seer in such desperate times—but no, things were so bad, apparently people didn't want to see into the future.

So he began casting about for anything, and the USO was about the only group still out there who still had any money.

He got booked on a tour of U.S. bases first, and played to the glummest audiences possible. It got so bad, he begged his contact at the USO to get him off the tour. Just his luck that the contact actually came through. If Zoltan wanted a change of scenery, he had just the place for him to go: 10 shows in Iceland.

Now Zoltan picked up his bags and began the long trudge toward the clutch of buildings way at the other end of the runway. He had to find some colonel here, the entertainment director for this place. The guy who'd be pulling his strings for the next two weeks. Zoltan had scribbled his name down somewhere. What was it again? Colonel Carpp? Colonel Crapp? Colonel Crabb? He wasn't sure.

He kept walking, and the wind and snow got worse and with each step he felt more miserable.

This was not good, he thought, looking out on the utter wasteland of snow and ice. He was feeling some really strange vibes here.

"I should have seen this coming," he whispered to himself.

Chapter 21

The next day dawned bright and sunny. There was no snow in the forecast for the region where the Circle Wing was located. It was perfect flying weather.

Yet no combat missions would be flown today. Or the next day. Or the day after that.

By orders of the new adjunct general, all 12 bases of the Circle were on stand-down until further notice.

Each base received a separate set of orders. Each set spelled out exactly what activities were to be completed during the stand-down. For just because the Circle bases would not be flying any missions against the enemy, that did not mean there would be nothing to do.

Things were going to change. That was assured once the new orders went out. The biggest change was the consolidation of 20 of the Circle Wing's 33 bomber squadrons. Now, instead of going in 33 different directions at once, the 20 squadrons would become the 101st Combined Heavy Bombardment Wing.

This new unit would contain no less than 750 bombers, both B-17/36s and B-24/52s, as well as 300 or so cargo planes, recon planes, weather planes, and training bombers.

The second biggest surprise was that 10 other bomber squadrons were being deactivated. Two would no longer exist. The eight others were to have their aircraft reconfigured in a very radical way. Their maintenance crews were told to weld their bomb bays shut. They were told to take anything having to do with dropping bombs—from the racks to the bombsights to the bombardier's station—off each aircraft.

In their stead, extra 50 caliber ammunition racks were to be installed. And each plane crew was ordered to cut 20 holes along each side of their aircraft's fuselage. At each of these holes, a glass blister would be placed, and then a .50 caliber machine gun. These weapons would be taken from the Circle's storehouses and from the two bomber squadrons that were being deactivated completely.

When done, each reconfigured bomber should have no less than 50 machine gun stations on board—20 on each side of the fuselage, as well as double guns in the nose, belly, roof, and tail.

One of the bomber squadrons that was wiped out completely was the 3234th, the all-female unit. Their ground crews were dispersed to the new 101st Combined. Their pilots were told to report to Dreamland base. They were now the nucleus of the 2001st Fighter Squadron.

About 20 miles west of Dreamland there was an island in the ice known as Krjnck Jel, or simply "Crank." For the next 48 hours, the sky above Crank was filled with female pilots flying the little-used Mustang-5s of the dormant 2001st. At first, the airplanes simply flew in circles in formations of twos and threes. Then, gradually, as the day wore on, the planes began engaging in mock dogfights with each other, using direct-beam radio signals as "ammunition," fired by squeezing bubble switches attached to their control columns.

Each pilot was rated on accuracy and skill, and those women who proved the best were then made combat staff officers in the 2001st. Their first job was to instruct the rest of the new fighter pilot corps.

On the second day, these instructors became "The Aggressors," the designated enemy that the rest of the squadron fought against. The only man involved was Hunter, playing the part of referee/guru.

By the end of this second day, the pilots were well schooled in the basics of fighter aircraft. The transformation was nothing less than remarkable.

On the third day, a new twist was added. The Aggressors flew very low patterns over Crank Island. Twelve bombers borrowed from the Combined Group flew over the island in a mock bombing formation. The Aggressors "attacked" the bomber formation, rising straight up out of the earth to do so, or so it seemed. But before they could reach the bombers, the Mustang-5s of the 2001st pounced on them. On the first few tries, the Aggressor pilots got through to the bombers every time.

But by the end of the day, the Aggressors were getting nowhere near them. Thus the new 2001st Fighter Squadron was reborn.

The changes didn't stop there. A great hoopla was put on surrounding the restructuring of the revitalized Circle bases. New unit patches were sewn, new flag decals were stamped out. All of the airplanes—bombers, trainers, cargo planes—were painted the same deep blue and white camo, an effective yet eerily chilling color scheme.

Now, instead of crews gathering separately on each base, trucks were used to bring people in to congregate in one big club, located in a hangar at Dreamland. This makeshift place was open to all, officers and enlisted men both. Here the crews would eat together, drink together, get to know one another.

In many ways, this might have been the most important change of all.

There was one squadron that didn't receive any instructions when the Wing first reorganized. Not flight orders anyway. Instructions eventually came through though. And now many of the drudge jobs usually done by the plane crews themselves had been turned over to the members of this last squadron.

This meant that in the new Circle Wing, the planes were cleaned, the bombs were moved, and the garbage taken out by members of what used to be known as the 13th Heavy Bombardment Squadron.

The fourth day of the restructuring dawned clear and crisp as well and it was spent with more training, more drills, more flying.

Then word went through the new groups that a mission briefing was scheduled for that night. Finally the crews would learn the reason behind the huge shakeup.

The trucks started arriving at Dreamland ops center at 1800 hours, six in the evening. It took nearly two hours for everyone to be dropped off from the individual bases. The room was overflowing by 1930 hours, and busting at the seems by 8 p.m. Even the hallways outside were packed. In the end, more than 4500 people were on hand.

At precisely 2015 hours, the room hushed and the lights went off.

Then, for the first time, the members of the Circle Wing saw their acting commander in his new position. Major A. Payne, Adjunct General, walked out on to the stage.

He looked nervous, and was fidgety as usual. Behind him the Main/AC computer whirred softly. The mission film screen was lowered as usual. The projector was turned on, and as usual a blotch of colors appeared on the screen. Payne reached down and focused the lens, and as usual, those gathered saw an animated map of Occupied England.

The clouds moved, the airplanes appeared, just like always. A huge gathering of airplane icons formed over Iceland, and as usual, they turned south. At this point, a wave of disappointment might have been detected by a Psychic Evaluation Officer, had one been on hand.

But then suddenly, moving quicker than he had in 10 years, Payne dramatically kicked the mission projector over. The thing fell off the stage and shattered into a million pieces on the floor. A gasp went through the crowd. *What the hell was he doing?*

"You know what?" he yelled to the crowded ops room. "We don't need this piece of shit anymore!"

The room was stunned. Mission film projectors were known to cost thousands of dollars.

Payne looked out at them. His face was creased in terror, but it was too late to turn back now.

"And you know what?" he yelled again. "We don't need this piece of shit anymore either!"

With that he took a crowbar, walked over the Main/AC and began smashing it to bits. Magnetic tapes went flying, switches began breaking, blinking bulbs began popping. A real tremor went through the crowd now. The men and women had never seen anything like this. The Main/AC was the guiding light of the U.S. military, the Holy See. Attacking it was like beating up the Pope.

Yet Payne tore into the machine with such verve, he reduced it to a smoking pile of scrap in less than 30 seconds time.

Then he returned to the microphone, out of breath, his face more crimson than usual. All the hate, all the sorrow he'd experienced in losing so many of his men over the last four months finally came to a head. It was the best thing that had ever happened to him.

"We've been doing it all wrong!" he announced. "Because the War Department doesn't know what to do and neither does that maniac piece of shit."

And at that moment, something changed. A murmur went through the crowd.

"You sick of seeing your friends killed for nothing?" Payne asked them.

"Yes!" came the reply.

"You sick of throwing bombs into a city for no reason?" The reply came back stronger. *"Yes!"*

"You think that maybe we can start thinking about winning this war again?"

"Yes!"

"OK then," Payne said, sweating up a storm, but working the crowd like a Saturday night preacher. "Let's get to work and do the job right!"

"Yes!" was the unanimous response.

The crowd was so whipped up, it was actually getting hot inside the huge room. Payne looked offstage to where Hunter and Captain James stood. Hidden, Hunter and Sarah were urging him on. He gave them a quick thumbs-up.

Payne took two steps back and dramatically tore down the very expensive movie screen to reveal a dark blue curtain.

"Starting tomorrow, ladies and gentlemen," he said *"This* will be our target . . ."

He pulled the curtain down to reveal another map. A real map. No fancy moving planes, no fancy moving clouds. One that didn't move, one that didn't look like a cartoon.

Payne took up an old-fashioned pointer and slammed the map once hard. "This, my friends, is where we're going!"

Every eye in the room was on the map. It looked so different, they didn't recognize it at first.

But then it began to sink in. And then, they began to cheer.

The map was of Germany.

Chapter 22

The dressing room provided by Colonel Crabb's Art Revue was actually a pantry in the kitchen of the 2001st Officers Club. The room was cold, had a poor lighting table and was so cramped the mirror had to be fitted in lengthwise. If an airplane took off anywhere within a 20-mile radius, the place shook right down to the stained floorboards.

At the moment, though, all these things were not on the mind of the man staring into the mirror. He didn't even care if there was someone on the other side of the glass looking back in at him. He just wanted to get his damn eyeliner right before he went on. And damn himself, he hadn't packed his new brush.

So his face was right up against the mirror and the old bristled eyeliner brush was smudging his forehead and now his foundation was running . . . and then suddenly, the door opened. There was no knock, no warning that someone was outside coming in.

The door just opened, and a man was standing there, looking in at Zoltan through the reflection of the mirror.

Zoltan gasped. "You? You're alive? You're here?"

"Yes—to all three questions," the man replied.

He squeezed into the pantry and somehow managed to close the door behind him.

Then he locked it.

Zoltan's heart went right up to his throat. This man was going to kill him, he just knew it.

The man pulled the only chair out from under Zoltan and sat down on it. Zoltan retreated, backing up as far as he could go against the opposite wall.

"Why so nervous?" Hawk Hunter asked him dryly. "Didn't you know I was coming?"

Zoltan began squeaking. "Well, yes, of course. But I think you got a wrong impression about me."

"And what wrong impression would that be?"

Zoltan took a breath. "You probably think I was involved in sending you to jail. But I wasn't . . . I *swear* it."

Hunter leaned back in the rickety chair. "Who was then? Not those old guys."

Zoltan bit his tongue. Did he really have to tell this guy about the OSS agents? Would he kill him if he didn't?

"No, not those old dudes," Zoltan replied finally. "Someone they were working for. They're the ones who sent you to the joint."

Hunter put his left foot up on the edge of the dressing table. It was just enough for Zoltan to see he had a huge double-barrel Colt .45 automatic strapped to his leg. It was his crash survival weapon, literally a hand cannon.

Zoltan began sweating, even though it was freezing in the dressing room. The guy was radiating strange vibes, though not negative ones necessarily. Just weird ones.

"Hey look pal, that was so long ago," he started. "And besides, you're obviously working for the military now. I don't have to tell you how screwed up it is. Does it really make much difference now who put you away?"

Hunter had to agree with him. It didn't. But that was not why he'd come to see Zoltan anyway.

"I will tell you this," Zoltan went on. "They didn't put much thought into it. The guys who put you away. They didn't have time for that. You were a nuisance. An oddity, true. But they really couldn't have cared less about you. Sending you to prison was just the easiest thing to do."

"Well, they did me a favor," Hunter surprised Zoltan by saying.

Zoltan calmed down considerably after that. Maybe this guy wasn't going to kill him after all.

"So?" he said. "Why did you come to see me?"

Hunter leaned forward a little. But he still kept his pistol in full view.

"It's simple," he began. "Out of all the people I told my story to back then, you were the only one who gave any indication that you might think it was true."

"I'm convinced it's true," Zoltan answered immediately. And he meant it. He did have psychic ability—he'd been tested for months by the military before getting his officer's bars in the Psych-Eval unit. It's just that his powers weren't always "focused." So he was usually either right big-time, or wrong big-time. There was no in between with Zoltan.

And he believed Hunter's story. He believed he was from another place. A place just like this place, but another place entirely. The question was—and he had thought about this for many months after first meeting him—was he right big-time about this Hunter? Or . . .

"Some of it has come back to me in dribs and drabs." Hunter was telling him. "You could help me out by telling me what I said while I was hypnotized. Do you recall any of it?"

"Are you kidding?" Zoltan replied. "I know it verbatim."

Hunter sat back and put his hands behind his head. "OK then, let me have it . . ."

So Zoltan told him everything he'd heard that night. About Hunter falling out of the sky. About his being a soldier for an outfit called the United Americans. About the crazy patchwork of wars they'd fought. Russians. The Mid-Aks. The Family.

"I didn't know you were a pilot," Zoltan said. "Not until you ran out and stole that Pogo. That's odd."

"It was like I was sleepwalking," Hunter revealed to him. "Until I got airborne that is."

His voice trailed away, thinking about that first wondrous moment of flight so long ago. When he took off these days, he still got the thrill, but everything around him was so crazy, it was hard to appreciate it.

"Well, they eventually found out you'd KO'd two subs," Zoltan said. "And that you saved a few thousands lives, but they covered it all up. They didn't have the concept of what a hero is. But I'll tell you, some of the whispers I've heard since . . ."

"Whispers?"

"It's the tippiest top secret in the country right now. And I only know it because I heard someone in the know blurt it out during a hypno session right before I left the service. I never put it in my report. In fact, they'd probably shoot me if they realized I know what I know."

Hunter leaned forward and looked the guy right in the eye. "If I guess it, will you tell me?"

Zoltan just stared back at him. "Maybe," he replied.

"Things haven't been the same since me and those two other guys were fished put of the water?"

Zoltan's eyes went very very wide. "God, man, how do you know?"

Hunter just shook his head. "I don't know," he admitted. "I just *know* . . ."

"Well, that's it exactly," Zoltan told him in a whisper.

The psychic nervously lit a cigarette, wondering if he had said too much—again. Instantly the small room filled with smoke.

"Those other two guys," he asked Hunter. "Has it come back to you who they were?"

Hunter shook his head. "Nope," he admitted. "Not

really, anyway. I do get a sense that one was my friend and one was my enemy, but I don't know who was who, or which was which."

Hunter paused a moment.

"Does anyone back in D.C. know who the two others were?" he asked Zoltan.

"If they do, I've never heard about it," Zoltan replied. "My feeling is, they're as much in the dark about it as you are. But the deep dark secret is that the German resurgence has something to do with the guy the Huns picked up that day."

Hunter just nodded glumly.

"How strange," he said. "How it happened. I mean, what if the Germans had picked me up, and the Americans had gotten one of the other two? Does that mean everything would be different?"

Zoltan reached into his makeup drawer and came out with a bottle of scotch. He quickly poured out two glasses, handed one to Hunter, did a mock toast, and downed his drink, all in one smooth motion.

"Take some advice, my friend, from one who knows," he said. "Don't dwell on what could have happened. You'll drive yourself crazy."

Hunter thought about that for a moment, then drained his glass as well.

"That's advice I think I'll take," he told Zoltan.

They sat in silence for a moment, then Zoltan spoke again.

"Are the crowds always so dead up here?" he asked Hunter. "That OC is like a funeral home out there."

"We've got a big mission coming up," Hunter explained. "The biggest, in fact."

Zoltan began applying his makeup again. "Oh yes, I felt the vibe," he said.

"Any predictions on how it will go?" Hunter asked him impulsively.

Zoltan stopped with the makeup, shut his eyes, and concentrated intently.

Then he looked up at Hunter, as if he himself was surprised by the message the cosmos had sent him, or that he got any message at all.

"Yes, I do," he said.

"Care to share it?"

Zoltan looked at him like he was a ghost. "What you do will change the course of the war."

Hunter was a bit surprised at just how bold a prediction it was. But then he asked another question.

"Change which way? In our favor? Or against us?"

Zoltan concentrated once again, but this time it was clear the psychic was getting a busy signal.

"I'm sorry," he said. "That I guess I can't tell you."

Chapter 23

There was a light snow falling the next morning.

The wind was at 20 knots, and more snow was expected by midday. The temperature was supposed to be minus 16 degrees Fahrenheit, but if it had been possible to take a thermometer sampling 1500 feet above the small south-eastern Icelandic island where the Circle bases were located, the temperature would have read a relatively balmy 28 degrees.

A combination of factors was responsible for this: increased heater activity at the seven still-activated air bases of the Wing; the combined heat from so many humans, in frenzied activity, exhaling carbon dioxide at an accelerated rate all at once; but mostly the high temperature swing was due to the massive exhaust being given off by the combined engines of nearly 1100 aircraft turning on their double-heat engines all at once.

So even the elements would be changed this day.

The first plane took off for Target Germany at exactly 0500 hours from Base Three. It was a B-24/52. The pilot was Captain P.J. O'Malley of the old 999th Bomber Group.

He would serve as the flight leader for the 1000-plus bombers taking part in the big mission today.

Aircraft took off at a rate of one every 10 seconds from all seven bases. Still, it took more than 90 minutes for all of them to get airborne and into formation.

The activity at the eighth base, that being the home of the 2001st Fighter Squadron, was also very frenzied. Fifty-six Mustang-5s, whipped into shape by Dreamland's revitalized maintenance teams, took to the air, forming up themselves and meeting the huge flock of bombers at the rendezvous point 55 miles southeast of the coast of Iceland.

The last plane to lift off from Dreamland was Hunter's well-worn Mustang-5. He flew low, as mandated by the crowded skies above the Circle, and by chance found himself roaring over Base Nine, the place where the hundreds of bomb magazines had stood dormant for so long. He couldn't help giving it the once-over as he flew past.

Base Nine was even more of a ghost town now. All of the magazines had been opened, and where literally thousands of tons of high-incendiary bombs had been stored just a few days ago, there were now just empty holes in the ground.

How lucky he'd been just to stumble upon it, Hunter thought as he began climbing to meet the rest of the fighters.

Almost as if it was meant to be.

One hour later

The German radar station was located on a small island off the north coast of Scotland called Toe's Head.

There were three main radar dishes set up there. They had the ability to detect targets up to 100 miles out into the North Sea. The station also had a smaller, limited electronic eavesdropping ability, but this device was not turned on. In fact only one of the three radar dishes was working at the moment. The power supply to this desolate part of Scotland had been erratic lately, due to a series of power station bombings down south. That's why they were operating at just one-third capacity.

But one dish or three, the activity inside the station itself was still the same. Five technicians of the German Defense Corps were assigned here. At the moment, all five were asleep.

This was against regulations of course, but there was no one in authority within 150 miles that would be able to discipline the sleepy radar crew. Sleeping late was the routine here on Toe's Head. The radar had a self-sensor unit in it; if a blip was picked up, a warning buzzer would sound and at least one of the techs would usually wake up. The way the system was set up, if two blips were detected, the warning buzzer's volume got a bit louder. Three blips, a little louder than that.

The volume of the warning buzzer that went off at 0735 hours this morning not only woke all five technicians, it knocked them off their cots. Then a second later, it blew out the speaker through which it was sounding.

The five techs were dazed—they weren't really sure what had just happened. One second they were asleep, the next, their ears were assaulted by a screeching buzzer, and then complete silence.

Finally the techs got into their trousers and sat at their radar screens. They switched on their main radar displays—and were even more confused. The screen showed one-quarter snow. In other words, the upper left hand quadrant of the round screen was all white. Only under two conditions could this happen: the most likely was a malfunction in the main screen power array. The device was overloading itself.

The second condition was highly unlikely: that there were so many targets suddenly being picked up, it would give the screen a snow-out effect.

The techs ran a series of quick diagnostic tests—oddly, they all came back indicating things were working fine.

Only then did they decide to switch on their two other

dishes, using backup power units to do so. To their confusion, and mounting dismay, these screens showed the white-out effect too.

Now the techs weren't sure what to do. They were used to seeing the irregular bomber streams flying down from Iceland to targets over Occupied England. Tracking these enemy flights and sending the appropriate warnings south literally could be done in one's sleep, or in a sleeplike condition. But these small formations usually showed up as a scattering of blips on their radar screens, never filling up fully one quarter of them.

They'd just never seen that many enemy bombers in the air at one time before.

The techs decided to try their only other detection device—the electronic eavesdropping array. This could, under the right conditions, pick up airborne radio traffic within a 50-mile radius. Occasionally, if the techs were bored, they would turn on the device when the American bomber streams were going over and sometimes listen in on the panicky, even inebriated voices of the crews as they pushed further south to their targets.

What would they hear now?

They switched on the listening device—and the noise was nearly as loud as the warning buzzer which had knocked them out of their sleep. The squeal was so loud, the techs turned the volume all the way down and still the racket hurt their ears.

It sounded like 10,000 voices talking at once.

Which is what it was.

The German techs' concern was growing at frantic proportions now. Something was happening here that they'd never experienced before. If the white effect was not a technical glitch—and with the sounds coming out of the audio sensor, it didn't look like it was—then there had to be many hundreds of enemy bombers heading south.

The techs all looked at each other—panic was beginning to set in. Then they made a quick decision. They had to call south, down to London, and warn headquarters about the oncoming armada.

But just as they were trying to raise their superiors on the secure radio, they heard another sound. This was not emanating from a speaker system, but was coming from outside the station itself.

The techs opened the door and found the wind blowing at a high gale. The station was on a small cliff, the stormy seas below. But the noise they heard was not the wind or the sea. The noise was coming from a spread of six Mustang-5 jet fighters sweeping over the waves—and heading right for the station.

The techs ran back inside and began broadcasting a red alert on all frequencies of their emergency radios. The jets went over the station seconds later—the techs couldn't believe they weren't blown off the map at that instant. But on the first pass, the American jets held their fire.

This gave the German techs the time they needed to contact London and warn them that a huge bomber force was heading south and that a major attack could be expected somewhere in Occupied U.K. within the hour.

The American jets roared over again, rocking the radar station down to its foundations, but not dropping any weapons this time either. This gave the techs time to confirm, repeat, and reconfirm their panicky report and then open the trapdoor which led down to the rudimentary bomb shelter in the station's basement.

But the five techs never made it. The American jets swooped in again, and this time, opened up with full machine guns and cannons. This first barrage killed all five techs instantly and essentially destroyed the station and everything inside.

Two more strafing passes followed, just to make sure. When the building caught on fire, the American jets finally pulled up and climbed back up to 27,000 feet. Here they rejoined the 40 or so other fighters leading the front of the massive bomber force now just 35 miles from the coast of Scotland.

Once the fighters had reformed, a general radio call went through the entire airborne force.

Five minutes later, the armada began a long, slow turn, not south towards targets in Occupied England, as the German High Command was now convinced, but to the east and south.

Toward Germany itself.

It so happened that a pair of advanced German jet fighters, having taken off earlier that day from a base in Germany, were just completing an hourlong shake-out flight off the coast of Occupied Denmark when they heard the commotion on their radios.

The planes were Me-999s, the latest long-range fighter in the German Air Force's newly burgeoning inventory. The Triple-9s, as they were also known, were one of 12 new designs put into service by the German military in the last month alone. The aircraft was a two-man, swept-back design able to carry bombs for ground attacks as well as machine guns and cannons for dogfighting. The Me-999 was Germany's first true dual-purpose airplane, a concept never really explored by either side before.

The pair of 999s had been trying out a new electronic package when they happened to pick up the very last vestiges of the emergency radio report from the now-destroyed radar station at Toe's Head.

A thousand enemy bombers? Also many American fighters? The report didn't sound real. In fact, the Me-999 pilots thought they had wandered into a drill of some kind, a doomsday training scenario being conducted by occupation forces in the U.K.

Still, they were within 100 miles of the enemy formation's supposed position and to scoot there and back would give their double-reaction engines a fair workout. After discussing it between themselves, the pair of Me-999 pilots decided to give it a try.

Both planes opened full throttle, and rocketed away at

nearly 1000 knots. Both pilots also turned on their long-range targeting radar, exclusive equipment inside the big dual-role jet fighter.

But like their crispy comrades back inside the Toe's Head radar station, the German pilots thought their equipment was fooling with them. The Me-999's radar systems indicated a huge blotch of something was heading right for them. Could there really be 1000 enemy airplanes coming this way?

The pilots relit engines and inside of three minutes, they saw with their own eyes what their radar screens could not convince them of. Breaking through a gigantic cloud bank, they found the horizon literally black with approaching aircraft. American aircraft. Bombers. Fighters. Even cargo planes converted to bombers. They were all flying southeast.

The German pilots were stunned. What the hell was this? An illusion? They'd never faced a situation like this before. Most of the Reich's air defense fighters were stationed in the U.K., as they should be. These guys were just test pilots really. They knew very little about front-line combat.

Still, both knew they had to warn the German High Command that there were at least 1000 American bombers on the wing and that they were not heading for the U.K., but for the Reich itself.

But with the speed of the oncoming armada, there wasn't much time to radio back to a secure link inside Germany— under normal conditions this would take several minutes at the least.

What should they do then? They knew they alone represented the first line of defense between the bombers and the heretofore unimaginable prospect of enemy planes bombing their homeland. They also knew there was little they could do to stop this many airplanes. But they had to do *something*. So they both powered up their weapons systems and began to climb . . .

Up they went, through 30,000 feet, through 40,000, up to 50- angels. Then, looking down on the wave of airplanes, they went right over the top of the bomber stream and dove down, angling for a position on the enemy's rear. Here they found what they were looking for. Of the vast number of enemy aircraft, they knew—just as jungle cats know when stalking a herd—that there would be stragglers. Planes with engine trouble or other problems that prevented them from keeping up with the main group.

And indeed, three bombers were trailing the vast enemy airborne force.

It was these airplanes the Germans decided to attack first. If there was no way they could stop the entire enemy force, it was better to pick off these weaklings and at least return to base with something to show for their efforts.

The pair of German planes tightened up their two-ship formation and launched their first attack from the 10 o'clock position. The three prey were flying in a ragged chevron about 10 miles behind the main bomber force. So far the covering American fighters had not made a move to defend their wounded birds. This was fine with the German pilots, of course. It would make their job that much easier.

The attack came in straight and true and from the first few seconds of it, the German pilots thought they would soon have a huge B-24/52 to their credit.

But just as the first of their bullet streams began making hits on the selected target, both pilots noticed something. This did not seem to be a regular enemy aircraft they were shooting at. Instead, there was a line of windows stretching from behind the gigantic wing all the way back to the gigantic tail. And now they could see gun muzzles sticking out of every one of those windows. And now they could see extra gun mounts on the top, the belly, and in the tail of the airplane as well. And now, all of those gun muzzles were pointing right at them.

The combined barrage that erupted from the American bomber a second later was, in a word, frightening. Each gun was loaded with tracer bullets, the better to lead the fast enemy airplanes with. And the combination of more than two dozen guns firing in unison at the Me-999s was nearly blinding. And of course, unsuspecting and greedy in their bid to shoot down a straggler, the two German pilots weren't at full power and thus stumbled right into the fusillade.

They tried to turn away; but only after it was too late. Both planes had more than 3000 rounds pumped into them within six seconds, perforating man and machine alike. The enemy planes did not explode as much as they just disintegrated. There was some smoke, some fire, and even some frozen blood drops blowing in the high winds at 27,000 feet. But the two airplanes simply ceased to exist seconds after the gunners on the bomber opened up on them. In all, only scraps of metal, rubber, wire, and bone hit the surface of the cold North Sea five miles below.

This was the only evidence left of the two spanking new Me-999s.

The newly-instituted In-Flight Protection Squadron— the gigantic flying fortresses reconfigured with many guns to protect the bomber stream—had claimed its first two victories.

The city of Bremen was the first target.

The city of 900,000 was selected as much for its geographical location as it was for its target value. If all went right, it would be the first major German city the American bombers would come close to. And if this bold plan was going to work, Bremen would be the first test.

The American air armada made landfall over the Reich itself at 0810 hours, exactly on schedule. The first piece of solid land the bombers passed over were East Frisians, a series of barrier islands which form most of western Germany's coastline with the North Sea. The planes picked up some light, panicky flak from this region, but it was way too low and way too scattered to affect the bomber stream.

Once over land, the 1000 airplanes turned southeast

again, passed over the Jade Busin area, and picked up the Aller River. Using this as a landmark, they steered directly south. Bremen was now just 20 miles away.

The city had air-raid sirens and a sizable civil defense force in place. But these things hadn't been used in years. So when word of the approaching American bombers first reached the city's defenders, they foolishly didn't believe it. They asked for endless verifications and confirmations, and by the time they were convinced that an attack was coming, the American bombers were already blotting out the horizon.

The first bombs started dropping on Bremen at 0830 hours, again exactly on schedule. They rained down from 100 specially designated aircraft layered throughout the stream. The bombs themselves were known as ATX-30s, a mix of high-explosive, magnesium, and petroleum jelly. On contact, the bomb would explode, due to the HE, then the magnesium would be ignited, and the pliable jelly would splatter the flames everywhere. One bomb could cover a 1000-square-foot area with what was essentially burning glue, a substance which would adhere to wood and skin alike. Bremen was an old city, noted for its many wooden structures. It had also been an unusually dry winter season. The city was like a tinderbox.

The first 100 or so bombs started a fire in the city square which was raging out of control less than two minutes later. A second wave of bombs came down further east, hitting the city's substantial riverside oil storage facilities, and igniting them as well. A third wave found kindling to burn in the city's outlying yet highly residential Southforest sector. The fourth wave of bombs struck a huge military barracks on the southernmost tip of the city.

In all, more than 2000 separate fires had been started by just 100 planes of the bomber stream. Fires, it would turn out, that would rage all that night, all of the next day, and well into the third.

And still, more than 900 of the American aircraft had yet to drop their bombs.

By this time, bells were ringing all over the German War Command headquarters in Berlin. It was evident now that some kind of an American attack was happening, and it was aimed at the Reich itself.

But the sheer size of the attack and the audacity of it served to confuse the Germans. Did the Americans even have 1000 bombers left? More importantly, did they have 1000 pilots? The attack was so unexpected, many German high commanders still believed it was a fake, even though they were receiving reports that Bremen was burning to the ground.

Finally, though, German War Command stumbled into action. They postulated a probable flight path for 1000 American bombers and reckoned that if they were sticking together, they would mostly likely hit the cities of Osnabruck and Munster next, then swing west again and head back to their bases in Iceland. This was actually beneficial to the German defense forces because, by happenstance, there was a huge airfield just outside Osnabruck, and it contained a training squadron of Natter rocketplanes being readied for assignment in Occupied U.K. The bomber force would have to fly practically right over this base if they continued their present speed and heading. The Natters would eat them alive.

The German High Command immediately contacted the training field and told them of the oncoming American threat. The field commanders were ordered to get every available Natter ready for action and launch.

The scramble alarm was sounded immediately at the Natter base. Pilots were suited up and running to their rocketplanes by 0845 hours.

A vanguard of American bombers was spotted approaching Osnabruck five minutes later.

* * *

The Natter was a rocketplane, its forward propulsion effected by the mixture of two highly volatile chemicals called T-stoff and S-Stoff blowing out the back.

The planes, then, did not need runways or long takeoff runs. They were launched by means of movable sleds, which carried the deadly rocket plane for about 200 feet over the ground until the thrusters had created enough velocity to get the craft airborne.

The training field at Osnabruck had 30 such sleds to service 300 flyable Natters. Each sled had 10 rocket planes hooked up to it, ready for loading and launch, just like bullets in a gun clip. Once the first Natter was airborne, the next would begin its sled ride and take off just five seconds later. Then the next one would be launched, and the next, and so on, until all 10 were up and away. In practice sessions, the German units at Osnabruck had launched all 300 Natters in less than 90 seconds.

But it was getting those first 30 Natters off the ground that was the difficult part. Lining up, firing their motors, getting clean takeoff runs. If for whatever reason the first rocket didn't get off the rails, then none of those behind it were going anywhere.

So there were two ways to fight Natters. Trying to tangle with them in the air, as they were rising into the bomber stream, their own guns blazing, was a tall order. Even for a jet fighter, this was a difficult task as the Natter could clock up to 1400 mph for short periods of time, a speed advantage even the fastest American plane could not overcome.

The best way to beat the dangerous little rocketplane, then, was the second way: get to it before it got airborne— while it was still on the ground, sitting still, its fuel tanks full of two of the most volatile substances on Earth.

This would be the American plan.

* * *

The American bombers were within sight of the Natter field by 0850 hours.

What the Germans on the ground saw was a group of huge aircraft seemingly coming straight for them. But two things were wrong here. The reports from Bremen said there were hundreds of American bombers, maybe even as many as 1000—plus substantial fighter support. But the skies above the field showed only a couple of dozen American bombers, and no fighter cover at all. At least none that could be seen.

This prompted the launch order from the field's commander to his Natter squadrons. Two dozen unprotected bombers would be easy pickings for the 300 or so Natters. In fact, the greatest danger might lie in the crowded-sky syndrome—there would be so many Natters aloft and so many returning at the same time, the chances of losing planes and pilots due to collisions was greater than that of enemy fire.

Still, the commander's orders were to launch all planes and that's what the ground crews began to do. Suddenly they were very busy getting those first 30 crucial planes up.

So busy, they did not see the line of American jet fighters approaching from the south.

Hunter was leading the group of 12 Mustangs which had peeled away from the small formation of B-17/36s about five minutes before.

There were only 25 bombers heading for Onasbruck and they were essentially set out as bait, a bid to get the Germans to expose their Natters at the worst possible moment, while they were still in their launching sleds. Coming in from the unlikeliest direction—south—the plan called for Hunter and the female pilots of the 2001st to tear into the Natters before they could even get off the ground.

If the attack on Bremen had been textbook quick, deadly, and efficient, then the attack on the Natter field was even more so. This was not 12 jets versus 300 rocket planes here. Again, all Hunter and the female pilots had to do was make sure the first 30 Natters didn't get off their rails. Destroying them would destroy the launching sleds, and thereby eliminate the threat completely.

So Hunter led the Mustang-5s in very low and very slow and again the order of the day was to make every shot count. The first sweep came in with complete surprise, and concentrated on the first 10 sleds, separated as they were from the fanlike arrangement of the main sled-launch array. Hunter went in first. He sighted a trios of sleds, gave a quick squeeze to his MG trigger, then another, and another. Three quick bursts, three Natters destroyed. But there was danger in this too. To get the right shot in the right amount of time, he had to hold the Mustang slow and steady, and then pull up quickly as the bullets ignited the T-Stoff/S-Stoff mixture.

So he fired three times quick, and then put the 'Stang into a massive climb. The trio of explosions that followed shook the jet from back to front, but caused no permanent damage. He quickly cleared out and let the next Mustang come screaming in.

This was Captain James herself. She got down low, fired once, twice, three times. Another three Natters iced, another three sleds wrecked. She climbed out fiercely too, the three explosions licking her tail as she ascended.

The next jet came in. This time, four short bursts. Four more sleds and four more Natters, up in flames.

The first 10 sleds were thus destroyed. The second wave of Mustangs was then able to concentrate on the main sled array. Mimicking the first wave's actions, they too used short bursts, low flying, and quick pull-ups. They took out eight of the next 10 sleds. Now the third wave came in. They had to fight their way through the smoke and constant explosions from the first two passes, but were quick and competent about tearing up the last 10 sleds.

In all, only two Natters were able to get airborne. Hunter got one, Sarah got the other. The Mustang-5s swung back around a third time, strafed the field's command facility, its training buildings, and its fuel supply for good measure. But then it was time to go.

On Hunter's call, the 12 Mustangs started to climb. Up at 20,000 feet they met up with the bombers, which had dumped a token amount of firebombs on the nearby city of Osnabruck. The fighters took up positions in the rear and flanks of the small formation. Then, as one, the group turned away from the smoking Natter base.

In all, the training field had been knocked out in less than two minutes.

By now the German High Command was convinced they were being attacked in a major way, and unlike ever before in this phase of the war.

The targets Bremen and Osnabruck showed a general southerly direction of the massive American bombing raid. Common sense dictated that the bombing force had to turn right eventually and head back west, to their bases. After all, how long could they stay over German territory practically unabated?

So the powers that were in Berlin became convinced the next target of the massive raid would be the city of Munster—where an alarming number of troop concentrations were located. After that, possibly the city of Essen, where a huge munitions factory was located. This way the enemy planes could take on another pair of targets and already be pointed at their direction of escape, over the Occupied Netherlands and then out to the sea beyond.

Working on these assumptions, the German High Command began frantically calling air units from Occupied Holland and France and even the U.K. itself, and ordering them to take off immediately and prepare for a massive aerial confrontation somewhere between Munster and Essen.

In all, more than 800 German fighters answered the call—new models like Me-999s, older ones like Me-362s, and many in between. By 0915, three huge German fighter groups were aloft and converging on the spot where the German High Command was sure the 1000 American bombers would soon be.

It was a good defense strategy, an almost chesslike reaction in light of a sudden, dangerous situation that just three hours before had seemed impossible.

The only problem was, it was the wrong move.

For the American swarm, against all odds and sound military thinking, had turned not west toward home, but east. Due east. Deeper into Germany.

They swept over the city of Hannover, unloading 2000 tons of incendiaries and setting its substantial downtown communications center on fire. The air armada next visited the city of Braunschweig, 80 miles east of Hannover and the location of a huge double-reaction engine factory. Another 1800 tons of fire bombs rained down on this city. Some home fighters rose in an attempt to drive off the bombers, but they were all dispatched either by Mustang fighters or the In-Flight Protection gunships. The conflagration in Braunschweig was aided by the fact that the factory was hit dead-on, as well as by a hidden fuel storage dump nearby. These fires would burn for a week.

It was now 0930 hours, and still the American raiders were on the move. Still, they flew east.

The planes were next spotted over Magdeburg, where an oil-cracking plant was located. But the Americans dropped no bombs here. Instead they flew right over the heart of the city—and continued east.

And it was only then that the German War Command realized the Americans weren't intending on turning around and going west at all—at least not until they hit what had been their main target all along.

For just 80 miles east of Magdeburg, sat the capital city of the Reich, Berlin itself.

Berlin was not undefended, of course.

There was an entire fighter wing stationed here—450 interceptors of the latest designs—plus another wing consisting of Natter rocketplanes, and an entire army corps of antiaircraft guns set in concentric rings around the city.

The flak batteries posed the first threat to the approaching bombers. A path had to be carved through these gun emplacements over which the bombers could fly. This difficult task had been given to the same 12 Mustang-5 jetfighters that had attacked the Natter base Osnabruck.

It was partly cloudy over the German capital now, raining in some spots, while others were perfectly clear. In other words, a typical spring day in the Reich. The clouds would help the bombers, at the very least they would give them some cover from the outlying AA guns. But the ceiling was only 2500 feet, and Hunter's group of fighters would have to operate way below that for nearly the entire bombing run.

The 12 Mustangs broke away from the bomber pack about 15 miles from the edge of Berlin. Picking up the Havel River, they quickly got down almost to surface level. Leading the way, Hunter was flying no more than 25 feet above the river, the spray kicked up by his plane's preceding shock wave actually covering his canopy with water. By now the German defense authorities should have sounded the air-raid sirens and all civilians should have been under shelter. But as Hunter and the other Mustangs screeched along mere feet above the river, they could see ordinary citizens lining both banks. Strolling, napping, having an early lunch by the riverside, there were hundreds of them.

What was this? Hunter thought.

Then it sunk in. Obviously, the Berlin authorities never

gave the air-raid warning. Why? Maybe that old stuff about the impossibility of the Allies attacking Berlin itself. But for whatever reason, Hunter and the others could see large groups of civilians pointing and even waving to them as they flashed by. Morbidly, Hunter and the others waved back.

About three miles from the city, the Mustangs pulled up slightly and turned east. Here was the first concentration of AA guns. Equally important, located alongside many of the guns, were radar stations, some of which controlled the air defense fighters for all of Berlin.

The American jets came in so fast, and so low, they caught the AA gunners practically unawares. Lining up in six two-ship formations, the 'Stangs ripped through the gun emplacements and the radar stations, their machine guns tearing into flesh and metal alike. Each formation went around three times. That's all that was needed. For a quarter mile in each direction, the targets were quickly destroyed.

Once over the first ring of flak batteries, the planes climbed, but just a little, up to 150 feet. The next line of AA guns was located in the Grune suburb of the city. Hunter picked up the towering snouts of the 288-mm radar-controlled monsters from two miles out. Again their perilously low altitude gave the Mustangs an advantage. Again, they came in quick, guns blazing, and caught the gunners by surprise. They were flying so low and the gunners had been expecting targets so high, there was no way the Germans could depress their gun muzzles quick enough to fire at the Mustangs. Once again the Americans tore a path right through the AA emplacements.

The third ring of AA guns was centered near the Wilmersdorf Plain, a flat piece of terrain just outside the new city limits of Berlin. Warned in advance, these gunners were waiting for the American jets. They had their guns cranked down all the way and they were loaded up with short proximity fuses on their shells.

But this is where the Circle Wing's ability to improvise came into play.

After attacking the second ring of AA guns, Hunter and his fighters did a strange thing—they began flying around in circles.

The commanders of the AA guns at Wilmersdorf saw this on their radar screens—and were baffled. What were the Americans doing?

The answer came a second later. First the AA gunners heard a mighty screech of engines. Then out of the clouds they saw a huge B-24/52 heading right for them. It was coming down so fast, at first the gunners thought the American bomber had been shot down and was about to crash. But that wasn't the case. This was on one of the bomber gunships from the In-Flight Protection squadron. It had been called on to fulfill a very special mission.

Knowing the AA gunners would be confused by the Mustangs' mysterious tactics, the gunship was able to roar right over the main flak emplacement, level off and then go into a low, wide orbit, tilting perilously to the left side. The pilot gave the order for all left-side gunners to open fire, and an instant later their fusillade began. Riding low and slow, the huge bomber resembled a flying dragon now. The waves of tracer fire pouring out of it were frightening, unreal. The stunned AA gunners, with the muzzle barrels deflected all the way down, simply could not fire back at the big plane. Once again, the Germans were cut down like wheat stalks by a sickle.

The bomber only stayed on station for 20 seconds, one complete revolution around the main gun batteries. Then it screamed for height, clawing its way back up to a safer altitude.

When Hunter and the other fighters arrived about a minute later—dizzy from their merry-go-round delaying maneuver—there was nothing left. Where once there was as many as 55 AA guns, now was little more than a smoking hole in the ground with no one left alive to fire the flak guns that remained. Hunter just shook his head and chalked it up as yet another strange event in this crazy life he was leading. The idea to use one of the gunships as a mighty ground suppression weapon had come to him the night before . . . in a dream.

Meanwhile, German interceptors were taking off by the dozens from bases all around the city.

The last reported position of the American bomber swarm had them flying due east at 27,500 feet—typical pre–bomb run positioning. The majority of German interceptors were immediately vectored to this height and positioning. But the first ones on the scene found . . . absolutely nothing.

Some of the German fighters climbed up to 30,000 feet. Still nothing. Others went up to 35-angels, while some went down to 20,000. Still nothing.

How was this possible? The German pilots frantically radioed back to base, trying to get radar fixes on the enemy bombers. But intercept information was now very scarce because many of the crucial radar stations had been knocked out along with the flak emplacements.

It actually took one, long strange minute for the Germans to figure out what had happened.

Then they looked up—*way* up—and finally spotted the American bomber fleet. They were up at 65,000 feet! They had all climbed at the exact moment the flak and radar stations were being hit, instead of descending as the Germans had expected them to.

Only about half the German fighters could fly to 65-angels; they were the old but rugged Me-362s. These airplanes left the Me-999s and others behind and started putting on the fire to get up to the enemy's lofty altitude. But none of this was making any sense. Why would the Americans be flying so high? They couldn't possibly hope for any kind of targeting effectiveness from 13 miles up. Plus, at that height, they would be sitting ducks for the Natters, hundreds of which were located at a base west of the city, their pilots in place, just waiting for the word to launch.

The ascending German fighters naturally attacked the first bombers they came to—those flying at the bottom of the pack. This was a mistake, of course, because these low fliers were the gunships of the In-Flight Protection squadron. The Germans had not yet caught on that some of the American bombers weren't bombers at all, simply because everyone who'd come up against the gunships so far hadn't lived long enough to tell anyone about them.

Immediately a six-pack of Me-362s were shot down by the gunships and twice that number sent fleeing.

Another flight of 362s arose and they too battled the gunships, now laid out like a blanket under the rest of the bombers. A third fighter group strained to get up to the nose-bleeding altitude and they began firing on the bombers themselves. But the guns of the tight formation and the rest of covering Mustang fighters chased them away.

A fourth flight of Me-362s roared in and here the bomber stream took its first casualties. Two B-24/52s were torn up by eight German fighters and were literally blown out of the sky. Their cloak of invulnerability now shorn away, the bomber formation tightened up even more.

They had to hold this dangerous position for just a few more minutes . . .

Meanwhile, Hunter and his group of fighters had circled around the city, dodging flak and small arms fire, heading for Templedorf Airport. This was where the wing of Natters was waiting to take off.

This time the field commander knew the American jets were coming, so he began launching Natters immediately. The tiny rocketplanes began going off like fireworks. Dozens of red, fiery smoke streams went shooting straight up into the sky in an exercise of controlled pandemonium.

Hunter and the Mustangs roared through this fire ball, firing at random and hitting Natters by the handful. But these were just a small percentage of the rocketplanes that were launching; hundreds more were heading up toward the bomber stream which was now passing 13 miles high over the center of the city.

That was OK. Hunter's flight was never expected to stop the massive Natter launch—just disrupt it.

This they did.

Very quickly the first wave of Natters was closing in on the high-flying American bombers.

But they found something curious, too. The bombers were no longer staying at 65-angels. They were dropping down from that altitude very quickly. Some were coming down so fast, the Natter pilots were also fooled into thinking the bombers had been shot down and were crashing.

But this was not the case.

The bombers were dropping as the Natters were rising making it extremely difficult if not impossible for the German pilots to shoot accurately simply because both sides were going so fast in opposite directions.

Two bombers were hit—both fatally—in collisions with Natters. But the dive tactic was proving exceptionally effective. For all their speed and firepower, the rocketplanes were still just one-shot charlies. They rose, they shot down bombers, they ran out of gas, they came back down in a glide. They couldn't do anything else.

So once these Natters had passed through the storm of diving bombers, they'd shot their load. They were ineffective. Spent. As it was, many would wind up drifting back to the ground with their guns and cannons still full, startled by the outrageous, dangerous, improbable American tactic.

The bomber force—still more than 1000 planes—leveled off again at 27,500 feet. At this point, Hunter's Mustangs linked back up with the covering force. The Wing was now over a mostly residential section of east Berlin, which was exactly where they wanted to be. They still had German fighters all over them, but the Mustangs made a good account of themselves, shooting down 12 of them, with the loss of only one bomber.

At point zero, O'Malley's lead airplane finally opened its bomb bay doors and began dropping its fire bombs. Stretched out now for 10 miles, more than 700 of the bombers began doing the same thing.

In seconds, tons of incendiaries were falling over eastern Berlin. The flaming jellied gasoline splattered all over the mostly wooden and plastic structures below. The firebombs came down exactly where they supposed to, in a section of the city where many of the German High Commanders made their homes. Soon enough, this quadrant of Berlin began to burn. The ultraaccurate bombing, especially after all the high jinks and maneuverings of the Americans planes, was aided greatly by having an enormous landmark to drop on: the huge swastika the Germans had painted onto their rooftops so long ago. It turned out to be a mile-long bull's-eye for the Americans.

The bombers emptied their loads, turned west and quickly accelerated out of the area. The German fighters stayed with them for a while, hanging on their tails, battling the Mustangs, but claiming only two more American aircraft to 24 of their own.

But then suddenly the German fighters gave up. Why? Because the German High Command came to believe that *another* wave of American bombers was approaching Berlin, and the *Reichcapital* would need every fighter they had to ward it off. But the second wave of bombers was just a ruse dreamed up by Hunter. As soon as they had dropped their bombs, he had many of the withdrawing bomber pilots actually start sending false radio messages to each other, creating the illusion that there was another bombing raid on the way in.

In the confusion and panic, the Germans fell for it and recalled their fighters. The rest of the surviving bombers got away unscathed.

Berlin would burn for days.

* * *

Throughout the battle, one man stood watching from a window in the New Reichstag, the headquarters of the German High Command.

The city was beginning to melt all around him. The glare of the fires, the scream of jet fighters above, the distant pounding of the antiaircraft batteries—war had returned to the Reich. Yet he could not take his eyes off the enemy planes, especially one American jet fighter that seemed to be everywhere at once.

The man recognized the almost impossible maneuverings of this particular Mustang. It ripped through the German interceptors, firing wildly yet hitting targets every time. Unconsciously, he licked his lips and tasted the salt from the Atlantic where he'd been plucked by the German Navy almost a year ago.

Strange, how things turn out, he thought.

He kept his eyes on the Mustang until the American bomber force had finally passed over. The jet fighter was the last one to leave, trailing behind the others, watching the rear.

That's when the man wiped his thin, bearded face, and started talking to himself.

"A thousand-plane raid. Firebombs. Gunships protecting bombers. Outrageous fighter tactics. I know these things. I know the thoughts behind them . . ."

Then as that last jet fighter finally disappeared over the horizon, he added: "And I know who that man is, too."

Two hours later, the bombers began returning to the Circle Bases.

Some were badly shot up, some were carrying wounded. Some were so low on fuel, they were forced to glide in. Two crashed on landing. Eight others were damaged beyond repair. Thirteen didn't come back at all.

But 1103 did, along with every fighter. They were all

home by 1200 hours straight up. Behind them they'd left six cities in Germany burning.

And the next day, the planes took off, went back, and did it again. This time they bombed Dresden, Bonn, Hamburg, Frankfurt, Cologne, and Berlin again. Like before, they stuck together. Like before, they fought off the increased enemy interceptors and destroyed AA batteries on the ground. They lost 17 more airplanes.

The day after that, they did it again. And the day after that, and the day after that. For seven straight days the Circle Wing rained fire and death on Germany. By the eighth day, when they finally rested, nearly 40,000 tons of incendiaries had been dropped, more than 22 cities had been hit, many more than once, including Berlin, which had been hit every day. Follow-up reconnaissance flights proved it: in one week, more than half of Germany had been set on fire.

On that eighth day, very late in the afternoon, after a special recon plane had been sent over the targets and instant-film from its cameras had been processed, Major Allen Payne, acting CO of the Circle Wing, walked into the darkened office of General Seth Jones.

Slowly, respectfully, Payne held the photos showing the widespread scorching of German targets up to the General's eyes. Then he read, very precisely, the combat report for the week, noting the number of airplanes put into the air, the number of miles traveled, the number of timely turn-arounds for the bombers, the tonnage of bombs dropped, and lastly, the relatively low number of crews and planes lost.

The general sat there, absolutely still as usual, and listened. And at the end of it, Payne saw two tears drop from the old man's eyes. Then the man came back to life again. He looked up at Payne, weakly shook his hand, then uttered two words: "Thank you."

Then the old man leaned his head back, closed his eyes, and finally died.

Chapter 24

Washington DC
One week later

The cab pulled up to the unassuming brownstone in the Georgetown section of Washington, D.C., at precisely 5 P.M.

It was raining, but just a shower, and the air was thick with the scent of leftover cherry blossoms.

A man in a black suit and trenchcoat got out of the cab, threw the driver a $20 bill and then went through the front door of the building.

He took the elevator down no less than 16 floors, finally arriving in the subsection of the basement.

This was yet another secret briefing area for OSS agents. One that was used when absolute top security was needed. Its location was known to less than 100 souls. This man was one of them.

It was Agent Y.

He went to a door marked 87 at the end of the corridor and entered without knocking.

It was dark within, as usual. One light at the end of a

very long table was the only illumination. Two men were already in the room, smoking cigarettes and murmuring to one another. It was X and Z. They hardly acknowledged Y's presence as he came in, closed the door behind him and joined them at the far end of the table.

"Why do you guys always insist on sitting in the dark?" Y asked them. "We're sixteen floors under the ground. Isn't that dark enough for you?"

They continued to ignore him. Y just shrugged.

"Well, cheer up, my friends," he said, mocking them. "I have some very encouraging news."

He removed a yellow envelope from his briefcase and slid it over to the two agents. They languidly picked it up and read together the single sheet it contained.

"Those bomber boys plastered Germany for the fifteenth time today," Y announced proudly, essentially telling the men what they were reading. "They hit Bonn, Dresden, Hamburg, Essen, and Berlin again. Their only problem seems to be that they're running out of firebombs—finally. They'll go dry in about a week. The Air Corps is scrambling to resupply them and if all the planes don't blow up trying to take off from Gander, they should be in good shape."

X and Z simply put the paper back down and stared at the ceiling.

"Again, let's see some smiles, my friends," Y urged them. "We're not quite winning this thing again, but the Huns are feeling—how shall I say it?—a tad warm this Spring?"

Though X and Z weren't aware of it, Y had every right to feel cheery. He knew that things had started to change back in America's favor the day Hunter landed at the Circle Air Wing, just as things had changed in Germany's favor the day the man they'd scooped from the ocean landed there.

True, the U.S. still had a long way to go, but it really did seem that Agent Y's great perception, that Hunter was a man whose very presence could alter the course of the war, had been dead-on correct. And the facts were there to back it up.

But his colleagues were not joining in his enthusiasm. Something was troubling them. Something that could override the encouraging battle reports from Europe.

"What is it my friends?" he asked them. "What has happened?"

Y sat down and Z slid a deep red envelope over to him. Red was the highest security level. Furthermore, the envelope was sealed with both green and red wax. This elevated it to Level 42 Security—the highest within the OSS realm.

The wax seals had already been broken however.

"And this is?" Y asked simply.

"The end of the world," Z replied.

X lit another cigarette and blew the smoke all around the dimly lit room.

"One week ago," he began, "a Sea Marine patrol on Block Island found the body of a dead German officer washed up on the beach. He was wearing the uniform of a German Air Force intelligence officer, but papers he was carrying identified him as a liaison officer with the German Navy."

Y reached inside the envelope and pulled out a photo of a man in a German uniform, laying dead on the beach. His mouth and nose were stuffed with sand.

"He may have been a courier of some sort," X continued. "He was carrying some very sensitive documents with him."

Y pulled out a three-page briefing paper.

"Sensitive?" he asked. "How sensitive?"

X looked at Z and then back at Y. "Would you believe the entire plan for a German invasion of the United States?"

Y just stared back at them. "Are these documents real? Have they been authenticated?"

"They've passed all the chemical tests, the printware analysis, everything the Main/AC could come up with as far as purity," Z said. "These things are real. We think . . ."

Y quickly read the document.

This is what it said: the Germans were planning to land 62 paratroop divisions along the eastern coast of the U.S. sometime within the next 30 days. They planned to concentrate on the Mid-Atlantic states. After establishing a beachhead there, they would drive inland, swing north, and capture Washington D.C.

At the same time, five major U.S. cities would be bombed—New York, Boston, Baltimore, Miami, and Atlanta—by high-flying Focke-Wulf 911s, carrying a new secret weapon, or by apparently enormous missiles, called DG-42s, which would be launched from Germany itself.

All this would be coordinated with an attack on Texas, New Mexico, Arizona, and southern California by German special unit troops infiltrated into Mexico from previous secret landings in Central America.

There would also be a seaborne attack on northern New England by some of Germany's numerous Scandinavian allies.

In the second phase of this invasion, another wave of German paratroop forces would come right over the North Pole, over Canada and land around the Great Lakes. A third phase called for a similar over-the-top attack on the midsection of the United States.

The Germans would be able to move all these troops and drop all these bombs and attack so many American cities due to a wide array of secret weapons that they'd apparently been building for almost a year. These included monstrous airplanes—bombers and troop carriers—that had somehow mastered the art of aerial refueling, and this prolonged their range.

Y stopped right there. At least that would explain the strange reports they'd been getting lately about mysterious groups of large airplanes seen flying odd formations way out at sea.

He began reading again. The first step in this invasion plan was actually scheduled to take place 24 hours before the main thrust hit. This preinvasion action involved a lightning attack on the island of Bermuda. Once they'd captured this island, and its several airports, the Germans would have the perfect staging area for the big attack on the American mainland.

In all, the invasion was expected to last less than a month.

Y was staggered by the report.

"Really, what are the chances any of this is true?" he asked Z.

The man just shrugged. "It's either all true or total bullshit," he replied.

"But we have to consider how we found this information," Y said. "Putting fake plans on a corpse and having it wash up on the beach is the oldest trick in the book."

"That is correct," Z said. "But I think we have to go on the assumption that it's all true, simply because to ignore it, and guess wrong, would be fatal."

Y looked at the calendar. The attack was supposed to go off in just 30 days. There was absolutely no way they could muster up any kind of effective defensive plan, not with the woeful state of the U.S. military these days. There could be no throw-em-back-into-the-sea strategy either. They didn't even have time to dream one up, never mind assemble the defensive troops needed to fight 62 divisions and have them fortify the coastline.

"Simply put," X said, "we are doomed."

Z numbly agreed with him.

But Y wasn't so sure.

"If this is still a month away, that might mean the enemy troops are still in their staging areas," he told them. "And because they are hiding the equivalent of a million men somewhere, I've got to believe those staging areas are in Europe. And if those troops are still at home, then we at least have some chance of interdicting them, stalling them, or maybe stopping them altogether."

X and Z just looked at him. Then they laughed.

"Always the optimist," Z said derisively.

"Well, we have to do *something*," Y shot back at them. "You said it yourself."

"That's right," Z countered. "I'm going to do something. I'm going to pack up the wife and the girlfriend, get my ass out to the Northwest Coast. Seattle sounds very nice at the moment. Or maybe the deep woods of Oregon. It's the only place the Huns don't intend to invade any time soon."

"You'll be at the head of a very large stampede," X said, leaning back to light a cigarette. "When word gets out about this, whew, boy . . ."

"All the more reason to leave sooner," Z said.

Y's face flushed red. It was obvious even in the darkened room. He turned on Z.

"If you leave now," he told his colleague through gritted teeth, "I'll track you down and kill you."

Z stared back at him with some astonishment. "When the hell did you grow such a big pair of balls?"

"It's our country, you fool!" Y bellowed at him. "And we've got to do our job."

X raised his hands, playing the peacemaker once again.

"OK," he said turning to Y. "How do you suggest we attempt to counter this massive operation, with all its weapons, and huge aircraft, and missiles that can travel ten thousand miles? Do you have a plan in mind? Something that can be implemented quickly, but also with just a very small number of people involved?"

Z sat back in his chair smugly. Y could hardly see his face for the low light and cigarette smoke.

"So? Do you have a plan of this caliber?" he mocked Y. "Great mind that you are?"

Y flushed with anger again—but then suddenly, a strange calm came over him. They needed a big operation quick, performed by someone who could both do the job and be trusted.

Maybe that wasn't such an impossible request after all.

"Yes," Z went on, joining sides with X. "Do you have a magic rabbit you can pull out of your hat?"

Y just glowered back at them both.

"Maybe I do," he said finally.

Chapter 25

Over the North Sea
One week later

It happened as Hunter was returning from the 21st air strike over Germany.

Hamburg, Hannover, Frankfurt, and of course, Berlin had been firebombed again this day. Only three bombers had been lost, all to Natters. Two other bombers had been damaged though, lucky flak bursts had caught them at the tail end of the Berlin run. As the rest of the Wing headed back for the safe haven of Iceland, Hunter stayed behind to guard the stragglers.

It was usually during this last stretch that Hunter settled back to do his daily breathing exercises. As always, he loosened his chin strap and his seat harness and began taking the long deep breaths of oxygen.

But suddenly, on his third breath, his body began vibrating.

He sat up immediately and began looking all around him. This feeling he'd come to associate with impending trouble was running through him very strongly now. Were enemy fighters approaching? Were they jets or rocket-planes? He scanned the sky above him, below him, behind him and to both sides—and saw nothing.

But still the feeling would not go away. He checked his position on the homing TV. He was exactly where he thought he was—just passing over the Faeroe Islands and now some 200 miles from the nearest enemy territory. He'd never encountered any German aircraft way out here. Yet his entire body was almost shaking at this point.

What was going on?

He radioed ahead to the stragglers that he was dumping some altitude and that he'd catch up with them. Then he put the nose of the Mustang-5 straight down and began to plunge.

Through 45,000, through 40, then 35,000 feet. The *feeling* became stronger with each mile he dropped. Finally, instinct told him to pull up at 22,500 feet. He did so and looked around him again.

And that's when he saw it.

It was an enormous jet-powered seaplane, about 20 miles off to his right. It was going very fast and flying very low. It was painted in polar disbursement camouflage, with large Iron Crosses hidden on its wings and tail.

Hunter had never seen an enemy airplane like this one. Its size was astonishing. It was at least twice the size of the biggest American SuperBomber. Maybe even three times as big. From the back of his skull came a flash of an ancient German seaplane called the Dornier Do.X. It had been enormous for its day, with a long top-mounted wing and no less than six propeller engines.

This flying behemoth he was now looking at had been built on the same principal, except there were no fewer than 28 jet engines adorning its wing. And he guessed it was at least five times the size of its very distant cousin. It was so big, it looked for all the world like a flying battleship.

Hunter had to take the next moment to think about what he should do, exactly. It appeared the giant seajet was heading right for Iceland. But no matter what direction it was going, the enemy plane had to be shot down. The problem was, the fighter group was already 100 miles ahead of him, and probably none of Sarah's Mustangs had enough fuel to double back, help him kill the beast, and then reach Iceland with the fuel remaining.

Plus, at the speed the seajet was flying, there was a possibility it would get away while Hunter was waiting for some help.

The question was then, could he do it alone?

He had taken out two AA sites, a flak train, five Natters, and a Horton Flying Devil today, so he was about half full on machine gun ammunition. And though Hunter had yet to use his cannon in any his combat flights so far, the bulky weapon still had its requisite 25 shells in place.

So did he have enough ammo to take on this giant or not? He wasn't sure. But perhaps more important, did he have enough fuel?

He didn't know the answer to that question either. But either way, he had to try. One more deep breathe, then he yanked on his control stick and dove on the huge airplane.

The enemy plane saw him coming from about a mile out. This did not surprise him. The giant airship had dozens of windows and glass blisters all over its fuselage. There must have been at least a hundred portholes on her. There were no side or top guns that he could see though, just a large gun station in the rear. But he was sure that with so many windows, someone had spotted him coming down out of the clouds.

It really made no difference whether they saw him or not. Hunter simply kicked in his double-reheat burner and bumped his speed up to 850 knots. The airplane's rear gunners began firing almost immediately, but he was moving way too fast for them to get a bead on him.

He flew under and then over and then back along the length of the thing, marveling at its enormity. The plane which had circled him the day he was plucked from the Atlantic looked like a glider compared to this craft.

Hunter looped again and placed himself on the plane's six o'clock. He pulled back his weapons safeties and did a system check. His four mgs were ready to fire, as was the dormant cannon. A quick look at the homing TV told him he was beginning the engagement 178 miles southeast of the tip of Iceland. It was exactly 1100 hours when he opened up.

On his first pass, he tried to find a vulnerable place under the big wing, where his bullets might hit a fuel tank. Some of his initial hits did produce telltale wisps of vapor, but nothing big enough to ignite. He looped and went around again. This time he threw some shells into the last two starboard engines. His bullets simply bounced off. The engine cowlings were obviously made of heavy duty steel.

Another loop. Another pass at the engines. Again, no hits to speak off. He tried the underwing fuel tanks again. Nothing. He tried pumping bullets into the underside of the giant fuselage itself, hoping to find a soft spot. But again, nothing. His bullets either bounced off, or had no affect on what they did penetrate. He was now down to half his remaining bullet load.

He made six more passes, again to little affect. He tried a pair of head-on strafing runs, zeroing in on the plane's bulbous cockpit—it had more glass than a skyscraper. But he saw most of his shots bounce off the thick, hardened glass. Even firing directly into the engine intakes had no noticeable affect. The air-suckers were obviously protected by heavy-duty screens inside the cowlings.

All this shooting and diving and looping was burning fuel and time. Hunter attacked the big plane for no less than 15 minutes, and other than making the pilots change course slightly to avoid him, he had not altered the big plane's progress at all, never mind shooting it down. It was like trying to stab a whale to death with a pocketknife. No matter what he did, the big plane simply continued plowing through the increasingly frigid air, its destination known only to those within.

The galling thing about the attack was that he had an audience. There were many faces pressed up against the numerous porthole blisters, watching him in an almost leisurely fashion as he broke his nuts trying to bring the flying giant down. He even detected some of the enemy airmen looking out and laughing at him, so sure they were that his attempt would be futile.

He did four more passes, all of them at the under-wing fuel tanks. And finally he saw a continuous stream of vapor leaking from at least one perforation. But no sooner had he started this leak, when his four machine guns went dry.

They were now 110 miles from the Icelandic coast, and it was obvious the plane was heading in that direction. Hunter began wondering exactly what the big Dornier might be carrying inside. It wasn't a bomber, it had no bomb bays. Could it be a troop carrier? A maritime spy plane?

He didn't know. But it was clear it was heading for American-held territory and that it was up to no good and that Hunter had to somehow knock it down.

He was desperate now. He looped again, got back on the big plane's tail and gingerly keyed his cannon's safety switch. He knew the backwash from the huge airplane would make it almost impossible for him to get close enough for a clear shot with the low-velocity cannon, but he was running out of tricks to try.

So he increased speed and opened up with the cannon for the first time ever. Immediately he heard an ungodly noise and the Mustang-5 began shaking so violently he thought it was coming apart of the seams. The nose-mounted cannon produced a cloud of smoke so thick, Hunter couldn't see for several hair-raising moments. And when it did clear, the first thing he saw was a gang of enemy airmen in porthole bubbles still laughing and pointing at him.

But the 25-shot cannon barrage had paid off. It had

taken a chunk off the big plane's tail wing before running dry. Hunter was now out of ammo and almost out of gas. But he'd scored a little wound on his target—and this gave him a rather desperate idea.

Hunter knew that as big as the plane was, like all planes, it needed all its critical surfaces to fly. And like all planes, it needed a tail wing to stay airborne.

Something in the back of his skull told him of a tactic the Russians used way, way back in some other place and time. When they were out of ammo, they would simply ram their opponent. Hunter decided he would do the same.

He pushed the throttle ahead, his engine sucked up a load of gas and he rocketed right into the left-side tail wing. The big Mustang-5 sort of bounced off, its nose crunched in, but it took a small chunk out of the extremely huge tail wing in the process.

Hunter dropped back, got steady, increased throttle and rammed the tail again. Another chunk flew off, producing another big dent in the Mustang's nose. He hit the huge seaplane again, and another piece of the tail broke off. He hit it again, and again. And again. The coast of Iceland was now in sight. The blisters were still full of faces looking out at him, but no one was laughing now. These faces were etched in confusion and horror as they watched the mad American pilot continuously ram their airborne ocean liner, picking away at their unsinkable flying ship, one piece at a time.

It took another 20 long minutes. But at last, more than half the tail section had been knocked away.

And finally, the big plane started to go down.

The Mustang-5 was on fire as it approached Dreamland base.

Its nose and right wing were smoking heavily. From mid-fuselage on back was totally engulfed in flames. The engine was scoring very high. Its screech sounded like it was going to explode at any moment.

Yet as the small crowd of concerned colleagues looked on, Hunter brought the huge fighter in low, wheels up, gunning his engine with the last of his gas, and succeeding in blowing the fire off his fuselage.

He turned again, intentionally draining off his airspeed and lined up on the far runway. He came in shallow, waiting for the last moment to pop his gear down. It was on fire too. The Mustang hit the frozen runway a few seconds later, bounced up, came back down heavily on its right wing, bounced again, and came down hard again.

It was the damaged nose that was causing all this oscillation; in the thick, cold air, it was as aerodynamic as a mallet. The plane bounced a fourth time, but at that moment, it finally ran out of gas. It came down for good on the fifth bounce, then went into a wild spin. But somehow Hunter managed to keep all three of its wheels on the ground.

And that's how he came to a stop—spinning. The emergency trucks were already rushing out toward him. Many of his squadron mates were running across the frozen tarmac too. Watching the drama from in front of the ops building, Payne threw his jeepster into gear and joined this mad rush. His vehicle was faster than the running men, faster even than the fire trucks. He was the first one to reach the crash site.

He found Hunter waiting for him.

His uniform was singed, his helmet gashed, his face painted with soot and snow, but he was alive, and in one piece.

The same could not be said for the Mustang-5. Fuselage scored, wheels collapsed, wings literally hanging off, and a nose that looked like a punch drunk fighter, the wind and snow would claim it before the base mechanics could.

The first thing Payne asked upon reaching him was: "Where in hell did you learn to fly like that?"

Hunter took off his helmet and washed his face with a handful of snow.

"I have no idea," he told Payne truthfully.

Payne drove him at high speed back to the ops building. A doctor arrived, and after looking Hunter over, just shook his head and said, "Wow." Then he departed.

Payne gave him a cup of coffee and together they sat in the empty ops room.

"So what the hell happened out there?" the officer asked him.

Hunter gave him a quick recounting of his battle with the huge airplane. Payne's eyes got wider with every sentence.

"I got a good spot on the wreckage," Hunter told him. "It came down right on the edge of the island. We've got to get out there and see what the hell it's full off, and what it was doing way out here."

Payne grimaced at Hunter's plan but knew it would be necessary. "I already called for a Beater from 999th; it should be here in ten minutes."

Hunter drained his coffee and got a refill. Finally, the cold was leaving his veins.

"I don't like this," Payne was saying. "They've never come out this far."

Hunter dumped a half a cup of sugar into his coffee. He would need some energy for what was coming up.

"Not that we know of anyway," he replied ruefully. "But we've been making a lot of noise lately. It was probably just a matter of time before they did something about us."

Payne refilled his cup too.

"I've got a squad of the Air Guards ready to lift off with us. Do you think we'll need them?"

Hunter thought for a moment, remembering the kids who'd flown in with him that first horrible day. They hadn't seen much action up here in the great frozen north, but

Hunter had come to admire them for their tenacity, their willingness to help out, and their general goodwill.

He finally nodded. "Yes, we should definitely bring them. And someone else too . . ."

The Beater arrived 10 minutes later.

Hunter and Payne were waiting for it out on the main runway. The squad of Air Guards—10 men in all—were waiting too. Each was wearing the heaviest in polar combatwear: Large hooded parka, thermal pants and boots, fur-lined helmet, and face goggles complete with radio and Boomer inputs. Hunter and Payne were dressed in similar PW gear as well.

The 13th member of this party looked very lost in his bulky outerwear, though.

Zoltan the Magnificent had never had to climb into one of these gorilla suits before, and he was swimming in it. He'd also never had to handle a weapon before, but one of the Air Guards had given him a mammoth M-25 semi-automatic battle rifle and a long belt of ammunition. The psychic looked very weighed down by all the necessities of this odd, upcoming mission.

Hunter wasn't exactly sure why he wanted the swami to come with them. The man had been playing to sold-out audiences every night since the bombing campaign had begun, and had become a favorite of everyone on the base. Hunter and he had had many discussions in that time concerning Hunter's rather odd background—something that no one else at the Circle Wing knew about. Not Payne, not Sarah. No one but Zoltan. In that time, he and the psychic had become friends.

Now his gut was telling him the psychic might come in handy on this strange mission and he'd stopped questioning his instinct a while ago. The psychic didn't look happy about it though.

And who could blame him? As the Beater came in, its

frightening set of rotors and flying surfaces and its immense size was enough to make anyone wince.

But the thing finally touched down and the gangway fell open and the Air Guards, Payne, and Hunter charged in. Zoltan was the last one up the ramp.

When no one was watching him, he made a quick sign of the cross.

It took them about half an hour to fly out to the crash site.

The perpetual storm grew worse as the Beater sloshed its way northeast. Hunter had flown over the crash site with the last fumes his Mustang had left, and had done a visual spot on it before limping the rest of the way to the base.

That had been more than an hour ago now, and with the way the snow was coming down, he was concerned the crash site would be covered over before they reached it.

But finally they were approaching a place called Krujeb-ackn Harbor, a deserted stretch of shore line about 35 miles northeast of Dreamland base. Hunter had his nose pressed up against the Beater starboard observation blister, scanning the frozen land and ice-clogged water way. And then he saw it, just as he'd left it. The huge airplane cracked up on a rocky beach, only about half a foot of snow hiding it from above. Oddly, it seemed as if this place had been the plane's destination all along.

Everyone on the Beater, from the flight crew to the Air Guards, was staring out at the crashed seajet, their mouths wide open with astonishment. Even in a world of big, bigger, and better, this airplane was a monster.

The Air Guards checked their weapons and prepared for what might be an opposed landing. Hunter estimated that there might be upwards of 150 people or even more on the airplane, judging from the faces he'd seen in the windows.

If any of them survived, would they still have the will to fight?

But as it turned out, there were no survivors of this crash.

The Beater set down with a bone-jarring thump and the Air Guards stormed down the gangway with admirable precision, weapons up, spreading out, ready for anything.

But it was quite clear quite quickly that everyone aboard the huge seaplane was dead. Those not killed outright in the crash had succumbed to the 30-below temperatures.

The wreckage, while scattered over a half mile, was actually in three large pieces. The wing had split in two, throwing the 28 engines in all directions. The tail of the aircraft was sitting in 10 feet of slushy water just off the beach. But the main compartment, the fuselage right up to the immense cockpit, was still more or less in one piece.

The Guardsmen surrounded the still, frozen wreckage, weapons ready. Hunter and Payne pried down a side gangplank, walked up and cautiously peaked inside.

Suddenly, a shock wave went through the frigid air.

From Zoltan's point of view, standing a bit timidly at the bottom of the plank, it seemed as if Hunter had been hit by a bolt of lightning as soon as he looked inside the crumpled airplane. His body shook once from head to toe. Zoltan felt the shock wave too even though he was at least 15 feet away from the pilot.

Hunter's reaction had been so severe, Zoltan found himself running up the gang plank, so sure was he that Hunter had been shot or electrocuted.

But when he reached him, Hunter was still among the living. He was breathing, his eyes were not rolled up to the back of his head. He was conscious.

He was, however, bordering on the verge of shock.

As it turned out, Payne was too—but not for the same reason as Hunter. No, Payne's mouth was hanging open because of what the compartment of the huge airplane contained.

There were some troops. Mountain troops from the elite Haussling Division. There was a half company or so and they had all either been crushed at the front of the compartment, or had died of exposure at other parts throughout.

But this was not the surprise. The surprise was the airplane was also filled with hay and about two dozen dead horses.

"Horses?" Payne was saying over and over again.

Zoltan looked in on this scene of grisly carnage and felt another psychic jolt go through him.

"Horses?" he parroted Payne's mutterings.

He turned back to Hunter, who was still standing frozen in place at the doorway. The breath was coming out of his mouth and nostrils very, very slowly.

"Jessuzz, Hawk," Zoltan said. "You OK? You look as if you've seen a gh . . ."

Zoltan knew better than to finish that sentence—but as it was, Hunter wasn't listening to him anyway.

"This," he was saying instead, surveying the compartment full of dead humans, dead horses, and bales of strewn hay, "this I have seen before . . ."

Zoltan looked at him as if he was cracking up. How could anyone have seen such an odd, grisly sight as this before?

Hunter was shaking his head. It seemed preposterous to him too. But from that place way in the back of his skull, the message he was getting loud and clear was that he'd seen something very similar to this bizarre scene some time back in that other place.

Payne was still oblivious to it all—only Hunter and Zoltan could feel the psychic disruption. The Air Exec, and now the Air Guards who were filtering in, were asking the same thing: *Horses?* Why would anyone want to fly all the way up here in such a large airplane under such dangerous conditions, just to bring a couple dozen horses into the middle of nowhere?

It didn't make any sense.

Not at first anyhow.

Hunter somehow got his legs moving. He stepped into the compartment, gingerly made his way around the accumulated, flash-frozen gore and began crawling up to the cockpit.

It took some doing just to get to the front of the wreck, but when he reached it, he found he had to climb up no less than five stories around a spiral ladder to reach the flight deck.

Again, a feeling of eeriness came over him as he managed to squeeze himself through the wreckage to the front of the cockpit.

The pilots were still in their seats; four of them in all, killed on impact and already frozen solid. Hunter found himself staring in the eyes of the one he assumed was the aircraft commander.

Then, completely on impulse, he began chipping away at the man's left breast pocket, intent on searching it. But what exactly did Hunter expect to find here? An ID of some kind? No, that was not important. The guy was a German pilot; that's all he had to know. Perhaps he was carrying documents in that pocket, something that might unravel this mystery. But again, Hunter didn't think that was the aim of this quest.

It seemed more personal than that . . .

Was he looking for a picture of a loved one? Was that it? Why would that interest Hunter? Why would he care what this guy's widow and kids looked like? Well, maybe the picture wasn't of the pilot's loved one, but of someone in Hunter's past. He stopped in mid chip, trying to make some sense of this thought. How weird was that? Why would a picture of someone close to Hunter be in this guy's pocket?

He resumed chipping away at the ice and blood and finally was able to unclasp the button and get the flap open.

But the dead man's pocket was empty.

A second later, he heard footsteps coming up towards

him. It was Zoltan. He didn't even have to say anything to the psychic, the man already knew.

"Is this familiar to you in some way too?" he asked Hunter.

Hunter just shook his head. "In some way, yes," he replied.

They both studied the cockpit for a moment, Hunter bringing his senses back to the matter at hand.

Payne crawled up to join them. He was astonished at the height of the flight deck. "This is a real high-rise, isn't it?" he commented.

"This is a seaplane," Hunter was saying. "It was probably meant to land off the beach. Then I guess they intended to off-load the horses and the hay and . . ."

"Yeah, and what?" Payne asked for all of them.

"That's a lot of hay for two dozen horses," Hunter observed.

"So maybe there were more horses?" Payne continued the thread. "Brought here earlier, maybe still nearby?"

"If this was just a dropping-off point, where were they going?" Hunter asked.

"They went thataway," Zoltan suddenly said.

Payne looked over at Hunter. "You mean he really does have psychic powers?"

But Zoltan was shaking his head. "No, look, you can see them, tracks in the snow, see?"

They pressed their noses against the glass and sure enough, from this height, it was obvious that a 10-foot-wide track had been made in the snow, leading away from the beach. From ground level it had all blended in with the frozen background. They would never have seen it if Hunter hadn't crawled up to the fight deck in the first place.

Then came shouts from behind them. The Guards had found something too. Hunter and company made their way back to the gory hold. Among the broken bodies and the hay, the young soldiers had found another strange item: a gigantic roll of bright red fabric. It seemed like

woven plastic. It was about 12 feet wide and the roll was
big enough to contain thousands of feet of the stuff, maybe
up to half a mile in length.

Again Hunter was nearly knocked off his feet.

"This," he whispered loud enough only for Zoltan to
hear, "This stuff, this tape. It's familiar too."

Zoltan just shook his head and did another quick sign
of the cross.

"Well, you've finally done it, Hawk," he said. "You're
finally giving *me* the creeps."

The Beater had some trouble getting airborne as the
wind and snow had intensified since they'd landed at the
crash site. But somehow, the octocopter got about 100 feet
of air underneath it and with all eyes pressed against its
many observation bubbles, they began to follow the tracks
in the snow.

They went on for miles. The tracks led them over hills,
through frozen valleys, across icy streams, and over more
snowcaps. The trail was littered with dead horses, some
hacked to pieces, their frozen bodies and legs sticking up
through the snow drifts. Strands of yellow hay could be
seen too, most of it plastered up on bare rock faces, the
amber color very alien against the frozen waste.

They flew along like this for nearly 45 minutes, the winds
buffeting the Beater's rotors, and causing metallic screams
that shuddered throughout the aircraft. The trail led back
toward the circle of American bases. It was soon evident
that the Germans—with their horses and their hay—were
heading for someplace close to the airfields. But again the
question was, why?

They finally found their answer on a frozen plain that,
when they would do their rough calculations, was located
in a spot exactly equidistant from all the bases.

Here they found the people who had made the first
tracks through the snow. They were all dead too. Men and

animals, frozen together. They had huddled for warmth, possibly waiting for the relief column that had never come.

The Beater landed and Hunter and the others got out to see it all up close.

Hunter pulled Zoltan aside. "This stuff, or a lot of it, is familiar too."

Zoltan pulled his collar closer to his neck. "A plane full of horses. Soldiers carrying red tape? None of this makes any sense. How can it be familiar?"

But then, beside the dead, one of the guards found something. It was the beginning of a long line of the same bright red tape. It was partially hidden underneath the snow. But it turned out it stretched for nearly one half mile, east to west.

It didn't take long to figure out this strip of red tape was actually part of what would have been a huge cross. The second column had been carrying the second half mile of fabric—and the horses had been used to pull the huge wad of tape across the frozen waste—and provide food for the troops.

But two long strips of plastic in the middle of the ice and snow? Why?

But Hunter knew exactly what was going on.

Two strips, crossed. Bright red against the white terrain, to be hidden under the snow until the last possible moment?

"It's a target," Hunter told them. "A cross, to be hit. A huge aiming point."

Payne and Zoltan just looked at Hunter then at each other.

"A target?" Payne said, yelling to be heard against the howling wind. "A half mile long? Why that big?"

Hunter felt the blood freeze inside his veins again. Then his body started vibrating.

"Because," he said, "whatever is coming down on this thing is big too . . ."

Chapter 26

Every airplane at Dreamland was either out on the runway or taxiing up to it by the time the Beater made it back to base.

Hunter was surprised at the number of aircraft. Not just the several dozen Mustang fighters, but a couple huge Boxcar cargo jets that had been hiding somewhere in the hangars way out back.

In all, there was at least 65 airplanes waiting to take off; even then some would probably be left behind.

They were bugging out. Payne had ordered it, via radio from the Beater. Every base around the Circle was evacuating. And doing so as quickly as possible.

There was no doubt in Hunter's mind that some kind of German weapons strike was coming. The partially constructed big X in the snow had been the bull's-eye—and the German military had gone to great lengths, and wasted some valuable troops, in its attempt to set it up.

It was also obviously an aiming point, and one whose location was not just a guess in the wind. If the point was equidistant from all the Circle bases, the middle of the necklace as it were, that meant to Hunter that something

big was coming—something that could hit in the middle
of nowhere and wipe out 12 airfields with its 20-mile radius.

Something very big . . .

Payne needed no convincing of this. That's why he sent
out a general order to all active bases to pack up everyone
and everything they could and get airborne. And do it all
in 45 minutes.

This was the shrinking time frame Hunter had figured
out on the ride back. He reached this number by back-
guessing when the Germans expected the second load of
men and red tape to arrive at the target site if their plane
hadn't been shot down.

In many ways it would have been better had they discovered the big X without shooting down the seajet. That way
they would have had the window of opportunity to work
with as the Germans were attaching the fourth arm of the
X.

But now, once the Germans realized their plane was
gone, and their intentions somewhat uncovered, they
would probably accelerate their plans and send what ever
they were going to send anyway, hoping the partially-
constructed cross would suffice as the aiming point.

These thoughts and his gut were telling Hunter they
had no time to lose, no time to sit around and figure out
what to do and when.

Something big was coming, there wasn't really much
they could do about it and so the prudent thing was to
get the hell out—damn quick.

The Beater dropped them in front of the Dreamland
ops building then its crew hurried back to Base Two to
gather its own stuff, pick up some comrades, and bug out.

The Air Guards scrambled to grab a few personal items
and then ran out to one of the big Flying Boxcars waiting
out on the runway.

Meanwhile Hunter and Payne hurried into the ops building and began unloading as many of secret documents
they could stuff into a duffle bag. Then Payne grabbed
pictures of his wife and kids, took his baseball glove and

ball and his last bottle of scotch, and ran back out again.
By the book to the end, he actually locked the door behind
him as he left.

People were running all over the base now, most of them
heading out to the waiting Boxcars. Calls had gone down
to Atlantic Wartime Command about the bug out, but
there was no indication they'd been decoded and read as
yet—and the people on the active Circle bases had no
time to hang around and wait for the official order to
evacuate.

Even details of where everyone was going hadn't been
worked out. The main thing was for everyone to get into
the air and as far away from the Circle as possible. Just
where to put down would have to be divined later.

Hunter had barely the clothes on his back to his name,
so there was no packing for him. He'd hailed a big jeepster
and loaded Payne and the secret documents into it. Zoltan
appeared and Hunter stuffed him inside the jeep as well,
along with Colonel Crabb and his eight lovelies. Each one
was crying and hugged Hunter before loading into the
vehicle.

Meanwhile the first of the squadron fighters was taking
off. The roar of their combined engines made it nearly
impossible to talk. One of them screamed right overhead,
wagging its wings as it did so. Hunter knew it was Sarah,
waving down to him. He felt a chill go through him. He
really liked her. But when would he see her again, if ever?

He got the last of Crabb's girls loaded into the jeepster
and then told the driver to head directly for the front of
the big Boxcar. They could all get access to the plane by
the forward cargo door.

Just as the driver was about to speed off, Payne reached
out and grabbed Hunter by the arm.

"What are you doing? Get in!"

Hunter just shook his head. "I'll catch up with you,"
he said hastily.

"Catch up with us?" Payne said, not getting it yet. *"How?"*

Zoltan was catching on.

"Where are you going?" he asked Hunter.

Hunter looked down the long line of open hangars.

"I'm not sure yet," he said.

With that he tapped the driver on the shoulder and the guy finally took off.

The last Hunter saw of Payne and Zoltan were their astonished faces in the rear window of the jeepster as it drove away.

Hunter now had 20 minutes.

He ran to the meteorologist's station and quickly studied as many weather charts detailing local conditions as possible. He got as much information as he could absorb in about three minutes.

Then he ran back out to the street.

Dreamland was really like a ghost town now. The last plane was just leaving. Its engines whined unbearably as it ascended into the frigid clouds. After that, there was nothing but the wind.

It was closing in on 15 minutes to go. Hunter grabbed an abandoned snow cycle and began screeching up and down the base's roadways, between the hangars, looking in each one.

It was lucky of course that just about every hangar door was open. The problem was just about all the hangars were empty. Hunter was beginning to wonder whether his gut had finally sent him the wrong message—and stranded him here just as the sky was about to cave in.

And that's when he found it.

He'd always suspected that some of the stuff kept in the hangars out back of Dreamland was top secret. Outrageous prototypes sent north to be tested in the harsh conditions and left to rust once the war started going against the Americans.

But this thing . . . what was it?

Hunter found it in a hangar whose doors had not been open. He just felt compelled to screech to a halt in front of a black air barn at the very rear of the airbase. There were no less than five locks on the front door—a good sign of a top secret place. There was a window though and three bullets from his massive survival gun took care of it forthwith. He crawled inside and found the strange aircraft.

It was sleek, it was small—and it had no rear end.

Its fuselage was cut off just a few feet from the end of the canopy. Here was a powerful pusher-type turbo-prop. The wings were swept way back. The nose was very long and sleek.

Hunter inspected the strange airplane anxiously. Maybe this was pushing the plot envelope a little; he had less than 10 minutes to get the hell out of here. Would he, could he, really expect to do so in a strange, rather bizarre looking aircraft, one that he had no idea how to fly, or even if it was airworthy? Or if it had gas in it—or any fuel around for him to load in, which alone would take more time than he had left on the ground.

And even if he was somehow able to get airborne, what he intended to do—what his gut was telling him to do— would require some weaponry.

This airplane was obviously a test model of some kind. The proper maintenance would call for it to have empty fuel tanks if it was in storage, and few test planes carried weapons.

But he checked its gas tanks and for some absolutely unknown reason, they were full. And then he checked for guns, and sure enough the plane was packing four cannons, two on each wing, an outrageous set of armament for a test platform, but installed nevertheless. Even more incredible, the guns were loaded and ready.

Hunter had no time to question the twists and turns which brought him here, to this place, and to the airplane that was exactly what he needed. He just whipped open the hangar doors, climbed into the airplane, and did a quick check of the instruments. They looked like they belonged in an alien spaceship. But he pushed the right buttons and threw the right levers and the engine started up, true and burning fine, on the first try.

He popped the brakes and the strange airplane screeched out of the hangar and into the wind and snow. Hunter fought the foot pedals and finessed the brakes to keep the thing pointing straight while taxiing as fast as he could go.

Meanwhile he was looking over the instrument panel. It was so old—or new, or whatever the word was that he needed to describe things in this place—that the panel-backing was made of highly polished wood, like that found in a luxury car. The seat was lambswool, the knobs and buttons all polished chrome. There was even a little name plate at the bottom. It read: XF-55/4, "SuperAscender" manufactured by Curtiss-Wright/McDonnell-Douglas company.

Hunter's head was filling with so much stuff now, it was getting hard to think straight. But the odd airplane's name rang another minor chord in his blocked memory bank. This airplane looked like a mutated combination of a World War II test plane and a funny-looking but venerable jet fighter the design of which he could just barely frame in his head. Funny nose, tail wings that pointed down while the wingtips pointed up. As if someone had closed the hangar doors on it. It was big. Fast, named after a jungle animal. The Rhino? Or was it called a Phantom? Or both? But why would an airplane share two names like that?

Hunter didn't have time to puzzle it out—he was approaching the main runway and now all his thoughts had to concentrate on the matter at hand.

If some kind of German weapons strike *was* coming, it was simply against his nature to just leave and not attempt to do anything about it. That's why he'd stayed behind, that's why he was lucky—so incredibly lucky—to find this airplane, gassed and armed to the teeth.

If something was incoming, Hunter intended to meet it—head-on if necessary. Why? Because the sad fact was this: while everyone at Dreamland might have been able to get out, there were still seven other active bases in the Circle and all of them were bigger, had more planes, and more people. The chances of all of them getting off the ground in time was small. By trying to affect the enemy's incoming, even just a little, Hunter believed he might be able to save some lives.

So these were his thoughts as he brought the Super Ascender out to the runway and ran up the engine. It was snowing hard of course, but he was able to get one last look at this place, the place that had been his home for what seemed like a century or so. The polar camo buildings, the rows of hangars and barracks, the blowing snow, the ice and the OC.

Damn, he surprised himself by thinking, he was actually going to miss the place.

He gunned the engine and felt the odd little fighter push its way down the runway. He reached takeoff speed in an astounding five seconds—the plane was incredibly fast for a turboprop. He yanked back on the control column and up he went. Nearly straight up and at an amazing speed.

"Super Ascender?" Hunter thought. "The perfect name . . ."

It was now 1300 hours.

A huge storm was brewing up north. The winds and the snow and ice were heading south like a tidal wave.

The Super Ascender reached 45,000 feet in less than 90 seconds, without losing its breath. Hunter was amazed at the airplane's technology, despite the fact it looked in many ways like an antique.

Still the words "Phantom" and "Rhino" kept going through his mind, though he would never be quite sure why. Not for a long time, anyway.

He passed through 50-angels, and the tiny little fighter still wanted to climb some more. Trouble was, Hunter had had so little time, and had moved so high so fast, he was still figuring out oxygen levels, the heating systems, and other settings. So he finally leveled out, did some yard work, then came back to the matter at hand.

The huge storm over his left shoulder looked like it was about to devour him at any moment—yet it was still 200 miles away. On the southern horizon, the bare wisp of smoke rising from enemy territory. He could just barely make it out, sooty and black against the bluish white clouds far, far away.

He turned the Ascender over and looked below. He could see planes taking off from the handful of Circle bases remaining. How much longer would it take them? Five more minutes? Five more hours? He didn't know. This made his mission even more difficult. What to do? He would begin a square holding pattern, loitering over the island, waiting for what he was certain would come at any moment.

But then a very dampening thought hit him: how foolish was this? How could he expect to find something if he didn't even know what he was looking for? In all this sky? With the perpetual gloom of dusk and a gigantic storm just over his shoulder?

Again, he didn't know—but he was certain that he was supposed to be in this place, at this time. His consciousness wouldn't allow him to be anywhere else, and from that perspective, he knew he was doing the right thing.

But what tidal wave of emotion inside him could control his very being so much? Every day since being picked up in the Atlantic he had learned just a little bit more about who he was before he came to this place. What was a rather more frightening thought—frightening in the sense of trying to know the unknown—was *what* was he before all this? He'd seen no evidence that other men he'd met along the way had these forces twisting, turning, pushing them in all directions at once. Who was he? That answer was getting simpler everyday. What was he? That was still locked in black, still way too deep in the back of his skull.

And just as he was thinking these thoughts—and wondering if there was any chance in a zillion that he really was an angel—his body began vibrating with unbelievable intensity. His breath caught in his throat—the sensation had startled him so.

"Jeesuzz—what is this?" he whispered, knowing trouble was on the way.

He got his answer just two seconds later.

It was a missile. Nose cone, first stage, second stage, steering fins, long fiery trail of exhaust coming from its tail.

It was way up there, probably at 100,000 feet or more, but it was coming down too, and an incredible rate of speed.

This thing was simply colossal, and its true size still was not apparent because it was growing bigger with each blink of the eye.

Hunter guessed correctly that it was at least as tall as the Empire State Building—the newer, *taller* one—and at least the same girth. He could only stare at it for what seemed to be the longest time, as if he was standing still and it was moving at twice the speed of sound.

Pictures flashed through his head and before his eyes. A V-2 rocket, he believed, was used in his version of World War II. This thing looked like that. But there was also something called a Saturn 5 rocket that was stuck in his memory banks too. Much larger, much more powerful than the V-2—but both had something in common. What was it?

Had they been designed by the same man maybe?

Hunter had no idea, but something in his brain was telling him that this thing coming right for him, this enormous stick of metal and fuel and fire, and no doubt high explosives in its nosecone, looked like both a V-2 *and* a Saturn-5. Just a dozen or so times bigger.

And now the reason for the big X became very clear. This giant had a TV camera in its nose, Hunter was sure, and the people controlling it back in Germany were steering it to its target—and looking for the X, or at least a partially complete one.

Had they had more time they could have dug out the miles of red tape from the ice—but Hunter knew it was useless to worry about that now. The flying monster would find the ragged target and if the people steering it were good and if something this big, and moving this fast was at all accurate, it would slam into the middle of the Circle within the next two minutes. And there really wasn't much Hunter or anyone else could do about it.

But that didn't mean he wasn't going to try.

He pushed his throttle forward, his steering yoke back and he was soon climbing again. Lining up the nose of the Ascender with the nose of the approaching giant, he test fired his cannons and was amazed at the kick as all four fired at once. And unlike his old Mustang-5's nose mounted noisemaker, these cannons were lively, accurate, responsive.

The missile was now passing down through 85,000 feet just as Hunter was climbing through 60-angels. He knew he really only had once chance: that was to try and hit the TV camera in the monster's nose and maybe affect its impact point—but at the same time realized this was just a crazy notion. The missile was coming down and the unfinished big X was just a matter of convenience now for the unseen controllers.

Still, as Hunter closed to within 5000 feet of the missile he pressed the firing button for all four cannons and a long stream of fiery sparks came pouring out of his gun ports. The stream filled the empty sky between him and the missile but only for a few seconds and not to much good.

But at least he'd accomplished one thing: whoever was controlling the big missile had undoubtedly seen him. Seen the defiance in his desperate attack.

So Hunter just kept firing and firing and thinking that knocking done the big seajet had been a breeze compared to this impossible task. Plus, he knew that in a million to one shot he actually hit something in the nose cone that ignited it, he and the missile would be blown in a million different directions—and his stay in this strange place would be a very short one.

And just as that thought was processing through his head, something very strange happened. He felt his hand go up to his left breast pocket, and pat it, as if his brain expected something to be in there, some kind of good-luck symbol. But his pocket was empty, just as the German's seajet pilot's had been.

His hand tried again, patted his heart three times, like some unseen force was moving it. This was a very frightening thing for him—more frightening than thousands of tons of explosive and missile bearing down on him.

An instant later, his guns ran out. The missile was no more than a half mile away now and he fought a sudden urge just to ride the little plane right into it—knowing in the same breath that it would be as futile as a gnat trying to stop an eagle.

So, in a final defiant act, he turned off right in front of the rocket and raised his middle finger—a last message to the evil hands controlling it. Then he finally banked hard and got the hell out of the way.

As far as Hunter could tell, the huge missile hit the partially completed X dead center.

The blast was yellow at first, quickly growing into an orange ball and then finally a brilliant balloon of blood-red crimson. It lit up the perpetual dusk for hundreds of miles around; its brilliant colors reflected off the snow and ice, intensifying its frightening beauty.

Hunter had put the Super Ascender on its tail and had climbed to escape the effects of the huge blast, but still, even at 55-angels, the shock waves buffeted the small plane for one long, terrifying minute. They were strong enough to send him toppling, head over tail, while still going straight up! He lost all power, lost his engine feed, lost all control. But he stayed conscious, knowing this tempest had to be a temporary one.

And finally, the world outside did calm down and Hunter regained control of his airplane. He leveled off, turned over, and looked down at what was once the island that held the Circle of 12 American air bases and saw that nothing was left. It was crater—melted snow, smoking chunks of ice, the seawater already pouring in.

In less than 60 seconds, the landscape had completely changed. Where just an hour before there were hundreds of planes and thousands of men and miles of runways and buildings and life was now little more than a new polar lake.

Hunter's heart fell to his feet. His toes became so numb, he couldn't work the airplane's pedals. The same was true for his fingers and the control stick.

There one minute, gone the next. Did everyone get out in time?

How would he ever know?

He turned the Ascender over again and pointed the nose south. He scanned the sky in all directions and saw nothing but cold dark clouds and the huge plume of smoke still rising from the titanic blast. He went through all the channels on the plane's rudimentary radio and heard nothing but static.

Then the question flashed through his mind.

"What now?"

He throttled back to 300 knots—he'd have to watch his fuel; it was dangerously low and the Ascender held only about one-third the gas the Mustang-5 had lugged around. And a lot of that had been burned up trying to get altitude on the big missile.

So now there was the possibility that he would find no place to land—and yet the circumstance didn't frighten him in the least. At that moment, all he could think about was how an entity like the Circle could simply be vaporized like that. Add the possibility that hundreds, maybe thousands of men he'd come to admire greatly were no longer alive . . . well, the idea of just running out of fuel wasn't that bad. Maybe this was the way it was supposed to end . . .

But then again, maybe not.

His radio crackled to life just a few seconds later.

"Dreamland One, do you read?"

The call surprised Hunter so much he began fumbling with the odd dials and levers, trying to find the way to respond.

"Dreamland One? Are you out there?"

Hunter finally found the send button and keyed the old fashioned hand-held microphone.

"Dreamland One here," Hunter replied.

"Dreamland, switch to course one-seven-three," the ghostly voice told him. "Maintain 20,000 feet for 25 minutes and await further instructions."

Hunter did a quick calculation as to where this course would bring him. It took him just a few seconds to realize that it would carry him about 150 miles out into the North Atlantic.

He rogered the call and repeated the instructions back to the mysterious dispatcher.

"And then what?" he asked the echoing voice.

But he got no reply.

The radio had gone dead.

Part Three
Flood

Chapter 27

The *USS Cape Cod* rose like a phantom city out of the mists of the sea.

It was a megacarrier, one of the last built by the American Shipworks Corporation. It was a mile long and almost a quarter of a mile high. Its deck was more than 2000 feet wide. Its crew numbered 23,000, not counting some recent unexpected arrivals.

The aircraft carrier was so immense, it was not unusual to have two entirely different weather conditions at either end. There were men who served on her who had never seen topside, never mind walk the deck. The steam used by the ship's 24 catapults in one day could power a small city for two years.

Seeing this floating monster from 20,000 feet was an exercise in optical illusion, as Hawk Hunter soon found out.

Somewhere back in his past he must have landed on aircraft carriers before—but never anything near this big. Even from four miles up, the ship was so imposing, it seemed only five or six hundred feet away. Hunter felt like he could reach out and touch the damn thing.

And the closer he got, the bigger it became. Until it finally filled his vision to nightmarish proportions.

You could never pull this thing with tugboats, he thought, oddly, not knowing why. *Not in a million years . . .*

He'd had no problem finding the ship. How could he? The ship was hard to miss, plus the instructions given to him over the radio carried him here directly. And now, flying over it, his heart brightened. He could see the deck was actually crowded—not with naval attack and fighter planes—but with B-24/52s, B-17/36s, Mustang-5s, Beaters, and the giant Flying Boxcars. It was all the airplanes from the Circle.

Somehow the Navy had come to the rescue!

The decks were so crowded, in fact, that Hunter had to fly by a second time, looking for a place to land. The ship *was* like a floating airport, but every runway seemed too stacked to set down on. Finally he found an unoccupied strip of deck on the large overhang island; it stretched diagonally for about 750 feet or so. A bright green landing globe was blinking furiously at one end of this strip. With his radio out, he assumed this was the only way the people on the ship could tell him where to land.

He went around again, then lowered his gear, put down his flaps, held his breath, and began a final approach. There were no arresting hooks on the Ascender, no trap wire on the deck would be able to catch his bottom to capture it. He would have to use the entire length of landing strip and his brakes to bring it in safely.

He dropped to 100 feet above the deck. He fought off a stiff crosswind, trying at the same time to compensate for the huge ship's roll. At 50 feet high and 200 out, he went full flaps and nudged the stick down. Twenty feet high, 75 feet out. The ship lurched up, Hunter remained steady. Fifteen high, 50 feet out—the ship went down again, but Hunter stayed glued to the stick. Ten high, 20 feet out. There were deckhands in orange uniforms with hand paddles frantically waving at him, but he had to

ignore them now. Five high, 10 out. Two high, five out . . .
zero, zero . . . *Wham!*

The next thing he knew, he was skidding along the slick,
windswept deck. He immediately killed the engine and hit
the brakes; there would be no bolter here. He was either
going to get down or go over the side. He pushed the
brakes all the way to the floor; they locked and held firm.
Then came much screeching, and lots of burnt rubber
and smoke. But finally the little Super Ascender slid to a
stop just 10 feet from the other side of the deck.

He'd made it.

There was a small crowd around the plane by the time
he popped the canopy. Many had familiar faces. Up front,
the maintenance guys from Dreamland, including his old
pals Dopey, Sneezy, and Sleepy, led a round of applause
for his slick landing. Members of the old 999th and even
the chicken-hearted 13th were on hand and applauding
too. Only later would Hunter find out the carrier's landing
officers had actually been waving him off and trying to tell
him to wait until a larger space of deck could be opened
up.

Waiting at the bottom of the access ladder were Payne,
Zoltan, and Colonel Crabb. They yanked him off the steps
and nearly squeezed him to death with bear hugs. Crabb's
dancing beauties were also on hand, looking lovely in lowly
sailor blues. They squealed when the saw Hunter and
pushed the three men aside to smother him with kisses.

But Hunter was at a loss as to what all the celebrating
was about. He didn't deter the German missile from oblit-
erating the Circle. He really didn't do anything but put
his own life in grave danger, and all for nothing, as it
turned out.

So why was he being treated as a hero?

It was Zoltan who read his mind, of course.

"Because everyone got out," he told Hunter. "No one
was left behind back at the Circle. No one. They owe it all
to you, Hawk. They've already flashed word about this back
to the states. In fact, you're famous back home already."

Hunter actually laughed at the sound of that word.

"Famous? Me?" he said, shaking his head. "I don't think so."

A tractor appeared and pulled the Super Ascender to a less crowded part of the very crowded deck. Then Payne, Zoltan, and Crabb brought Hunter down to one of the carrier's 33 mess halls. The assembled sailors gave him a standing ovation when he walked in; there had to be 2000 of them at least. One of the mess officers brought him a huge bowl of vegetable soup, a loaf of bread, and a pot of coffee. Then he asked Hunter for an autograph.

The food looked great and smelled great. Hunter felt like he hadn't eaten in years. But no sooner had he grabbed his spoon than the mess hall came to another standstill. The thousands of sailors jumped to attention. Through the door walked a rugged yet regal officer wearing a smart white uniform, He was the captain of the *USS Cape Cod*. His name was Jack Norton.

He walked over to Hunter's table, and Hunter managed a salute. But clearly, it was the aircraft carrier's CO that was impressed. He too greeted Hunter as if he were some sort of hero. Then he asked permission to sit with him. Embarrassed, Hunter immediately said yes.

"You prevented another Dunkirk," Captain Norton told him, a cup of coffee appearing in front of him. "That's what they're saying back in the states."

Hunter's head was spinning. How could that be? The evacuation of the Circle bases had happened less than two hours ago.

"How could I become famous so quickly?" he finally asked.

The answer was simple, Norton explained. For the past week, the aggressive wartime media back in the states had been covering the firebombing missions to Germany—and featuring Hunter as the mastermind behind them. The American people, starved for a hero in dark times, now had one. His picture was on the front of every news-paper, on every TV news broadcast, and on the lips of just about every American citizen. So the answer to his question was what Zoltan had said earlier: He was famous already.

Norton motioned to an aide who produced a Boomer, the combination shortwave radio, TV, film-player, and music box that everyone in this strange world seemed to own. He switched the TV to a U.S. world-beam station. Sure enough, there was a story about the attacks on Germany, featuring file clips of the huge B-17/36s and B-24/52s taking off, burning German cities, and a shaky film of Hunter climbing into his Mustang-5 and taxiing away in the snow. Just when the footage was taken, he had no idea.

"And they haven't even heard all the details about the evacuation of the Circle Bases yet," Norton told him. "Wait until that story hits. There will be books. Movies. Talk shows. They're talking Medal of Honor for you already."

Hunter just looked across the table at Payne, Zoltan, and Crabb. All three were grinning and shrugging at the same time.

"That's showbiz," Crabb spoke for all.

They ate lunch, Hunter stuffing himself with two bowls of soup and two loaves of bread. Norton asked him for details about the final minutes of the Circle bases, and Hunter happily supplied everything he wanted to know.

When he'd finished eating, the CO told Hunter he'd been assigned an officer's berth in a very good part of the ship. Then he surprised him again by telling him a visitor was already waiting for him there.

Again, Hunter was stumped. How could he have a visitor on the carrier? Who would have expected him to be here? Less than three hours ago it seemed like he'd be at Dream-land forever.

He voiced this to the captain, who just shrugged.

"Don't bother even thinking about it," he said. "These things just happen."

And after taking a moment to consider this, Hunter decided it was good advice. Maybe it *was* best that he stop trying to figure out every strange twist and turn that seemed to be routine parts of daily life here in this new place. Really—why would a prototype model of the Super-Ascender be fully gassed and armed and waiting for him at the exact moment he needed it? Why would he suddenly stumble upon 50,000 tons of firebombs, again just when they were needed? There were no coincidences in this place, he had to keep reminding himself of that. But if that was the case, then didn't that make every strange thing that *did* happen to him here even more mysterious?

Don't think about it . . .

They left the mess and Payne pointed him in the general direction of his berth. They made plans to link up later; the air exec now had to confab with the ship's officers about what they would do next. But that was another strange thing. The massive aircraft carrier had actually been heading for Iceland when the refugees from the Circle dropped on board. When the bug out occurred, it too had been in the right place at the right time.

Before they parted company, Payne slipped a small flask into Hunter's hand.

"It's the last of my scotch," he told Hunter. "I figured you deserve a sip or two. Just don't let the swabbies catch you with it."

Hunter thanked him and headed for his assigned berth. It was on 16th deck, just about midships. A nice part of the city. He checked a series of maps along the way and he didn't get lost at all. Still, it took him nearly a half hour of trudging down the crowded passageways to reach the place.

By that time he'd come to realize that he hadn't slept more than three hours in one time in nearly two weeks. What was the likelihood that now, as he really didn't have anything to do in the near future, he'd be able to sleep for about 24 uninterrupted hours and recharge?

Less than zero, as it turned out.

* * *

He finally made it to his berth. And yes, someone was waiting there for him.

Someone very unexpected . . .

It was Captain Pegg. The elderly officer who had sprung him from jail.

"Hey, Pops," Hunter said. "What the hell are *you* doing here?"

"Following orders," the man answered wearily.

Hunter did a quick recce of the cabin. It was very tiny, ironic for such a big boat. He had a bunk, a chair, a desk, a boomer, and a small sink. His jail cell had been bigger.

He collapsed onto the bunk, his weary bones sinking deep into the one-inch mattress.

"Orders, eh?" he asked Pegg, who was slouched in the chair across from him. "And they are?"

"I have a package to deliver to you," Pegg said.

"From your bosses, I assume?"

The old man just nodded. He looked a little ill.

"Rough trip out?" Hunter asked him, surmising the man's distress came from a bumpy carrier landing.

"The roughest," the old timer confessed. "I'm fifty-six years in the Air Corps. I never wanted to get anywhere near one of these damn things. They're too big! But when I'm called on, I serve. I have since 1942."

Hunter had to admit some grudging respect for the man. Anyone who would give more than a half century of service to his country—and not get above the rank of captain—he had to feel for.

Hunter looked around the cabin again. "This place reminds me of my suite back in Sing Sing," he commented.

Pegg shifted in his seat.

"I'll bet there've been times lately that you wished you were back there," he told Hunter.

"More than I can count," Hunter replied.

Next to the sink was a coffee machine. Hunter reached

over, filled it with water, dumped in a pack of grounds, and set it brewing.

Then he located two cracked coffee cups.

"You take it black, Pops?" he asked the old man.

"If I have to," he replied.

The machine poured out two black coffees just five seconds later. Hunter gave one to the elderly officer. Then he retrieved Payne's flask from his pocket and gave them both a splash. Pegg was surprised, but thankful.

Finally Hunter sat back down.

"OK, pal," he said to the man. "Let's have it."

Pegg took a sealed envelope from his coat and passed it to Hunter.

"This is an animated mission film containing details for a very secret mission," he said sipping his coffee noisily. "It's so secret, you can't open it until I leave."

Hunter shook the envelope as if this would reveal some of the secrets inside.

"What do you know about it?" he asked Pegg.

The old guy just smiled and sipped his coffee again.

"Nothing," he replied.

"Absolutely nothing?" Hunter pressed him. "Or just officially nothing?"

Pegg smiled again, and this time the grin stayed on his face.

"Every soldier hears rumors," he said with a shrug. "Especially where I work."

Hunter settled back, put the envelope to his forehead, and said: "Tell me the best one you know."

Pegg pulled out a pack of Golden Luckies, and offered one to Hunter, who declined. He lit one up for himself.

"Well, it's no secret the war is still going very badly for us," he said soberly. "Losing the Circle is a big blow, but not exactly an unanticipated one. Still, there are some very ominous things being whispered about . . ."

"Like what?" Hunter asked.

"Like the Germans being ready to invade the U.S.,"

Pegg said starkly. "Like we won't be able to stop them if they ever make it off the beaches."

Hunter just stared back at him and let this information sink in. It really wasn't that much of a surprise. They'd bombed Germany almost every day for three weeks and set half of the Reich on fire. But even with the success of those missions, it was still not enough to win the war or even turn the tide back in their favor. And now with the Circle bases gone, hitting Germany would be that much tougher.

Or so Hunter thought.

"So where do I fit in?" Hunter asked him.

The officer pointed to the envelope.

"That's over my head," he replied. "And probably over the heads of ninety-nine percent of the people running this war. All I know is that mission film came from the highest level of the intelligence community."

"The same guys that locked me up?" Hunter said with some disgust. "What's their problem now? They upset that I just got out of the last hellhole by the skin of my teeth?"

"They're asking you to serve," Pegg told him. "It's your country, isn't it?"

Hunter started to say something, but stopped. Was it his country? Or not?

"I don't know," he finally murmured. "Sometimes I think it is; other times I'm not so sure."

Pegg thought about this for a moment, then finished his coffee with one big slurp.

"You know what your problem is?" he asked Hunter out of the blue.

Hunter just shrugged.

"No, you tell me," he said.

The old guy got up and put on his coat.

"You think too much," he said. *"Way* too much."

With that, he saluted and went out the door.

*   *   *

Hunter made himself another coffee and opened the envelope. Inside was a small film reel about the size of a cigarette pack. He turned on the Boomer, inserted the reel and hit play.

Then he sat back and watched what America wanted him to do next.

It was actually quite simple.

A big hit had to be laid on Germany. Something bigger, more destructive than a month of firebombing. This time another element would be used. Several years back, the Germans had consolidated all of their dams in the Ruhr Valley into one gigantic hydroelectric plant, the Merne-Sorpa Dam. They had diverted no less than five major rivers and emptied 16 lakes into one massive body of water, and now that water, running through the monstrous hydro-electric turbines of Merne-Sorpa, supplied Germany as well as parts of Occupied Holland, Belgium, and France with nearly 75 percent of their electrical power.

If that dam could be knocked out, then the German war effort would grind to a halt—theoretically, at least.

And if the rumors Pegg told him were true, then blowing the dam would at least delay any U.S. invasion plans.

But a dam, especially one this immense, could not be taken down with firebombs, or even conventional iron bombs, as the mission film clearly pointed out with a car-toonish sequence showing B-17/36s slamming bombs into the side of the dam—with no effect.

The plan that had been formulated went like this: the Merne-Sorpa could be breached only if at least 20 tons of high explosives were detonated on its face all at once. In other words, all in one big bomb. But there were no 20-ton bombs, not even in this bigger-is-better world. How-ever, one B-17/36 could carry 20 tons of high explosives. If such an airplane could be flown into the dam face, and the HE detonated, the dam would be breached, and the Reich's extensive hydro-power capability destroyed.

No one was suggesting a suicide mission here—not a typical one anyway. The idea was to have a drone bomber packed with HE flown into the dam by radio control. But the aircraft would have to hit the dam wall at an exact point in order to crack it and kill the power-making ability. To hit this exact point with an immense drone ship meant a homing device would have to be fitted on the dam face, one that would heat up and thus guide a radi-seeker in the nose of the bomber. Then, all that would be needed would be for someone who knew what they were doing to get control of the airplane by radio, get its nose lined up with the heating ring and wham! The plane would hit the homing device and explode, the dam would splinter, and the lights would go out all over Germany.

The plan mentioned diversionary bombing raids all over western Germany to cover the dam-busting mission. Where would the planes needed for this part of the plan take off from? From the *Cape Cod* and four other megacarriers that were secretly steaming into the North Atlantic. Now this was a dangerous piece of business, especially since the Germans had already shown what their DG-42 missile could do, both on the Circle and on Paris. But one last bit of U.S. military secret technology made such a risky operation somewhat less so. The Navy had come up with a way to artificially cloak a ship, not electronically, but by creating artificial fog banks, ones that could reach nearly a mile in width and height. One thing about the DG-42, it couldn't hit what it couldn't see. The fog would keep the five mega-carriers somewhat elusive, at least until they could launch and recover the week's worth of diversionary and follow-up bombing raids.

And that was the strange thing about this strange plan. It was obvious to Hunter that it had been in the works for a while. Had he not found himself aboard the carrier this way, he would have been spirited out of Dreamland and briefed very soon anyway. So the fact that the *USS Cape Cod* was nearby when the Circle was iced had simply been . . . well, a "harmonious" event.

The mission tape ended with some projected weather forecasts, estimated mission time frames, and other malarkey. Then, surprisingly, the authors of this wild idea signed their names to the plan. And for the first time, Hunter found out who was behind it all. It was America's premier intelligence agency, an outfit called the OSS.

Their final conclusion was this: Someone had to get to the dam, set up the heat ring, then direct the drone ship via radio into the target, all while a series of massive fire-bombing raids were taking place on a dozen cities nearby.

The person to do this would need good infiltration skills, piloting ability, and the sense to keep his mouth shut should they get caught.

According to the OSS planners, that person was Hunter.

After leaving Hunter's berth, Captain Pegg headed for a place called the Third Forward Officers' Mess Portside.

The journey took him nearly 45 minutes. Once there, he got another cup of coffee and then walked over to a table located in the far corner.

A man was waiting for him. He was dressed like a Navy Commander, but Pegg knew he was not a naval officer.

"How did it go?" the man asked him.

Pegg just shrugged.

"OK," he replied. "I gave him the clip. I'm sure he's watching it now."

"Do you think he's up to it?"

Pegg noisily slurped his coffee. "Well, he seems to be the adventurous type. He's patriotic too, I think. I have a good feeling about it."

The man poured a cup of coffee for himself.

"Good," he said. "Then maybe the whole idea to come up here was not such a waste."

Pegg sat forward a bit and then spoke again. "May I ask you a question? Why don't you just brief him yourself? I mean, after all that's happened . . ."

The man drained his cup of coffee and then sat back in thought.

"I'm not sure," the man known as Agent Y finally

replied. "But I guess there will be time for that soon enough."

Hunter spent the rest of the day watching the mission film over and over again. Occasionally, he would cheat and switch the Boomer over to world-beam TV broadcasts. Just about every time he saw some kind of reference to the German fire-bombing campaign and his part in it. They kept showing the same film of him climbing into his jet over and over again. Even he got sick of it after a while.

Finally, after watching the mission film 10 times and thinking he knew all that was expected of him, he showered, shaved, climbed into a clean set of overalls, and met up with Zoltan, Payne, and Crabb in the Second Aft Officers' Mess Starboard.

They spent the evening eating, drinking coffee, signing autographs, and talking about the "good times" back at Dreamland base. It seemed more like a dream to them now.

For the time being all three would be staying on the *Cape Cod*. The four other megacarriers would be in position by morning, each one carrying a huge contingent of Air Corps bombers. These planes—and the very raw pilots who would be flying them—would continue the firebombing campaign against Germany. These attacks would continue for seven days. After that, it was anyone's guess what would happen. But because the trio had been exposed to parts of this secret mission, they were all staying put.

Midnight arrived and it was time for Hunter to catch some sleep. He'd just spent the longest of days and he had to be out on the deck at 0600 hours to begin his mission. If the others knew anything about the dam-busting aspect of the plan, they didn't let on. But the three sensed Hunter was going somewhere soon and that it was important.

So when he got up to leave, each man shook his hand warmly.

"Good luck." Crabb told him, "My girls and I are working out a dance interpretation of all this, you know. I guarantee it will be very entertaining."

Hunter just shook his head. "Some things maybe I don't want to know about."

Zoltan was next. "Be safe, my friend," he told Hunter. "And remember, don't think too much. It's bad for you."

"I promise," Hunter said.

Then came Payne. Hunter felt bad for the officer because he deserved as much credit for the firebombing campaign of Germany as Hunter did, maybe even more. Yet the unassuming major didn't seem bothered by it at all. He'd fulfilled his promise to himself. He'd gotten his men out of Dreamland alive and in one piece, what was left of them anyway. Therefore he was very much at peace with himself.

"We'll see you soon, Hawk," he told Hunter simply. "The best of luck."

Hunter thanked them all again, left the mess, and began the long walk back to his berth. Three thoughts were running through his head: *Don't think. Do the mission. Everything else will be sorted out in time.*

But at the end of the trek, as he neared his berth, his body began vibrating. He stopped just two feet from his door and examined the feeling. This was not an enemy-approaching vibe, thank God for that. No, these shakes were telling him something else. Maybe something was waiting for him on the other side of the cabin door.

He opened the hatch and found the place was dark except for the light from a single candle. And someone *was* waiting for him. A sultry shadow reclining on his bunk. It was definitely *not* Pegg, thank the cosmos.

Just the opposite, in fact.

Clad in just a T-shirt, and a short one at that, was Sarah.

Hunter stepped in and closed the door.

"Is this a briefing, Captain James?"

Sarah smiled. "An off-the-record one. I've been hearing some funny stories about you."

Hunter sat down in the chair next to the bunk. She looked so beautiful he couldn't take his eyes off her.

"Funny as in ha-ha?" he asked.

"Not exactly," she replied.

She reached out to him and he took her hand. The next thing he knew, he was in the bunk with her. Her body felt incredibly warm. Warmer than his thermal flight suit. Warmer than the sun itself. Hunter couldn't remember ever feeling so warm. After swimming in the Atlantic, after sitting in his prison cell, after a hellish month in Iceland, he never thought he'd be this warm again.

"You know what I heard?" she whispered in his ear.

"Tell me . . ."

"I heard you're from another planet or something."

Hunter laughed. "I think the 'or something' is more accurate."

His body was really shaking now, and yes, the quakes were coming from south of the border.

"So," she asked with a smile, her T-shirt slipping off, "How do they make love where you're from?"

Hunter thought about it for a moment.

"Beats me," he said.

Sarah smiled again. "Oh, kinky, huh?"

"Kinky?" Hunter replied. "I'm not sure I . . ."

His words were cut off by her kiss. Then they got closer. Her T-shirt came all the way off. Hunter saw the two most luscious breasts. Not too big, with small nipples. And suddenly, he felt a lot warmer.

They kissed again. And again. And again.

"Oh yeah," Hunter murmured. "I remember this . . ."

And then the huge aircraft carrier began rocking, even though it was sailing in very gentle seas.

It would continue that way all night long.

Chapter 28

By the next morning, the *USS Cape Cod* was again at rest.

Its Surface Defense teams had created a fog bank which extended for nearly a mile around the huge aircraft carrier. With unusually still winds, the hiding place would remain intact for as long the weather cooperated.

Hunter was standing out on the flight deck by 0545 hours, breathing in the somewhat-artificially cool air. The mission film told him to meet his transport at 0600 hours, 15 minutes from now. He had no idea what kind of an aircraft to expect, no idea who the crew would be. All he knew was they would be OSS-trained and the airplane unique to undercover insertion operations.

It was amazingly still on the flight deck now. As he understood it, they were about 250 miles west of the Shetland Islands, approaching the North Sea. The idea of course was to get as close to Germany as possible, for both his infiltration and the covering bombing attacks.

He closed his eyes and took a deep breath of the sea air and still smelled Sarah's soft perfume. She was so nice, and beautiful, and sexy, and warm. Very, very warm. He let out a long breath again. That was a night he would never forget, no matter what world he found himself in.

Just then he saw three people approaching him through the faux mist.

They appeared to be carrying a lot of equipment. Though the mission film said he'd get his gear on board the OSS plane, maybe there'd been a change in plans.

But then the three people got closer and Hunter was astonished to see they were, in fact, a TV news crew— cameraman, sound guy, and a guy with a microphone. They walked right up to Hunter and stuck the microphone in his face.

"Hello Flight Officer Hunter, can we have a few words?"

Hunter was stunned. *What the hell is this?*

"We understand you are leaving on a secret mission soon," the reporter went right on rapping. "Care to say a few words to the folks at home, maybe tell them what it's about?"

Hunter was speechless. Was this a gag?

"I can't tell you anything," he finally blurted out. "It's top secret . . ."

The reporter laughed a very false laugh. Then he turned to the camera and said: "Self-effacing, maybe even shy. Just as we've been told to expect him."

He turned back to Hunter and stuck the microphone even closer to his mouth.

"You realize you have a lot of fans back in the States," the reporter said. "How about a word or two for the folks at home."

Hunter kept his mouth shut. Did these guys have authorization to do this?

"Or how about telling us something about your mysterious past. What do you say? How about giving us a scoop?"

Hunter just shook his head. Tell us about it? Where he came from was supposed to be one of the darkest secrets of the U.S. military, deeper and darker than the mission he was about to go on. And these guys wanted him to talk about it?

"I think I'd better not," he finally blurted out.

"Well how about this mission today," the reporter insisted. "We hear it's a really top secret one—c'mon, let us in on it."

"I can't," Hunter replied. "It's *top secret.*"

The reporter just laughed his fake laugh again. Then he looked back into the camera and said: "OK, there you have it folks. An exclusive interview with the famous Hawk Hunter. And remember you saw it first here on WSUX . . ."

And with that, the three men disappeared into the fog again.

Hunter's head was spinning now. Did that just happen? Was that real? But then, something else caught his attention. Something big.

He stared out into the fake fog and saw a gray outline. It was so gigantic, Hunter was distracted enough to forget the reporters for a moment. It was another megacarrier just a few hundred yards off the starboard. It was so big, it blotted out whatever morning light that was getting through the artificial fog. The second carrier's presence underscored the fact that the other ships supporting the mission were moving into position. He studied this floating city for a moment and then the big ship vanished into the fog again.

At exactly 0600, Hunter sensed an aircraft approaching. It was a small airplane, not a jet, not a big chopper or anything even close. No, this was definitely a piston-driven prop plane. One that was very, very quiet.

Interesting, Hunter thought.

The aircraft got closer. But he could just barely hear it. He'd been told to expect a unique infiltration aircraft. That's exactly what it sounded like coming out of the clouds.

It was strange, because while he sensed the airplane's approach, he was surprised when it finally came out of the mist at him. It was not in the air at all, it had already landed on the near end of the deck and had rolled up to him without him realizing it. The plane was that quiet.

And he'd been right; it was a piston-driven prop plane. The propeller was enormous and thus the engine must have been too. But there were a series of dampeners around the cowling to keep the noise down. In fact, painted in scroll letters on the cowling, it read; WHISPER-ENGINE.

The aircraft itself looked like a biplane, one with its bottom wing missing. It had big squatty tires like a German Stuka of old. The fuselage was thick and boxy. The tail was painted with Zebra stripes and the ID number 333. It was about half the size of a C-47, Hunter figured. In this strange place, that was rather small indeed.

The plane was a Westland Lysander-XX. An odder airplane has never been built, here or anywhere else.

The side door opened and Hunter ran towards it. The plane wasn't going to stop, that was quickly apparent. So Hunter jumped aboard even as the pilot was turning around and heading back to take off again.

Hunter just made it in before the pilot gunned the single engine. Suddenly the plane was moving very quickly. Hunter was barely able to close the door behind him when the plane was lifting off the carrier deck. He could see the huge carrier start to fall below him as he finally jammed the door closed.

The pilot put the Lysander into an incredibly steep climb. Hunter was nearly thrown to the back of the airplane cabin, it was so severe. He held on and waited for the climb to end. It took about a minute and it was a bit hair-raising. But finally the plane passed above the artificial fog bank and leveled out.

Only then could Hunter climb up to meet the two-man crew.

They gave him a sort of quick but friendly salute.

"Captain Lancaster," the pilot said.

"Lieutenant Moon," the copilot added.

Hunter gave both men the once-over. Unlike many other people he'd run into during this strange adventure, they did not seem familiar to him. At least, he didn't think they did. They were not wearing any insignias on their flight uniforms, but Lancaster looked and sounded British; Moon was definitely an American. Both had special ops written all over them.

"Hunter," was the extent of his introduction to them, along with a quick handshake. "How's the weather look?"

It was an important question.

If the weather was against them, this wouldn't be a pretty flight.

"Weather is about a four," Lancaster yelled back to him. "We could do better."

Hunter strapped into the third seat in the plane's roomy cockpit. He took a look around. The Lysander *was* a very odd aircraft. Inside there were berths for four, plus a stove, a kitchen, an eating table, even a head with a door on it. As a military airplane, it was more like a flying house trailer. What a concept!

He found his gear next to his seat. It was all stuffed into one backpack. Inside, he found the heating ring, three batteries, a Boomer, a rope, and a radio control set for steering the drone. He lifted the pack for weight. It seemed to be made of some kind of indestructible material and would fit snugly on his back. But the thing was heavy. Damn heavy.

They broke through the real clouds at 7000 feet, and for the first time in a while, Hunter actually saw the sun.

Both Lancaster and Moon put their oxygen masks and helmets on, so did Hunter.

They flew on in silence. Hunter settled back and sucked in some pure O—it helped wake him up a bit.

He'd gone over all the plan a hundred times now, but felt it wouldn't hurt to do it again.

The first phase would be the most dangerous. Getting into Germany undetected. The bombing raid, launched from two other megacarriers nearby, would be a great cover, but the plan called for them to land practically in the middle of it.

The dam itself was only two miles from one of the bomb impact zones. From the air, and with bad weather, that might as well be inches. Their timing would have to be precise.

Once down, Hunter would leave the plane and set up the heat ring on the target. The batteries to be used were the most important element and they weighed a ton. But the heat ring had to reach at least 150 degrees Fahrenheit for the heat-seeker in the nose of the drone to work. Thus two batteries had to be placed in tandem, and hooked up just right. That's why his pack was so heavy. He had to carry two main batteries plus a third as a back up.

Once the heat ring was attached, Hunter would find a safe place not too far away from the dam itself. The bombed-up drone would arrive overhead. At this point Hunter's flying expertise would come into play—indeed that's the real reason he was here. He would essentially be flying the big drone once the radio contact was switched over to him.

He unpacked some of his equipment. All these switches and tubes and radio equipment worried him. Like everything in this strange world, it all seemed to be bigger and bulkier than it should have been. He was certain that much of it could have been built smaller, but he had to work with what he had.

Oddly too, there was not much discussion about what would happen after the drone went into the side of the dam. Certainly the bomb-packed airplane would explode—but would it really be enough to make a crack in the thick dam wall? And would the crack be big enough? Or could it be too big? No one was really saying.

The OSS planners were sure though that the cascade of water from the busted dam would knock out most of the power in the western half of the Reich's territory. If the Huns lost power for as long as a month, it would be a significant blow to the pumped-up German war machine. And it would give the Americans another 30 days to some-how figure a way to turn the tide yet again.

Once the deed was done, Hunter's escape plans were fairly straightforward. The dam blows up, he climbs aboard the Lysander, and off they go. A flight of Navy long-range attack jets from the *Cape Cod* was promised to meet them and ride air cover for their getaway.

If all went well, Hunter could be eating soup in one of the carrier's mess halls by dinnertime.

He made that his most immediate goal.

The flight passed for the next two hours without incident.

The plane was flying slow, and the wind was against them, but that was OK. They were still on schedule.

Then, about 0815 hours, things began happening.

They had just broken through a massive cloud layer when they saw them. Way off to the east and south. The bomber formations from the two other megacarriers. Again there were the two prime Air Corps types, B-17/36s and B-24/52s. There were at least 10 packages and each package had least 25 planes in it. And these were just the ones that Hunter could see.

"Lot of airplanes just for the three of us," Hunter heard Lancaster murmur.

"Lot of people chewing our asses if we fuck up," Moon replied.

Hunter took another gulp of oxygen and remained silent. The formation of huge bombers looked impressive; he would have loved seeing them take off from the huge carriers. And he was sure they were chock full of firebombs—all of them. This sent him gulping for more O.

There were some fighters too; they were flying so high above the bombers that it looked like they were expecting an attack from Heaven itself. Hunter could only wonder if Sarah was up there flying with them. He took in some more oxygen; they hadn't discussed anything about the mission the night before, which was good. He really didn't want to think about what danger she might get into if she was involved.

The Lysander moved over and took up a position underneath one of the bomb groups.

They flew on in formation like this for the next half hour. The weather got worse the deeper they went into the east. By the time they made landfall over the European coast, the clouds above Germany itself looked like they were miles high, and blacker than black.

Storms of the most incredible kind must be taking place beneath them, was all Hunter could think. He'd never seen clouds so big and so dark.

At least, he couldn't remember doing so.

They flew for another hour, the huge bomber formation all around them, the fighters above them.

They ran into some flak around Dokken in Occupied Holland and then again near Bacholt, inside Germany itself. But they were flying too high for the weak AA. And no German fighters showed up even to probe them.

Obviously there were all assigned to protect the bigger cities of the Reich.

Twenty minutes out from their target area, Lancaster began shutting down some of the aircraft's electronic systems. They would aid anyone with a detection unit on the ground in finding them, plus it was always a good idea to shut off anything electrical you could spare if you were about to attempt a hairy landing.

And the plan called for this landing to be an especially hairy one.

The dam itself was three miles wide, and nearly one half mile high. Next to its western edge, there was a service road which ran through a woods for about 100 yards before flowing into a larger highway nearby. But the term "road" might have been used a little too quickly. It was essentially a path lined with trees on both sides. Its main advantage was that it was open at either end. In theory the Lysander could fly in at one end, and fly out at the other.

But once they got a look at the road from the air on the long-range TV screen, they all knew this would not be very easy.

First of all, the road was not just *near* the dam—it was right *beside* it. This increased their level of exposure to guards thought to man the small outpost on the dam's western side, as well as to those in a much more substantial force, quartered on the eastern side. True, it would take these troops some time to get across the three-mile-long dam to the far side. But if the Lysander got stuck or was slow to take off for any reason, it could be a problem.

The second bad sign was the weather over the landing zone. Those huge dark clouds were now pouring sheets of rain over the target area, the dam, and the city of Heidiberg, just a few miles away. It was the bombing of this city that was supposedly providing the immediate cover for the Lysander to set down.

But the weather was so bad, there was a possibility that the local military might not even realize their city was being bombed, which would make the diversion meaningless. Hunter didn't like this either.

But it was no time to complain. It was time to just go ahead and get the damn job done.

So Lancaster began pulling back on the throttle and then put the nose of the Lysander nearly straight down. They started dropping like a rock. The engine got quieter as they went down. This impressed Hunter; there was some cool technology at work in that Whisper-engine.

Lancaster was able to bring the plane down almost vertically; Moon was working, hard too. It was a precision thing and again Hunter was impressed. They were dropping very fast however and none of them was wearing a parachute. But again, it was too late to think about that now.

He figured they were about 200 feet in altitude now. One group of bombers was going over them very low, and he could see the first bombs falling out of the lead plane heading for their targets in Heidiberg.

"One-fifty altitude," Moon called out, somewhat calmly. "One hundred . . ."

Hunter hugged his equipment bag and once again held on. It seemed that was all he'd been doing since arriving in this strange world: trying to make it through one more heart-stopping landing.

"Seventy-five," Moon called out. "Fifty . . ."

Hunter took a quick look outside but now couldn't see anything, with the rain and the trees. Still it felt as if he was coming down in a helicopter rather than a fixed wing craft.

"Twenty-five," Moon intoned. "Twenty . . ."

At that moment, Lancaster pushed something and pulled something, and suddenly they were going forward again and a second after that, they were down.

Just like that. Down on the road, under the trees, just like it said in the mission film. Lancaster was able to stop the Lysander from rolling in less than 25 feet. Hunter was simply amazed. He reached up and slapped both pilots on the shoulder. Both men returned the gesture with a quick thumbs-up.

Then they just sat there for a few moments in silence, in the rain. They could hear booming and rumbling and Hunter wondered if it was the bombing of the nearby city or real thunder.

Or both.

Or neither.

Lancaster turned around and looked at Hunter as if to say: Well, sport, time for you to go . . .

Hunter got the hint and climbed down into the hold of the plane. He picked up his heavy gear and went out the door, securing a GI combat helmet to his head.

The downpour was incredible. Hunter could barely see his hand in front of him. He crouched down, picked a direction and started running.

The roar around him was so loud now, it hurt his ears.

The sound of the bombers going overhead, the sound of bombs hitting Heidiberg nearby. But there was another roar. The roar of water. Hunter picked it out of the cacophony and ran toward it.

He broke through the tree line and found himself looking across a huge body of water. It was so wide and the wind and rain so fierce, there were waves topping it that were as high as any in the ocean itself.

The water was moving to his left. He ran along the shore and soon was able to see the edge of the dam itself through the sheets of rain.

Suddenly there was huge explosion off to the southeast and Hunter saw a gigantic fiery mushroom cloud rise above the hills and trees. The ground rumbled so violently, he was knocked to his ass and almost wound up in the water.

It looked like the world was ending right over the tree line. What the hell were they dropping over there, he wondered.

He regained his footing and started running again. Finally the western end of the dam came into view. There was a lone guard in a small guard house watching the far end of the dam. He was standing outside, using the roof for protection, having a smoke, watching the bomb blasts in the distance. Hunter came right up beside him and knocked him out cold with one punch to the jaw.

The man crumpled to the ground. Hunter took his gun and threw it in the water. Then he ran up to the road that went across the dam itself.

The road dipped a little and when Hunter got to the top of it, he discovered that the body of water on his left looked bigger than the Atlantic Ocean. The wind and rain were so intense, the waves were six or seven feet high and some were crashing over the stout retaining wall itself. It was a little unsettling when seen at eye level.

In complete contrast, to his right there was a sheer drop of at least 2500 feet. Hunter made the mistake of taking a look down and nearly lost his equilibrium. The dam was simply immense—10 times larger than he'd imagined it.

Just the size of the thing made him a little dizzy. At the bottom was a trickle of a river which flowed down into what became the Ruhr Valley. Many trees and hills ushered it on its way. A small village stood about a mile down on the right. Hunter could see lights in the windows of the houses. There was no doubt in his mind this was a place where civilians lived—but it was way too late the dwell on that either.

Hunter took another look down the side of the sloping dam and gulped. What really sucked was he now had to climb down the side of this thing.

He hooked up his rope to a convenient tie-ring on the wall and then just threw himself over. Down he went, half falling, half rappelling. Twenty feet, 30 feet, 40 feet. More. The convex winds were fierce; they were blowing him back and forth, up and down. Down 50, then 60. The air was shuddering with the concussion of the bombs falling just a mile or so to the south. The shock wave from each explosion would slam him into the concrete wall. Already his hands, elbows and knees were scrapped and bloody.

Like so many times in the past few weeks he asked himself, over and over: *What the hell am I doing?*

He finally reached a spot he judged to be 120 feet down from the top. It was a guess, but the plan after all was to slam a huge aircraft packed with explosives into the wall, so how precise did he really have to be? He fought with his backpack and finally got the heating ring out. He picked a spot, yanked off the adhesive cover and jammed it on to the cement. It stuck—thank God.

Next came the oversize batteries. They both contained enough stored juice to run a small village for a day, that's why the damn things were so heavy.

He ripped the adhesive off the first battery, and thankfully it stuck too. The second one gave him a problem; he had to tie it to the first and then winch it up, using the heating ring itself. Finally it was in place. He did a quick test on both, saw they were at full power, then happily dropped the backup battery. It bounced and cracked and shattered itself all the way down the side of the dam.

Feeling lighter than air now, Hunter did a quick systems check and convinced himself the heating ring was connected properly. Then he climbed back up the side of the dam, lifting himself up and over the small wall and landing in a very ungraceful heap back up on the roadway.

Phase one done, he thought. Now for the fun part.

He jumped to his feet and ran back down the road, off the dam, and into the woods again, this time further down from the dam face. He found a spot from which he could see the heating ring and the Lysander waiting patiently, engine running, in the clutch of trees about 100 yards away.

He took the radio set from his backpack and quickly turned it on. It was slow to warm, but at least it was still alive. He dialed in the prescribed frequency and after a minute of searching, finally found the explosives-laden drone-bomber. According to the homing signal, it was right overhead.

Hunter was mildly astonished. Would all this crap really work? Curiosity alone would have pushed him on.

He took out the remote control switch for the heating ring, pointed it in the general direction of the device about 500 feet away and clicked it to on. It was hard to see through the pouring rain, but damn if he didn't detect after 10 seconds or so a faint glow coming from the one-foot diameter ring.

Jessuzz, that was money, he thought. He snapped on the homing beacon to full power and pulsed the bomber drone again. The readout said it was 4400 feet right above him, waiting for his order to come down.

Hunter just shook his head. Was it really going to be as easy as this? He hit the arming switch on his radio set. A green light blinked to life. All 22 tons of blockbusting explosives were now fully armed and fused.

He pushed the radio throttle control ahead a bit and listened hard to see if he could detect the sound of the drone's engines burping a little at 4400 feet. But between the downpour, the wind and the nonstop bombing of Heidiberg nearby, it was impossible even for Hunter's ultrasensitive ears to discern the sound.

No matter, he thought. The radio set said the plane was up there, and at this point, that was good enough for him.

He did one last visual check of his area and surroundings. He was about to bring down the wrath of God here; he wanted to make sure he hadn't forgotten anything in the rush.

The heating ring was now shining very brightly through the bad weather, like a neon halo in the upper left hand corner of the immense dam face. There was absolutely no activity coming from this side of the dam—the guard was still knocked out, and the Lysander was still snuggled into the woods nearby, its prop spinning, its feather-sound engine living up to its rep.

Hunter took out his hand beacon and blinked it twice in the direction of the Lysander. This wasn't in the plan, but he wanted to at least warn Lancaster and Moon that all hell was about to break loose. His two blinks were returned with two in kind. They saw him, they got the message. Everyone was now waiting on him.

He moved a little closer to the edge of the cliff, out from under trees, for a clearer look at the stormy sky. He pulsed the drone again and everything came back as OK. He activated the plane's heat-seeking beam, and instantly a red light popped on the control panel. The plane had a lock on the heating ring. That *was* easy!

Hunter threw the main activation switch and then gave the drone full throttle. The bomb-laden plane started on its way down . . .

He heard it a moment later. Sixteen big engines screaming for life as gas flooded their fuel injectors. The combination of full throttle and gravity would give the airplane an impact speed of nearly 800 mph—this was going to make quite a show.

The scream of the drone's engines was blotting out all

other sounds now. Hunter unconsciously moved back into the woods a bit. He was expecting the plane to come out of the clouds off to his right. It would pass about eye level with him and then plunge into the dam wall to his left.

He closed his eyes and envisioned the plane hitting the dam, exploding an instant later, and when the smoke and debris cleared, a good-sized crack would be on the dam face. Most of the debris would be blown downward, he was sure, but he still had to keep his helmet on, for that stray chunk of concrete that might not know the principles of Newtonian physics.

The drone's engines filled his ears now—he looked at the radio set. It was 15 seconds away. One last look around. Did he have enough time to blink Lancaster and Moon again? No, and what was the point? They might take it the wrong way and think something had gone awry.

Ten seconds. The wind screamed, the rain increased, but the drone's engines were growing incredibly loud. Seven seconds. The heating ring was glowing so much, Hunter thought he could feel its warmth. Five seconds. Engines screaming. Ears hurting. He peeked out from the trees again, eyes glued on the mass of clouds up to his right. The drone should appear through them . . . right . . . now.

But it didn't . . .

And in that instant Hunter knew something had gone wrong, knew all this bulky crap *was* crap and that he'd been foolish to believe it could all work.

But the airplane's engines still sounded like they were right above him. *Where the hell was it?*

He got his answer a second later.

There it was. Not off to his right as he anticipated, but off to his left. Coming in over the dammed water itself! It was flying wildly, nose wobbling, wings stunting, tail wing twisting. And it was going very, very fast. It hit the surface about 100 feet out from the dam wall, plowed through the waves, sending sheets of water on either side. Then hit the wall from the opposite side.

Then it blew up.

In the next microsecond all Hunter could see was water. Water was everywhere. It was as if he was looking up at a faucet that someone had turned on full blast. He couldn't see. He couldn't hear. He couldn't breathe. He was tumbling, flying through the air while water was all around him. Water was going in his mouth, up his nose, in his ears. There was fire around him too, and smoke, and very large pieces of concrete and metal and trees. Tree limbs and leaves and dirt and roots were passing him by at high speed, flying and crashing through the water, just like him.

It was strange how much consciousness he retained in those first few seconds after the blast and the catastrophic dam burst. He knew what had happened. The plane had come in the exact opposite direction as it should have and had blown a huge hole *outward* in the dam wall. This had instantly created the effect of an enormous tidal wave and destroyed the *entire* dam. The water surge went hundreds of feet into the air, and the gigantic wave was now careening down into the Ruhr. And Hunter knew it was all happening, for he could see it all around him. *What a way to die!* the thought flashed across his saturated brain. Flying through the air while still under water.

But there was even more strangeness in this, the last few watery moments of his life. Like Dorothy in the tornado he saw houses, cars, cats, dogs, people flash by him. And then he saw the Lysander too. It was caught in the tidal wave and it went by him tumbling and upside down. And he even caught a glimpse of Lancaster and Moon at the controls, fighting them, like they could actually get a handle on this thing.

Hunter's urge was to scream out to them, but they were gone in a swirl and flash, and then more water hit him, and he began to go under.

And then finally, everything just went black.

Chapter 29

More than 70,000 people were killed by the flood.

A wave of water 600 feet high roared down the Ruhr Valley at more than 100 miles an hour. It leveled everything in its path. Three major cities, dozens of villages, and countless farms and camps were washed away in the deluge. All electrical power from the edge of the Rhineland to the Wuttenberg area in the south was gone. Sewage systems, water ducts, drainage, and fresh water supplies were all destroyed in the immense thousand-square-mile area.

The wave had a life of more than an hour before dispersing into the Boden Spee lake on the border of Switzerland.

It left many places covered in water. Villages, valleys, bridges, tunnels. Cemeteries.

Once the water settled deep on these places, things began to rise.

The great flood was only one of the problems for Germany.

The simultaneous bombing raids had resparked fires in several major cities—Hamburg, Dresden, Frankfurt, Essen, Bonn, Wiesbadan, among others—and dozens of smaller ones, like Heidiberg. Few military installations were hit by the firebombings. The targets this day were mostly population centers. Twenty thousand died in Dusseldorf, 32,000 in Cologne. Thirty-three thousand in Mainz. And, as planned, the bombers kept right on coming, some making two and three flights from the hidden carriers within the 24-hour period.

When it was over, at the end of the horrible day, nearly a quarter of a million people were dead in Germany, killed by either fire or water.

That's why it was so strange that, when the next morning dawned, the skies were clear, the sun was bright, and the temperature balmy.

When Hunter woke up, the first thing he saw was a cow.

It was lying right beside him, eyes open, tongue out, water lapping at its chin. It seemed to be smiling at him.

Hunter lifted himself up slightly. It was painful but he had to see where he was this time, Heaven or Hell. His eyes cleared and he could see far enough to realize that he and the cow and tons of rubble were all clinging to the top of a very small mountain peak, which was now an island in the middle of a very big, very wide Teutonic lake.

He was somehow able to lift himself up further, to his knees at least, where he took a deep breath, and then collapsed again. His mouth went under water when he did, and the cold water shocked his system enough to have him scramble up some logs to the rocky peak itself.

Heaven *or* Hell, he didn't want to be in the water anymore, ever again.

He crawled up to the driest patch of land on the peak, dragging his backpack with him. He took in many deep breaths now. He looked down and saw the cow's head was without a body. Only then did it hit him. He was breathing. He was alive.

He had survived what tens of thousands hadn't.

He spent the next day there, clinging to the one tree left on the peak, drying out both inside and out. He'd dispatched the cow's head soon upon arrival, but more stuff came floating along, and some of the bigger pieces were drawn in by the eddys around the new island. There were some body parts mixed in here too and they didn't all belong to cows. But Hunter found out soon enough that the water was moving very swiftly and if anything disgusting did wash up, it usually washed away again very shortly afterwards.

So he ignored the flotsam and concentrated on the eerily magnificent lake before him. He was at least 100 miles downstream from where the dam broke, of this he was sure. And he seemed to be very high up too. In the distance he could see smoke plumes, rising up from many places. To the north and east of him were many new lakes, one being particularly enormous, about 10 miles away.

It was a miracle he had no broken bones, no major cuts or bruises. He spent much of this day drying out the contents of his backpack and trying to calculate exactly how he had made it here, to this place, alive. Had he caught a hold of a piece of driftwood—or had some driftwood snagged him? If so, how had he been able to keep his head above the water? And how did he manage to avoid getting crushed, like the cow, in the thousands of uprooted trees and logs moving so swiftly in the fast current?

He didn't know, and after a while, he didn't care. He was here. He was alive. He was unhurt and still reasonably sane.

But now what? He had to get off the small island. But how? And where would he go once he'd left?

He made getting off his first priority. He wasn't too keen on trying to snag a large piece of driftwood and hoping it would serve as a raft. And it really was way too far in any direction to attempt a swim.

What to do? He finally realized that if he just sat back down and watched the long line of debris float by, eventually the answer would come to him.

That's what happened just as the sun was rising on the second day.

Like the previous one, the sky was crystal clear, and the sun rose warm and dry. He was experiencing his first hunger pangs when he looked off in the distance and saw it. Floating among sodden bales of hay and an army of black wooden boxes, was a boat.

It was small, and it was upside-down, but it was still afloat, and that's all Hunter needed. He watched it for hours, tracking its movements like radar, urging it on as it bumped and skidded and stalled and made its own way through the flotsam.

Finally it reached a point about 100 yards off the east end of the island. Hunter didn't even think about it. He plunged into the very chilly water and started swimming. Twenty exhausting minutes later, he reached the boat and managed to flip it over. Then he threw in his back pack and climbed inside.

He bailed with his hands for the next two hours, darkness fell, and the sun's warmth went away. He got to the point where he could bail no more. There was still six inches of water in the 12-foot scam, but he was so tired, he just lay down in it and went to sleep.

When he woke the next morning, he was three miles away from the island that had saved his life.

It was the beginning of his third day without food, but this did not bother him much. He felt that in his previous place, he'd gone for long stretches of time not eating too. This was just another one of them.

He floated along somewhat peacefully, bailing routinely, moving with the still-rushing water, no need for paddles or oars. He passed church steeples, the tips of monuments, empty flagpoles he imagined were sitting atop a submerged school or hospital. He saw floating caskets and thought that perhaps they might be a little more seaworthy than his leaky boat. But he had no intention of playing Ishmael. He let each casket pass him by without a second glance.

Hunter drifted for hours like this. He came to imagine that the entire Ruhr Valley had been filled. Was that possible? How big was the Ruhr? He wasn't sure; to him it was a distant point of history. Ruhr Valley. Lots of people. Lots of industry. That's where it ended for him.

At about noon that day, he had some luck. He caught a fish, with his hands and his shirt as a net. It was a big one—God knows what type. And it was probably a little stunned from the sudden turn of events in its formerly peaceful watery world, and this made for an easier prey.

. Hunter had been to Japan several times, but he didn't remember any of them. Still, he knew enough to slice open the fish, and skim the inside of meat and throw the rest away. Then he allowed these slices to dry for about an hour and then he ate them. It was good. Freshwater sushi.

He'd just finished his feast when the water took him around a steep, dark bend. He was now passing by a towering mountain that still had snow at its peak. It had been spared being covered by the flood by 3000 feet or so.

He turned the bend and then something caught the corner of his eye. Suddenly he was hand-paddling the boat madly towards the shore.

Sticking out of the far side of the mountain was a chalet. It was built of stone, was colored yellow, had many spires and towers and windows. It was very German, almost like the picture on the wrapper of a candy bar.

He reached the shoreline, and very carefully secured the boat to a partially uprooted tree trunk. Then he moved quickly but silently up the embankment and was soon peering over the short yellow wall that surrounded the place.

This wasn't a military installation. There were no gun turrets or spotlights or any sign of a guardhouse or guards. The place looked empty, and maybe was so even before the flood came. Hunter scaled the wall and went inside.

The first thing he found was the gun. It was a monstrous carbine, hanging from the wall, with a full belt of ammunition. Hunter took it down and was surprised by its weight. Not only was it huge, it had a barrel that flared out like a blunderbuss. He sniffed one of the bullets. It was dry. He sniffed the barrel. The gun hadn't been fired in a while.

He immediately took it and draped the ammo belt around his shoulder.

So far, so good.

He went through the hall, through a dining room, where the table was set, and into the huge kitchen. There were mountains of food in here. He started grabbing anything that came in a box. He wound up with a lot of crackers and a container of chocolate. There was a man's sturdy denim work coat hanging from a hook on the back of the door. Work pants, too. Hunter quickly got out of his uniform and into these clothes. It was the first time he'd been dry in almost four days.

He stuffed his mouth with chocolate and then discovered the liquor cabinet. He took some brandy and a bottle of Schnapps. His load was getting heavy and he didn't want to stay too long. The house didn't look very used; still he felt like someone had been here recently. A photograph on the wall showed a family. Father, mother, young daughter with red hair, infant son. They were well-scrubbed Nordic types.

He scooped up more candy, but then saw a cruel clue as to the whereabouts of the owners. There was a pair of very tiny shoes at the back door. Beside them the shoes of a young girl. Beside them, a woman's sports shoes. And a pair of men's work boots.

Hunter took a step into the backyard—and that's where he found the family. They were in the swimming pool, all four of them, in bathing suits, floating face down. The water had come up to this point so quickly, it trapped them, and then receded.

He looked at them for a long time. Then he took the work boots and left.

Hunter returned to the boat, cast off, laid down in the back, and ate chocolate and crackers and drank the brandy.

Night fell, the stars appeared overhead. The glow from

the hundreds of fires all around him lit up the sky on every horizon.

He could hear explosions going off in the distance and the sky above him was filled with moving lights. Some white, some red. Some were very high up; others were not.

Hunter sipped the brandy and just watched the lights go back and forth. He was sick, not in his stomach, but in his heart. He wasn't exactly sure why. After all, he was a soldier, a military person, he knew that much about himself at least. Yet all the death he'd seen recently, especially up close, was like a claw in his chest, ripping at him. How could he be a soldier and yet have all this death bother him so much? It sure didn't seem to bother anyone else he'd met. But then again, he couldn't exactly look into the soul of everyone.

He drank more brandy and ate more crackers and loaded up the gun and began shooting at the lights overhead. Would he ever know exactly what had happened to him? How he'd gotten here? Where he'd come from? He fired off another round at a red light skimming above him. Would he ever know whether he was married or not? Or if he had any kids?

He didn't think so . . .

There was one thing of which he was certain: the German resurgence began shortly after he, and the other two people in the water with him, arrived in this world. At least one of the other two was picked up by the Germans. Had this person been the instrument for the German turnaround, as Zoltan had indicated? Hunter had guessed it back then and was even more sure of it now.

He loaded the gun and fired it again; this time the target was a very white light flying very high above him.

In their subsequent conversations, Zoltan had also told him that certain things might jog his memory as to what had happened before, but he was finding those things few and far between. Many times he'd just closed his eyes and tried to conjure up some piece of his past, but it was nearly impossible to do. And every time he closed his eyes now, he saw those four people face down in the pool and wondered how many more he'd killed. And those were things he was sure he'd never forget, as much as he wanted to.

He fired the gun again, this time at the planet Venus. Then slumped further down into the boat and went to sleep.

It was the sound of someone else's gunfire that woke him the next morning.

He was still sick and groggy and his new dry clothes now seemed wet and old. But he was smart enough to stay low, and listen closely to the sound of guns going off nearby.

There were several different kinds. The pop-pop-pop of a high caliber rifle. The sustained boom-boom-boom of a large machine gun. Then many, many cracks, indicating pistols.

Hunter got his own weapon loaded and ready and then finally peeked over the side of the boat.

He was approaching a narrows between two mountains and people on one side of it were firing at people on the other. They were German soldiers.

He squinted in the morning sun and found it to be a very confusing scene, at first. Why would these German soldiers be firing at each other?

He drifted a little bit closer, not daring to paddle or move at all. Then he saw what the fight was about. Stuck against a rock between the narrows was a very valuable commodity—so valuable, a small internecine war had broken out for it.

It was a boat. It was smaller than Hunter's, and more narrow, with a wrecked motor still attached. But it could float and that was the important thing. Apparently, one group of German soldiers had been stuck on one mountain, the other group on the other. Now they were fighting each other over which side would get the skiff.

Hunter sank back down behind the gunwale. This was

not good. If the Germans were desperate enough to kill *each other* for a boat, what would they do to him for his?

He looked in every other direction, searching for a way out of this sudden predicament. But there was none.

He was one with the water and he had to go where it was going to take him, and at the moment, it was taking him right into the thick of this strange battle.

But as he lay there, looking up into the sky, trying to come up with a plan, an unusual sound came to his ears. Above the din of the gun battle now just 100 yards away, above the sound of the distant explosions, still going off like rumbles of thunder, he heard another sound.

It was so familiar, but he wasn't sure why. Whirring. Mechanical, but soft, almost.

Like a whisper.

He lifted himself up and looked off to the clouds in the west and way, way out there, he saw the outline of an airplane. Long flat wing, jumbo-booted landing gear, plowing its way through the air, as opposed to flying through it. Zebra stripes on the tail wing and fuselage.

It was the Lysander!

Hunter was astonished. How could this be? He'd seen the airplane tumble by him a second after the dam broke. Even then it had been breaking apart and the two crewmen just seconds away from death. But now there it was, about two miles off to his left, just flying along as if it were on a pleasure flight, same zebra-striping, same 333 tail numbers. Hunter watched it go, wondering if this would be finally, the last unsolved mystery of his strange life.

The gunfire got his attention again and a peek over the bow found him not 50 feet away from the battle. Some of the German soldiers were up to the waists in water now, shooting at their comrades across the gap of 40 yards or so. Others were throwing rocks. The Germans on the left had a small cannon, a single-shot affair they were using with mixed results. The gun had a loud *whoomp!* for a report, followed by the scream of the shell and then the dull explosion of the impact.

This was now mixed in with the machine gun fire and the rifle shots and even the sound of rocks hitting the water. Hunter got as low as he could inside the boat. What should he do? He couldn't jump out now—he was much too close. He couldn't fight both sides—he didn't have enough ammunition for that.

The boat drifted closer and the sounds of the battle got louder and louder. Hunter loaded the gun and just waited for whatever was going to happen.

And what happened was . . . nothing.

The boat simply drifted through the gap. He could see the German soldiers right above him, on either side, their faces locked in a grip of madness, firing away at each other. But it was like they didn't see him. He floated right by them, unnoticed. As if he were invisible.

As if he were a ghost.

It was a long time before the sounds of the gun battle finally faded from Hunter's ears.

His boat meandered along, occasionally being bumped by driftwood and debris, pushing it this way and that. He knew he couldn't drift like this forever, as much as he would have liked to. At some point, he had to get to a piece of reasonably dry land. Then he would have to find a working aerodrome, steal a plane, and fly away, to somewhere.

After a while, these thoughts were interrupted by the sound of water rushing. He looked up and oddly enough, saw his piece of reasonably dry land just ahead of him. It was a large, pastoral valley, surrounded by mountains covered with pine trees. It looked very odd to him. In this land of water, why was this place so suddenly dry?

The answer was in the noise he'd heard. Water, rushing forward. Water, going through narrows, turning itself into foam and spray.

Water, going over the side of a cliff.

It was the strange physics of water that had created the

enormous waterfall. A lot of the water from the busted dam had stayed tucked in these mountains, seeking its own level. But eventually it reached a point where it began to pour out again. No wonder the water had been moving so swiftly the three days he'd been in the boat.

He saw the top of the falls and the great splash of German countryside beyond and knew immediately he was in big trouble. Funny then that in the four or five seconds he had left, he grabbed the bottle of Schnapps and the chocolate first, then the gun, his backpack, and the ammunition second.

Paddling was useless; this he knew.

So he just held on and . . . and it became very strange. Time *did* stand still. Not the tired expression he had apparently read in many bad books and seen in many bad movies. No, to him, to his consciousness, things really did go into a sort of slow-freeze.

He started going over the falls. He could really see the countryside beyond now, And he was able to look down and see that the drop he was about to take was steeper than the side of the dam he'd blown up. This waterfall, newly created by the flood he had started three days before, was probably close to 3500 feet high. A mammoth drop.

Out beyond, taking in everything as things moved slowly forward, he could see a few villages, bombed-out, true, but still dry and safe from the flood waters. He also saw a wide highway and many roads running off of it. And then, several miles from the heart-stopping falls, he saw the most interesting thing of all: it was an air base. Or at least two runways with a few buildings nearby. Even in this split second, he got the impression that the base was not used regularly, abandoned. Oddly, he thought it might even be a top secret place, where not much activity happened, at least in broad daylight.

Now, as if this wasn't enough for him to observe, in this frozen moment in time, he also saw two other things in the sky. First, just as the front of the boat was tipping over the top of the gigantic plume, he saw a million contrails suddenly flash overhead. They were American bombers on their way to targets again. Had they been there all along? Or was he just noticing them now, in this dire split second? He didn't know. All that was certain was the huge bomber formation was going right over his head, and heading even deeper into the heart of Germany.

And he was sure that their holds were filled with incendiaries again. In an instant within an instant, he felt a hot flash sear his face.

Now the boat was almost completely over the top of the falls, and he was just beginning to go over when he saw one last thing—possibly the most bizarre, and in the end, the most startling.

Way off in the distance, flying very low and somewhat erratically, was the Lysander again. Wings battered, smoke pouring from its power plant, the whisper-engine sounded just a bit louder than the last time. It was flying over a small woods about two miles to his left and within a second or two disappeared behind the tall trees.

In Hunter's last conscious moment, just as he started on that very long plunge down, he got the feeling that the two pilots inside were looking for something.

Chapter 30

There were no dreams this time.

No peeks into other dimensions. No communing with angels or devils. No long tunnel. No bright light. No warm shining figure bidding him on.

No, this time Hunter simply came within a half pint of getting enough water in his lungs to drown. And die, forever.

He hit the water so hard that it dented his helmet. But it was the helmet that saved his life. Without it, the impact would have surely split his skull, a fracture he could never have recovered from.

As it was, the waterfall was so high and so powerful, it had in three days dug itself a hole at its base that went down several hundred feet. After hitting the water at about 80 miles an hour, Hunter plunged into this frightening pool, the boat and all its contents following him about half a second later.

He went into the water like a bullet, traveling so far down into the dark swirl, when he finally stopped, he could not see any light above him. It was pitch black, with only an occasional tree root, clump of dirt, and yes, even a few skulls floating around him.

For one very scary second—the one that followed the sheer astonishment that he was still alive—he almost started swimming in the wrong direction, thinking he was upside down. But he was smart enough to stop, calmly put his hands to his sides and let the air in his body do the rest. Slowly, but surely, he began rising.

How long it took for him to ascend just to the point where he could see light again, it was impossible to say. He was holding his breath with all his might and was thankful for the breathing exercises he'd done to stay awake during those long flights in and out of Iceland. His lungs were use to holding in a large amount of air for a long period of time, and again, this was the difference between Hunter's living and dying.

His lungs finally did burst about 20 feet from the surface, though, and he did suck in a huge amount of water. But he popped up about two seconds later, and by the sheer action of his breaking the surface, was thrown up onto the shore, his backpack, still in place, cushioning the blow.

Like a big fish had just spit him there, he lay on the cold, slimy shoreline, throwing up water, phlegm, undigested chocolate and pieces of cracker, but no blood.

When his stomach was finally purged and his lungs empty of most of the water, he still did not move.

Instead, he remained motionless, drifting in and out of sleep and unconsciousness, knowing the difference only by the fact that in sleep, he dreamed of ice and not water.

The next day—his fifth inside Germany—it was raining and cold, but Hunter didn't mind.

He woke with a mild headache, but happy if a little confused as to why he was still alive.

He looked up at the gigantic waterfall and winced. Shivers went down his spine. The thing looked unreal, it was so big. How could he have possibly survived such a fall?

He fooled himself by pretending to study the air currents at the bottom of the falls, weakly throwing pieces of grass into the raging mist and watching them quickly go sky-borne. Yes, he mused, maybe the air currents actually helped cushion his impact and thus helped him survive.

But he really didn't buy it. It was not an act that would have been permitted by the ordinary laws of physics, not to the degree that it would actually save his life. But Hunter felt oddly comfortable believing it. In fact, he felt rather good. Strong. Ready to take on the world.

But there was a reason for this: He would later find out that for this day and the next few he would be suffering from what was called postimmersion narcosis, a condition caused by a shutoff of oxygen to the brain, but only for a second or two. Translation: he would remain at the mercy of a somewhat accidental "high" which could lead to spells of euphoria, hallucinations, fits of grandeur and the illusion of superhuman strength.

But in Hunter's mind, nothing seemed changed. Everything was the same.

He finally got to his feet and miraculously—or not—found the box of crackers floating nearby. The contents were water-logged but Hunter ate the mush anyway. Then, even more amazing, he found the gun and his ammo imbedded in the river bank about 50 feet away. The gun was bent, but still usable; the bullets incredibly dry. Finally, he found the bottle of Schnapps bobbing in the turbulent water. He retrieved the bottle, took a huge swig, and felt the alcohol warm his entire system, one bone at a time.

Now brightened by two intoxicants, he resumed his strange journey.

It took him about an hour to get far enough away from the waterfall that he didn't hear it anymore.

This time consisted of his climbing down the mountain of debris that had been spit out of the falls just as he had been.

At the bottom of this enormous pile of dirt, rocks, tree trunks, and the occasional human and animal body part, the bare if damp German countryside around him resumed unabated. He found a road by mid morning; he found the highway an hour after that.

It felt good to walk again, to be *able* to walk again. He swigged the Schnapps until the bottle ran dry, telling himself it contained vitamins he needed for strength and sugar he needed for energy. At this pace, he arrived, staggering slightly, at the gate of the small air base, just about noontime.

The place was deserted, just as he had thought while frozen on the precipice of water.

And actually, he'd been right on two counts about this place. It was abandoned, and it was a top-secret facility. Hunter could tell by its muted appearance. The lack of oil spillage on the tarmac. The unmarked buildings. The rows of barbed wire.

Obviously anyone who had been stationed here had gotten word about the oncoming flood in enough time to get out. Little did they know the great deluge would miss swamping this place by little more than a quirk of topography.

So, here it was—secret and abandoned. But what did it contain?

The soldier within Hunter told him it was his duty to find out.

It took him one hour, and more than a dozen cuts and scrapes, to make it over the tall barrier of concertina wire. Then he had to scale a 20-foot-high chain link fence that had been doused with oil. Only after this was he able to get inside the compound itself.

The first place Hunter went was the chow hall. He knew many clues as to why no one was here, and when they might return, could be found where the food was served.

He found the place in the basement of one of the hangars. It was Goldilocks all over again. A meal was on the table, some kind of breakfast porridge. Coffee cups were still full, even little cups of some powdered orange drink. Everything looked to be about three days old.

The table was set for 15 people; Hunter assumed that like all places such as this, the occupants ate in shifts. Quick deduction had him estimating about 45 people had been assigned here.

But there was an odd thing about the mess hall. He could find no special section for the officers or pilots. There was no senior mess.

This told him something too. There probably were no officers or pilots assigned here permanently. Yet it was undoubtedly an air base. So what kind of air base has no pilots?

One that is being used as a storage facility for aircraft, he guessed correctly. Airplanes fly in and wait here for pilots to fly them back out again.

He went back up top and took a long look at the two runways. They were each about 10,000 feet long—fighter length, and maybe long enough to handle some cargo planes. But he doubted they kept heavy bombers here. The hangars weren't big enough, besides.

He found what he believed to be the main hangar, the place where the goods probably were. It was bigger than the other buildings and painted all white.

He broke a rear window—and no alarm went off. In fact, there was no electricity at all at the base. That was obvious by now.

Hunter went in through the window and found it absolutely dark inside. He stood still and took a long deep sniff. Aviation fuel. Oil. A little bit of burnt rubber. No doubt about it, there were airplanes in here.

But what kind?

He started walking, slowly but surely, making sure he didn't crack his head or his knees on anything sharp. Soon he could tell by the reverberations of his boot steps that he was in a big open area, the guts of the hangar itself. It was cold in here and all the smells were more intense. He took a moment to analyze the odor again and guessed there were at least a dozen airplanes in here.

Top-secret airplanes.

Still following his nose, he walked over to the first airplane, drawn there by its mass and smell. He put his hand on its nose and closed his eyes—and instantly his body began shaking. He saw red before his eyes, the vibrations were so intense. He drew a breath and tried to settle down. This was something very important here, he could *feel* it.

He ran his fingers down the plane's long snout, past the belly-mounted air intake, past a couple of small strakes along a leading wing edge that flared out into a delta shape. There was a missile, wingtip-mounted, that was about seven feet long, and about eight inches around. Along the back edge of the wing he found steering surfaces, and clunked his ankle on what he supposed was a wing-mounted bomb or a reserve-fuel drop tank.

At the rear end, the strakes flared in to the exhaust tube. This itself was huge, with movable vanes. Hunter took a very deep sniff now. This engine had been fired up and flown only once in its life, he guessed. Probably just for the flight from its place of manufacture to here.

He noted all this and then walked to the next plane. It was exactly the same. So was the third, the fourth, the fifth, and the sixth. All of them, 12 in number, were the same kind of airplane.

But the question was, what kind of airplane was that?

Throughout all this Hunter's inner being was vibing to the max. He was shaking, the back of his skull was pounding, like many of the secrets and lost memories in there were ready to get flushed out. He took another sniff. Yes, this place, the smell. So familiar. He was sure he'd been in a place just like this one before—not in this time. But definitely in another one.

The sheer curiosity of it all finally got the better of him. Maybe where he was really from, he would have handled it differently. But this version of him was still light-headed from his experience on the flood, from his experience of nearly drowning, and from his experience at the bottom of the bottle of Schnapps.

He wasn't too good at the moment at not feeding an impulse—especially one as strong as this one.

He wanted to see these goddamn airplanes and he wanted to see them now! But to do that, he needed some light, and the only light available here would be daylight. And the only thing standing between him and some illumination was a row of big, thick-paned windows that had been painted black so as not to let the slightest bit of sun into this place.

Now the "other" Hunter might have taken the time to feel his way over to nearest window, somehow climb up to its sill, feel around until he would find some kind of locking mechanism, and then somehow solve it in the pitch dark, scrape away whatever paint buildup might be on it, and then, probably very slowly and painstakingly, get the window to open, maybe just a crack to allow in just enough light.

Well, he just didn't have time or patience for any of that crap now. So he simply aimed his huge rifle about 35 degrees from the floor and pulled both barrels. The explosion was enormous, the cloud of cordite thick, the blast of the gun muzzle in the completely dark room almost blinding.

But the cloud of buckshot hit the window straight on, and punctured it in 274 locations.

Hunter reloaded and let another blast go. Then another, and another. Now there were more than a thousand points of light flooding into the hangar. And only then did he turn around. And only then did he see what kind of airplanes they were.

Long snout, cranked wing, high tail. Red, white, and blue color scheme. Sleek, dangerous-looking, and fast.

"Jesus Christ," Hunter whispered, never more astonished in his life.

They were F-16s.

And that was it.

That was the moment when everything came rushing back. It came in a torrent greater than the flood he'd just survived. The feeling suddenly building up inside him felt hotter than the fires he had set on German cities.

These were F-16s! He used to fly one, back where he was from. He flew one for the Thunderbirds. He flew one for the 16th Fighter Squadron of the old U.S. Air Force. Then, after World War III, he flew one for the Zone Air Patrol, then the United American Air Corps. In this airplane, he'd fought air pirates, Mid-Aks, the Family, the Russians, Nazis, skinheads, white supremacist groups, and the KKK Air Force. This airplane was him, and he was it, an extension of himself in his other world.

He was so staggered by this revelation, he found himself sitting down in the middle of the hangar floor, holding his head in his hands. Spurred by the touch of his beloved airplane, everything was coming back to him now in a big way. At last he knew exactly who he was: Major Hawk Hunter, the best fighter pilot who ever lived.

The one they called The Wingman.

But Jessuzz, where the hell was he? On another planet? No—this was definitely Earth. But it was *another* Earth. Same time, different place. A parallel place. The same, but different.

How did he get here?

He actually squeezed his head with his hands and let the memory come. A huge comet had been spotted, it was on a collision course with Earth. He was in space, in the captured Zon space shuttle. There was a string of nuclear bombs; he flew out to lay them in the comet's path. His close friend Elvis Q had gone with him on this suicidal mission—and someone else too. The bombs went off. The comet was diverted—and then . . . then what?

What happened after the bombs exploded?

He remembered a bright white light. And a long tunnel. And something drawing him up into that light. And when he reached it. the next thing he knew, he was falling . . .

Then he hit the water. And *that's* how he found himself floating in the Atlantic Ocean!

But three of them fell out of the sky. He and Elvis and someone else. Who was it?

That's when his stomach began to tighten, his fists did too. Yes, this memory was coming back as well. He was the Wingman and his arch enemy was Viktor Robotov, world terrorist and Satan on Earth. Hunter had been chasing him forever, or so it seemed, and even went so far as to steal his space shuttle and go into space to capture the supervillain up there!

But then, just at his moment of triumph, just as he had the devil in his clutches, the comet was spotted, and the world had to be saved.

But on that last ride to put the bombs in place, he and Elvis had kidnapped Viktor and took him with them, certain they were all going to die anyway.

So then, the two other people in the water with him: One was Elvis.

And the other was Viktor.

Then suddenly another memory came flooding back— one that was even more powerful than the last. It was so intense, Hunter felt like someone had fired a Stinger missile into his chest. That ache in his heart, he'd felt it almost since the first second he'd arrived in this place. A woman was there. Her name was Dominique. She was the beautiful love of his life. But she was dead. He knew this, he felt it in every fiber of his being. His eyes began to water as this, the most painful memory of all, began to sink in.

Dominique was gone. He was without her.

Damn . . .

The next thing he knew, he was running. Out of the hangar, out of the air base, up the side of a small mountain nearby. He seemed to reach the top in minutes, though it should have taken an hour or more. And at the top he collapsed.

Out of breath, out of life, he just lay there, numb from what had happened.

The flood of memories was almost too much now, but he knew he had to let them flow. So for hours he stayed perfectly still, looking up at the sky, letting it all come back to him. His parents. His schooling at MIT. His colleagues, his enemies. The wars he'd fought, the friends he'd lost.

And those planes down in the hangar, the trigger for letting his memories back in. He knew them too. They were F-16 Fighting Falcons, originally designed by the General Dynamics Corporation. He knew more than their name. He knew every inch of them. Every bolt and rivet, ever panel and every wire. He knew exactly how many gallons of fuel one plane could carry, knew how many bombs could be hung from beneath the wings, knew how many cannon shells were needed to feed the huge front-mounted gun.

He knew how the thing flew, how fast, how high, how low. He even knew the correct tire pressure for the gear wheels in both hot and cold climates.

But what he didn't know was *how* these planes could have gotten here. In this place. They certainly hadn't fallen into the ocean along with he and Elvis and Viktor. Those airplanes had to have been built in this time, in this place, by hands belonging here. But how? For all its quirky advances, this world didn't have anywhere near the technological smarts to put out one of these airplanes, never mind 12 of them. Besides, even the greatest minds of this era wouldn't have been able to dream up this exact design, not in a million years.

But if someone *told* educated and skilled people how to put them together—well, that just made more sense.

So what Zoltan said and what Hunter had suspected all along was true then: Everything changed in the war the day Hunter and the two others were found in the Atlantic. And one of the people who dropped in with him was responsible for the resurgence of Germany, and for these weapons and for God knows what else.

And Hunter had no problem at all determining who that person was.

It was a devastating thought to behold, but now, with night fallen, staring up at the stars, mind almost numb from overload, Hunter felt it had to be the correct one. Like a deadly virus, a common germ, he believed right down to his bones, that Viktor had infected this world as well. And because he was responsible for bringing him here, then it was his responsibility to stop him, somehow, before he tainted this world any further.

So these were the thoughts he dwelled on all that night— these and the pangs of loss for Dominique.

He stayed on top of the mountain, wide awake and thinking, until the sun came up the next morning.

Chapter 31

Hunter began the next day by studying the F-16s.

He finally managed to get himself to climb up and get inside one of the cockpits. It was a huge psychological leap forward for him, even though at first he'd feared it might be a traumatic event. But once he'd squeezed in and settled down and took a deep breath he knew it was OK. His body fit the contours of the seat perfectly. His hand went to the side stick controller so naturally it was scary. Yes, this was familiar and it felt good. Back in his other world, he'd spent more time in one of these things, than he had walking around upright on two feet.

The cockpit control panels were different though. They were very spare. All the essentials were there: altitude, AOA, fuel gauges, oil pressure lights, and so on. But the panel had none of the sexy bell-and-whistle connections. No radar mapping, no terrain avoidance, no NightVision capability.

The jets were stripped down inside, but in an odd way, this made them better, and more dangerous. These airplanes were pure fighters. Engine, wings, and weapons. He would have loved to turn one on, but that would be impossible. There as no fuel at the base—not a drop. He'd checked. Same with weapons. There were no bullets, no cannon rounds, no bombs anywhere. These airplanes were virgins. Hunter would have bet none of them had more than an hour's flight time between them.

Which was really too bad. Because, as painful as it was, he knew they had to be destroyed.

And quickly.

Of all the decisions he'd made up on the mountain the night before, this was probably the most difficult.

These airplanes were his strongest link back to the place where he came from. In many ways, his only link. He would have loved nothing better than to keep one somehow, fly it, be with it.

But he knew that couldn't be.

For despite his own odd circumstances, he was still in a military situation here. And the right thing had to be done.

He knew these airplanes could have a huge affect on the outcome of the war. No weapons in this world could catch up to a 1600-mph fighter, not one that could sustain that speed for long periods of time, unlike a Natter, which blew its load in two minutes. These airplanes would be able to shoot down the huge American bombers with impunity then. They would make the other German wonder weapons look like toys once they became operational. These 12 airplanes alone could possibly win the war for Germany. And who was to say there weren't any more of them?

So they had to go . . . and go quickly, before the Huns realized this part of the valley was still dry and came back to reclaim their prize.

But how could Hunter do it exactly? There was no fuel, no flammable liquids at all at the base. No weapons, no explosives, nothing combustible. There was nothing to burn them with really.

He'd found a sledgehammer, and thought for a while that he might be able to batter the planes to the point where they could never fly again. But he quickly came to the conclusion that this would be impossible. He could bang on these things all day and really do only superficial damage. He'd have been better off if he'd found a screw-driver.

No, there really wasn't anything here with which Hunter could destroy the airplanes quickly, all at once. Not directly anyway.

But he still had his Boomer, and amazingly it still worked.

And with it, he might get lucky.

It took him more than an hour to climb back up the mountain this time.

His heart was heavy, that's why it took so long. The adrenaline rush from the day before had dissipated, and the full effect of the narcosis had not fully set in yet. So now he was just tired, cold, hungry, and heartsick. He missed his world, as crazy as it had been. He missed his friends.

He missed Dominique.

By the time he topped the hill, night was falling. He ate a handful of mush from the four-day-old supply found in the mess hall, and drank a container of water.

Then he lay back and looked up at the smoky sky again and waited for the stars to come out.

And the bombers too.

He knew the in-flight combat radio frequencies for most of the bomber groups from the old Circle. He'd used them so many times during the operations over Britain and Germany, they came back to him like prayers. He was sure some of the old Circle planes would be taking part in the new bombing campaign now.

If he could just get a message through to one of them.

It took three more hours of scanning the skies, but then, right around midnight, he saw them. The contrails showed up first. Very high, coming out of the northwest. There were so many of them, they were filling the sky with long white stripes from horizon to horizon.

He saw the lights on the bombers next. It was the absence of any fighter opposition to and from the target that allowed the American pilots to boldly illuminate themselves with a single red light, just to stay safe in the very crowded and tight bomber streams.

He did a quick count, just of the bombers he could see, and came up with 554. God knows how many were behind them.

He cranked up the Boomer, snapped on the short-wave radio and started twirling the dials. Above him now, the sky held more contrails than stars.

It would take him more than half an hour of trying, but then finally, he actually got someone to answer his call.

It was a bomber pilot attached to what once was the old, sodden 999th, now flying off the *Cape Cod*. Hunter read out a list of code words he remembered from his time riding shotgun for the bombers, and finally the pilot believed Hunter was who he said he was. A fellow American who was on the ground looking up.

The pilot said he had about a six-minute window to talk so Hunter had to be quick. The pilot assumed Hunter wanted to arrange for a rescue pickup.

"No," Hunter replied. "I have a target down here that has to be hit."

"How big is the target?" the pilot asked. "You know we're restricted to one-square-mile hits. Anything under that can't be done by one package."

"I don't want a package," Hunter told him. "I want one bomber with six bombs. No firebombs either. Someone will have to round up some iron bombs."

"This all sounds highly unusual," the pilot replied.

"It's a highly unusual target," Hunter called back, running out of time. He quickly gave the pilot the coordinates and then asked him to repeat them.

"Hang on," the pilot replied instead.

Hang on? Hunter wondered.

There were 20 long seconds of static, then finally another voice came on.

"This is Captain Dan Raycroft," said the new voice. "I'm the air intelligence officer for this group. Please repeat your code signs."

Hunter did.

"This is unbelievable," Raycroft exclaimed.

"What is?" Hunter wanted to know.

"If you are who you say you are, then you are the most famous person in the world right now."

"What? Repeat?" Hunter couldn't really hear too clearly. But he could tell the guy at the other end was flipping out.

"You are everywhere, man," Raycroft told him. "You're in every newspaper. On TV. On Radio."

"Yeah, I know," Hunter said. "But . . ."

"You're the guy who blew the dam, right?"

"Yes, but . . ."

"And you gave an interview to the press recently, right?"

Hunter had to think a moment. Did this guy mean the camera crew he'd met on the flight deck of the *Cape Cod*?

"Yes, I did," he replied. "But listen . . ."

"Well pal, that's been playing everywhere," the intell officer interrupted him again. "As your last words."

"What?"

"Yeah, man," Raycroft replied. "That's what I'm trying to tell you. Everyone thinks you're dead."

Hunter was stunned. He couldn't believe what he was hearing.

"Turn your TV receive button to quick-flash," the intell man told him. "Hurry . . ."

Hunter did as told and soon the little screen on the Boomer was showing bits and pieces of news footage— obviously some kind of an animated briefing reel the intell officer was carrying with him. The first image was Hunter's picture. Then the same old clip of him climbing into the Mustang-5 jet in the snow and taxiing away. Then a clip of damage to Ruhr after the dam break. It was even more catastrophic than he'd thought. Then came his brief comments on the deck of the carrier to the camera crew. Then a huge memorial service in Washington, D.C. And then a casket burning in the middle of Berlin square!

Hunter could barely speak.

"The country is in 30 days of mourning for you, man," Raycroft told him. "You're as dead as dead can be. In fact, the Germans are calling you the *Himmelgeist*."

Hunter just couldn't believe it. There was only one thing better than a real live hero to perk up a country's morale— and that was a dead one. And now, he was it.

"Well, you've got to let people know I'm still here," Hunter told the man in the plane high above him. "That I'm still alive."

But then the transmission began to fade.

"I'm losing you," he heard Raycroft's voice say, weakening with each word.

"Jessuzz, wait!" Hunter yelled into his microphone. "Did you get my message. About the air strike?"

"Air strike? What air strike?"

Hunter nearly dropped the phone.

"I told your pilot," he yelled back. "I need a bomber to drop six bombs, low and slow on a very important target down here. I gave your pilot the coordinates. Is he going to pass them on?"

"I'll pass them on," Raycroft said, his words fading badly.

"And are you going to get someone out here to rescue me?"

But that's when the connection finally died away. Hunter tried and tried and tried, but he could not raise Raycroft again. The line was dead. He looked up at the million or so contrails passing right over his head. Which plane exactly had he been talking to?

There was no way he would ever know.

He started beating on all the switches and buttons on the Boomer—looking for a replay button. But this particular machine didn't have that function. So the clip showing his memorial services in both Washington and Berlin was lost forever.

Finally, he just sat back and began sucking in the night air. How weird was this? Every time he thought things couldn't get any stranger here, they did.

He waited a couple of hours, then began trying again to raise one of the hundreds of bombers that were going over his head, this time heading northwest, going home.

But he couldn't get through to any of them.

By morning he knew he had to prepare for the air strike, even though he wasn't too optimistic that his message and the important coordinates all got through in one piece.

He climbed back down the mountain, regained the base, and went to the white hanger. He closed the windows and any doors he could find. He did this to the six other buildings as well. Closed windows and doors spread bomb blasts around better than open ones, and Hunter wanted as much destruction at this base as possible.

His work done, he went back to the white hanger one more time and gave the 12 F-16s one long last look.

He felt like a man throwing his family off a bridge.

Finally he just turned and walked away.

Another debate he'd had with himself was where exactly he should stay for the air strike.

Good sense said as far away as possible, but Hunter knew that couldn't be the case. Air strikes were always chancy things, even if the pilot knew what he was doing. Hitting a ground target from any airplane was just not an easy thing to do.

There was a chance then that all of the F-16s would not be destroyed in the first attack; a follow-up might be needed. If this was the case, then Hunter would have to do a quick bomb damage assessment and then call in a follow-up strike if necessary, meaning he would have to contact the attacking bomber before it left the area.

So he had to find a place not too close to the target,

but not so far away as it would take him a long time to do the poststrike evaluation.

As it turned out, there was just the perfect place about 2000 feet away from the hangar.

It was a pillbox, an old one, possibly dating back to World War I. It was built into the side of a hill nearby. Maybe at one time it guarded the approach road to the secret base. It was made of cobblestone and mortar and wood, and it looked damn sturdy.

It faced the white hangar, so Hunter would have a good view of the bomber's approach. If he was able to make contact with the pilot beforehand, he could walk him right in. Plus, if one or two bombs fell short, the thick walls would protect him from harm.

So this is where he would stay and wait for the bomber's approach.

He had salvaged the last of the porridge and the orange drink from the mess hall and brought this as his meal to the bunker. He also had his flight suit dried and repaired by this time, so he climbed out of the denims for the first time in a while and into the more comfortable speed jeans.

His gun was holding up well too. The ammo was still dry, and a quick cleaning brought the barrel and muzzle up to snuff.

He used the denims as a mattress and pillow and sat down for the first time in a very long time. He ate the hardened porridge and sipped the orange drink. He had the Boomer nearby, turned on with the batteries switched to low.

He positioned himself so he could look out one opening of the pillbox and see the secret air base, look out another and have a clear view of the northwestern sky, the direction from which the air strike bomber would come. Out the third opening he could see the tall, narrow waterfall, its water falling hundreds of feet, still kicking up a perpetual cloud of vapor and spray several miles away. It looked rather peaceful at the moment.

He finished the porridge and drained the orange water.

He set the Boomer's DHF radio to scan and leaned back. The sun was coming through the western opening now and hitting Hunter right in the face. It felt warm, drying. Drowsy.

He tried to fight it, but he couldn't. He hadn't stopped in what—seven days? Heroes had to sleep too.

Even dead ones.

Still, Hunter never felt his chin hit his chest, or his eyes begin to close.

He was asleep before the empty cup of porridge hit the floor.

Hunter dreamed many things that long afternoon.

Things that his mind would only allow him to deal with in a sleeping state, things too troubling to come to the surface, even now. One was the fact that he had met several people since arriving in this world that reminded him of people he'd known back in his old one.

Now, in his dream, he met them again briefly. Captain Crunch. Colonel Crabb. Even Wolf, the commander of the destroyer that had picked him up out in the Atlantic. Was it possible that they were here, as different people, but at the same time like the person he knew? He didn't know, so he began asking each one. But after a while, this became too complicated for his psyche, even for his dream state. So his subconscious urged him to move on.

He dreamed next about swimming in very cold water, even though his hair and hands were on fire. Then he saw the dead horses near the huge red plastic German target again. They were encased in ice, legs sticking up, but now they were breaking through the frost and coming back to life. Then he was back in the Pogo, and feeling that exhilaration of flight running through him for the very first time in this lifetime. Then he was suddenly back in his old F-16, flying the same heart-stopping maneuvers, yet this time, he was over his old base at Cape Cod, back in his ZAP days. Damn, it had been Otis Air Force Base! he just realized. The same place that'd he'd been brought and questioned soon after appearing in this world.

But the strangest dream of all came at the end. He dreamed a swarm of bees had flown into his left ear and were coming out the right. Their buzzing was far off—but getting louder.

Closer.

Hunter shook himself awake a second later and oddly the first thing he did was grab the rifle and sweep the room.

He was alone, but was still frozen in horror. The sun was gone, it was night. The buzzing, far off, was the American Air Corps coming back to firebomb Germany.

Hunter couldn't believe it—he'd fallen asleep!

He grabbed the Boomer and turned it on full scan. What he heard was a wave of voices getting stronger, clearer as the hundreds of contrails approached again from the northwest.

Damn. Damn. Damn.

Hunter screwed back to the frequency on which he'd spoken with the bomber the night before. But it was empty. There were people talking on just about every other channel but the one he was concerned about—the one that he should have been monitoring all afternoon instead of falling asleep. It was clear.

But to Hunter's way of thinking, that was a good sign. The omission of voices on that channel might mean his message had gotten through and the air strike was on its way.

He carried the Boomer over to the window and studied the huge air armada scorching the night sky once again with long white tails above his head.

He could see red streaks off to the west—flak rising not quite high enough to affect the swarm. Then he saw blue and green streaks falling through the bomber streams— these were the fighters, their guns full of ammo, going in to attack the flak sites. A series of explosions just over the horizon told him some hits were made. The flak stopped rising after that.

The first line of bombers was nearly right over him now. He checked the Boomer again and found the specified frequency was still silent. He briefly visited the window looking out on the secret base. Everything was still, and the slight wind blowing through the place, gave off an eerie howl.

And beyond, the majestic waterfall was still throwing clouds of mist up into the night sky.

That's when the Boomer finally crackled with life.

He was back at the window looking out on the bomber stream. He zeroed in on the Boomer's frequency, then slapped the scramble arm down.

"This is Zebra Delta . . . are you there?"

"I'm here," Hunter replied hastily. "Are you my air strike?"

"Yes we are," the voice came back. It sounded confident, very self-assured.

"You got my coordinates? You got the dope on the target?"

"Yes, we do . . ."

Hunter was surprised. It seems like his request had been filled to order. But what were they carrying?

"May I ask what your bomb load is, please?"

"We are carrying six eight-hundred-pound bombs, high explosive," was the reply. "Is that what you asked for?"

Hunter was amazed.

"Yes, it is," he said, looking up at the second wave of bombers and wondering which one he was talking to.

"Let's talk this through, OK?" Hunter asked. "You got the map coordinates. Let me give you some landmarks. You come in from the dead west, you'll see a rise out of a valley. Then the target—it's a two-runway base with a bunch of support buildings and one big white hangar. Beyond that, there's the biggest waterfall you've ever seen, and after that the flood. OK?"

"OK . . ."

"Now, line your nose up with that waterfall and put your bombs into the white hanger, then we're money, get it?"

There was a crackle of static.

"Got it," came the pilot's reply, but Hunter thought a moment. Does he really? He searched the next bomber stream, way out, figuring at any moment he would see one plane start to drop down and . . .

"Zebra Delta? What is your position right now?" he asked the pilot.

"We are approximately one half mile away from target . . ."

One half mile?

"Jessuzz, what is your altitude?"

"Altitude at 100 feet, coming in from the west . . ."

Hunter shook his head and then looked west, and sure enough, here was a huge B-24/52 coming in, full engines, smoke billowing, rocking back and forth in the thick air. Right at that instant, Hunter knew the plane was too big, too fast, too low to attempt this mission.

"Jessuzz, you're way too low!" Hunter screamed into the Boomer, but it was way too late. The huge airplane was bearing down on the target at more than 500 knots.

"Roger," the pilot continued radioing mindlessly. "Line up our nose on the white hanger and let bomb string walk right up the waterfall . . ."

Hunter's jaw dropped. *What did the pilot just say?*

"No, abort! Abort!" he started screaming again, but it was too late.

The bomber went right over the pillbox. He saw the bomb bay doors open and a string of bombs tumble out. They missed the white hangar by a mile, impacting—all 4800 pounds of them—up the side of the waterfall.

The explosion was tremendous—the waterfall was instantly blasted apart. Tons of rock and dirt were thrown high into the air. Fire and smoke filled the sky. It seemed like the whole mountain came apart, which is exactly what happened. And over the top of the dirt and rock came a tidal wave of water as high as the waterfall had been. It hit the previous mound of rubble first—and kept on coming. It hit half a dozen rolling hills next—and kept on coming. It hit the outside of the base, then the fences and the support buildings and tower—and kept on coming. It swamped the white hanger and tore it right off its foundations.

Then, maybe two seconds after the explosion, the water hit the pillbox where Hunter stood simply transfixed.

And then, for the third time in six days, he found himself tumbling again, out of control, being swept along by the deep, dark water.

Chapter 32

When Hunter woke up this time he was absolutely, positively convinced he was in Heaven.

The sun was shining. The birds were singing. He was laying in a pool of warm water, some of it trickling over his face. It felt so good against his skin. And there was a beautiful girl standing over him. She looked just like an angel was supposed to look. Golden-red hair, soft skin, almost luminescent. The sun was hitting her in such a way that she even seemed to be wearing a halo.

This is cool, Hunter thought hazily, knowing somewhere deep in his mind that beating the flood three times would have been just too much to ask. So he was dead, for real this time.

At least now he could get some sleep.

But then someone was talking to him, trying to get him to move, but he really didn't want to move. The water was warm and comfortable and . . .

"Please!" he heard a voice plead, and this got him to open his eyes again. "We don't have much time."

It was the girl standing over him.

Hunter lifted himself up and for the first time got a good look around.

He was in a small stream, one of many that were coursing through a wide, flat, now treeless valley.

But what kind of a place was this? He looked around and saw that the muddy path of destruction stretched for miles. And odd as hell, on the stream banks all around him were the 12 crumpled F-16s. Nearly all of them were sticking nose down into the mud, though a few were flipped belly-up, or resting against downed trees, their noses pointing skyward, as if they were ready to take right off.

Hunter's eyes almost watered on seeing the airplanes. They were all total wrecks, twisted and battered and in pieces from the water's incredible force. He and they had tumbled down the same flood together.

Finally he had to look away.

But then he saw scores of other wrecked military equipment littering the soggy valley as well. Tanks, armored cars, helicopters, artillery pieces. They were all twisted and torn and battered and ripped up worse than the F-16s. They all bore the Iron Cross of the German Army.

He stared up at the sun and the young girl again.

"Please," she was saying again. "We don't have much time."

She was cute. Delicate features, petite body wrapped in only a soaked nightgown. But Hunter had to blink twice. Damn, he couldn't believe he was thinking this, but this girl looked very familiar to him too.

"Please," she was saying to him, "I will run out of time and then it will be too late."

Finally Hunter got the message.

He rolled over and finally got to his feet. He was very wobbly, and his hands were scraped and cut. But he didn't think he was badly injured and a quick self-diagnosis confirmed this. And somehow he'd had the presence of mind to strap the rifle onto his back before the waters came, because it was still tied around his neck. He still had his steelpot helmet on too. But everything else was gone.

He shook his head and got his bearings and caught his breath and then looked at the girl who looked familiar to him and asked:

"What are you doing out here?"

But she ignored him. She turned instead and began walking out of the stream.

Hunter followed her and briefly collapsed on the bank. It was now just sinking in—the girl had saved his life. Somehow she had made her way through the devastation to reach him.

"What is your name?" he asked her.

But again she didn't answer him.

"We don't have much time," she said instead. "We have to hurry."

Hunter got back to his feet, gave his injured ankles a few steps and, though a little woozy, knew he was OK.

Where the hell am I? he asked himself, looking around at the field littered with wrecked equipment again. It was almost as if some huge battle had been fought here. But how? And when? Hunter had no idea.

He pulled the rifle from his back. He checked the chamber—two dry charges were inside.

"Come with me," the girl was telling him, standing about 20 feet away from him now. "Hurry. I don't have much time."

"OK, OK," Hunter said, trying to stretch some of his aches and pains away. "I'll go with you."

With that, the girl started running.

What followed now was a foot race. The girl was running as fast as her bare feet could carry her. At times she looked like she was gliding above the devastated ground, that's how fast she ran. Hunter tried his best to keep up with her. But no matter how fast he moved, the girl always managed to stay about 50 feet or so ahead of him.

They ran over hills, into valleys, across washed-out river-beds, and through fields of wheat and corn that had been shorn away.

Finally they topped one hill and Hunter came upon an

astonishing sight. Before him, stretched throughout a wide valley, were at least two dozen enormous wrecked airplanes. They were as big as the seajet he'd shot down over Iceland, bigger even. He quickly studied one of them. Inside he could see dead crewmen, still strapped to their seats. Equipment, tools, boots, helmets, and other supplies filled the wrecked cargo holds.

These monsters were obviously troop carriers. And he had no doubt they had been intended to be used in the rumored invasion of the U.S. that Pegg had spoken about. But, just like the devastation he'd seen back in the other valley, no battle had wrecked these airplanes. The flood waters had done it instead.

The girl was standing at the top of the next hill by now, beckoning Hunter furiously. He left behind the graveyard of monster airplanes and scrambled up the hill. But when he reached the top, the girl was not there. And now he was looking down into another valley. This one was full of bodies. Dead soldiers. Thousands of them.

He slid down the hill and made his way over to one clump of corpses. He looked into the eyes of three dead men and realized they were German paratroopers. They were in combat uniform, parachutes still attached to the backsides. They were wearing full equipment belts and ammo loads. There must have been at least 10,000 of them scattered throughout the valley, most floating in the many pools of water the flood had left behind.

He reached inside one man's pocket and came out with a map. He opened it and saw it was not for anywhere in Germany or Europe, but for the state of Maryland. That was all he needed for proof. These soldiers were obviously connected to those wrecked airplanes, possibly even the advance landing parties for the U.S. invasion. Yet the flood had killed them all too.

Hunter's stomach was nearly turned inside out by this time. Some kind of animals had already been feeding on the bodies and he imagined what a nightmare this place would be once all the water was finally gone and the sun got around to baking all these corpses. He began running again.

The girl was at the top of the next hill by now and yelling to him.

"Hurry! I don't have much time left . . ."

It took Hunter 10 minutes to climb out of the field of death.

Finally, he reached the top of the last hill and saw before him a long concrete bunker. Two wrecked vehicles were smashed against its front door. A huge antenna lay crumpled across its roof. Two rings of high concertina wire had once surrounded the structure, indicating that it, just like the hangar containing the F-16s, was probably a very secret place.

But the fences had been washed away. And the front door was wide open. And the girl was standing next to it, beckoning him inside.

Hunter stumbled down the hill, fell once, got up, fell again, and got up again.

He climbed over the two rolls of barbed wire and the wrecked fence and was soon standing at the front door. The girl was inside. Her voice was echoing now.

"Please, look in here, I have to go . . ." she was insisting.

Hunter stumbled inside. The first thing he saw was a BMW FlyBike, a kind of combination motorcycle and small airplane. He'd seen a few of them around the Circle bases, though they weren't the transportation of choice in sub-zero temperatures. They had big motors, loud mufflers, lots of chrome, and a twin set of turbine jets which could move the bike through the air at about 40 knots, pretty fast considering it was an open ride.

Beyond the bike were six boxes. They were made of plastic and wood and each one was broken open at the seal. Hunter examined the first one. Beneath loads of packing paper and straw matting, he found another smaller box inside. It was black and made of lead. It was also very heavy. He managed to lift it out and get it open.

Inside was a bomb.

It was about 30 inches long, maybe seven inches around, and had small wings in the back and a tiny fusing propeller on the front.

But this was not a typical aerial bomb, as even Hunter's groggy, spinning head could tell him. He lifted the thing out of its case and cradled it on his lap. There was lots of yellow stenciled lettering on its side. Some of it identified the bomb as an Mk-175, low-detonation, high-yield strategic weapon. Low-detonation? High-yield? Hunter almost let the thing roll off his lap. He was that startled.

These words, and words like them, he had not heard here in this strange world. Why? Because nuclear power— and atom bombs—didn't exist here.

At least, not until now.

He turned the bomb over, trying to divine more information from all the letters and numbers stenciled on to it. But the only phrase he could make out clearly was both simple and ominous. Up near the nose, there was a yellow box with these words in German printed within it: READY FOR USE.

He opened the rest of the big boxes and found five more bombs, all of them exactly the same. He just couldn't believe it. In this building was probably more destructive capability than all the bombs both sides had dropped on each other for the entire 59 years of this version of World War II!

And obviously, just like the F-16s and the other so-called German wonder weapons, these bombs had been introduced to this world by the same person who'd revived the Reich shortly after arriving here.

"How did you know to bring me here?" Hunter called out for the girl. The last he'd seen of her, she'd walked deeper into the bunker.

But he got no reply. So he started walking toward the end of the structure himself. It was pitch-dark and empty except the bomb crates themselves. Perhaps they'd been carried here in hurried anticipation of the flood.

He walked all the way to the end—and found no sign of the girl.

He called out to her, but got no reply.

He went back to the front of the building. She was not there either. He looked in all directions, but could not see her anywhere against the absolutely flat terrain. He went back into the bunker, walked its length again, and found nothing.

She was really gone this time.

Vanished into thin air.

Just like that.

Chapter 33

It took Hunter more than two hours to fasten the six bombs on to the aerial motorcycle.

Ever since he'd been here in this other place, he'd been able to tap his ability to fly just about any kind of aircraft he'd been faced with.

From the Pogo to the Mustang Jet to test-flying the Bomber Gunship, Hunter had been able to climb in, take a look at the instruments, and go.

But this strange machine, this was different. This flying bike had no instruments, save a fuel gauge and a speedometer. It really was like a kid's bicycle or even an earthbound Harley; it came with no instructions, no parameters. You learned at your own pace.

Trouble was, Hunter had to learn this lesson real quick.

Plus, he'd be doing it with a terribly overloaded takeoff weight, assuming, of course, that he could get it off the ground at all.

These bombs, he realized, were compact hydrogen weapons. Each weighed at least 80 pounds—not bad for a potential destructive power of many thousands of megatons. But for Hunter's purposes they were way too heavy, especially since he had to carry all six of them. There was no alternative to this. He couldn't leave any of them behind, not as dangerous as they were. He *had* to bring all of them with him, somehow, some way. And that way was on this flying motorbike.

He was able to remove some of the unnecessary weight from the strange aircraft. He took off the chrome exhaust guards, the chrome front grille, and the heavy rubber seat. He was able to take one tire off of each of the four landing struts, and this freed up space for him to attach two of the bombs.

The second pair had to be strapped alongside the seatless saddle. There was just enough room to slot them in between the engine mounts in back, and the wide steering column in front.

It was the fifth and sixth bombs that were such a bitch to hang. Finally Hunter was able to winch both of them up under the nose. No rope would hold them here. He had to strip out the metal bindings of the plane's saddlebags to get wire strong enough to mount each bomb.

Then, he had to push and pull and ultimately drag the flying bike up to the top of the hill, a distance of maybe 500 yards that took him more than three hours to cover.

But his timing couldn't have been better. By the time he got to the top of the hill, night had fallen, and a huge moon was rising.

He was higher than he thought; the view of the German midlands was incredible from here. To his right, flooded farmland and pasture. Over the horizon, the glow of the still burning cities. To his left, nothing less than a small sea—the one created by the burst dam. In front of him, more burning cities. Behind him, the same.

Now he had a real question to consider, one he hadn't really given much thought to: Where was he going exactly?

He didn't know. Way in the front of his skull, the place where everything now percolated, a voice was telling him to wing it, use his instincts, fly away and see where it gets you. But the part of him that actually did his rational thinking for him was questioning just how wise this course would be.

It was a long drop down just about any place in the Ruhr Valley these days, and where it wasn't solid ground, it was square miles of lake water. And Hunter knew this crate, packed as it was, would sink like an anchor should he find himself forced to ditch into the wet deck.

He'd also have to watch out for enemy aircraft, though he already had two up on any German pilot who happened to spot him. Hunter would certainly be flying way too slow and way too low to interest any pilot in engaging him.

But said pilot would probably have a radio and just spotting Hunter in the pokey flying machine could be catastrophic. For a helicopter or a smaller prop-driven airplane, Hunter would be meat on a hook. If the enemy's bullets didn't light off one of the H-bombs first, that was.

So, this would be an interesting flight, to say the least.

He started the preflight stuff on the FlyBike. The engine came to life with just a few foot-pumps. It roared, quieted down, and then roared again. It had excellent throttle control and the engine was more powerful than Hunter had first surmised. At last he'd be a firsthand witness to some of that vaunted German engineering he was always hearing about.

He extended the wings and brought the control surfaces to trim. Everything looked to be working fine. His fuel gauge read full: 25 gallons in the main, two and a half in the reserve tank. Hunter's mind briefly recalled a time in his other past where one notch of the throttle would burn that much fuel in a matter of two seconds. That was in his old F-16XL. He felt another pang in his chest. That was another thing from his old world that he'd never see again.

He yanked his mind back to the matter at hand. He revved the engines just one more time and guessed the oil system must be vacuum-controlled, because the engine sounded both juiced and lubed.

OK, then, there was nothing to hold him back. So he

climbed on, hit the throttle, pinched the brakes, and started rolling.

Off the cliff he went, his airspeed barely 10 knots after the running start. He immediately dipped dangerously low. The bombs were not only heavy, they were unstable, and thus wreaking havoc with the craft's center of gravity. Hunter instinctively pulled back on the steering bars and raised the nose. This immediately ended the juggling act. Then he increased throttle just slightly and the FlyBike stopped dropping. He went hard right to get some sideways momentum and, once gathered, pulled back on the steering again and at last began to climb.

He'd been right. The loaded-down FlyBike was slow and he couldn't get more than 200 feet under its ass, but at least it was flying. And one thing Hunter had found out here, in this strange place, as well as the other: he was always better off when he was airborne.

His head began to clear as he pointed the FlyBike's nose right at the rising moon and laid on a little more gas.

He was achieving his first objective. To get the six nuclear bombs away from the Germans. He was sure they were trying to get to them too, but because he was the only living soul inside the area devastated by the flood, he'd somehow beaten them to it. Thanks to the young girl. Whoever—or *whatever*—she was. His mind curiously turned blank when he thought about her. Try as he might, her image was fading quickly from his memory. What was she doing out there? How had she found him? How did she know to take him to the bombs? He didn't know.

But because of her, he might be able to get the H-bombs into American hands and perhaps someone would be able to pull them apart and figure out a way to disable them so they could never work again.

Or something.

OK, but where was he going? He didn't know if anyone was still looking for him—or if anyone even came out at all after the dam burst. From the conversation with the bomber that night, everyone just assumed he'd been killed from the start. But if the rescue units had been sent out, and if by some grace of the Cosmos they were still looking for him, then they would probably expect him to stay near, or get back to, the last location he was seen alive. That would be the busted dam itself.

And just like that, he had his goal, his destination. How far away was he? He couldn't be sure. But he was certain he wouldn't have any trouble finding it. All he would have to do is follow the coastline of the new inland sea and eventually find its source.

He climbed a little more and took in the moon for a few moments. Even though he was only a couple hundred feet off the ground, it still felt like he could just reach out and touch it—it seemed that close.

He began thinking about how he felt when he was airborne. He'd flown a hell of a lot in his other life—he felt like that's all he did. Just the same here as there, being on the ground was the unnatural state of affairs for him.

He climbed just a little more, and soon he was at 400 feet. He steered over to the coast of the inland sea, and then completed a sluggish yet effective 45-degree turn to the left. Now his nose was pointing north, up where the big Merne-Sorpa Dam used to be. If his calculations that he had about two hours flying time in the bike were correct, there was a chance he might actually make the dam site with fuel to spare.

He looked over at the moon, now brilliant and dazzling on his left. The airbike's motor was humming right along. The bombs seemed secure. His head was remarkably clear.

This was going well, he thought.

Too well.

His body started vibing just a second later.

Damn—something bad was on its way.

He quickly sorted out the sounds around him. Take away the wind, take away the burping FlyBike motor, take away his own heart beating. What was he left with?

A high-pitched, sizzling sound. And sizzling meant fuel being burned. It was getting louder, higher pitched. He looked to his right. Nothing. Behind him, nothing. In front, all clear. And then his left—and that's when he saw it. A plume of smoke and fire coming right up at him.

Someone was shooting rocket-propelled AA at him!

The flak shell exploded just a second later, no more that 50 feet off his left wing. The blast went off about 15 feet below him though—and ultimately, that's what saved his life. The flak shell blew down, and most of the shrapnel went that way as well. But the concussion itself was enough to knock Hunter on his side and drive the FlyBike horizontally. He came very close to going inverted, a dive from which he knew he could never recover. So he fought the FlyBike's controls viciously, yanking the plane all over the place, overcompensating one way, while fighting to keep it from going over the other way.

Somehow, he was able to level the plane out and even get the nose elevated again. That's when the second flak burst went off. This one was closer and about even with him in altitude. It threw him nearly an eighth of a mile to the left, and at the end of the spin, he actually did go 180 degrees over.

The force of the unexpected maneuver righted the Fly-Bike almost instantly though. Hunter looked down and saw shrapnel burns scoring the entire right side of his body. Yet, somehow, none of the bomb's jagged pieces had pierced his skin.

He recovered again and managed to look behind him and saw two more flak trails. But both shells exploded too high and too far away from him to do much damage. Still, the shock waves had him fighting for control once again for the next few anxious seconds.

Hunter had to think quick. He pushed the nose over and was able to bring the airplane down to about 20 feet; now he was just skimming along the top of the water of the inland sea. He thought he'd be safe from the flak from here—and he was. But now he saw a storm of luminescent streaks coming out of the woods. They were cannon shells, lighting up the night, and coming right at him. He threw the FlyBike into a climb, but heard two distinctive pings on the bottom of the frame.

One round had hit his rear left tire, blowing it out and sending him momentarily out of his skin. The next tracer round bounced off one of the nose-mounted bombs—and nothing happened. Hunter couldn't get the air in and out of his lungs fast enough. He began climbing again, a flood of tracers following him up as the FlyBike screamed for altitude.

Somehow he managed to escape all this too, and was huffing and puffing as the bike climbed to 300 feet again. He steered his way further out over the water, away from the shore-based ground fire. Either these guys had been waiting for him, or he had chosen to fly over what must have been a large contingent of German soldiers hidden in the woods, quite possibly troops who'd somehow survived the carnage in the flood.

This thought was driven from his mind by the roar of an angry engine behind him. He turned left and was horrified to see a German helicopter had flown up right beside him. It was a troop carrier, a big, strange, gangly thing sprouting rocket-assisted rotor blades and a gaggle of side-mounted weaponry.

Now there were about a dozen gun barrels pointing at him. Somehow Hunter managed to lift his own gun up and squeeze the trigger. The gigantic cloud of shot hit the flying machine in the worst place possible: its fuel tank. Gas was suddenly leaking down onto its hot engine. The pilot banked steeply away from Hunter, but the machine blew up seconds later.

Riding the shock wave through this, Hunter's ears were filled with another sound. He turned to see an even stranger German flying machine on his right. This was a flying platform, circular in shape, four separate helicopter-like rotors barely keeping it up. Standing out on the platform, like the deck crew on a submarine, were six men

crowding around what looked to be a 88-mm antiaircraft
gun.

A flying flak wagon? Really?

But Hunter didn't have to time to think about it. The
thing was so close to him, he could see the gunners looking
right down their sights at him. He flipped the big rifle
over, somehow slammed a shell in, and fired.

The storm of shot scattered the gun crew; three were
hit seriously. The others naturally tried to get out of the
way. In doing so they must have violated one of the
operating rules of the platform because it quickly became
unstable and unbalanced. It began to wobble and then
flipped over and disappeared below him.

Hunter flew on, still trying to control his own unstable
airplane. Now more flak was coming up from the woods
on both sides of the lake. He could clearly hear the *pomp!
pomp! pomp!* of an 88-mm AA gun firing at him from the tree
line. He was almost moving too slowly and too erratically for
anyone to get a real bead on him. But how long could
that last? Even now, more machine gun tracers and large-
caliber carbine rounds were whizzing and pinging all
around him. But still he flew on.

Up ahead, he could see a huge gun muzzle pointing
out of the woods near a narrow in the inland sea. Suddenly
fire started coming out of this barrel like water out of
a hose. It was blocking his flight path—and he was too
wounded, and too low, and too underpowered to attempt
a climb over it. He would have to go under it instead.

He rammed the steering column down and gave the
throttle a goose and he was soon looking at the water
coming right up at him. Just as quickly, he yanked the
steering bars back and gave the throttle another goose and
the nose went up. The engines coughed, the flame was
right above him, but he made it through. He reached up
to his helmet and found the top of it was sizzling hot.
That's how close he'd come.

Now it seemed like every gun in the woods was firing at
him. The sky was lit up with tracer rounds, pom-pom shells,

lak, fire-shells, concussions blasts. The FlyBike's engines vere perforated in several places now, one of his fuel lines vas leaking directly onto one of the H-bombs. The tiny jet urbines themselves were beginning to cough badly, and ae could feel their power slowly ebbing away.

The bombs were shifting all over the place too, one of hem was hanging by just one strand of wire. What hap-ened to a hydrogen bomb's fusing mechanism when it s soaked in fuel and exposed to a spark? He didn't want o know.

Hunter yanked back on the throttle—fuel was his most mportant commodity now, but it was draining out of his anks quicker than it was flowing into his carburetors. This vas the problem.

He was slowly going down, too injured to stay airborne ny longer.

But where or how could he find a safe place to land? With the sky filled with bullets and AA rounds, only water elow him and thick forest on either side.

This was getting very hairy . . .

But then he heard yet another familiar sound. A high whine among the whizzing of bullets. An engine, but it vas very quiet, almost like a whisper.

He managed to turn to his right and saw an aircraft iding just off his wing. Hunter could see right into the arge bubble canopy at the two pilots looking back out at aim. The big engine. The long top-mounted wing. The hick fuselage. The heavy-handed landing gear.

Jesus Christ, he whispered.

It was the Lysander.

Flying was a matter of essentials.

Any aircraft that hoped to stay in the air must have a wing, for instance, one that was big enough to provide he lift needed to keep the plane's weight airborne. The uselage itself had to have a certain integrity too, so as not to interrupt the airflow too much to make the aircraft unflightworthy.

Most important though was the pilot. He had to be alert, aware.

Alive . . .

At this moment, with Hunter staring back at the Lysander as it got closer to his tail, he wasn't sure the airplane met any of those essential requirements.

First of all, its wing was battered, its fabric torn and rippling mightily in the wind. And its fuselage looked as if it had taken several broadsides from an ack-ack gun at close range. There were giant gaping holes up and down the length of it. Wires were dangling, fuel lines were drooping. It seemed like every critical control link had been severed long ago. Yet the airplane was still flying.

But it was the view inside the cockpit that Hunter found most disturbing, frightening even. Lancaster and Moon were there, staring blankly back out at him. Not moving, not blinking, and from all evidence, not really flying the airplane. They were just staring out at him, the glow from their instrument panel lighting their faces in a very eerie way.

Hunter felt a shudder go through him, more violent than the flak waves that were still throwing his little flying bike all over the sky. There was something else very strange here. Both Lancaster and Moon, looking out at him with their unflinching gaze, appeared to be dripping wet.

Suddenly the sounds of the battle came back to him. More flak was exploding to his right; shot too high and too fast, it went whizzing right by him. But now the Lysander was moving ahead of him. They wanted him to follow them, so he did. Perhaps they knew a place where he could set down . . .

But then the airplane began climbing, and as it went up Hunter went up too. He passed through 400 feet, 450, 500 . . . Hunter couldn't believe his failing FlyBike had enough gumption left to go this high this fast, but it did. Maybe he draft behind the Lysander was such that it was helping he FlyBike along, Hunter didn't know.

All that was apparent was, he was getting beyond the range of the huge guns and gunfire from the woods.

Then up ahead, Hunter saw a very odd earth formation. Whether it was a result of the flood or whether it had been out here in the Ruhr Valley for centuries, they were coming to a mountain that had a strange flattened-off top.

The closer he got to it, the more it seemed to Hunter like a giant had taken a knife and simply lopped off the mountain's peak, leaving it unnaturally smooth and level.

The Lysander made right for the mountain and Hunter felt the FlyBike just go along and follow.

He actually had to climb to land so he pushed the throttle forward and yanked back on the handle bars and up he went again, one last ride in the elevator, up the side of the strange mountain. He reached the plateau, kicked the engine, leaned heavy on the handlebars and *boom!* he was down.

The FlyBike nearly tipped over on contact with solid ground, but Hunter was not displeased. There was no such thing as a bad landing, especially if one's mode of transport was as shot-up as his was. He simply fell off the bike, rolled once, and then slowly got to his feet.

Somehow all six bombs were still hanging on the bike. What would have happened if one had fallen—or had gotten hit by a stray flak shell? Hunter shivered again. He really didn't want to think about what a dangerous thing he'd just done.

The flattened mountain was a very strange place, too. It was not a result of the flood—this place had been here for years. Hunter could tell by the hardness of the ground and the proliferation of fully grown pine trees anchoring its northern face. It was a forest above the forest, with sheer cliffs protecting it on all sides.

Now he heard the Lysander again and looked up and saw the airplane circle once overhead and then come in for a landing. Hunter started waving his hands madly—

he wanted the pilots to see where he was. But they came in at the other end of the flattened-out peak, forcing Hunter to run about 300 yards over to them.

The plane was down and taxiing by the time Hunter reached their landing spot, still waving his arms and screaming like a madman. The Lysander pivoted perfectly on its left wheel, and as Hunter approached he saw the rear access door swing open. The plane's engine never shut off and it was clear that the pilots simply wanted him to jump on board and leave with them immediately.

But Hunter couldn't do that. He couldn't leave the six H-bombs up here. As protected as it was, it would been a simple matter for a German rotorcraft to fly up here and find the cache. And he wasn't going to let that happen, not after what he'd just gone through to swipe them from the Germans in the first place.

But there was another reason he stopped short of climbing aboard—even just to speak quickly with the pilots. It was the plane itself. When it first came up beside him in the midst of the ack-ack storm, it had looked to be very badly damaged. Now, seeing it up close, Hunter realized what an understatement that had been.

There were such gaping holes in the fuselage and wings, Hunter couldn't see how it was possible the airplane could fly. There simply wasn't enough wing surface for it to stay airborne. Plus the holes in the skin had severed all of the critical steering controls, as well as the fuel lines and hydraulics. All this hit Hunter like a kick in the stomach and he skidded to a stop just a few feet short of the plane's open door.

Don't get onboard, something was telling him. He chose to take the advice.

So he ran to the front of the plane and began waving madly up at Lancaster. Finally the pilot saw him and dreamily pointed him out to Moon.

Now both men were looking down at him. Not waving, not shouting, just staring at him.

Hunter cupped his hands and started screaming: ''I've

got some extremely powerful ordnance I swiped from the Huns! You need to get word back to my ship that we need a heavy lifter out here as quick as possible. OK? Got that?''

Lancaster and Moon made no response. Could they hear him? Hunter didn't know. So he yelled it all over again to them.

This time, after a few seconds, the two pilots just kind of shrugged, smiled, waved, and nodded their heads.

Then Lancaster must have given the plane full throttle because it started rolling again. Hunter watched as it began kicking up dirt and dust and smoke. It went into a short takeoff roll and quickly lifted off.

And that was it. There was no wiggle of the wings, no flashing of the navigation lights.

The shot-up airplane simply continued to climb, higher and higher, until it disappeared into starry night sky.

Chapter 34

Hunter spent the rest of the night making plans.

There was a job for him to do here, in this strange but not so strange place. It involved more than just his trying to win this screwy war, or prevent a German invasion of the United States, or even keeping his own sanity intact.

This job, his life's mission, no matter which universe he found himself in, was to track down and stamp out the person who had caused so much suffering and human misery back in his old world that he made the most notorious dictators of history look like puppy dogs. And now, that embodiment of Evil itself was here, in this world, a place that needed no more suffering than the one he just left.

Again, in a way Hunter felt responsible for this human Satan being here in the first place. He had forced him to go on that long ride up toward the comet with him, knowing that they'd all probably be blown to smithereens and thus, at least, the world would be spared two catastrophes, one natural, the other fairly supernatural.

But how was Hunter to know that they would all fall through a black hole, or a rip in the fabric of time, or whatever the hell their means of entry to this place had been? How could he be expected to know the most hidden, most secret quirks of the universe?

Still, the facts were these: This piece of human vermin was here, and Hunter's pledge to find him and kill him back in his old world had made the jump to this place with him as well.

So he planned, and stayed huddled with the six H-bombs, and waited for the day to come.

And when it did, the first sound he heard was that of eight engines arguing with each other. The racket was on the wind, blowing across the top of the flattened-out mountain, and Hunter might not have heard such a wonderful sound in either of his lifetimes.

It was the unmistakable screech of a Beater, the eight-rotored monster that passed for an ultraheavy lift helicopter in this world. He knew the Germans did not fly these machines—they certainly would have built them better than this. That could only mean one thing; his message had somehow gotten through. And his plan, his *new* plan, was one step closer to fulfillment at last.

The only surprise was that there were actually two Beaters coming for him. This was even better for him. He could now fulfill his quest on his own, without endangering anyone else.

He heard them and then he saw them. The pair of gangling monsters, descending out of the cloudy morning sky, above the faint roar of American bombers heading deep into Germany to attack more targets within the Reich once again.

Hunter was out in the middle of the flattop, waving his arms like a crazy man as the first octocopter set down.

The doors on this one opened quickly and 10 heavily armed soldiers poured out. Their weapons up, ready for anything, they were his friends, the squad of young Air Guards from the Circle bases. He recognized them right away. They, in turn, looked at him like they were seeing someone who'd risen from the grave.

Behind them, another familiar face came off the Beater. It was Payne, looking very smart in a combat uniform and actually carrying a weapon, a first for the bookish officer. He and Hunter greeted each other warmly. Like everyone else, Payne thought Hunter had died a long time ago.

He quickly put the Air Guards to work, hauling the H-bombs onto the first Beater. Hunter hastily told Payne how he'd acquired the weapons and where, and briefed him on what he'd seen during his days in the flood-soaked valley. Payne seemed rather startled by the appearance of the H-bombs though, as were the Air Guards.

One little bomb that could blow up an entire city? What kind of devilish weapon was that?

Hunter assured Payne he would explain it all later, that the most important thing now was to get the bombs out of Germany—but still, none of it seemed to be sinking in.

"Didn't Lancaster and Moon brief you on this?" he asked Payne.

Payne's face nearly went white. "Who? Brief us about what?"

Now it was Hunter's turn to be stumped. "Isn't that why you came here?" he asked Payne. "Didn't they tell you?"

Payne just shook his head.

"We've been out here every day since you disappeared, looking for you," the officer told him. "When you contacted the bombers the other night, we intensified our search. We went up and down this valley—but it seems no matter where we searched, you were always in another part of it."

Hunter was very confused right now, and something in his head was telling him, just forget it, don't think about it, it will work itself out.

But he just couldn't let it go that quickly.

"Are you saying it was just luck that you spotted me down here?" he asked. "I mean, I must be a hundred miles away from where I was the night I talked to the bomber."

"Yes, *luck* is what you'd call it, I guess," Payne replied, as confused as he. "I can't think of another word to describe it."

Now Hunter was speechless; not quite sure what was happening here. But then his attention was directed to the second Beater, just setting down nearby.

"You've got a very special guy out here looking for you as well," Payne told him. "Shocked the hell out of me when he said he wanted to come along. I figured he'd be too busy to spend hours doing search patterns, but he insisted."

The ramp to the second Beater was lowered.

"Who the hell you talking about?" Hunter asked Payne.

"Well, from what I can understand, he's the guy who's been pulling your strings since you arrived in Iceland, if not before."

With that, Hunter watched as a figure emerged from the second Beater. He was bent over, with gray hair, and a pipe stuck permanently between his teeth. He moved like a very old man—because he was a very old man. It was Captain Pegg.

"Him?" Hunter exclaimed.

But Payne shook his head. "No, not him," he said. "I mean the OSS guy. The top spy in the country. *Him* . . ."

Hunter looked up to see another man standing in the doorway of the chopper.

"He's only known by the code name Agent Y," Payne told Hunter, but the Wingman wasn't listening. He was staring at this guy and the guy was staring right back at him, and in a flash Hunter recognized him. In fact, he'd been good friends with him—not in this world, but in the one before.

He walked over the man just as he was coming down the ramp. They just stared at each other for the longest time. The man obviously felt some strong connection to Hunter too—but he just didn't know why.

Hunter, on the other hand, knew *exactly* why.

This OSS man. This mysterious agent Y. There was no mistaking it this time. Hunter definitely knew him back in the other world.

His name was Stan Yastrewski.

His friends called him "Yaz."

"How you doing, Yaz?" Hunter asked him.

The OSS man looked absolutely astonished and confused at the same time.

"How could you possibly know my name?" he asked Hunter.

But Hunter certainly didn't have enough time to explain it all to him now—if in fact there was anything to explain.

"Let's just say it was more than a lucky guess," Hunter finally told him.

"Yes, much more," Y told him. "I was there that first day. I saw you being questioned. I saw you take off to attack those subs. From that day on I was certain that we knew each other before—but I couldn't remember how or when."

"Well, set aside a few days when this is all done and maybe we'll be able to figure it out," Hunter replied. "But the important thing now is for you get these bombs back to our guys—and out of Germany."

Agent Y seemed to accept this, and told the crew of his Beater to help the Air Guards in securing the six bombs.

"I think the important thing is that we *all* get the hell out of here and back to the ships," the OSS man said. "The Germans will certainly spot us down here, out in the open like this."

Hunter took a deep breath. Pegg and Payne had joined them by now.

"Well, there's a slight problem with that," Hunter said.

"What is that?" Payne asked him.

"I can't go back," he told them. "Not yet. There's something else I've got to do."

"Got to do?" Pegg mimicked him. "You've been out here for seven days man. The Huns would love to kill you, and all of America thinks your dead. You've got to get back right now."

Payne and Agent Y were nodding in absolute approval. But Hunter was just shaking his head no.

"I need this Beater," he said. "And about four hours. I'll meet you back at the ships then."

The three men all looked at him like he was crazy, which in reality, he was, due to his near drowning three days before.

Payne especially began to protest—but then Agent Y just held up his hand.

"No," he said. "Let him go. He knows what he's doing."

Hunter shook hands with them, and then climbed up the steep ramp to the Beater. He took a look at its eight rotors and its very ugly shape and stopped for a moment. He had to fly this thing a long long way.

"I hope I do anyway," he whispered to himself.

Chapter 35

The trip east was one of dodging American firebombs and staying low enough so as not to attract the attention of any German fighters.

Flying the Beater was probably the worst experience Hunter had endured in this strange world. The thing was an unforgiving beast, not appreciative of his infallible piloting skills, and always just one nut and bolt away from going down in a horrible crash.

But it carried him to where he wanted to go. It took more than two hours, and he'd had to dodge smoke, bad weather and the occasional flak burst to do it. But finally Hunter arrived at his destination.

He landed the Beater not far from what used to be the Berlin Military Airport.

Hit particularly hard by American firebombers, the immense airfield was now littered with the remains of the German Home Air Defense Force. More than 200 fighters of all types lay charred or burning up and down the melted runways. The place had been abandoned days ago. With incendiary bombs raining down on it endlessly for nearly a month, the nonstop conflagration had caused the people who used to work here to flee.

Hunter left the Beater and began walking. The streets leading into the center of the city were empty as well. Blocks upon blocks of architectural oddities, opera houses, museums, and sex bars. Murals of fake heroic war scenes, painted like advertisements, next to neon signs hailing the best little whorehouse in Germany. All of them burned or burning.

This place was even stranger on the ground, Hunter thought.

He walked the streets quickly, seeing everything, looking everywhere. His huge double-barrel .45 pistol was loaded and ready. But there was no one to shoot at. The burning city was deserted, too. Except for one person, Hunter believed. That's why he was here.

There was still no doubt in his mind that Viktor had been the impetus behind this latest German attempt to conquer the world. In this strange and different place, Viktor's brand of evil was still all-powerful. He'd almost accomplished here what he'd almost accomplished back where he and Hunter first came from.

How ironic then that Hunter would have to cross over into an entirely different universe to finally catch him.

Or so he thought.

He reached the center of town, the grand plaza of the New Reichstag. It was enormous, of course—five times the size of the version Hunter had seen in photos from his version of World War II. All Roman columns and white cement, there was a huge Iron Cross centerstage in the roof. The encrustation of steel and cement was pockmarked and scored from all the firebombing, but was rigidly in place nevertheless.

Hunter studied the plaza from the cover of a nearby building's front door. It too was completely deserted. A few huge Supertanks sat empty in the square, tracks broken, engines charred and ruined. A crashed Focke-Wulf bomber was nearby too. It looked small in the vast plaza, almost like a broken child's toy.

Hunter rechecked his ammo load and began to move out when he saw the tiger.

It was about 25 feet off to his left, pawing through a garbage pile looking for food. Hunter hadn't anticipated this—but it wasn't that hard to figure out what had happened. Berlin had a large zoo. It had obviously been caught up in the firebombing and now hundreds of exotic animals were on the loose in the enemy capital. The tiger spotted Hunter a moment later. He growled and showed his teeth. But clearly he was more afraid of Hunter than Hunter was of him.

He grabbed something from the trash and then ran off. Hunter began moving across the plaza.

He reached the enormous steps and was mildly astonished to see a small herd of zebras run by off to his left. Above him, three condors were circling. He hoped that they weren't looking down on him. At least not yet.

He finally reached the top of the stairs of the Reichstag and pulled one of the enormous wooden doors open. It was dark inside—no surprise there. There hadn't been any electrical power in Germany for more than a week. Hunter walked in, and shut the door behind him. He wanted his eyes to adjust to the darkness before he went any further.

Strange that it would come to this, he thought, inching his way forward again. His foggy memory seemed to recall that more than once he'd hunted down his nemesis through dark hallways, approaching yet another final confrontation. And what would he do when he found the Devil himself this time? He'd vowed to kill him on the spot many times back in his old world. Nothing had changed that now.

He walked through the dark hallways, hand cannon up, sensing that he was getting very, very close now.

Then he turned the corner and saw before him the doors of a huge office. There was a light inside this room, and he could hear it flickering. It was battery-powered; the juice was wearing thin.

Hunter walked into the room, pistol raised high. The place was a mess. There were many war gaming boards thrown about with thousands of black and white wooden pieces representing armies scattered everywhere. There were hundreds of battlefield photographs and instant-news reels thrown about too. And the paintings on the wall, originally intended to depict glorious German victories on sea, land, and air, were now all scarred and ripped, and even fading. Particularly ironic was one showing a massive bombing of New York City; German bombers overhead, the Big Apple, entirely engulfed in flames, below. It was, of course, an attack that never took place.

History is made up of the lies that historians all agree on, Hunter thought as he quickly studied the mural.

In the far corner of the room was a desk, and at the desk, there was a man. Head down, back to Hunter, it was as if he'd spent the last few days just looking out the window as the city of Berlin burned down around him.

Hunter slowly moved towards the man; his sixth sense was vibrating him madly. At the same time he could tell that there was no other danger about. Just this man was here, the one who had foisted this latest version of German Imperial misery upon the world. Hunter had vowed it would never happen again, in this world or any other. He was so sure that he was close to fulfilling that pledge, he could feel it in his bones.

Strange were the thoughts that went through his head though. That day, in the middle of the Atlantic. It seemed like many years ago now, when the truth was, it was barely nine months ago. What would have happened if the Germans had picked him up—and the Americans had gotten this man? Or any other permutation of three? Hunter just shook his head; there was no sense thinking about it. This was how the dice fell here, in this place. Who knows where they were falling in another place entirely.

He crept even closer, being as quiet as possible. But he

sensed that the man knew he was here, knew why he had come, and wasn't really going to do a lot about it. The scent of crushed human spirit was almost a stink in the air. This man was a failure—he'd rebuilt an enormously powerful war machine in such a short amount of time, only to see it crash almost as quickly as it was born. That would break anyone's spirit, no matter how clever, how cruel, how cunning.

He was but 10 feet from the man now. His back was still to him, but Hunter saw the characteristic black clothes and long black hair.

The last time he'd seen Viktor was up in space. At that time, he'd been dressed in an outfit that look liked a cross between the pope's finest garment and those of a drag queen. But now this man, this broken human being who was about to have his life taken by Hunter, was dressed simply in a black uniform, almost bereft of ornaments or insignia.

Hunter took three steps closer and then stopped. He was about six feet away from the man now. He raised his weapon—it would be a clear shot to the head.

Hunter's fingers began to tighten around the gun. He was finally a microsecond away from completing a task that took nothing less than a transuniversal dispersal to accomplish.

It seemed almost too easy.

And as it turned out, it was.

Hunter was loath to shoot the devil himself in the back— so he took a deep breath and then spoke.

"You know I'm here," he said. "And you know *why* I'm here. So just turn around, slowly, and take it like a man."

The person stirred, but did not move in panic. He wasn't that surprised to hear Wingman's voice or the unmistakable click of an automatic pistol getting ready to fire.

"We've been through a lot," said the muffled voice from the desk. "And I knew it would be you who would come after me. I knew you would figure out what happened to us, how we found ourselves swimming in the middle of the ocean—and I knew it was just a matter of time before we met again.''

Hunter clicked the safety off his gun.

The man started to turn around. Hunter tensed, and tightened his finger on the trigger just a bit more.

"I'm not a religious man," he started to say. "But I hope there's a hell, Viktor, so you can have front-row seat."

That's when the man swung around finally and their eyes met and Hunter's hand went so numb he nearly dropped his weapon.

"Viktor?" the man said, looking at him with a twin expression of bemusement and astonishment. "I'm not Viktor . . ."

It was true. It wasn't Viktor.

It was Elvis.

Now what passed was the longest minute of Hunter's life.

They just looked at each other, not talking, not blinking, just staring, and putting the pieces into place.

Finally it was his old friend who began to talk.

"Many things happen when you go through what we did," Elvis said, tears beginning to form in his eyes. "It's not guaranteed that you stay the way you were. That you will remain a good guy. *You* stayed the way you were. I changed. And Viktor . . . God knows what happened to him."

Hunter could barely speak. "But how do you know all this?"

Elvis just shrugged.

"I don't know," he replied. "It's just in my head, just like I'm sure a lot of things are in your head. But when I got here, people thought I was a god or something. And that was my reality. I just remembered everything quicker than you."

Hunter had lowered his gun by now; inside him, his very soul was being torn in two.

"Don't worry about it," Elvis said, wiping the tears away. "At some point I guess I knew it would end this way."

He reached into his desk drawer and took something out.

"So let's just leave it at this," he said. "See you next time."

With that, Elvis put a gun to his head and blew his brains out.

Chapter 36

New York City
Two Weeks Later

The first thing Hawk Hunter saw when he woke up was an empty bottle of champagne.

He rolled over on the massive bed, the silk sheets clinging to his body, and felt the very warm form of Sarah sleeping softly beside him.

He wiped the sleep from his eyes and stared at the very ornate ceiling above the bed. They were in the Presidential suite of the Ritz Carlton Hotel, New York's finest. They had been here for three days now, and all Hunter had done was eat, sleep, drink champagne, and have sex. He had to admit that so far, the sleeping part might have been the best. He'd been that tired.

Today was the big day. There was going to be a ticker-tape parade down Broadway in his honor. More than 2 million people were expected to attend. For while the rumors of his death had been greatly exaggerated, they did nothing to quell the excitement and sheer disbelief when it was announced that he was in fact still alive.

America simply went nuts and the War Department, citing the good of the country, urged him to go along with it.

They were giving him the parade because they were saying he was the person who had finally won the war. But Hunter knew this wasn't true.

The war was over—completely and finally. It had ended three days before. But its conclusion had taken place while he was on an airplane, heading back to the States.

The end came when five B-17/36s left the deck of the *Cape Cod* and headed for five separate targets around Occupied Europe. At precisely midnight, May 1, each plane dropped an MK-75 thermonuclear bomb on its targeted city, the same weapons Hunter had discovered in the washed-out ammo bunker in the Ruhr.

Berlin, Rome, Madrid, London, and Moscow had been utterly destroyed, any last vestiges of Germany's High Command reduced to radioactive sizzle. Millions had been killed as well, of course, and millions more wounded or burned by radiation. The war was over simply because there was no more Reich; no one was left to tell what remained of Germany's troops what to do. So they surrendered in droves.

Added to this were the tens of thousands who had died in the Great Ruhr Flood, and the hundreds of thousands who had died in the firebombing campaign, and the death toll for the victory went into the tens of millions.

Not exactly something Hunter would consider throwing a parade for, but such was life here in this strange but not so strange place.

He rolled out of bed and quietly padded into the other room. The suite was enormous, but frankly it reminded him of a mausoleum.

He stared out the window at the crowds already starting to gather below. They said he was the man who won the war because he was the one who brought the battle back to Germany, the one who firebombed the cities, the one who caused the great flood, the one who found the H-bombs. But Hunter did not feel like a hero.

His mind had ached so much in these past two weeks, he believed his head was about to burst.

No one really knew what he had lost in this long strange adventure. He'd lost an entire universe, full of friends, life, history. And the only friend who had come through to this place with him was now dead, an innocent victim of the unpredictable twists of transuniversal travel.

He shook his head and felt the sick feeling in his stomach again. No, he was not a hero, and anything he might gain from this day, or whatever days lay ahead, would not change his mind one bit. For what he wanted, he believed he could never get—that was, a way back to where he had come from.

He just wanted to go home.

A knock at the door disturbed these thoughts. He threw on a bathrobe and answered it.

It was a man wearing a pair of huge sunglasses and carrying an easel covered by a small curtain.

He introduced himself as the person who was writing the story of Hunter's exploits in the war. Though the details of how Hunter actually got here to this world were still top secret, everyone across the country knew just about everything he'd done since being assigned to the Circle Wing, thanks to Amerca's rabid media.

Which led him to ask this writer a question: If everyone knew how many times he'd blown his nose in the past 10 months, and everything else in between, why would anyone want to publish a book detailing all these events?

The writer just shrugged and said: "Beats me, that's just showbiz, I guess."

He unveiled the easel to display the cover art for this book. It showed a huge air battle taking place over London. Big Ben was in evidence, surrounded by lots of smoke and fire, and two German warplanes were zooming around, all seen from the view of a third airplane's cockpit. But if this was meant to depict one of Hunter's many exploits, then somehow, something had been lost in the translation.

"So, how's it look to you?" the writer asked him.

Hunter just shrugged. "Well, if it's supposed to be me, that looks to be the inside of a Pogo's cockpit. I didn't fly any Pogos overseas. And we never really bombed London. And those German planes, they're not Natters, or Me-362s, or Horton flying wings, which were the airplanes that we usually fought against. And I'm not sure London even looks quite like that."

The writer laughed. "Well it doesn't look like much of anything anymore," he said.

With that, he shook Hunter's hand and quickly went out the door.

Hunter closed it behind him, but then heard another knock.

He opened it to see his old friend, Zoltan the Magnificent.

"What am I disturbing?" the psychic asked him with a smile.

"You should know," Hunter told him. "Absolutely nothing."

Zoltan stepped inside but indicated he was only going to stay a moment.

"I had to tell you something I heard from a friend of mine who is still in the Psychic Evaluation Corps," the mystic began. "Apparently there is a very secret project the government has been working on that may be related to your experience."

Hunter ears started burning when he heard this.

"Jessuzz, where is it?" he wanted to know.

"That's just it," Zoltan told him. "No one really knows. The location is so secret because of the sensitive work they do there. But I hear it is a group of researchers trying to find other people who have fallen in, just like you. In fact, what they are trying to prove is that people have been doing this throughout our world history. And get this: they think these incidents are the origins of all stories about angels."

"Angels," Hunter exclaimed, the very word having some difficulty rolling off his tongue. "Tell me more . . ."

But Zoltan put his hand to his lips, indicating the universal sign that now was the time to shut up.

"I will find the location of this place, I promise you," he told Hunter. "Until then, be well my friend. And don't think too much. It's bad for you."

Then he shook Hunter's hand and went out the door again.

Head swimming now, Hunter went to close the door once again when suddenly, there was another person knocking on it.

Hunter opened it and found himself staring into yet another familiar face.

It was, of all people, Captain Wolf, the commander of the Navy destroyer that had scooped him up from the middle of the ocean that day long ago.

"I'm sorry to bother you on this busy day," he told Hunter, his voice reverent and low. "But I felt I had to come and see you."

Hunter let him in.

"I've been following your exploits, of course," he told Hunter. "Just like everyone else. It really makes me wonder what would have happened if we hadn't picked you up that day."

"You and me both," Hunter told him. "And I don't think I really thanked you properly. So let me do it now."

He shook hands with the man, who finally broke into a smile.

"Well, thanks," Wolf said. "But that's not why I came up here."

"Why then?" Hunter asked him.

The Navy officer reached into his pocket and came out with a small cloth bundle. He handed it to Hunter, who slowly unraveled it.

It was a tiny American flag, one with 50 stars on it. Inside was a picture of Dominique.

Hunter tried to say something, but couldn't. He tried to take a breath, but had a problem doing that too. He tried to move, to do something, but he was frozen, staring down at the picture wrapped inside the flag.

"We took these off you that day," Wolf explained. "I just thought you should get them back."

Hunter finally looked up at him; his eyes were really misty now.

"Thanks," was all he could say.

Wolf smiled again, saluted, and then went back out the door.

Two hours later, Hunter was dressed in a uniform of Air Corps blue. He was standing at the mirror, and Sarah was brushing the lint from his jacket.

A knock came at the door. Hunter opened it, and Agent Y—his friend, Yaz—walked in.

"Ready?" he asked Hunter. "All of New York City is waiting to see you."

Hunter just shrugged. Inside his breast pocket was the photo wrapped in the flag. He tapped it twice.

"Ready as I'll ever be," he said.

Yaz checked his watch. "Well, good, because it's time to go,"

Hunter turned back to Sarah and gave her a quick kiss.

"You'll be here when I come back?" he asked.

"You can be sure of it," she replied sweetly.

He kissed her again and then followed Y out the door.

They rode the elevator down to the lobby which was now cordoned off by hundreds of New York City police. A huge jeepster limo sat idling outside the door. A giant crowd waited beyond. Hunter took a deep breath, tapped his pocket again, had one more fleeting wish to be back in his cell at Sing Sing, and then walked out with Yaz.

The crowd erupted at first sight of him. He waved and then ducked into the limo, Yaz right behind him. Here they would wait until the front part of the parade passed them by. This gave Hunter a rare opportunity to talk to the OSS agent, who he hadn't really seen much of since that day on top of the flattened German mountain.

"So, how are you adapting?" Y asked him. "Figuring out things?"

"Trying to," Hunter replied, still uneasy.

"I can understand your predicament," Y told him. "And who knows what theories our people will come up with concerning universe transfer once you've talked to them."

"It should be interesting," Hunter murmured, wondering if Y knew of the secret research project Zoltan had just told him about.

Y continued: "But you should be aware. Though everything here might seem almost the same, I suspect you'll be finding differences, both big and small, for many years to come."

"That's for sure," Hunter said.

In fact, that was the most encompassing thing on his mind at the moment. And it prompted one question he'd wanted to ask Y for a long time.

It had to do with several incidents that had happened to him in the Ruhr. The Lysander pilots, he saw them, but they were never found again. He explained this to Y, telling him exactly what happened after the dam broke. Then he told him about the young red-haired girl who had led him to the H-bombs. This was stuff Yaz had never heard before, and his eyes went wide with each word.

"It's true about those pilots," he said. "We searched for them, just like we searched for you. But we never found them, and they certainly didn't tell us you were on the mountaintop."

"But I saw them, they were flying off in the distance during the flood," Hunter insisted. "And they landed on the mountaintop. And then this young girl. I swear I saw her in a photograph hanging in a house I'd taken food and clothes from. Yet, it couldn't have been her, because . . ."

Hunter let his voice just trail off. He didn't want to speak the words.

Agent Y pulled his chin in thought.

"This is very interesting," he said as the limo finally started to pull away.

"Why?" Hunter asked him.

"Well I guess I should be the one to tell you if no one else has," Y replied. He turned to Hunter, lowered his voice and said, "You see, in this world, we see a lot of ghosts."

The parade wound its way down Broadway. The throngs of people were screaming and waving at the sight of Hunter, a blizzard of ticker tape raining down on his car.

From a window in a building high above it all, two men were sharing a drink and looking down on the festivities with a measure of bemusement and disdain.

It was Agents X and Z.

In front of them was a very secret OSS report that surprisingly enough, had nothing to do with Hunter, nothing to do with the recent defeat of Germany. What it said, was that in the next two months, a far-flung American naval base, way out in the Pacific, would be attacked by Japan. The place was called Pearl Harbor.

Both men were trying to digest the report which they had just read. Was America ready for another war so soon after this one? Neither man could tell. But more importantly to them was what their role would be in the upcoming conflict.

"It will certainly be a rich payday for us, if the Japanese go ahead with this plan," Z said. "But how can we be sure we'll be on the winning side?"

X looked out the window just as Hunter's limo was passing by.

"Well, we know what kind on an effect *he* had on the last one," he said. "And with the second man dead, I guess that leaves us with only one thing to do, if we want our futures guaranteed."

"And what is that?" Z asked him.

"Well, there were three men in the Atlantic that day," he said. "Each one extremely valuable in his own way. We know where this Hunter guy is. We know what happened to the guy in Germany."

"True enough," Z agreed.

"Then," X said. "I suggest we try like hell to find the third one."

Somewhere in the South Atlantic

The ship was the strangest one in a whole fleet of strange ships.

It was huge, an old cruise liner, and it was powered by steam engines, sails, and oars. It was crewed, like all the ships in the fleet, by the descendants of Jewish people who had been released from Germany's extermination camps years before and had been sailing the seas looking for a homeland ever since.

At the bottom of this ship, where no less than 500 men and young boys rowed for up to 12 hours a day, two officers were talking. There was an opening for a job on the upper decks. The women up there needed someone who would help them watch over the hundreds of young children who lived on the great ship. The person had to be kind, trustworthy, a hard worker, and willing to sacrifice long hours in service to the women and the kids.

"Do you have such a person down here?" one officer asked the Oarmaster, the man in charge of the rowers.

The Oarmaster thought a moment and then replied yes, he did.

He recommended Rower #1446798.

"Ah, the man we picked up at sea that day?" the officer said.

"Yes," the Oarmaster replied. "He's the best man we've ever had."